THE PRINCE

THE PRINCE
R. M. KOSTER

THE OVERLOOK PRESS
NEW YORK, N. Y.

This edition first published in the United States in 2013 by
The Overlook Press, Peter Mayer Publishers, Inc.

141 Wooster Street
New York, NY 10012
www.overlookpress.com

For bulk and special sales, please contact sales@overlookny.com

Cataloging-in-Publication Data is available from the Library of Congress

Book design and typeformatting by Bernard Schleifer
Manufactured in the United States of America
ISBN 978-1-4683-0117-5
1 3 5 7 9 10 8 6 4 2

For Otilita and Herbert

PREFACE

This is one of three independent but interlocking novels—technically the first volume of a trilogy but, to my mind, more like the left panel of a triptych, since each of the three is complete in itself, since they need not be considered in the order of their publication, and since *The Prince* and *Mandragon* are of a size, while *The Dissertation*, which they flank in time, is one and two-thirds times larger.

The Prince is my seventh novel. The first six were stillborn. It was taken for publication while still half finished. It was kindly received: I could scarcely have written more favorable reviews myself. The hardcover edition sold out without being remaindered, and a National Book Awards jury nominated it for a prize. It was not my first love but my first conquest.

Warner did a paperback edition. So did Morrow and Norton. Grijalbo and Éditions Denoël brought the book out in Spanish and French respectively. Overlook will publish *The Dissertation* and *Mandragon* beginning next year.

The trilogy depicts imaginary people and events in the imaginary Republic of Tinieblas. There are some glances back and forth toward past and future, but the temporal focus is mainly the seventh decade of the utterly unreal 20th century. The same themes play in variation through all three books. Major characters from one book appear as minor characters in the other two. One character, Alejandro Sancudo, has intermediate status in all three. There are sorties in all directions into actual localities, but the main setting is Tinieblas. A good case may be made for its being the main character.

How does a fellow from Brooklyn come to invent a Central American country? I went to Panama as a soldier in 1957, having been drafted a year before. By enlisting for a third year I got into counterintelligence and thereby out of uniform. Because of my languages I was offered postings in France and Panama. I had no overcoat, so the choice was easy; if I went to France I'd have to buy one. Before my enlistment was up I married a girl from Panama. This union is now in its fifty-fourth year and likely to last. On being discharged I taught at the University of Panama, then joined the faculty of the Florida State University Panama Branch. Meanwhile I was writing unpublishable novels. Two shootings caused the hero of this book to gestate inside me.

In 1964 deputies to the Panamanian National Assembly, the country's legislature, chose *suplentes* who took the seats, cast the votes, collected the salaries, and enjoyed the privileges of their principles when the same were absent. No suplente-ship was so valuable as that offered by Roberto "Tito" Arias. Tito, son and nephew of two presidents and husband of the great dancer Margot Fonteyn, was essentially an adventurer and playboy and would likely spend more time on Aristotle Onasis's yacht than in his seat in the assembly. Prospective suplentes were expected to help out with campaign expenses, so Tito, chronically short of funds, promised the plum to two gentlemen and collected accordingly. Once elected, however, he had to choose, and the man not chosen expressed his disappointment by firing four bullets into the back of Tito's neck as he waited in his car at a stoplight. This was in late June, 1964.

Word of the shooting flew about the city. I was stringing for the Copley News Service and was at Santo Tomás Hospital when Tito was brought in. Good doctors saved his life, but he was paralysed from the neck down and in his face partially. Two or three years later my wife and I were invited to an event at the British ambassador's residence. Tito and Margot attended. His man Buenaventura carried him up the stairs and deposited him in his wheelchair. I was able to observe him for a few minutes.

The second shooting came in 1968. The Panama Canal Zone was still in existence then under United States jurisdiction, and the local Democratic organization had representation in party councils. In 1967 I became a national committeeman, the youngest of 110. Members were ex-oficio delegates to the 1968 national convention, and that March I became Robert Kennedy's first delegate in his campaign for the Democratic nomination, the only member of the national committee to declare for the him between his announcement on March 16th and President Johnson's withdrawal from the race on the 31st.

The Canal Zone had five convention votes. I set about electing a

Kennedy delegation by the ancient strategem of bringing in an unsuspected horde of new voters. By June 5, the day of our meeting, we had a majority. At four that morning, however, I got a call from Los Angeles. Dun Gifford, my liaison with the Kennedy campaign, told me the senator had been shot.

"How is he?" I asked.

"He's either dead or a vegetable," said Gifford.

The manuscript of my sixth novel was returned to me a day or two later. Not by a publisher. My agent was ashamed to send it out under his name. Over the course of the next months, during which I was preoccupied with events—the riotous Democratic convention was followed closely by an armed coup in Panama that imposed a nasty dictatorship—I decided to quit writing and invest my ambitions in politics. I would go to law school, pick a state, be in Congress by 40 and the Senate by 50. I did the necessary applications and gave notice to FSU that I would leave in June 1969.

In December 1968 I began fiddling with a pair of books. Writing wasn't my thing any more, so a little fiddling couldn't do much damage. Your typical Panamanian has two households. When his wife, for whatever reason, isn't properly attentive, he goes to his girlfriend, and vice versa. I had two typewriters and two books.

One book was a comic novel in the manner of Waugh about a congressional delegation that junkets to a tropical republic to inspect U.S. bases. The other was . . . I didn't know, except that it was first person, that and that the narrator was parapliegic, a vegetable, due to an attempted murder. I spent weeks writing the first two pages over and over, about how he could move one finger a few centimeters. When I couldn't any more, I went to my other typewriter and book. There was nothing wrong with the pages. They ended up being paragraphs two and three of Chapter 3 of *The Prince*. I wrote them over and over to see if the narrator would tell me more about himself. At length he did. His name, for instance, was Kiki Sancudo. Tito Arias, whom I'd had a chance to observe, plus Bobby Kennedy, in whose dream I'd entangled myself, yielded Kiki as in a chemical reaction. The comic novel, which had been romping along in perfect health, died unattended. *The Prince* survived and thrived. And I realized that, for good or ill, I was a writer.

As I discovered more and more about Kiki, I discovered Tinieblas, which had a geography and a history, as well as social, economic, and political peculiarities, and was somewhat a *bouillabaisse* of Central America and the Caribbean. Some months before I finished Kiki's story, I realized that I could not depict his country in one book. When I was about a third of the way into *The Dissertation,* I realized I was doing a triptych. The writing of *Mandragon* completed the work.

But not the imaginary world I'd made, what Tolkein called a "sub-creation." Another book has called me back to Tinieblas, and I'm discovering more.

Is *The Prince* dated? I think not. Revenge is still a popular passion. The man of action forcibly thrust into the contemplative life (c.f. Machievelli) can compete thematically with the intellectual who is forced to act (Hamlet). Besides, as I realized late in its composition, *The Prince* is plugged in (as it were) to the myth of Prometheus, where the hero is bound for an altruistic impulse. As for the American tropics, they remain lands drenched in sunlight yet places of darkness. All change in the last 40 years has been superficial, so that the marvelous Nicaraguan expression applies: *"La misma mierda con distintas moscas"*—"The same shit with different flies."

A word on the cover. It was done by Guillermo Trujillo, the best (to my mind) of Panama's many fine painters. In the early 1960s he and I had workshops on the second floor of a decaying tenement off Plaza Catedral in the old quarter of Panama City, he dabbing with exemplary vigor at a dozen canvases simultaneously, painting a little on one, then moving along, I pecking languidly at yet another unpublishable novel, both of us arting away next door to each other like Marcello and Rodolfo in *La Bohème,* except that we were tormented by heat, not cold, and never (alas!) interrupted by pretty women. I made him promise that if I ever had a book published, he would do the cover. At the time it seemed unlikely he would ever be called upon, but he fulfilled that promise not once but three times.

Gracias, Guillermo! If the wise purchaser of this elegant edition finds my words as good as your picture, I shall be quite satisfied.

—R. M. K.
Panama, August 2012

Y la tierra estaba desordenada y vacía
y las tinieblas estaban sobre la faz del abismo.

Genesis 1:2

NOTE

The purpose of literature, and every other art, is to translate us from the so-called "real" world into others more carefully organized. Hence the people in this book are imaginary.

Similarly, the only way to reach the Republic of Tinieblas is via this book.

I have given my chief character a nickname, a diminutive of Enrique. It would normally be spelled "Quiqui," but I have transliterated it "Kiki" so that the reader may hear it correctly in his mind's ear.

—R. M. K.

PRESIDENTS OF TINIEBLAS
(Independent Republic Declared 1821)

1821–1828	SIMÓN MOCOSO *(elected by constituent assembly)*
1828–1830	JULIO CANINO *(deposed)*
1830–1848	ISIDRO BODEGA *(military dictator, died in office)*
1848	ADRIANO MOSCA *(resigned after one month in office)*
1848	MANUEL GRILLO *(resigned after two months in office)*
1848	FRANCISCO PIOJO *(resigned after three weeks in office)*
1848–1853	JUSTO CANINO *(deposed and fed to sharks)*
1853–1860	EPIFANIO MOJÓN *(military dictator, deposed and crucified)*
1860–1866	ALCIBIADES ORUGA *(first popularly elected president to serve full constitutional term)*
1866–1872	BOLÍVAR CEBOLLA
1872–1875	GUSTAVO ADOLFO PUIG *(deposed)*
1875–1878	SATURNINO AGUI.LA *(deposed)*
1878–1883	LÁZARO TORCIDO *(died in office)*
1883–1893	JESUS LLORENTE & FELICIANO LUNA *(presidency jointly claimed, Luna hanged, Llorente resigned)*
1893–1896	RUDOLFO TÁBANO *(resigned)*
1896–1897	HILDEBRANDO LADILLA *(fled to Portugal with National Treasury)*
1897–1898	ERNESTO CHINCHE *(resigned)*
1898	ILDEFONSO CORNUDO *(voluntary exile)*
1898–1904	RAMIRO AGUADO *(elected by Chamber of Deputies)*
1904–1905	MODESTO GUSANO *(deposed by populace)*
1905	AMADO DEL BUSTO *(deposed by U.S. Marines)*
1905–1908	MODESTO GUSANO *(reinstated by U.S. Marines)*
1908–1912	ASCANIO PÍCARO
1912–1914	RAMIRO AGUADO *(resigned)*
1914	MODESTO GUSANO *(deposed by populace)*
1914	FRANCO TIRADOR *(resigned after three weeks in office)*
1914–1916	RAMIRO AGUADO *(finished term originally elected to)*

1916–1917	EUDEMIO LOBO *(resigned with the encouragement of the United States Ambassador to Tinieblas)*
1917–1919	ARMANDO CABEZA LOZA *(died in office)*
1919–1920	VICTORIANO MOSCA
1920–1923	HERIBERTO LADILLA *(resigned)*
1923–1924	FELIPE GUSANO
1924–1927	HERIBERTO LADILLA *(resigned)*
1927–1928	LUIS NAPOLEON TÁBANO
1928–1930	ABÚNDIO MORAL *(deposed)*
1930	ALEJANDRO SANCUDO *(held office for thirty-six hours, resigned when his ammunition ran out)*
1930–1932	EFRAÍN ANGUILA AHUMADA *(Moral's Vice President)*
1932–1936	JUAN DE A. TÁBANO
1936–1940	ERASMO SANCUDO
1940–1942	ALEJANDRO SANCUDO *(deposed by U.S. Army)*
1942–1914	EFRAIN ANGUILA AHUMADA *(appointed with advice and consent of the U.S. Ambassador to Tinieblas)*
1944–1948	LUIS GUSANO
1948	OLMEDO AVISPA *(died in office after twelve hours)*
1948	FERNANDO COMEJÉN *(died in office after six hours)*
1948–1952	ALEJANDRO SANCUDO *(election ratified retroactively, deposed after three years, seven months in office)*
1952	BELISARIO ORUGA *(served out remainder of Sancudo's term)*
1952–1956	PACÍFICO PASTOR ALEMÁN
1956–1960	ENRIQUE ABEJA
1960–1962	JUAN DE LA CRUZ ARDILLA *(special two-year term)*
1962–1964	LEÓN FUERTES *(assassinated by plastic bomb)*
1964-1965	BONIFACIO AGUADO *(assumed office as Fuertes' Vice President, deposed)*
1965	AIAX TOLETE *(president military junta, resigned)*
1965–1966	NARSES PUÑETE *(president military junta, resigned upon new elections)*
1966	JOSÉ FUERTES

1

Jaime will get him. No, Alejo will have him delivered. An officer and two guardias will bring him to the ranch, smartly wrapped, in one of those vans with the Alliance for Progress handshake stenciled on the doors. The guardias will set him down on the porch, and Jaime will sign the receipt. Then he'll carry him over the threshold.

Will he struggle? No, not after that long ride, and he'll be very scared. But not completely terrified. It will be too much like mashing a roach unless he remains rational. He will not foul himself, for example. I'll stipulate that the officer have him attend to his necessities in some secluded spot on my property.

Jaime will carry him to Edilma's room and lay him on the bed. Gently, and a pillow under his butt. Jaime will take the iron off one ankle and clamp it to the leg of the bed under the spring. Rope or electrical cord for the other. His hands will be manacled under him behind his back, and Jaime can run the cord through his armpits and truss him to the head of the bed. He will curse and struggle, but Jaime will neither speak nor treat him harshly. I'll be out of sight of course. I'll have Jaime wheel me to the bedside once Ñato is locked in.

When he sees me, Ñato will plead, beg me to forgive him, even say he didn't mean it. I'll simply let him look at me, or perhaps just say, "I've missed you, Ñato," to let him hear how I speak now. That and the sight of me ought to obliterate any hope of mercy, and yet Ñato's been in so many tight spots and always wriggled out, he won't despair completely. I can count on that to keep him from going insane with terror. He will whine and blubber. Curse and threaten. Collect himself and try to make a brave front, then break down and beg.

"Please, Kiki! For the love of God! On the life of my mother, I didn't mean to do it. I lost my head, Kiki. You know I've always been impulsive, never cool like you. I didn't know what I was doing until too late. And, Kiki, you had me crazy. You pushed me too far. You didn't treat me correctly. Let me go now, Kiki. You won't regret it.

"Why don't you say something? Why don't you answer? Stinking cripple! Faggot! What do you do now, give your hole to Jaime?

"You won't get away with it. I have friends. They'll make you wish you died four years ago.

"You can do what you like, you and your husband. I'll show you what it is to be a man!

"I'll show you! I'll show you! For the love of God, Kiki¡ For my mother, don't kill me! Let me go!"

Jaime will take out his revolver and unload it. He'll cut off the sight with a hacksaw. No, take the sight off with a grindstone and buff the barrel smooth. Then he'll take one round and grind down the slug till it's flush with the cartridge case. I don't want any bullet tunneling up to hit the heart or cut the aorta, just the blast in his guts, burnt powder and splintered lead to bring him peritonitis in two or three days.

Jaime will poke the barrel in a jar of vaseline. I want Ñato to see that, and he'll say, "What are you going to do to me?"

"You don't look well, Ñato, so we're going to take your temperature." If I speak very slowly, he'll understand.

That's the moment I want to watch, before Jaime starts, after Ñato knows. Guesses but can't bring himself to believe it. I want to watch him turn into an insect. I'll stipulate that they give him a bath and a shave and a haircut before they deliver him so he will look as human as possible at the start. I'll have them go to his house and pick up one of the silk shirts he likes to wear buttoned al the neck with no tie and a pair of his made-to-measure beltless slacks, so that he'll look his own natty self with his little mustache and brilliantined hair. Powdered and perfumed for his wedding night is how he'll be, and I won't miss the look on his face when he sees the vaseline.

When I nod, Jaime will open Ñato's pants and pull them down

as far as they'll go. He'll probe with the smeared barrel. I expect there'll be a lot of twisting and thrashing about, perhaps a few "Hijos de puta!" for Jaime and me, snarled between clenched teeth, but how much will Ñato be able to do in his ribbons and bows?

"Keep knocking till he opens, Jaime," and Patient Jaime will find the strait gate and the narrow way.

Now, when the trigger guard rests against the base of his spine, will he curse or cry? He'll cry, mourn himself and moan, "No, no, no." I'll nod, and there will be a dull pop, a seismic bulge in Ñato's belly, a rainbow arc from heels to shoulders and pig squeals stabbing at the ceiling.

I suppose the gun will be blown free. In any case, Jaime will withdraw it. He will undo all the cords and irons, put the pillow under Ñato's head and dress him neatly. Then he'll bring a chair to wait with me for Ñato to regain consciousness. With any luck he'll last for days.

2

That's the way it'll be. That way or some better way. I've time to think about it. There are so many details to arrange that a fitting execution often seems more trouble than Ñato's worth, and I decide to have Jaime give him a simple bullet in the brain. Or strangle him with a coat hanger, or cremate him, or break his bones with a sledge, and it works back up into something elaborate, lengthy, and picturesque. Composing and revising while I wait for sleep, or during the day as I sit in my wheelchair, or, as now, when I wake early. A new method comes to me, or some small fact springs to mind making what I had supposed to be a sound plan impractical or unsatisfying. Then I begin anew. Right now a lead suppository seems the medicine for Ñato, but I won't rest complacent. When the thrill of creation has faded, I'll go over each detail, consider alternative prescriptions, compose, and revise.

When one spends as much time as I do on a single problem, it is impossible to conceal it completely from those nearby. I don't babble about my plans, but my household is generally aware—and I hope *he* is too—that I intend to chastise Ñato for so magically changing me into a vegetable with his nine-millimeter autoloading wand. They also suspect my deep contentment that President Fuertes protects instead of persecutes Ñato, thus reserving me the pleasure of a personalized revenge. Jaime agrees with me. Edilma, whose crooked claws can diaper me again now, thanks to Ñato, as they did almost forty years ago, understands, though I think she would rather Ñato were officially tried and punished. My wife Elena would have me dream of some miraculous cure, nerve transplants, say, that will have me up on skis again, though after seeing me poked and tickled by the diplomaed superquacks of three continents, even she has lost hope. Marta says I'm obsessed and considers this dangerous. In accord with her forced declination from mistress to secretary, she thinks I ought to have stayed in California and dictated my memoirs. Sound plan on the face of it, for writing is a compensation for life. And she assumes the tender lips of metaphor could leach me of all hate. But though I have been exiled from my body—strength, motion, sex, and other valuables, confiscated at the frontier—I refuse to give up living, which for me is action. It would be no substitute to add to the knowledge of bananaland politics, peeling back the foreskin of ignorance from some university department of Greaseball Affairs; or to compile an annotated record of my best games with the brilliancies marked with exclamation points—six thousand M-2 carbines fianchettoed from their New Orleans warehouse to a hardware deposit in Tinieblas, for example; an apparent blunder which, after a few quiet moves, reveals itself a masterly positional posting for their diagonal plunge into Costaguana; or to take up pussiography and map out my plowings in ten thousand dry humps of the mind, to end up like poor Casanova ("For me the age of miracles is over") dipping limply with a pen where I can no longer put a penis; or to keen poetically over my loss; or, worst of all, to pick at the scab of the past: If I had done this, if I had said that; if I'd given Ñato his due and recognized him as a dangerous coward instead of a harmless one I'd be whole now; if I'd had the patience to teach him how to shoot or taken him campaigning with me in the interior, where there's no decent hospital, I'd be safely dead. No. I am perfectly right in being obsessed; it gives me the will to action. I shall help my father beat Pepe Fuertes and take delivery of Ñato Espino and treat him to a spectacular agony—say, impalement on a greased .38.

3

Something to think about as I watch the day creep through the louvers into my bedroom. I wake early from very active dreams. This morning I was riding a bay mare through a field some distance from Penonomé in the Republic of Panama, the very field which several years ago I planted in red pot marijuana. I merely rode through the field at a *trote*, admiring the crop and savoring the sun on my face. But as in most of my dreams, I was immediately aware that I was dreaming, for I could not reach up to wipe the sweat and dust from my neck. I went on and enjoyed the dream as best I could, but I was already planning Ñato's execution when my eyes opened.

I have the use of two fingers. Not complete use, but I can raise the index and middle fingers of my left hand a good three centimeters. I can turn my head fifteen degrees in either direction, open and close my eyes, roll them with bold abandon. I cannot bite, not even the hand that feeds me, but can mush soft morsels. I learned all this in a year, and also to stand firm at the sphincters until Jaime comes to put me on the pot, but in the last three years I have not been able to learn anything more.

I can make noises which are more or less intelligible to those who study. A scholar like Marta can translate my grunts and hisses. Jaime and Edilma grasp requests. Elena can interpret social conversation, but she lacks patience. Grabs the first clear phrase to gloss on; warps it into something of her own. Her directors make the same complaint, but they can cry "Cut!" and start over. I grunt denial, try to shake my head, but she purrs on. Marvelous voice that a famous androgyne has likened to the caress of a panther's tongue, but not what the paraplegic said. The cripple didn't mean that. The dribbling basketcase didn't have it on his impacted mind, and he hoists the corner of his mouth into what he does for a smile while rage kicks against the backs of his eyeballs. Strains for control. Seeks special powers lest head flop and eyes goggle. Begs bowel and bladder stage no protest demonstrations. Persuades his mouth to smile.

I can smile by hauling back the left corner of my mouth.

4

So with all these abilities I have returned to the independent and sovereign Republic of Tinieblas, which occupies a slice of the lost continent of Central America first touched by Palmiro Inchado de los Huevos. All the Spanish *adelantados* were crazy. Inchado believed himself possessed by devils and spent insomniac nights on deck. Just before dawn on November 28, 1515, the helmsman heard him cry, "Jesus of the Great Power, free me from this darkness!" ("Jesús del Gran Poder, líbradme destas tinieblas!"). Then Inchado jumped into the sea. His shark-surgered head was found washed up on a beach in what is now the Reservation.

Inchado's men didn't stay, but other Spaniards came some years later and founded a colony which stood three hundred years. Then Bolívar cockadoodledooed outside Lima, and when the echo reached Tinieblas, the governor slunk off to Cuba with his garrison, leaving the creole gentlemen—merchants and lawyers of the capital, ranchers and planters of the interior—to declare independence and proclaim a republic founded on the rights of man. They formed an assembly, drafted a constitution, and chose Simón Mocoso President.

Meanwhile Bernabé Sancudo, younger son of a Malaga notary, emigrated from Spain to Santo Domingo, where he became a hide factor.

When Mocoso's term was up, Julio Canino was elected President of Tinieblas by the free vote of male landowners and was immediately overthrown by General Isidro Bodega, who proclaimed a state of siege, dissolved the assembly, suspended the constitution, and remained president for eighteen years. Then Bodega died of gastroenteritis after a banquet of fried cuttlefish and was succeeded by Adriano Mosca and Manuel Grillo and Francisco Piojo, all within four months, whereupon a junta was formed, which convoked an assembly, which drafted a new constitution, which provided for elections under a liberalized suffrage, and the people elected Justo Canino, Julio's nephew. But Justo Canino was overthrown by General Epifanio Mojón, who proclaimed a state of siege, dissolved the assembly, and suspended the constitution.

Meanwhile Nicanor Sancudo, Bernabé's younger son, had immigrated to Cuba, where he dealt in tobacco.

General Mojón was President of Tinieblas for seven years. At first he suppressed the pamphlets of his opponents; later he confiscated their property; still later he put them in prison. All this time General Mojón, who had been a slim young artillery lieutenant at the Battle of Ayacucho—he is the only general in Tinieblan history who actually took part in a battle—and was still quite trim when he seized power, grew fatter and fatter until he could no longer sit a horse and his eyes were like thumb prints in soft dough. Also he began to smell, a sweet smell like gladiolas left overnight on a grave during the rainy season. When he was very fat and very smelly, he ordered two crosses set up opposite the President's Palace on the mud flats which reach out three hundred meters from the sea wall at low tide. They were tall enough so that the cross pieces hung a meter or so above the water at high tide, and on the following Saturday morning Don Justo Canino and Licentiate Jorge Washington Chinche, who had been Canino's Vice President, were taken out there from the prison where they had been for almost two years, and chained to the crosses.

The idea was for the sharks to eat them when the tide came in, and General Mojón ordered his noon meal to be served on the awninged balcony of the palace, so he might watch and listen. Numerous members of the Canino and Chinche families were there also, by General Mojón's invitation, not on the balcony, however, but below on the sea wall, and of course there were many other spectators because it was at that time a unique entertainment, even in Tinieblas. But the tide came in, and no sharks arrived, so when it started to go out again, General Mojón ordered his Mexican aide-de-camp to let some of Don Justo's blood down into the water, but if he killed him, he would take his place on the cross.

The Mexican had a muzzle-loading rifle made in the United States, and he laid it on the parapet of the balcony and knelt down behind it and allowed for windage and distance—the range was about one hundred twenty meters—and shot Don Justo through the palm of his left hand. At first it didn't seem that any blood would come—Don Justo was pretty thin after two years in General Mojón's prison—but then some did begin to dribble out of the wound and fall into the water, which was a little below the level of Don Justo's belt. Several sharks arrived presently, cutting around the crosses with their dorsal fins, and suddenly Don Justo let out a terrible scream, and then another, and Licentiate Chinche screamed as well, though some say he called out "Cabrónnnnnnnnn!" toward the balcony, and their heads strained back against the crosses and then flopped forward onto their chests, while the sharks lunged as far as they could out of the water to snatch steaks and chops.

Many of the spectators left then, but the families of the eaten men stayed on till dark at General Mojón's invitation. As the tide went out they could see Don Justo and Licentiate Chinche down to the fifth rib or so, and below that skeletons, though as the activity of the sharks subsided, buzzards flapped down to the arms of the crosses to restore symmetry.

The bones hung there for a week, then were replaced by men from the prison. This went on every Saturday until there were no more political prisoners and common criminals were used. After the first time there was no trouble attracting sharks; they even cruised around the crosses during the week.

Then, for the seventh anniversary of his regime General Mojón decreed that each of the seven provinces of Tinieblas would send two virgins to the capital for use on the crosses, and their parents would have special seats on the balcony, four seats set aside each day for those whose daughters the sharks would eat, and instead of chains they would be hung on the crosses with ribbons of the finest silk, and the girls would be naked, and two of them would be eaten every day for a week, and there would be no work at all in any part of the country so that the populace might come to the capital and celebrate. This decree went out a month before the anniversary, but the provincial governors had difficulty procuring the virgins. It seemed there were none in the entire republic, even little girls of twelve and thirteen had, their fathers said, been debauched and were not fit to serve in the celebrations of General Mojón's rise to power. So General Mojón sent his Mexican aide-de-camp with a company of troops to get the daughters of the most prominent men in each province, and while some hid and others committed suicide or were murdered by their fathers, the Mexican returned on the appointed day with fourteen nubile girls.

The Mexican aide-de-camp was master of ceremonies and personally stripped the girls and tied them to the crosses with silken ribbon in the national colors of purple, green, and yellow. The first pair were from the Province of Otán, where General Mojón had been born. One of the girls wept and tried to hide her breasts and triangle with her hands, and the Mexican cuffed her smartly on the ear to get her quiet. This drew a hiss from the spectators and even some mumbling from the battalion of soldiers whom General Mojón had stationed on the sea wall to keep order, but the Mexican got both girls up the ladders and onto their crosses without further trouble, and the tide came in precisely as predicted and the sharks, of course, with it. There was a sizable crowd, for while the citizens of the capital were used to seeing men eaten by sharks on Saturdays, naked virgins were another story, and besides General Mojón had installed a string quintet on his balcony along with the parents of the girls and dignitaries of his government, and then there were many people from the provinces who had never seen a human being, male or female, dressed or naked, eaten by sharks.

So it went that week. General Mojón had the table of tides published on wall posters throughout the town, and one by one the provinces of the republic honored the president: Otán, Remedios, La Merced, Salinas, Tuquetá, Selva Trópica, and, finally,

Tinieblas. And on the seventh day, when the seventh pair of virgins went to the crosses, there was a larger crowd than ever, for these were daughters of the capital itself, and one of them was Blanca Mariposa del Valle, the most beautiful girl in the whole country and daughter of Dr. Diogenes Mariposa, who had been eaten the week after Don Justo Canino, and Liria del Valle de Mariposa, whose brother Licentiate Dantón del Valle had been eaten too. And when the Mexican aide-de-camp went to strip Blanca Mariposa, she waved him back disdainfully and drew her white frock over her head herself and stood with her hands cupped under her lovely breasts. And the crowd wept, and the soldiers gnashed their teeth, and the colonel of the battalion ordered his men to train their rifles on the balcony, and General Mojón was deposed.

Then Blanca and the other girl were brought back from the mud flats, and General Mojón and his Mexican aide-de-camp were chained to the crosses, though a kind of seat had to be built on to General Mojón's cross, for he was so fat his arms wouldn't hold him. The tide came in, and with it the sharks, and they began eating the Mexican aide-de-camp as soon as they could reach his feet, but none of them would bite General Mojón. The tide rose and fell and rose again, and the sharks swam round and round General Mojón's cross, but none of them would touch him, used as they were to human flesh and hungry too, for the Mexican was a short wiry man with little meat on him. General Mojón went mad from fear and sunstroke, and people on the sea wall could hear him raving all night long. The next morning he died; by noon his flesh was rotting off him, but the buzzards wouldn't eat him either, so at low tide that evening a group of men went out and chopped down the crosses and buried them, with General Mojón and the Mexican's skeleton still on them, there in the mud.

Then a new junta was formed, a new assembly convoked, a new constitution drafted, a new election held, and a new president selected: Dr. Alcibiades Oruga, founder of the Tieblan Conservative Party. Dr. Oruga became the first popularly elected President of Tinieblas to serve his full constitutional term, and when it was over, he stepped down in favor of a Liberal, Licentiate Bolívar Cebolla. Cebolla was succeeded by another Liberal, Gustavo Adolfo Puig, who was committed to an insane asylum by his Vice President, Saturnino Aguila, and while this was going on, Nicanor Sancudo's younger son Pablo was arrested for advocating the independence of Cuba and exiled to Colombia, where he was first a journalist and then a timekeeper on the French canal in the Colombian province of Panama.

When Saturnino Aguila was in his third year as President of Tinieblas, Sarah Bernhardt came to perform at the Municipal Theater in the capital. Aguila took his whole government to the theater and paid his respects to Madame Sarah before the performance. During the entr'acte an officer went to her dressing room saying that the President of the Republic would like to make her acquaintance.

"I have already had the honor of meeting your President," said Madame Sarah.

"You have met the former President," replied the officer. "It is the new president who wants to meet you."

While Aguila was at the play, Dr. Lázaro Torcido and a group of Conservatives had occupied the palace.

After this, civil war broke out in Tinieblas, with the Conservatives holding the capital and the Liberals controlling much of the interior. Both Aguila and Torcido died, and the presidency was simultaneously claimed by Monseñor Jesús Llorente, a Conservative of course, and General Feliciano Luna, a Liberal, who moved his provisional capital between the towns of La Merced and Angostura, depending on the location of the columns of regular troops Monseñor Llorente sent out after him. Luna wasn't really a general, but rather a ranch foreman who collected a group of riders behind him. He raided towns, dodged regular columns, and was never actually brought to battle. This war went on for five years until Llorente lured Luna to Ciudad Tinieblas under a flag of truce and had him hanged. Then peace was negotiated through the good offices of the American Ambassador and signed on the veranda of the American Embassy.

At this time Eladio Sancudo, Pablo's younger son, who had come to Tinieblas and rode with General Luna, settled in Angostura, capital of Remedios Province, where he married the daughter of a storekeeper.

Now elections were held and won by Rudolfo Tábano, but during our civil war Tinieblas had contracted a huge debt to Germany, and as Tábano could find no way to pay it, he resigned in favor of his Vice President, Hildebrando Ladilla. Then Ladilla fled to Portugal with what was left of the treasury and was succeeded by his Minister of Justice, Ernesto Chinche. Then the German Emperor announced that he was annexing Tinieblas in payment of the debt and sent a cruiser, and the President of the United States invoked the Monroe Doctrine and sent two cruisers, and Chinche resigned in favor of his Minister of Agriculture, Dr. Ildefonso Cornudo.

Ildefonso Cornudo, who was bald as a doorknob and wore a spade beard in compensation, was a doctor of veterinary medicine who had emigrated to Tinieblas from Spain and was not even a citizen of the country. People said he had been named to Chinche's cabinet in return for professional services to a Black Angus seed bull which Chinche had imported at vast expense and which the tropical climate had rendered impotent. As soon as he became president, he went to Washington on board one of the American cruisers and signed the Day-Cornudo Treaty, under which the United States agreed to pay all debts owed to the German Emperor and Tinieblas agreed to grant the United States a nine-hundred-and-ninety-nine-year lease on a tract of land adjacent to the capital. After this Dr. Cornudo went by train to New York and from there by Cunard steamer to Paris, where he lived in conspicuous splendor until the flu epidemic of 1919.

When the terms of the treaty were published, some Tinieblans felt they had been betrayed, but when the second American cruiser trained its guns on the capital and prepared to debark marines, the members of the Chamber realized that the treaty was fair and ratified it. Then they proclaimed their Speaker, Ramiro Aguado, President of the Republic.

During Aguado's term the United States began building bases on the leased land, which they called the Reservation, and when Aguado's successor, Modesto Gusano, was overthrown by Dr. Amado del Busto, American soldiers from the Reservation reinstalled him. The Gusano Administration leased a tract of land in Tuquetá Province to an American banana company, and the government of Ascanio Pícaro, who followed Gusano, granted exploration rights in Otán Province to an American copper company.

Pícaro was succeeded by Aguado, who resigned in favor of

Gusano, who was deposed by Colonel Franco Tirador, who withdrew after three weeks in favor of Aguado. Then the people elected Eudemio Lobo, but he sympathized with the Central Powers and was, therefore, replaced, after the sinking, of the *Lusitania,* by Armando Cabeza Loza, who died of the same flu that killed Dr. Cornudo in Paris and was succeeded by Victoriano Mosca, who served out the rest of the term.

There followed a famous election between Dr. del Busto and Heriberto Ladilla, Hildebrando's son. Most people gave Dr. del Busto the advantage, but every one of the fifteen thousand indians in Tuquetá Province voted for Ladilla. So great was Ladilla's appeal to the indians of Tuquetá that little babies voted for him, and men long dead, so that when Dr. del Busto spoke demanding a recount, he could declare, "Tinieblas is the first democracy to extend suffrage beyond the grave." But as Ladilla controlled the Electoral jury, the count stood, and Ladilla took office.

During Ladilla's term various foreign companies began negotiating for oil exploration leases in Salinas Province, and Ladilla felt that the country ought to have the benefit of his leadership when it came time to grant a lease. But the constitution forbade a president to succeed himself, so five months before his term was up, Ladilla resigned in favor of his vice president, Felipe Gusano, Modesto's cousin. Then he ran again against Dr. del Busto, and the indians of Tuquetá remained loyal to him, and he won and signed a bill granting the oil lease to an American company. Then he retired and was succeeded by Luis Napoleón Tábano, who was followed by Abúndio Moral, who was overthrown by Alejandro Sancudo, Eladio's younger son.

5

My grandfather, Eladio Sancudo, never owned anything but the clothes on his back, a .45 caliber Martini-Henry rifle, and a photograph of General Feliciano Luna accepting a counterfeit presidential sash from the splendidly mustached mayor of La Merced. He clerked in the store which belonged to his wife's father, lived in

a house which belonged to his wife's mother, and died from a rup-
tured spleen after having been kicked by a roan mare which belonged to his wife's brother. This dependence on his in-laws in no
way curtailed his self-esteem. He had a bold stare for every man
and a leer for every unattended woman, and he refused to let himself be patronized, even by those who were buying him drinks. He
was sullen when sober and murderous when drunk, though as few
men crossed him, his wrath usually fell on his wife and elder son
Erasmo, my Uncle Erasmo, who were so perpetually bruised that
the people of Angostura decided that wife- and child-beating were
hallowed customs of Colombia, where my grandfather was born
and reared. After Uncle Erasmo ran away to the capital on his
twelfth birthday, his younger brother Alejo, who was only four,
came into the patrimony and wore rainbows about his eyes for
three years until my great uncle Simón Montes' mare Cucha, whom
my grandfather beat with a stick, made him an orphan.

Almost as soon as he arrived in Ciudad Tinieblas, Uncle
Erasmo was taken in by Don Fernando Araña, who was famous for
his generosity to orphan boys, and some say Uncle Erasmo became
his catamite, but then there is no Tinieblan public figure who has
not at one time or another been accused of being impotent, cuckold, or homosexual, if not all three. Whatever his motive, Don Fernando began by giving Uncle Erasmo a home and his first pair of
shoes, and sent him to school, and later to Coimbra to study law,
and finished by willing him a small legacy, so that when Alejo was
eighteen, Uncle Erasmo was able to bring him to the capital for a
year at the Instituto Politénico. This was the pinnacle of Tinieblan
education—we had no university then—a French lycée which had
withstood transplanting to the tropics. Alejo took his *bachiler* in
science. He wanted to be a surgeon, the only professional licensed
to mangle and maim in peacetime, but Erasmo, who was still
searching for a rich family to marry into, calculated the cost of a
medical education and instead sent his younger brother to agricultural college in Kansas.

Almost at once, surely before his English had roped its way much
above the kindly-direct-me-to-the-water-closet plateau attained at
the Instituto, he found night work as a keeper in a madhouse. His

biographer can decide—it's not my worry—if this choice of work reflected an already budded interest in government, or if the job itself led Alejo—the old fox campaigned in Salinas yesterday and will stop in half the towns in Tinieblas Province on the way in to his speech this afternoon—to believe he was fit (he would say *destined*) to rule. Clearly four years of tending the demented, deluded, and deranged is too valuable a preparation for politics to be coincidental. And all he read was political philosophy. I myself have fingered that college library's kidnapped poli sci collection, mold-scabbed volumes with the school crest—razorback *statant* in a maize field—that he left in the house when he sold La Yegua to me, and plotted his annotations, arrows sailing out from the reality of abstract theory to pierce the concrete Tinieblan dream, so that on only a pressed disaster ration of my high-energy paralytic's imagination I can see him swotting Mosca in the Soils Lab and opening Locke in the Schiz Ward. Somehow he still managed to get an agronomy degree and keep the lunatics in line. Or usually keep them in line, since one swollen-mooned midnight in his senior year he sat too rapt in Hobbes to react when a maniac, who believed himself to be a Siberian timber wolf, broke howling from his straps and bit him deeply on the throat. It is the scar of this wound, I think, not his contempt for the common man, which keeps him necktied long after other politicians have adopted the sport shirt or our Cubanstyle *guayavera,* for it has a way of glowing royal purple and dripping blood as though it were only an hour old. The first time I noticed it—at Medusa Beach, August, 1950—I thought Angela had done it to him, and I asked her why she hadn't bit me. Was my father's sting that much more toxic, or intoxic?

"I don't bite, darling," she replied. "Sometimes I scratch when I want more action. Cats don't bite, they scratch. Only bitches bite."

Then she told me the story, which my father had told her after she, assuming as I had that it had been some woman, asked him if it excited him to be bit while he made love.

When he returned to Tinieblas, he rejected offers to manage various farms, plantations, and ranches whose owners could afford to live in the capital, if not Paris or Madrid. The Tuquetá Banana Company, a subsidiary of Galactic Fruit, would surely have hired him; Uncle Erasmo, who had married Beatrix Anguila Ahumada, could have found him a post in the Ministry of Agriculture. Instead he went back to Angostura and nailed two partitions up at right angles in a corner of his grandfather's store and stenciled a sign:

ENGINEER ALEJANDRO SANCUDO MONTES
Agronomist and Surveyor

Each morning he put on his white suit and straw fedora and walked across the street from his grandmother's house and hung his jacket and hat on a nail and sat down on his chair, which had a stretched cowhide seat and back, and read political philosophy all day long, except for those occasions when a rancher or planter would come in with a problem; then he would put down his book and put on his hat and jacket, and perhaps take up his transit and compass or the narrow spade he used for spearing soil samples, and go out to practice his profession. In 1926 he married Angustias Maldonado, whose father had one hundred and sixty head of cattle on a well-watered ranch called La Yegua half a day's trot northwest of Angostura between the border of Tuquetá Province and the Ticamalan frontier, and altered his daily routine in that instead of walking across the street from a house belonging to his mother's family, he now walked down the street from a house belonging to his wife's.

At nights things were less orderly. At night Alejo put on a black double-breasted shirt and black trousers and black leather Mexican *charro* boots which he wore inside his trousers and drifted off into the shadows which flowed even to the center of the town, lapping against the oil lamps of the two cantinas, to return well after midnight, often with his face scratched as though by brambles and the corners of his mouth flecked with dried foam. During the months after his return to Tinieblas, ranchers began noting losses in their herds, a calf found wreathed in vultures the forenoon after a night of full moon, a cow ripped from throat to udders, gutted and with half a haunch torn away, sometimes three or four beasts mauled and slaughtered in different pastures on the same night, a bite of rump gone from this one and a shoulder missing from that. Once a *vaquero* on the ranch of Don Belisario Oruga—he raised beef, but his bulls had been used for *corridas* in the capital when the fighting bulls that were usually brought by boat from Mexico proved unfit—found a *novillo* half dead from ragged wounds about the neck but with three inches of blood on his left horn, and that same afternoon when Don Belisario, who was considering planting a pasture in pangola grass, went to consult Alejandro Sancudo M., Agronomist and Surveyor, he found the office empty and Alejo at home in bed, complaining of a terrible boil on his groin. Then a *campesino* was attacked by what he said was a wolf, though clearly it was some kind of cat—it chewed a cube steak out of him before he cut its left paw with his machete—for there are no wolves in Tinieblas, whereas we have plenty of jaguar (mostly in Otán Province, which borders on Remedios, and, of course, in Selva Trópica), as well as wildcat (*gato montes*), puma, and tigrillo. An expedition was mounted to track down and destroy the marauder, but Alejo, who was easily the best shot in Angostura, if not the entire province, had to decline a place in it, for he had cut his left hand seriously while sawing wood, and the men turned up nothing very big though they shot a lot of game and had a good, comradely week. The depredations slacked off then, and then took up again a few months later, and then stopped completely as mysteriously as they had begun at just about the time when Alejo Sancudo formed a secret society whose purpose was to seize power and reform the state.

He called the movement Acción Dinámica—a phrase which might have made him an American fortune as a detergent tout—though its members became known as the *remedistas*, derived from Remedios where they came from, and the explosive dose of salts they prescribed for the body politic. They were recruited from among the restless sons of provincial physiocrats, but for some time failed to outnumber the society's symbols—a Tinieblan fasces (machete poking from sheaves of rice), a swastika (or swavastica, the mirror image of Adolf's) etched in gold, a fiery cross, the sign of Cancer (under which Alejo was born), and a pet's corner of birds, fish, mammals, and reptiles, some zoologically possible, some imaginatively combined. Then the sorrows of the New York Stock Exchange depressed the banana market and put the Tinieblan economy in mourning. Young men watched their patri-

monies wither and sought dynamic action. They wore sheets to
meetings, held torchlight rites on horseback, formed cabals against
the merchants of the capital. *Grafters and libertines who grovel to
the gringos! Kick them out, and the foreigners with them! Republic
of virtue based on land!* Their leader, a grave, pencil-thin young
man with olive face and careful mustache, was already convinced
of his mystic mission to save the nation, whereas I always did a
thing for the joy of it, without deluding myself that it was part of
an august destiny written somewhere in a golden book.

So for five years Alejo bayed the moon, sublimating bestial urges
in the beastlier group therapy of revolutionary conspiracy, confecting
a doctrine by collage—gob of Gobineau glued to gloss on Guizot—
and a program by astrology—he had begun to study Nostradamus
now, along with theosophy, numerology, and occultism. (When I
think of all the verbal underpinning Alejo needs to support his will
to power, I hold it to my eternal credit that when I reached for the
brass ring, I never bothered myself, my opponents, or the public with
ideology.) Alejo is not unique (*See* Lew Garew, *The Latin American
Lycanthrocrats*), but—give him his due, he's going to win in April
and have Ñato delivered—there have been very few in his class this
century. Nutrillo, Macho Delmonte in Cuba, Dubonet the Haitian
witch doctor, and perhaps the Argentine Peñon. And Alejo already
had all his super powers there in Remedios: the gleaming bronze eyes
that sear men and spear women, the aura of sacred untouchability
(even the richest planters called him only by his title), the utter fear-
lessness (born, perhaps, from the knowledge that Tinieblans do not
load silver bullets), the hoarse, compelling voice, the pitiless frown
in adversity, and, for brighter moments, the demonic grin. How terrible to nurse talent in obscurity! He needed cheering crowds and
fawning ministers, and all he had for audience were some provincial
townspeople and for followers a scruffy pack whose adulation was
barely sufficient to keep him in human form. White by day he read,
tongue lolling from the corner of his mouth, in the dusty heat of his
office; black by night he schemed, hurling mute howls at each full
moon that found him still unknown. There he sat in that absurd
nightcap, wondering if the country was ever going to put on its red
hood and set out for grandma's.

6

In the end he decided to meet the country halfway, which accounts for my being born in the palace. Alejo feared the *moralistas* might harm my mother if he left her at Uncle Erasmo's, and my mother, who was nervous enough all by herself, panicked at the shooting and dropped me a week ahead of time.

An easy birth, according to Edilma. Squirted into the world just before midnight in a maid's room at the back of the building. Alejo came in, gun in hand, as I came out, peered at my groin, thanked Doña Angustias for a second son, found the sack of bullets he'd been looking for, and went back to the action.

Edilma has always maintained that I was not the least frightened by my father's warlike aspect or the fusillade without. Used to torment my brother Alfonso with it.

"Three years younger and more than a man Kiki didn't cry the night the *moralistas* almost murdered us."

Poor Alfonso got left in Remedios. He must have wished many times Alejo had made his attempt earlier.

As it was it was premature, but he could wait no longer. He was almost exactly Napoleon's age on the eighteenth of Brumaire and had, besides, discovered amazing correspondences between his own horoscope and that of Mussolini. More, he had been listening so long and so acutely to the discontented rumblings of his own brain that he believed the whole country in turmoil. He led his group down to the capital to seize power.

My mother was then extremely pregnant with me, and she went along to deliver in the hospital. Actually she was supposed to be Alejo's cover for making the trip, though he didn't need one. No one paid any attention to his movements, which was why he wanted power in the first place, wasn't it? In those days you went by road to Otán, then by narrow-gauge train to Puerto Ospino, then by boat, so that if the government had cared at all about Acción Dinámica, they would have been well-prepared for the *putsch.* Only one official in fact remarked the conspirators' arrival, Licentiate Erasmo Sancudo, Vice Minister of justice. He knew his brother would scarcely tramp all the way to Ciudad Tinieblas just for a pregnant wife—was there not a doctor in Angostura, as well as several practiced midwives?—and all his lunatic disciples were in the capital—for the christening, no doubt—along with a score of their field hands, who never went anywhere unmacheted. Uncle Erasmo winked at Alejo and offered to do what he could, consistent, of course, with the delicacy of his position.

There is a story which illustrates Uncle Erasmo's poise in delicate positions. When he was first practicing law, a bank clerk came to him with a sad but familiar tale. He had embezzled two thousand inchados and spent them on girls and lost them at the cockfights. Uncle Erasmo consented to accept him as a client on condition that he do exactly as told, then told him to take four thousand more and bring the money to his office. Uncle Erasmo then had coffee with the manager of the bank and after commenting on the weather, the political scene, and the price of bananas, got around to mentioning a client of his who had embezzled six thousand sound blue inchados from the manager's bank. The fellow had been prodigal—*contempt for husbandry is the gravest defect of our people, don't you agree, Señor Gerente?*—but was able to make immediate restitution of half and would gladly pay the rest back out of his salary if the bank agreed not to prosecute. If not, he was resolved to flee the country —*you must surely be aware, Señor Gerente, that professional ethics forbid me most sternly from revealing a client's name*—in which case his poor mother—*a saint, Señor Gerente, who takes communion every morning and never misses a funeral*—would never see him again, or the bank its money. The manager accepted, the lad was saved, and the odd thousand stayed in Uncle Erasmo's safe. So it is not strange that Alejo told his brother nothing of Acción Dinámica's intentions—one cannot say plans, for all anyone, Alejo included, knew was that they were going to take power; no one had any idea how—until Uncle Erasmo guessed.

The first thing Uncle Erasmo could delicately do was take Alejo to a reception given by President Moral on the eve of the four hundred and fifteenth anniversary of the discovery of Tinieblas. We may imagine a slick black snake of Pierce Arrows and Packards threaded through the porte-cochère and looped about the statue of Simón Mocoso in the little park opposite, head and tail dangling through narrow streets to the Plaza Cervantes while the rain leaps upward from the pavement and chauffeurs swab the insides of windshields with balls of newspaper. In the open patio a bronze faun (destined to become, eleven years later, a target for BB's aimed from the gallery) pisses superfluously into the pool installed by General Mojón to nest a quartet of piranhas (to whom he fed cats and puppy dogs) and now occupied by vegetarian goldfish, but only first-time guests pause to admire his tassel on their way to the ballroom. Let us forego the commonplace device of following Alejo down the receiving line toward an ironic handshake with President Moral, sashed in purple, green, and yellow and crucified with the Order of Palmiro Inchado de los Huevos, in favor of a portrait in the manner of Velázquez's *Meninas*. An ignored Alejo regards himself in a full-length mirror. In the foreground we see his straight shoulders and the seal-sleek back of his brilliantined head; at middle distance his reflection from widow's peak to wasp waist, eyes stern, thin lips firm under circumflex mustache as he paints an imaginary sash across his breast; and over his shoulder in the background a frieze of guests: ladies in silk print dresses of ankle length—hemlines have plummeted along with stock averages and coffee futures—men in white flannels cut very full in the trousers, the papal nuncio with a thick gold chain suspending a pearled crucifix over his cassock, an American naval officer from the Reservation in a high tight collar like Lieutenant Pinkerton's, and, at the far left, emerging from the mirror's rococo frame, the open carp's mouth and boneless chin of Abúndio Moral.

Perhaps one or two of the more lascivious ladies wondered who was the slim, intense young man who came in with Erasmo Sancudo, but certainly no one else paid Alejo any mind, so while the three violins, cello, and bass that Moral's protocol secretary had borrowed from the officers' club at Fort Shafter sawed out selections from a four-year-old Madrid *zarzuela*, he slunk off into an empty suite of rooms and unlocked the windows. Then he left the palace and went—on foot, for the rain had stopped and the

clouds thinned off enough to give snapshots of a rising full moon—
to Uncle Erasmo's, where he changed to black clothes and picked
up his pistol, and then to the town house of the Oruga family,
where his pack was gathering. Two hours before dawn members of
Acción Dinámica adfenestrated themselves into the palace. They
shot one guard and disarmed the three others while Alejandro Sancudo bounded up the marble staircase, kicked in the door of the
presidential bedroom, pointed his pistol at Abúndio Moral, whose
wife had pulled the sheet up over her head, and said: "You have
served the fatherland, now go home."

Moral left, but came back at dusk with a number of his
cronies. They got as far as Simón Mocoso's statue when the shooting started. Meanwhile both he and Alejo had called on the people
to rally. In defense of the constitution or the revolution, depending
on whose manifesto one read. These were printed in *EXTRA!* edi-
tions—it was a national holiday—of newspapers now defunct,
Moral's in one sheet, Alejo's in another, and distributed around
noon by boys on bicycles. The capital's two radio stations were
gagged by what was later called a mechanical breakdown in the
steam turbine of the Compañía Tinieblina de Electricidad y Gas (a
subsidiary of the Yankee and Celestial Energy Corporation), whose
legal counsel, the firm of Anguila, Anguila, y Sancudo, had recently
advised appealing a tax increase levied by the Moral Administration. Nor did the telephones, which were operated by the same
company, work very well that day, and this may have contributed
to Moral's difficulties in recruiting followers for a counter-coup.
He had, in the first place, delayed organizing this stroke, having
been assured by his Vice Minister of justice that the Civil Guard
would take all necessary steps. Don Abúndio had no idea until he
read Alejo's proclamation of a new era in Tinieblan history who it
was who had thrown him out of bed, and office, and by that time
my mother and Edilma had been brought over to the palace and
Uncle Erasmo had had coffee in the Civil Guard barracks with
Colonel Miltíades Garrote. After lamenting the shameful fact that
while the gringos had three generals and an admiral in the Reservation, the ranking officer in Tinieblas was only a colonel, Uncle
Erasmo reviewed the carcers of the great captains of history, all of

whom, it seemed, shared a concern for the welfare of their men, never allowing them to be uselessly slaughtered in unimportant skirmishes but rather holding them in concentrated readiness for the decisive blow. Colonel Garrote was persuaded that no steps were necessary at the moment; the Civil Guard remained in its barracks with the gates locked.

November 28–29, 1930, was amateur night at the palace. The *moralistas* blazed away from the park; the *remedistas* replied from the windows. At eleven-fifty three *moralistas* were riddled in a rush on the gate, the volley spurring my mother to her final contractions. Of the *remedistas* Santiago Pájaro was killed and Gaspar Oruga wounded in what he called the upper thigh and everyone else the buttock. A ricochet no doubt, for all the *remedistas* were men of honor. There were certain intranquilities in other parts of the city, particularly a cantina combat between hands from Enrique Marañon's coffee plantation and a group of stevedores armed with bailing hooks, but the general uprising Moral had called for never took place, while the gringos in the Reservation stood neighborly aside because Hoover had already instituted the policy that Roosevelt would name and take all the credit for.

Around eight the next morning, when it was clear that the people would rally to neither group, Uncle Erasmo went to the palace and arranged a truce. First he promised Moral that he would get his crazy brother out of the palace; then he spoke to Alejo. Moral, he said, had forfeited all right to the presidency when he left his post, where he might have stayed and died like a man, but Alejo's claim, which was proportional to his supply of ammunition, was weak. Governments ought to enjoy a little legitimacy or a lot of force, both if possible. Couldn't Alejo content himself with having ousted Moral and yield to Efraín Anguila Ahumada, who was constitutional Vice President (and Uncle Erasmo's brother-in-law and partner)? As men had died, no one could call the coup frivolous. People would say that Alejo was a brave man who had deposed a corrupt and retrograde despot. As for Acción Dinámica's program, couldn't he, Erasmo, expect to be a prominent member of the new regime, and wouldn't he see to it that the spirit of the revolution did not perish?

Powerful logic, sustained by Doña Angustias' pleas and the arrival of Garrote with a company of guards and Anguila himself, who had Garrote's general's stars in his pocket, along with a memo to have bars installed on all the palace windows. The *remedistas* retired in good order, with Alejo still brandishing his pistol, and little Kiki, traveling in Edilma's arms, the last man out.

7

Jaime, who carries me now, comes for me at six. He shuts the door softly and stands squinting in the groom. Sees my eyes open and pads over, smiling.

"Good morning, Kiki."

I blink to acknowledge, like a warship at sea.

He switches off the air conditioner and peels back the bed-clothes from where they have lain all night just under my chin. Kiki's no bed-making problem, except when he makes wee-wee. Don't do it often, and I'm condomed each night to be fail-safe. Like stuffing soft tripe into a sausage skin, and the item's furnished dildowise with latex thongs that tie about my hips. I like Elena or Marta to perform this sacrament, for old time's sake. Not that I was ever partial to rubberized romance, but both ladies were—and no doubt still are—experts with the stick shift, each in her own style.

Short flight to the toilet in Jamie's knotty arms. He holds my shoulder so I won't fall off. Wipes me.

Edilma makes cooing sounds around infants. Marta would be disgusted, and might even show it. Elena, who plays every role with grace, has won international raves in the somewhat Disneyfied casting of mother hen to my broken-winged capon, but I don't give her the bathroom scenes, which would cost the part much of its subtlety and weaken the memory of an earlier opus when I was cock of the walk. Jaime has to be around to fly me back and forth, and I feel no shame with him. Didn't I scoop vomit from your mouth, Jaime, when you almost drowned at La Yegua? You went wading after my son Mito's toy boat, stepped in over your head, and went down like a rock. I was hammocking on the terrace after a matinee row with his mother Olga—lucky for you we weren't inside screwing things back together—and dolphined in after you with all my clothes on. Had to dive twice before I found where the current had filed you between two boulders. Pulled you off the bottom by your black hair, and when I asked you later if you'd been scared, you said, "No, Kiki. I knew you'd save me."

8

Brown toes splayed on the tiles as he derricks me from pot to wheelchair. Our indians never wear shoes when they can help it, and I let Jaime dress as he pleases around the house. Loose shirt and trousers tied at the waist, revolver tucked in over his appendix. Used to carry it only in the street, but since my assassination it never leaves him.

Smith & Wesson .38 Special, nickel-plated with a six-inch barrel, the very weapon we'll mate with Ñato unless I change my plan. A dealer in Alexandria, Virginia, gave it to me as a sample. It came in a a flat brown cardboard box with a cleaning rod and a wire brush and a scrolled guarantee which I suppose one's heirs could forward to the factory with their reimbursement claim if, say, the firing pin broke at a touchy moment. Too fancy for my customers, but I took it anyway, thinking of you, Jaime. And when I returned to Tinieblas, we went to La Yegua. You drove the Cranston with me beside you and Olga in the back with Edilma and the kids, and the revolver in my briefcase though no one knew it.

That was in 1957, the year before you almost drowned, just after I'd bought the ranch. Eighty thousand dollars—he wouldn't take inchados—into my father's Panamanian bank. It was Uncle Erasmo who showed him how he could have a hank in a steel filing box in the closet of an accountant in Panama City: officers, shareholders, assets and liabilities, all in that little box, and no one but the accountant to know who owned it. I paid without a qualm, for there'd been a lot of target practice in Costaguana.

When I took the gun out, Olga got up from the hammock and went inside and asked Edilma where she'd put the aspirin. Mito asked if it was real, and I smiled yes and said he could hold it. He touched the cylinder and backed away—Olga's child—and I mussed his hair and sent him for you. We left kids on the terrace and walked down toward the river, you rubbing your palms on the seat of your pants, I dropping shells into the cylinder. You said I ought to fire first, and I laughed, thinking of feudal barons and *droit de seigneur.*

Olga had ordered a railing put on the terrace, and the carpenter had left a scrap of two-by-four on the grass. I flung it out into the river, thirty yards at least, a little upstream of where we were standing, and when it bobbed up and the current took it, I put my left hand in my pocket and thumbed back the hammer and held and squeezed once and the wood jumped like a tarpon.

Olguita squealed—she was only three—squealed with glee, "You killed it, Daddy! You killed the stick!" and Mito kept his hands over his ears even while we were walking back.

Rust at the butt where you've filed off the number; the nickel's worn where it rubs your skin. But I taught you to keep the bore clean and the action supple, and I know you'll sweep up my smashed life with it if I ask you to.

9

Jaime bastes me with lather from the badger brush, scrapes with my safety razor. His own flat mahogany face has never needed shaving, but he's grown quite expert using mine. He suspected the barber's blade at my throat and would lurk in the doorway, ready to blast at the first knick. Barber reluctant to visit me, and Jaime said he'd learned from watching.

Better with the razor than with comb or toothbrush; better

with these than at dressing me. I'd rather Edilma did it, but it's hard
to tell him now. Angry when I see my legs now, thin and white like
a notary's, and Jaime lifts first one, then the other, fumbling with
my shorts and trousers.

"On the left side, cretin!" grinding mashed words through fury.
As if it matters now where he stuffs those dried prunes! Worthless,
mirthless, helpless cripple! Can't put on his own pants. Can't wipe
his own bung. Wasted, white, flaccid! Why isn't he dead?

My head flip-flops like a gaffed tuna, acid foam around my
teeth. You can get more exciting tantrums from a healthy baby, but
it impresses Jaime, who frowns contritely.

"Sorry, Kiki."

"Nothing." Sane again, I make my smile. "Hard life, eh,
brother?" Sounds like a pig rooting.

Jaime nods.

"Harder for El Ñato when we catch him."

Jaime nods fiercely, showing teeth. "Yes, Kiki. Harder for
him," and he lifts the mannequin back into the chair to dress its
torso.

Philippine shirt of yellow-white silk, Elena's idea and very practical. Long sleeves for waxy forearms, french cuffs for shriveled
wrists, closed collar to hide the scars. No tie needed for embroidered front, and tailored to hang outside the trousers in lieu of a
jacket. Though in this case it doesn't hang. Draped neatly in the
dummy's lap, display cloth for pink plastic fingers.

Jaime rolls me through the house to the front balcony, then
slinks off to breakfast in the kitchen. The bay is a five-mile horse-
shoe with my house in the middle, right prong the naval docks in
the Reservation, left prong the old city with the sunshine-bouncing
gold roof of the President's Palace. A few early cars zip along
Avenida de la Bahiá. Sun still tame, affectionate like a lion cub
who'll grow up to maul you. Breeze enough to ruffle the bay and
one cloud, size of a marshmallow, hung out over the departing
shrimp fleet.

Pelicans wheel beyond the sea wall. Tuck wings and plummet.
Surface to brood over bulged beaks. Thrash back into the air.
Boomtime, thanks to the Humboldt Current. Six weeks till April

brings deep water for the fish, rain for parched fields, elections for Alejo, a lien on Ñato for Jaime and me.

Edilma brings my coffee; holds the thermos for me to sniff.

"See, Kiki. The way you like it."

Olga thought strong coffee bad for my health, or my disposition, though that's not why I divorced her. Edilma has always given me what I want. Every woman has in fact, though some, like Olga, gave and resented.

Pleasant smell. Little Kiki used to hang around the mill enjoying it. One roast for Tinieblas, another for the Reservation. Gringos like their coffee weak for some reason, so they can see through to the bottom of the cup. Take the perfume out and drink it like medicine, but even theirs smells good in the bag. Stacks of blue paper sacks with my mother's picture on them. *CAFE SANCUDO*. Something to trust about the family.

Smile for Edilma. Pours me a cup. Two spoons of sugar. Milk from the green carton. Holds the cup for Kiki to sip through a glass straw. Two cups that way while I watch the pelicans. Something that's as good as before.

10

Edilma believes Alejo put my mother's picture on the coffee sacks out of remorse for having driven her insane, but as far as I am concerned it was a political move. In this culture the leader ought to be respectful to his wife, as well as ardent to his girlfriends, attentive to his mother, stern with men, firm with horses, arrogant with the masses, and unchummy with gringos. Since Alejo was President when word came that my mother was dead—the Italian Ambassador delivered a personal sniffle of regret from Il Duce— and had recently forced Don Moisés Levi Mendes to sell him his coffee *finca* for about one-tenth what it was worth and had built his own mill with a generous loan from the Ministry of Agriculture, he put her picture copied from a wedding photo, on the blue sacks.

They continued to sell briskly, in the Reservation as well as in Tinieblas after the Japanese bombed Pearl Harbor and the gringos had Alejo deposed and exiled, though that probably had less to do with the coffee's excellent flavor than with national pride. Few Tinieblans were very contrite when they packed my father on a plane for Paraguay, but once he was gone he became something of a symbol of violated sovereignty, and those Reservation sales of *CAFE SANCUDO* were no doubt made to Tinieblan employees who were willing to stomach the gringo grind for the sake of nationalistic protest.

People like Alejo more when he's out of power. He's been out for eighteen years now, so they love him. Even the pelicans would vote for him if they had the vote. Fuertes would go on television and promise a new program, elaborated by the Presidential Planning Commission and funded by AID, for keeping the cold current inshore all year round, and the pelicans would still favor Alejo. Alejo would go out on the sea wall and hold up his hands with the palms out and say, "Pelicans of Tinieblas," and they'd all stop fishing and gather in to listen. "Pelicans of Tinieblas," he'd say, running his words together and then pausing. "I am Engineer Alejandro Sancudo Montes. I have been your President and will be your President again. History is a spiral which winds always to higher convolutions. Our destinies are intertwined. The stars guide my footsteps even in the wilderness. Nothing happens by accident. You will vote for me." And of course they would, all but the few who tried to understand what he said, and maybe even some of those because he's got so many parties behind him this time and looks like a winner. And as he'd promised the pelicans nothing, he could perfectly well expect to get the fish vote too.

He can always count on the women, not because he put through the law giving them the vote, but because he is still personally magnetic, irrational, and, as the picture on the coffee sacks proves, respectful to his wife's memory as he was to her person in life. Only last week I chanced to mention my mother to Doña Rosario Largo de Cristál, once Alejo's grade school teacher and now, at eighty, president *emerita* of the Woman's Auxiliary of the Tinieblista Party, and was reminded that no wife was more respected by her husband than Angustias Sancudo. There she was, a gibbering neurotic, yet Alejo always carried a little bottle of the rubbing alcohol she liked to sniff for her anxiety seizures and would leave any social gathering, no matter how heated the discussion, the moment she grew restless among the women and came whimpering to him. More, he didn't rut with *chola* girls or go whoring to the capital, but kept a Ticamalan woman discreetly in the village near La Yegua, visiting her only two or three times a week and never staying late into the evening, much less all night. (My mother's father, Don Augustín Maldonado, died shortly after the *golpe* of 28 November 1930, leaving the ranch to her, and Alejo was able to manage it from town since one of the first acts of the Anguila Administration was to put a road—"a vital stimulant to good relations with our sister republic," said Erasmo Sancudo, the new Foreign Minister—right by the ranch from Angostura to the frontier.) And because of poor Angustias' nerves Alejo abandoned politics for five years, returning to public life only when he was named Ambassador to Italy, an appointment which love of country made impossible to refuse.

No point in trying to tell Doña Rosario that he never abandoned politics, not even for an instant, that he simply preferred, instead of trudging toward the center of the stage, to make his entrances *en grande jetée brillante*. He pretended to disband Accion Dinámica in deference to Anguila, but continued to plot as earnestly as ever and was all set to overthrow Juan de Austria Tábano, Angela's successor, when Uncle Erasmo, then vice president and destined to become President the next year, had Alejo dispatched to the farthest decent embassy Tinieblas then maintained. As for attentions to my mother, he destroyed her pets with his basilisk stare. A bull terrier named Pepe ran off yelping as though kicked and never came back, and the white rabbit had convulsions and died in my mother's arms when he trained his gaze on it. Once he seized Alfonso by the ankles and hurled him into the river before my mother's eyes—when he tried it on me, I bit his thumb to the bone—while in the privacy of the house he usually addressed her in the third person as *La Inválída*. In Rome he often popped home early in the afternoon to stand in the doorway of the bedroom where my mother lay crocheting and glare at her for above five minutes, snarling incomprehensibly and making weird faces. Then he would stride out and return at six, all tenderness, and go in and fondle her and say, "Are you feeling a little better, love?" And she would smile weakly and ask, "Why were you so terrible to me before?" And he would shake his head sadly and sigh and say, "What are you saying, heart? I've been all afternoon at the Ministry of Trade, trying to get them to buy Tinieblan coffee. I've only just left the place."

So Edilma believes he stole my mother's mind like one of those precision-planning movie bandits and then felt sorry when it was too late, and I think he did it haphazardly and never felt responsible. She had to impersonate a whole country, reacting to him and paying him deference, so he alternately pampered and terrorized her, hardly remembering the one policy when the other was in effect so long as he got a response. If you asked him, I think he'd say sincerely that he was a good husband, that his wife was just too weak to absorb the great benefits he'd offered her. That's what he says about the Tinieblan people, after all, and he treats them the same way.

I don't recall the incidents myself, not even biting his thumb. I recall a soft woman who wore a lace bed jacket and smelled of lemon-scented soap, who grasped the fingers of her right hand in the palm of her left hand to stop them from shaking, who held her head a little to one side as she wandered distractedly through a flat in Rome, who lay in bed crocheting most of the day and would like as not crumble in sobs when her short-pantsed, scuff-kneed, boy-sweat-smelling younger son flung himself over her to embrace her. One day she was no longer there—I can reconstruct the time as being shortly after my father's 1937 visit to Berchtesgaden—and Alfonso and I were informed that she was ill and that we must be men. Alfonso cried, I didn't, though at the moment we both thought she was dead. She lingered, actually, for four years in a sanitarium near Como, a model patient—according to the file I had them exhume for me in 1963—until the morning she broke the bathroom mirror with her forehead and cut her throat with a shard.

11

Marta drops into a chair by the railing and slings one leg over the other. Sunglasses on, newspapers in her lap.

"Sleep well?" Sounds like a bullfrog.

"So, so."

"Gringo's no good?" Last night she went out with the director of the documentary crew Elena has brought from Hollywood.

No smile. Shrug. "How are you?"

"Fine. Watching the pelicans. Coffee?"

She shakes her head. Jaw set angry-worried, like the day she came to see me at the embassy in Paris. Her scholarship check hadn't come through, and she suspected I'd filched it. Her family were very anti-*alejista*—still are, except for her, and she's really a *kikista* and can't stand my father. At that time you loathed me too, didn't you, Marta? though your uncle Lazarillo, my cellmate in 1950, always spoke well of me, giving a romanticized version of our imprisonment in his column at least once a year to remind everyone how he'd suffered for democracy. Actually my father admired Lazarillo's wit and was secretly flattered by "*Hagiografía Tinieblina,*" an extended quibble on the illusory sainthood in our family name.

Lazarillo didn't get jailed until he revived the old rumor that Alejo has only one testicle with a satirical romance called "The Presidential Ball" in the English section of *Diario de la Bahía*. I was being held, without a formal charge: my real offense was getting caught humping Angela. We weren't treated badly, and after ten days or so my father shipped us out of the country.

But Lazarillo's tales of our comradeship in adversity cut no ice with you, Marta.

"How did you get your scholarship?" I asked, just to make chitchat, while my secretary was checking the mail.

And you said, "More honestly than you got your embassy."

Which made me notice you—slim girl with wide brown eyes that flashed marvelously and lovely long legs in crazy-colored tights.

"Perhaps you can get one to study etiquette."

She regretted her rudeness but wouldn't apologize and sat glaring at me, her little white fist clenched over the wooden button of her duffle coat. She always gets angry when she's wrong.

When my secretary came back without the check, I dictated a cable to the Ministry of Education. Then I offered to loan her five hundred francs.

"I don't want anything from the Sancudos!"

It was then a question of throwing her out or taking her to bed.

"The loan's from petty cash, but I'll give you a dinner on what we Sancudos have stolen from the poor."

"And your wife?"

"Will be furious. She'll scratch my face and throw figurines and call me filthy things in Italian."

"All right," she said, smiling at last. "I was pompous."

I took her to an unromantic place where provincial businessmen read their dinners from newspapers clipped to brown sticks, and she ate like a horse and recounted my iniquities. The gossips had taught her my story better than I'd lived it, and I learned that I'd been heartless to Olga and was now living off Elena, that I'd had ten kilos of heroin plucked from my bags at Miami airport and was making deals with neo-Nazis in Bonn. Also opinions of her own: that I was egotistical, staging a coup against the Aguado Government just to get power, and unprincipled, taking an embassy from the military junta just to get out of jail. She built a little pirate isle of Spanish in that Sargasso of bourgeois French grunts and won me there, singing of my sins and escapades. I'd got used to being known in Paris as Elena Delfi's husband, but my vanity was always sensitive until Dr. Espino removed it. I left half my steak, nourishing on your interest in me, Marta, and when the bill came I took you down the street to a hotel.

My arm around your shoulder as we crossed the avenue. Headlights shearing yellow over rain-glazed cobblestones and February wind tangling your hair. I felt like singing then. Each new girl was like the first time, and I couldn't believe my luck.

It was warm in the bar, but she wouldn't take her coat off. She lit my cigarette with book matches from the table and laid the match in the ashtray—a white ceramic triangle with RICORD printed in red and black—to see if it would burn to the end. I asked the waiter for brandy and registration forms, and she filled out mine from my passport. No coy protests, no romantic gush, as though that were what she always did after dinner.

"I thought you were older than thirty-four."

"Disappointed?"

"No. Thirty-four's a good age."

I sent the forms in with the waiter and could have drunk another brandy, but she'd only half sipped hers when he returned with the key. The elevator rose sedately like an upright glass coffin as I fumbled for her icy hand.

I didn't think you'd be a virgin, Marta. You were almost nineteen and had been five months in Paris. And you were so calm downstairs.

"I'm glad to be rid of it. I haven't thought of anything else for months. I could hardly study."

"No boyfriend?"

"There's a French boy. But he asks me and then lets me say no."

"So you seduced me."

"Until this evening I hated you. Then you didn't seem so nasty, though I'm sure everything they say about you is true. And you didn't ask, you just brought me here. I thought at least you'd do a good job. And you wouldn't have to talk about love."

Not a syllable. Nor a mention of how terrified I was that you might turn and flee down the stairs and that my fingers shook when I unlocked the door. I turned you by your firm haunch and cupped you where you flowed warm yolk; took you again and can still taste those first bites, though it's five years since that night and four since I was murdered.

At first I hadn't thought of having her again, or maybe just once or twice more for the novelty. But she was like one of those sweet fruits from home, a barely ripened mango or wild pineapple, which are impossible to get in wintertime Paris, even at Hediard's in the Madeleine for fantastic prices, and whose remembered savor can haunt an exile's dreams, so I decided not to give her up, at least not until spring. I would go by her room on the way to the embassy, striding up the Rue Racine in my chesterfield coat and ambassadorial homburg, a bunch of roses—the only gift she'd take from me—swathed in tissue paper in my gloved hand and my breath wreathing out before me in the windless morning, to spring three flights into Bohemia for a breakfast taste of youth and the tropics.

Elena sniffed it on me at once, that special jauntiness a new girl confers. Olga always tried to block it out, but Elena could hear it in my telephone voice all the way from Rome or Los Angeles and would ask, half serious, half in joke, if she ought to come and defend her territory. She treated me with particular kindness at such periods, enjoying my good spirits, for she believed a man ought to have adventures as a woman ought to be faithful. But when the thing of Marta had gone on above three weeks, which was a record, Elena said she wanted to meet my little friend.

This disturbed Marta; in Tinieblas wives and girlfriends converse mainly with fingernails. But I pointed out that Elena wasn't a fishwife and that the meeting was as difficult for her, since whenever she went out people gawked at her, despite veils and dark glasses. I didn't have to press, for she was no coward and as curious about Elena as Elena was about her. As for me, I waited to see what would happen. While I was married to Olga, I tried to organize and was always twisted up in unentanglable intrigues. By the end I had learned that women always make the final dispositions where love is concerned, and I relaxed and let them arrange themselves where they felt most comfortable. I left Marta and Elena to make their rendezvous and went to play squash with the British. When I returned home, I found them together in the living room.

"Marta and I are going to St. Moritz tomorrow, Kiki," Elena disclosed. "She ought to know how to ski."

"Am I invited?"

"Perhaps you could come on the weekend. We need a little rest from you."

And Marta poured me a cup of tea.

"I was afraid she might be a little whore," Elena said later. "I didn't want you to stay too long with one of those."

"And she's not."

"Not at all. I like her."

And Marta, the next morning: "I expected her to be a snob."

"And she isn't."

"No. And not jealous either. She congratulated me on choosing you and said it was better to share a man than own a boy. She says one can't own a man and shouldn't try."

"I wish I'd been there."

"You're conceited enough as is."

Four nights later, when Elena and I were in bed in the hotel at St. Moritz . . . Wait. I want to remember how it feels to have your legs tired but toned by skiing and your mind eased yet stimulated by the proximity of a lovely woman. We'd had dinner and a drink or two, and I'd danced with each of them and kissed Marta's smiling cheek at her door. I'd left the window open half an inch in the sitting room. The bedroom had rococo molding where the walls met the ceiling and a marble mantelpiece with a porcelain clock, roman numerals for the hours and a shepherd and shepherdess pushing absentmindedly on either side. I was reading about the battle of Ramillies in Churchill's *Marlborough,* probing foot reconnaissances into the frigid no-man's-land at the bottom of the bed, and had just dropped some Gauloise ash on the white coverlet, yellowed by the merged circles of the reading lamps, when Elena put down the script she'd been studying and asked:

"Do you want to keep this girl?"

"Well, she pleases me. But if it's a question of choosing . . ."

"Oh, Kiki. You're so pretentious. If I thought there were any question of a choice, I'd leave you at once as unworthy of me."

"Well, then, yes; I'd like to keep her."

"It's not to feed your ego, is it? I know we're all supposed to feed your ego, but I hope with Marta it's not just that."

"She has an excellent ego of her own which I, in my small way, have gorged like a Strasbourg goose."

"All right. She might do you good, settle you down a little. But remember, Kiki, I turned down a chance to play *Les liaisons dangereuses.*"

"Which means?"

"Which means I'm understanding you and the way you need other women, and not trying to find perverse stimulation or act out some sadomasochistic lunacy. And if you get tired of her, don't drag it out. I won't have you hurting her."

"Feeling maternal? Is it time we had a kid?"

"No. She's more like a younger sister, or a memory of myself at that age."

"Nine years ago. You make it sound like ninety."

"Being married to you makes one age quickly."

"It does, eh? Then come here, you big Istrian bitch. It's time for your hormone injection."

And the three of us lived happily until death did us part.

When I went back to Tinieblas eight months later, Marta asked me to take her with me. Her family disowned her, and Alfonso told me to let her go, let her finish her studies or get married.

"I'm not holding her. What should I do, throw her out? She likes it here, and I need her in the campaign."

"You're an egotistical bastard, Kiki."

"Well, yes. But as long as the girl's happy, what do you care?"

And when I was bungled into the plant kingdom, you stayed with me and learned to translate my noises.

"Is it that you feel sorry for me?" It must have been a year ago I asked her that.

"Do you feel sorry for yourself?"

"Sometimes."

"I don't. You don't either. If you did I'd leave you. I stay because you're a man."

12

"Shall I read or hold?"

Angry at something. Or just sick of life, as we get now and then. It's nice to sit in the sun and have her read to me, but not when she's bitchy. "Hold."

She pulls her chair beside mine and spreads Alfonso's *Correo Matinal*. My father has had a triumphant tour of the interior: "Tumultuous multitudes recall the great campaigns of 1940 and

1948." Picture of him speaking from the back of a truck in the Salinas oil field: kind of white suit that went out of style after León Fuertes became President; desiccated face under wide-brimmed hat; false teeth snapping at the wind; and all around a sea of aluminum helmets.

"'The maximum leader of the Tinieblista Party will speak this afternoon in Bolívar Plaza,'" Marta reads, "'accompanied by his son, Don César Enrique Sancudo Maldonado, and his daughter-in-law, Elena Delfi de Sancudo, the famous actress.'"

"Tears for the freak and cheers for the lovely lady."

"Why do you do it?"

"You know why."

"You should have stayed in California and continued the treatments."

"When I've seen Ñato. That's the treatment for me."

"Just see him?"

"'If Alejandro Sancudo is President, all is permitted.' That's what your uncle wrote day before yesterday."

"It's true."

"It's true where Ñato is concerned. It's not as though anyone cared about him or would miss him much if something happened. I imagine he's sweating now. Watching the campaign and worrying, and if he leaves the country, Interpol will get him. His only chance is if Pepe Fuertes wins, Pepe won't win. Alejo has the people. And the Electoral jury, and in this country it's not who votes, it's who counts. And he's made his deal with the Guardia, and Washington won't interfere. That's what you need: the people, the jury, a deal with the Guardia, and the OK from Washington, and he's got Nacho's money and Alfonso's papers and a TV station and four radio stations and the same white suit he had on when they threw him out in '52. And he's got Elena Delfi who won an Oscar three years ago, and a vegetable on wheels who can sit out in the sun making people feel so sorry for him they'll cry their way to the polls, who can whinny and drool and shit in his pants if it'll get votes, because when we win we're going to divide this country up, and my share is Ñato Espino!"

Came out heehaws. Only a few circuits left, and they overloaded. Cool hand on my check. Wipes my chin with a napkin. "Ya, papi. Cálmate, corazón."

Resting. Like a bug on flypaper. I want to do something again, mean something. People wondering why I'm back in the country. *What's Kiki up to? Is he planning something?* Expectant and afraid. *He's only a cripple. Cripple, hell! He's up to something.* It's the last chance for Alejo too. He's always been sure only he can save the country, but he really wants the kick of being in. He wants to feel the country under him and make it wiggle and twitch. Stick it in deep for the times they threw him out, for the months in jail and the years in exile.

"Do you know what it's like, Marta, to be in prison with your enemies in power? It's like how I am now. They used to poke their fingers in his food. Major Azote used to come every morning and piss into his cell. 'Good day, Señor Presidente. I have the honor to urinate on you.'"

"He shot Azote's cousin, didn't he?"

"Yes. And Ñato Espino shot me."

"And someone had León Fuertes blown up with a plastic bomb. Who had Fuertes killed, Kiki?"

"There are always people who want to kill a strong President."

She gives me a look. "You were supposed to be a minister, and you didn't get anything."

"Would it make you happy if I said it was me?"

"No."

"What's wrong with you this morning?"

"Nothing. I hate this politics."

"You used to like it."

"I never liked it. I liked you, and you wanted to be President."

"Everyone wants to be President. I wanted to be President, and I got shot. León Fuertes was President, and they blew him up. His brother Pepe is President, and he wants to stay President. My father was President twice—three times if you count one day in 1930—and he wants to be President again. They threw him out in 1952, and now the same people are trying to put him back in. Lucho Gusano's son-in-law wants to be President, but Pepe wouldn't give him the nomination, so Lucho's backing my father, and Meco Avispa wants to be President and is backing Pepe because Pepe's promised him the nomination next time. Nacho Hormiga wants to be President and figures the best way is to be my father's Vice President because my father always gets thrown out before the end of his term, and Lino Piojo wants to be President and is running as Pepe's Vice President because, after all, León Fuertes got blown up, and the same thing could happen to Pepe. Do you know that even Alfonso wants to be President? Only last week he told me, 'Kiki, I think I'd make a good President.' Can you imagine? Even Alfonso wants to be President. If they hanged Tinieblans for wanting to be President, rope would be worth more than rubies."

"I hate it."

"Give me *La Patria*."

"It didn't come."

"Then send the girl for it. I heard a kid hawking it on the street a little while ago."

"Why do you want to read *La Patria?*"

"To see what the other side says, of course. What the hell's the matter with you?"

"Of course! Something must be wrong with me. Not with your wonderful politics."

She flings out of her chair. Back in a minute with the tabloid. Holds it under my nose. "Here! Are you happy now?"

MORE HORNS FOR KIKI across the top. Full page picture of Elena from one of her movies; lying in bed, ecstatic face craned toward the camera and her fingernails in some actor's naked shoulders. *La Donna è Mobile* underneath. Inset at the bottom, a small shot of me laughing; caption *The Complacent Cuckold*.

"The story's inside."

Sun warm on my closed eyes.

"Don't you want me to read it?"

"No, thank you."

"'Elena Delfi has built a new set of horns for Kiki Sancudo, who isn't up to his conjugal duties any more. The latest lover is a well-known French singer, who flew all the way to Hollywood to keep her company on and off her cinema set. The Italian sex goddess married Don Kiki seven years ago in hope of becoming First Lady, but since he is no longer active as a man or a politician, she takes diversion where she finds it. Kiki doesn't complain. She pays the bills, after all.'"

Boy crying *Patria!* up the street. Marta's suffering, so she has to hurt someone.

"'La Delfi, who never tires of Tinieblan politics, arrived from California yesterday to take part in the current campaign. She's casting a local stand-in for Kiki, and since the lady is nothing if not a democrat, the post is wide open. Good luck, boys.'"

Pelicans wheel and plummet. Avenue filling up with cars.

"I'm sorry, Kiki."

Sit quiet and watch the cars. Wonderful place for a traffic survey. Great line of work for me, but they only have them in developed countries.

"Kiki?"

Can't teach a coward to shoot. Afraid of the gun, so he never learns to hold and squeeze. Think he'd be able to hit the head with four shots at three yards. When the man's unarmed and his back is turned. Jerked the trigger and pulled them low. Neck, shoulder, scapula, kidney. First one did the damage, and if it'd been four inches higher there'd be no problem.

"You're more of a man than any of them!"

Make my smile. "Don't worry, Marta. We're going to get them all."

"I don't care about them. I care about you. Let's leave, Kiki. Why don't we leave?"

"Because then it would just be waiting. This is the only place where I can do something."

"You can let people gawk at you. And snicker at you and write filth."

"That's the way it's done here. Tonight our radio will say that Pepe's withered leg is the result of syphilis inherited from his mother."

"And if they shoot you again? Ñato would shoot you again. Do you want to be dead, Kiki? Is that it?"

"No. That's why I came back. So I could feel as though I were still alive."

"Stop trying, Kiki. Stop trying to be like before. You're paralyzed. You can't smuggle guns or blow people up or overthrow the government or run for President. It's all fantasy. They're only using you. Everybody's using everybody, and I hate it. Give it up!"

And she goes out crying.

13

In the bedroom to my right Marta is dabbing her eyes with a handkerchief and choking sobs into anger,

And in the bedroom to my left Elena is dreaming (*Patria*, please copy) of that now-extinct hominid *Kikianthropos erectus* with her left hand clasped between chiffon-swathed thighs and the base of her thumb nestling Mount Pubis,

And next door fluffy-bearded Phil the documentary director who, I hope for both their sakes, laid Marta last night, not in my house, of course, but in one of the pushbutton assignation nooks on the airport road, while a poorly maintained air conditioner wheezed at them and (keep copying, *Patria*) she pretended it was the old Kiki putting it to her—and Carl the cameraman and Sonny the soundman are tenting their bedclothes with piss-rods,

And opposite them Edilma's niece Modesta is making up my bed without disturbing the corded buzzer that lies taped to the bottom sheet under my left index finger every night,

And downstairs Modesta's daughter Neira has cleared off Marta's toast crusts and tea cup and is setting places for the movie men,

And in the kitchen Modesta's sister-in-law Franca is cleaning shrimp for the noon meal, and Jaime is packing the last eggsoaked knob of bread into his jaw,

And at the service entrance on Justo Canino Street Edilma is buying Otán oranges from a pushcart man,

And in the back patio Modesta's husband Otilio is spraying the grass around the swimming pool, and earth and grass are drinking politely because they get their rations every morning while most of the country is sun-scorched brown and breathless, and a forage column of parasol ants is strutting up out of their rock-hard nest, quick-timing off on the long haul to the plants that flourish by the kitchen wall, while another column marches back, each ant holding a sheet of leaf three times its size so that the second column looks like a line of sloops beating closehauled through the grass,

And—what else? because there's no one to read to me or help me smoke a cigarette, and I will not, repeat, will not shout, and I don't want to get nervous nervous nervous because when you're trussed up (truss and trousseau from the same root, eh, Ñato), trussed up tight, it is imperative to keep calm calm calm,

And in the pink and white school bus of the Instituto de la Virgen Santísima, Olguita is drenching her classmates with envy telling them her plans to take tea and cakes with Elena Delfi, and some little bitch is trying to get even by mentioning the lead story in this morning's *Patria*, and Olguita is putting her down with a contemptuous phrase,

And all over the city newsboys are crying *Patria! Patria!* and citizens are staring at the front page and gobbling up the story inside and smiling to themselves or chuckling or laughing out loud, poking their neighbors, "Have you seen this?" because there's nothing so funny as an impotent paralytic cuckold, especially if he used to give himself airs, and others are shaking their heads and clucking about the yellow press but reading on all the same,

And perhaps that story is giving the readers of *La Patria* a faint impression of being alive, but I doubt it because that sensation doesn't pounce unless you joy or suffer personally, and the readers of *La Patria* make do with vicarious experience, sweaty sneering bleary swine, nutless gutless thoughtless zombies; run five-inch needles up their spines and they'd come to life, truss them up and they'd understand; and would they laugh then? would they chuckle? read them stories from *La Patria* and see if they'd laugh; all those who laugh this morning, and those who cluck and read on shall be turned into plants, trees for dogs to piss on and weeds for dogs to dump on and smear their bungs across!

And something else, please, because the spit is slobbering down my neck under my lovely Philippine shirt and I can't wipe it off and my shoulders ache and a vein beside my nose is throbbing and I can't press my finger against it,

And in a room at Lawrenceville, where *La Patria* is not distributed, Mito is hunching under the blankets the way he used to hunch up against Olga's warm flank on nights when the thunder cracked and he came droop-shouldered and chatter-toothed into our room, and I always let him come in and crawl up against his mother, though sometimes I was angry and let him feel it in my voice, and I'm sorry for that, Mito, because being afraid has nothing to do with heing a coward, or perhaps he is up and on his way across the muddy snow to a class in political science, a class where the teacher lectures about forms of government in sanitary, abstract terms,

And over to my left, two floors under the gold roof of the Presidential Palace, Pepe Fuertes is rocking in the high-backed, red-leather swivel chair he had carried over from his dental clinic four years ago, resting bis wasted leg in its aluminum brace and twenty-pound shoe in a half-open desk drawer, listening to Meco tell him about my father's swing through Salinas and trying to figure a way to steal the province this year since he doesn't have the strength to win it or the money to buy it,

And in my Aunt Matilde's house in Córdoba my father is chewing a stick of cane sugar with the false teeth Pepe made for him ten years ago when my father was urging loyal *alejistas* to vote for Pepe's brother León,

And outside in the street the motorcade is forming behind Nacho's bulletproof Lincoln (turned over to my father for the campaign as part of the price of Nacho's vice-presidential nomination), eight cars or so full of Tinieblista Party people first, then Nacho in one of his unbulletproof Cadillacs, and behind him cars full of members of his Partido Reformista Patriótico, then, five or six cars back, the Partido Campesino Libre, and behind them the Movimiento Civilista Conservador and the Partido Soberano Revolucionario and the Frente Defensora Nacionalista,

And at precisely eight o'clock Alejo, who is the only punctual man in Tinieblas, will spit his sugar cane on to Aunt Matilde's tile floor and smear his smile with the back of his hand and stride outside with his Westphalian bodyguard Egon behind him, and all the horns will toot,

And he will walk straight on without looking down the line of cars and duck into the Lincoln, whose door a boy briefed two hours before by Alejo's Florentine secretary Furetto will swing open at the last minute to let none of the air conditioning out, while

Egon does a *Seesoldat* doubletime around the car with his stock-fitted Mauser pistol at the high port,

And the second Alejo's shriveled seventy-year-old butt touches down on the Lincoln's ostrich-leather seat, his Rhinelander chauffeur Gunther will tramp on the accelerator, and the car will lurch off, rear wheels churning dust and graves, with Egon still half out the right-hand front door and Furetto clutching the hand strap in the back,

And the other cars will light out behind, out of town and left onto the Pan American highway, sixty miles an hour, twenty feet between bumpers, with horns blaring and party flags fluttering from radio antennas: red with black border and white hydra for the *tinieblistas,* yellow with green alligator for the *reformistas,* green with black bull for the *campesino libristas,* white with red jaguar for the *civilistas,* sky blue with orange fighting cock for the *soberanistas,* orange with purple Ozian winged monkey for the *frentistas,*

And the column will stop at each town large enough to provide a platform for the maximum leader and in Aguascalientes for a barbeque rally on the baseball field, and more vehicles will hitch on the end at each stop, so that by three o'clock when they hit the Guardia control-point west of Ciudad Tinieblas there will be eighty to a hundred cars strung out behind the Lincoln, plus trucks full of campesinos (to each one of whom Nacho's factotum has slipped a five-inchado note for his big time in the capital) and at least three busloads of Juventud Tinieblista,

And right now in his office in the Civil Guard barracks General Puñete is wondering whether he ought to order that motorcade halted at the checkpoint, whether it might not be safer to double-cross Alejo and not keep the Guardia out of the election than to trust Alejo to keep him on as commandant after he wins, and of course if Guardia support is enough to beat Alejo then the double cross was right, whereas if Alejo wins anyway, gets so many votes that all the ballot boxes the soldiers can dump into the bay and all the imaginative counting an intimidated Electoral Jury can invent still don't matter, then Puñete ends up as military attaché in some place like New Guinea and the double cross was wrong, while for the short run he has to worry about the possibility of a rising in the city when word gets out that Alejo's rally has been forbidden and the certainty of being nagged to distraction by the gringos, who might even cut off their fifty-thousand-dollar-a-month subsidy to the Guardia rather than be accused in the newspapers of encouraging a military force to meddle in a democratic election,

And in his headquarters at Fort Shafter in the Reservation, General Shortarm is getting a report from his G2 on the scheduled demonstration in Bolívar Plaza of the National Patriotic Alliance, six political parties supporting the presidential candidacy of Alejandro Sancudo, and hearing advice from the political officer seconded to his Command from the State Department and deciding whether to declare Tinieblas City off-limits to United States' military personnel and United States' civilian employees of the Reservation and their dependents, guests, and household pets,

And the ministers of Pepe Fuertes' cabinet, some already in their offices, some still in their homes or girlfriends' cottages, some in their air-conditioned chauffeur-driven limousines, are wondering if there might still be any people on the government payroll who will vote for Alejo, trying to find spots for supporters of the five-party Independent National Coalition which is backing Pepe,

And the seven-hundred-odd candidates for the fifty-five seat Chamber of Deputies—because besides the nine non-ideological parties we have Socialists and Christian Democrats too—are already on the phone scrounging money for their campaigns,

And the two-thousand-odd candidates for the various city councils are doing likewise,

And in his mother's house in the brand-new middle-income suburb of Esperanza paid for by the Alliance for Progress and built by a construction firm owned by Pepe Fuertes' brother-in-law out of cement blocks made by a firm in which Pepe himself is a principal stockholder, Ñato Espino is receiving my telepathic proclamation of his death sentence, manner of execution carefully described, and is shivering and mewling and twisting in his sleep, troubled sleep, unquiet sleep, sleep without repose or refreshment that comes only in the damp hours of pre-dawn darkness to flit on bat wings through his heart,

And here on this balcony, I, Kiki Sancudo, am watching it all with my eyes closed against the morning sun, watching and understanding and gathering my prancing mind under firm rein.

14

I was in school, at the Politénico on Avenida del General Enrique Guderian—changed from Avenida del General Jorge Washington and later, of course, changed back—the day they threw Alejo out of the palace for the second time. It was in January of 1942, the second day of class after the Christmas-New Year's holidays. The capital was particularly colorful those days because of the Decree on the Dignity of Occupations. Taxi, bus, and truck drivers, trolley motormen and conductors, and government chauffeurs wore purple coveralls and green kepis. Market workers were dressed according to what they sold: grocers in green, butchers in red, fish vendors in marine blue. Laborers wore khaki shirts, trousers, and forage caps; government functionaries, attorneys, businessmen, and doctors wore white suits and black ties; secretaries and shopgirls wore purple skirts and white blouses; teachers, even those in kindergarten, wore academic gowns and mortar boards. It was up to the individual to acquire and maintain his uniform, and penalties for improper dress were strict. The Vanguardia Tinieblina, a paramilitary formation organized by Alejo before his election and active enough in the campaign to chase his principal opponent into the Reservation, kept watch for violations. They wore green shirts and white duck trousers and purple berets, carried carbines slung across their backs and twirled leather quirts. The Guardia Civil had new uniforms of field gray—jodhpurs for the officers and black jackboots for all ranks—while the Young Patriots, which replaced the Boy and Girl Scouts and which was popularly though covertly known as Alejo's Little Bastards, had miniature outfits of the same stuff—skirts, of course, for the girls. All members of the Partido Tinieblista wore red and black armbands and had to be saluted with the right arm held stiffly forward, fist clenched, thumb up, and cheered with the cry *Arriba, Tinieblas!*

The city had the aspect of a gigantic costume party, but one which had gone on too long and which the guests weren't all enjoying. People had begun to slouch, to forego customary courtesies, to look the other way when party members approached. The salute was often given with the middle finger instead of the thumb raised, while the salutation sometimes came out *Arriba, tu Madre!* It was uncomfortable for waiters and bartenders to wear cutaways in that heat, and the cantina hostesses and barmaids resented having to wear the same uniform as the full-time whores—scarlet dress with white P for PUTA embroidered over the left breast. It got so a party member couldn't have a friendly drink without getting a Mickey Finn. Many formerly well-dressed business and professional men got doctor's certificates of goiter trouble and went about without neckties, and Lazarillo Agudo showed up at the offices of *La Prensa* one morning in his obligatory white suit and black tie but without shirt, socks, or shoes. He was reported by a party member, hauled from his desk by a quartet of Vanguardistas, quirted a bit in the face for resisting, and turned over to the Civil Guard, but as there was nothing specific in the decree about what journalists ought to wear in the way of linen and footwear, he was simply given a beating and released. The Ministry of Justice got the decree tightened up that afternoon.

Many who didn't mind the uniforms were annoyed by the Decree on the Protection of Labor, promulgated the day after General Guderian's tanks crossed into Russia, which abolished all existing trade unions and professional organizations and created a host of new groups with sonorous titles, altruistic aims, stiff dues, and compulsory membership. A more universal source of joy was the Decree on the Preservation of the Tinieblan Race, which was necessary, in the words of Alejo's radio address, "so that this noble race, born of the union of Mayan princesses and Castilian aristocrats, be preserved in its purity and not corrupted by the degenerate blood of mongrel breeds." This means that Jews and Chinamen were forbidden to marry non-Jews and non-Chinamen, and, more excitingly, deprived of citizenship, laid open to insult and abuse, subjected to vague but terrifying threats of deportation, and encouraged to sell out cheap to people judged racially pure by the Ministry of justice. That went for Don Moisés Levi Méndes and his coffee *finca*. But after dealing briskly with Jews and Chinamen, the decree grew sluggish, since when the Castilian aristocrats had killed most of the Mayan princesses' husbands, fathers, and brothers and chased the rest into the jungle, they brought in Negro slaves, and everyone in Tinieblas had at least one black grandmother, including Alejo, for the Colombian woman who bore Eladio Sancudo to Pablo Sancudo was surely black, or where did Erasmo get his squashed nose and Alejo himself his somewhat kinky if close-cropped hair? Instead of calling the slaves African chieftains, he set up a commission in the Department of Racial Purity of the Ministry of justice to determine how dark your skin could get and how pendulous your lower lip before you stopped being a member of the Tinieblan Race and became a mongrel. As the darker citizens owned little property, the question was not too pressing. The commission, which was in lengthy communication with scientific authorities in Grossdeutschland, hadn't come in with its findings.

Science aside, however, I was sure the Department of Racial Purity would never pass our social studies teacher, Dr. Abstemio Filos, whose skin was the color and texture of a Civil Guard's waxed boot, whose brow hurried back in furrows toward his steel-wool hair, whose nose was mashed like a gorilla's, and whose lower lip drooped like a baboon's, and so I felt free to bait and harry him, strutting about the room in my lieutenant of Young Patriots' uniform—Alfonso was a colonel—when he tried to bring the class to order at the beginning of the period, and pumping gales of glee from my classmates by beating my chest while he lectured. That day I had one of my sycophants—and it was delightful how the class sucked up to me, despite the fact that I was weak and unathletic—get him talking about natural selection and man's descent from the apes (titters, sputterings, and choked guffaws from the vicinity of Sancudo's desk at the absolute rear of the room), and when he was called out suddenly at about nine-thirty, I sauntered to the blackboard and wrote:

DARWIN WAS RIGHT.
THE MISSING LINK EXISTS.
IT LIVES IN TINIEBLAS AND TEACHES SOCIAL STUDIES.

This got applause, but less than I'd expected because a number of my fellow scholars had gone to the window to observe some unaccustomed activity across the avenue in the Reservation. A company of troops was being marched down the black-top road from the three-story, olive-green, screened-in, wooden-barracks square toward the main gate of Fort Shafter—puttees buckled at the ankles, Springfields slung from right shoulders, and instead of high-crowned campaign hats, steel helmets with slightly sloped brims. And as they swung down the road—captain at the front looking neither right nor left, sergeant out to the right about twelve men back from the point belching *Hut, hut, hut, hut, hut,* lieutenant with his pistol slapping his thigh sprinting up from the third platoon—a line of trucks headed out of the motor pool away over to our right and swung toward the gate, preceded by three high-silhouetted light tanks, certainly no match for one of General Guderian's, but General Guderian was at the moment fully engaged, giving ground, in fact, before Moscow. From the turret of the lead tank protruded the bust of a monster from one of the gringo football films: immense shoulders, flint chin, and leather helmet. It defined itself when the tank hippoed nearer as a gringo major—gold leaf on the brow of the helmet—who patted the receiver of a machine gun mounted on a trolley that ran around the hatch as though calming a Doberman whose leash would presently be slipped. The tanks growled up to the gate, waddling parallel to the avenue just inside the barbed-wire-topped cyclone fence, and then squirmed through, the lead tank crunching with its left tread in reverse, the other two each making slightly wider turns, so that they halted in a row with the front plates of their treads just toeing the avenue and their cannons aimed under our window at the classroom below. The major waved his left hand (palm forward, as though pushing an imaginary butt) at the sentry, who stood in a little stucco shelter just inside the gate. Such jolly fellows those sentries had been only four weeks before, lounging in their shelters (there were two boxes, one on either side of the gate), shouting foul taunts at each other, slinking out to flirt with the little whores who carne wiggling by the base every afternoon around four-thirty, jabbering in pidgin English, reaching down to pat a hip or pinch a titty, grinning to show the gum gaps left by cantina brawls, then looking up to howl a genial *Fuck you, Greaseball!* as we jeered them from our departing schoolbus, but now they were all business. Check every individual's ID card. Search the trunks of civilian vehicles. Stay alert and no grab-ass with hoors. So when the major waved, the sentry double-timed out with his rifle at port arms to stand straddling the centerline, and the other sentry did the same on his side, halting traffic along the avenue. Meanwhile the head of the infantry column disappeared behind the line of trucks, which had halted when the first one drew even with the gate, and then the squads came clambering up over the tailgates, unslinging their rifles and filling up the benches on either side, eight men to a bench, shoulder to shoulder with their rifles sticking up between their knees, until the last truck was loaded and the lieutenant pounded back along the line between the trucks and the fence and braced in front of the captain who stood by the cab of the first truck and saluted and reported, his jaw jerking the chin strap of his helmet. The captain snapped about-face and marched quickly and stiffly, as though he were trying to hold a rectal thermometer in place, three steps and then left-flank along the side of the major's tank, and then halt and right-face. He craned his head back and threw up a salute so that his hand quivered near the brim of his helmet and called, in a voice that rang across the avenue into our window, "Sir, B Company mounted and ready to move out, Sir!" The major nodded at him and lifted his hand off the machine gun and waved an answer to the salute. Then he looked straight at me and balled his hand into a fist and poked it slowly into the air ahead of him three times, and his tank jerked forward onto the avenue and then clanked around to our right bruising the asphalt, and the second tank crunched after it, its engine roaring, and then the third, and the first truck pulled ahead and turned through the gate, the captain swinging up into the cab from the right running board, and turned again, gathering speed to draw up behind the third tank, and all the line of trucks rolled on out the gate, their motors groaning and heat waves dancing above their khaki-painted hoods. And just as the sentries were about to turn back to their stucco shelters, two soldiers on motorcycles with rifles slung across their backs came stuttering down the hill, followed by a Dodge staff car with a white-starred blue pennant fluttering above the right front fender, and this group swept through the gate and took off after the column of trucks toward the old city, from which direction we schoolboys could now hear firing.

For three years, and no doubt even while Alfonso and I were in Italy, the students of the Instituto Politécnico had played war every noon, stalking each other in the cloister and clashing hand-to-hand in the quadrangle. When I first enrolled in May, 1939, the Spanish Loyalists, defeated on the peninsula, were still the favored group at the Instituto. That fall most boys wanted to be Frenchmen. After my father's election, it became more fashionable to be German, and by September, 1940, no one would be French except the son of the French Ambassador, and he had joined us Germans in our skirmishes against a diminishing band of Englishmen. The following summer a few of the former Spanish Loyalists became Russians, but they switched back to being Englishmen and two even became Germans after they were ambushed and badly mauled on their way home from school by a group of Young Patriots from the upper forms. But when, the week before the Christmas holidays, one boy suggested introducing new teams of combatants, there were plenty willing to be gringos and not one aspiring Japanese, not because we liked gringos—we knew all about imperialism from being chased out of the Reservation when we climbed the fence to pick mangos there—but because they were too palpable there across the avenue not to be feared and respected. As an eleven-year-old I couldn't help feeling scared when that gringo major looked at me; as a Tinieblan I was angry when those gringo sentries held up their rifles to halt our traffic and those tanks and soldiers violated our city, but as a noontime *Wehrmacht* officer, I had to admire the smooth, confident way the operation clicked off, and as Alejandro Sancudo's son I was aware that hard times lay ahead. When the American Ambassador called on my father the morning of December 8th to request that the Tinieblan Government take steps to black out the capital, my father kept him waiting for three hours and then announced that he was ordering flood-lights set up in the park opposite the palace and special illumination for every important public monument. On New Year's Eve he gave a huge reception in honor of the Japanese Ambassador, and on January 5th, the day schools opened, he published the Decree on the Defense of Tinieblan Sovereignty, which prohibited the sale of foodstuffs to the Reservation and forbade Tinieblans to work there under pain of loss of citizenship. The decree was not unpopular. The people who earned their livings in the Reservation and the merchants who sold milk and vegetables there didn't like it, but most Tinieblans resented the Reservation, many disliked gringos, and some thought it had been wonderfully clever of the Japanese to give them such a kick in the nuts. But no one thought my father had much of a future. A good sample of the prevailing opinion was given to me on the bus that morning by Aquilino Piojo, a classmate and friend of Alfonso's, a major in the Young Patriots, and the mid-day leader of von Piojo's Death's-head Storm Troopers.

"Your papa's crazy, Sancudo." Along Avenida Bolívar shop-keepers were boarding up their stores. "He's organized the country and put the kikes in their place, but if he thinks he can shit on the gringos he's crazy. It isn't done."

"The Japs are doing it."

"The Japs are crazy too. And they've got an army and a navy. Did you see the guns on that gringo battleship?"

The week before an American cruiser had put in briefly at the Reservation, up from Panama on the way, I suppose, to San Diego, and hundreds of Tinieblans had gone down to the sea wall opposite the naval docks to see her. Lino went on about the guns and the squadron of P-40's stationed at Potter's Field and all the other things that gringos had, and when I put in a halfhearted word for the Japanese, he said:

"You'll see. Those gringos are a serious thing. Boom! Boom! Boom!"

Now, of course, what we heard was pop! pop! pop!

"It's the Civil Guard fighting the gringos," said one junior pundit.

"Don't be a bobo," said another. "The gringos just left."

"It could be other gringos. The Civil Guard is winning and they had to send reinforcements."

"Jerk! Even if another bunch had left by the back gate they'd have had to pass by here to get downtown."

"They could be marines landed by boat. Or parachutists."

"Don't be such a pubic hair. What's happening is they're throwing out Alejo."

"Who?"

"Who? Anybody. Joaquín Araña [he was the candidate the Vanguardia had chased into the Reservation], the Guardia, the people."

"I bet the gringos are behind it."

"That's what you say. The people don't like Alejo any more."

"Then what are the gringos doing with those tanks?"

"They have no right to take them out of the base."

"They go where they feel like, the bastards."

"Alejo shouldn't have messed with them."

"Alejo has guts."

"Alejo's finished."

I did not participate in these speculations, and no one looked at me.

Dr. Filos came back then and told us to take our seats. I noticed immediately that he had taken off his gown and his mortar board, but I had no desire to call this infraction to his attention or even to report him to the Vanguardia that afternoon. He begged our pardon for his absence but added that in Tinieblas a class in social studies did not necessarily stop when the teacher left the room. Tinieblas was, in fact, of all the world the best place to teach social studies, for students had only to look out the window to learn, for example, that there is no morality among nations and no law except that of the jungle, and if they listened at the same window they would understand, far better than from a lecture on Machiavelli, that a ruler who makes himself hated and does not possess a strong city may be easily assaulted. He turned then, perhaps to put these precepts on the blackboard, and saw what I had printed. There was no laughter from my friends. Dr. Filos looked at the

phrases carefully. When I had written them, I had been immune
from punishment; now I was seared, but I resolved bravely to
answer any comment from Dr. Filos that it was mongrels like him
who made our country weak. Or perhaps I would cry "Arriba,
Tinieblas!" and die like a patriot, for it seemed to me suddenly that
the writing of those phrases had been a courageous and patriotic
act. But Dr. Filos said nothing. Finally he smacked his lips like a
monkey and began to laugh quietly, nodding his head. Then he
erased my phrases neatly and wrote in their place:

> *INTRABIT UT VULPIS*
> *REGNABIT UT LEO*
> *MORIETUR UT CANIS.*

When he turned, grinning sadly at me over the heads of the class,
the nine-fifty bell rang, and he said classes would continue as
normal.

My father did not die like a dog, however; he went out like a
legitimate politician, covered with someone else's blood. The night
before, the gringo commander in the Reservation had met Colonel
Genaro Culata, Commandant of the Guardia Civil, at the home of
Doña Artemisa Gusano de Fink, the widow of a gringo who had
come to Tinieblas in 1907 with the Copperhead Mining Company
and had married and stayed on after the copper deposits in Otán
Province were totally scraped out. As the niece of a Tinieblan president and the widow of a gringo empire builder, Doña Artemisa
could provide the sort of discreet liaison needed in such troubled
times. Both officers wore civilian dress, but strict protocol was
observed: no handshake and an aide-de-camp at parade rest behind
each chair. The gringo general was slight, gray where he wasn't
bald, with thin lips and steel-rimmed glasses; no doubt he sat stiffly,
as though taking a square meal in the dining hall at West Point.
Colonel Genaro Culata was the last of General Feliciano Luna's
fifty illegitimate sons, the only one to bear his mother's surname,
for General Luna, who was generous enough to recognize all his
male progeny, was hanged a week after Colonel Culata was conceived. He was tall for a Tinieblan and heavy, swarthy like his fa-

ther with a drooping mustache which I imagine he chewed during the interview, sitting with his legs spread and feet stretched out, permitting himself an occasional clawing at his crotch. The conversation was in Spanish, which the gringo general, who had spent long years civilizing his little brown Filipino brothers with a Krag rifle, spoke excellently. Colonel Culata's aide has left a record.

The gringo general told Colonel Genaro Culata without bluster that the United States of America could no longer tolerate the attitude of the Tinieblan Government. Responsibility and authority for the conduct of United States affairs with the Republic of Tinieblas has been turned over to him. Alejandro Sancudo would be deposed the following morning. If Colonel Culata cared to accomplish this with his own forces, the United States of America would furnish all necessary assistance and promptly recognize Culata himself. If not, the United States had sufficient force in the country to take all measures necessary to defend its national interest. Colonel Culata said that "measures necessary" sounded like a fancy way to threaten armed intervention, and added that it wasn't worth the pain to dip a turd in perfume. The general said that he would determine what steps might be necessary according to the circumstances which prevailed, but pointed out that the United States had intervened, reluctantly perhaps but none the less effectively, at Vera Cruz in 1915 and more recently in Nicaragua, Haiti, and the Dominican Republic—all this in peacetime—and now the United States was at war. Colonel Culata said he would have to consider the matter and consult with his officers; the general said that he must have an answer at once, and if Colonel Culata could not speak for the Tinieblan Civil Guard, would he please put the general in contact with an officer who could. Colonel Genaro Culata then said that Alejandro Sancudo didn't matter a donkey's prick to him, but that it was more in keeping with the honor of his profession to die at the head of his troops in defense of his country. The general said that he could certainly respect such a decision but that if the colonel had the good of his country at heart, he might consider the possibility of civilian casualties and the advisability of putting Tinieblas as soon as possible on the winning side of what was going to be a long and bitterly fought World War. Colonel

Genaro Culata stood up and said that since the general had him between the sword and the wall, he would throw Alejo out of office, but that the general could go to shit with his offer of recognition since he, Colonel Genaro Culata, had lived all his life, and until this moment with honor, without being recognized by his own father. Some civilian would turn up to form a government acceptable to the United States. The general said he would hold a force in readiness should the Civil Guard need help.

"You may do what you like," said Colonel Genaro Culata, "because you are the stronger. But if you come before I call, come shooting."

Then he went back to the barracks and told his officers: "We're going to throw out Alejo to please the gringos. I was born a son of a bitch and I'll die a son of a bitch, but that's what we're going to do."

The next morning Culata ordered the Guardia confined to the barracks and sent his second-in-command, Lieutenant Colonel Domingo Azote, to the palace with the two platoons he could trust. Azote left them under command of Captain Dionísio Espada, who was married to Azote's sister and was rumored to be faithful to her though he was easily the most handsome officer in Tinieblas, with orders to surround the building as discreetly as possible and went himself to the main gate. In other times the Guardia Civil had furnished men for the presidential escort, but Alejo, who had already been thrown out once by the Guardia, replaced them with members of the Vanguardia Tinieblina. These stopped Azote at the gate— no one was allowed inside without a written order—and told him to go back to the barracks. When the Leader (they liked this title better than President) wanted to see him, he would be sent for. Azote told them that the palace was surrounded, the Leader in the process of being deposed, and that he wished to avoid bloodshed and give Engineer Sancudo the courtesy of a personal notification. One of the Vanguardistas ran into the palace; the others leveled their carbines at Azote's chest. At length the first returned, relieved Azote of his pearl-handled, gold-chased Browning pistol, and began prodding him inside. On the steps Azote took the precaution of tying his handkerchief to the riding crop he always carried stuck in one boot.

President Alejandro Sancudo received Lieutenant Colonel Domingo Azote in his office, in the presence of Dr. Fausto Maroma, the Minister of justice, and the President of the Assembly, Don Francisco Caballero de la Rosa. He waved the guard outside but did not rise.

"Well, little Colonel. What have you got to say to me before I have you shot?"

"I have the honor to inform you that by authority of Colonel Culata and for the good of the state, you have been relieved of your duties as President of the Republic. The palace is surrounded. For your own safety and that of your collaborators here have the kindness to accompany me to the barracks."

"By the authority of President Rosenfeld and for the good of the United States. Ha! Do you think it was for this that I have given this country order? The law on social security? The franchise for women? Is it for this that I am purifying the Tinieblan Race and defending our national sovereignty, so that a packet of cowards who lick the gringo's backsides should put me down?" He stood up and placed both palms on the polished top of his desk, leaning toward Azote. "I am the Gauleiter of Middle America, named by Adolfo Hitler himself I will brook no indignities! All those who defy my authority will be shot! I will give you one chance, little Colonel. Pledge your royalty to me and put yourself at the head of the Guardia Civil. If the gringos dare put one toenail outside their base, I will crush them! They are mongrels. Their day is over. They will not fight. And should they dare to interfere, should they dare, Chancellor Hitler will send the finest soldiers in the world to help us bury them! He has promised it. He has given me his personal word. All of Middle America will be united under one order. One nation from Peru to Mexico. The dream of Bolívar!"

Lieutenant Colonel Domingo Azote blinked his eyes. "Mr. President," he said, "you're crazy. Consider yourself under arrest."

President Alejandro Sancudo reached into the top drawer of his desk and pulled out the pistol he had pointed at President Abúndio Moral and shot Lieutenant Colonel Domingo Azote through the chest. Then he ran around the desk and emptied the pistol into Lieutenant Colonel Domingo Azote's face. He threw the gun into

a corner of the room, picked Lieutenant Colonel Domingo Azote
up on his shoulder and carried him out onto the balcony from
which General Epifanio Mojón had watched the sharks feed and
threw him over the railing onto the sea wall. Then he rushed back
into the room to find his pistol and reload it.

When Captain Dionísio Espada heard the shots, he ran out
from the side street to the sea wall promenade in time to see Lieutenant Colonel Domingo Azote come sailing down from the balcony like a sack of feed. He then ran another hundred meters down
the promenade to a café that overlooked the bay and called Colonel
Culata at the barracks. Culata decided that if men were going to be
killed, it would be better if they were gringos. He told Captain
Espada to hold his positions and let no one in or out of the palace;
then he called the gringo commander in the Reservation. But when
Espada returned to the palace and saw Lieutenant Colonel
Domingo Azote lying in his own blood, he could not contain himself, and he drew his pistol and rushed around to the little park
with the statue of Simón Mocoso and gathered the squad he had
posted there and charged the gate, firing on the Vanguadistas, and
they fired back, joined by three others on the roof of the porte-
cochere, and the Civil Guards around the building began firing into
it, and Vanguardistas fired back at them from the windows, and
while Dr. Maroma and Señor Caballero ran up to the maids' quarters to see if they could dress themselves as women, Alejo himself
went back onto the balcony and fired down with his pistol. That
was the firing we schoolboys heard over at the Politécnico.

Now I have slides. The first one, snapped by my Uncle Erasmo
from the window of his office in the *Correo Matinal* building on
Bolívar Plaza, shows the gringo column rolling out of Avenida del
General Enrique Guderian—and the story goes that an official in
the Ciudad Tinieblas town hall was already instituting a search for
the old street signs with Avenida del General Jorge Washington on
them—and around the square into Avenida Bolívar, with a few private cars run up on the pavements on either side and the major's
tank about to smatter a pushcart full of casaba melons abandoned
on the corner by a fleeing, green-suited vendor. In the next we see
the tail of the column, with the two soldiers on motorcycles and the

staff car in the wrong lane trying to get past, disappearing down
Bolívar toward the Plaza Cervantes, while in Plaza Bolívar a platoon
is dismounting from four trucks, those already down fixing bayonets and a lieutenant seeing to the placement of a light machine gun
on the steps of the Hotel Excelsior. Now a series taken by Edilma
(who had gone out with two of the palace maids to do some mar-
keting) as she crouched in the portico of the general post office on
Plaza Inchado at the far end of Avenida Bolívar: first a view of the
square, littered with field gray Guardias lying under benches, kneeling beside bushes, craning around the kiosk on the side of which a
Correo *Matinal* poster with the words PRESIDENT SANCUDO AFFIRMS
NATIONAL SOVEREIGNTY can be clearly seen, and standing behind the
pedestal of the statue of Palmiro Inchado de los Huevos, all pointing
rifles at the side of the palace, from whose unzipped windows carbine barrels poke. Then the same scene, but at the extreme right a
tank with the major up, holding his Doberman by its steel ears and
aiming its perforated muzzle at the windows, while turret and cannon swing toward the palace. Next a shot of the tank, four or so
yards further into the plaza, with the staff car swung half in front
of it and a brigadier general in a khaki cap with polished visor,
khaki jacket with polished brass buttons, white shirt and tan tie,
polished Sam Browne belt, tan riding breeches, and polished brown
riding boots, standing beside the car pointing a little stick with a
polished fifty-caliber cartridge case fitted over the thicker end at
the major, who holds his right fist straight up in the air above him
and looks down contritely at the brigadier. Next, please; ah! The
brigadier and a captain dressed the same as he only with a pistol in
a polished leather holster, flap closed and lanyard rising from the
butt and looped through his epaulette, strolling across the square,
the captain with his shoulders a bit hunched, the brigadier quite
erect, left hand clasping his right wrist behind his back, right hand
holding his stick, which dangles by his left leg like a tail, and beyond
them a Civil Guard sergeant in field gray, sitting with his back to the
pedestal of the statue of Palmiro Inchado (between whose legs
another Guardia is aiming his rifle), holding both palms toward the
gringo officers, his mouth wide open shouting and his face smeared
with fear, and just to the left of the two gringos a Civil Guard rising

off his knees with his head jerked back and his Argentine Mauser held up the length of his two arms and pointing back over his shoulder. And finally the captain talking to the Civil Guard sergeant, who is on his feet now but crouched behind the pedestal, pointing with his left hand around it toward the little park whose trees can just be seen in the background between the corner of the palace and the façade of the Alcaldía, while the brigadier stands, still erect and quite exposed to the right of the pedestal, looking in the direction the sergeant indicates.

So when the brigadier learned that the officer in charge was over in the little park—for that was where the Civil Guard sergeant had last seen Lieutenant Colonel Domingo Azote—he and his aide walked back to the major's tank, both hunched a bit forward now as carbine bullets scuffed the dirt about them, but not running or even trotting, because the captain had to walk if the brigadier walked and the brigadier walked, not to set an example for his men or the Tinieblans but because he had been at Saint Mihiel with the Second Division and hadn't the slightest intention of being killed or even knicked in a banana republic. He told the major to button up his hatch and take his tank forward to the left side of the plaza near the Ministry of Education and send the second tank forward to the right of the plaza near the Alcaldía and to have his gunner load a round of high explosive but not to do any firing except on radio order from the brigadier. Then he told his driver to take the staff car, which had developed three moth-holes in its left front fender, back up Avenida Bolívar and take the cyclists, who were straddling their bikes in the lee of the major's tank, with him. Then he walked back to the first truck and told the captain who walked like he was having his temperature taken to give him the first two trucks and a smart sergeant and to be ready to send his men into the plaza if and when the tanks started shooting but not to shoot any Civil Guards and in the meantime to keep everyone sitting tight out of the line of fire. Then he put his aide in the cab of the first truck and climbed up on the third tank and told the sergeant who sat with his head and shoulders out of the hatch to have his driver swing right down the side street. The tank moved ahead, getting a bullet ping under the driver's slit window, and humped up on the curb, getting a bullet ping on the turret in front of the brigadier's chest, and turned down the narrow street, one tread on the sidewalk, with the first two trucks full of soldiers following, and then swung left and trundled round into the little park. Almost as soon as the tank came in view from the palace and before the cannon had a good field of fire, a white flag appeared on the roof of the porte-cochere (white flags were also waving in the windows facing the Plaza Inchado), for as a Vanguardista whom Alejo found waving a handkerchief told him, the Civil Guard was one thing, but they were not going to fight gringos in tanks.

The brigadier sent a soldier running back for the staff car and told the smart sergeant to get his men down and into fire positions and, not making the mistake of Lieutenant Colonel Domingo Azote, stayed by the tank, whose cannon and machine gun were trained on the palace, and had his aide call out in Spanish for President Sancudo to come out. So Alejo came out, his white suit drenched in Lieutenant Colonel Domingo Azote's blood, his right cheek twitching a bit, holding his pistol by the barrel (which was still so hot he had to wrap a handkerchief around it), not looking down at the bodies crumpled by the gate, giving no sign that he heard the curses of Captain Dionísio Espada, who was dying of a stomach wound, and stalked up to the brigadier.

"I surrender," he said, holding out his pistol, "to the superior weapons of a foreign force. I protest the unprovoked attack upon my country's sovereignty. I have resisted to the best of my ability and demand to be treated as a prisoner of war."

The brigadier waited for a translation from his aide, then shrugged his shoulders, took the pistol, put it on safety and handed it to his driver. "Tell him to get in the car."

Alejo got in, and the brigadier after him, and the aide in the front seat beside the driver, and they drove as quickly as possible back to the Reservation and through Fort Shafter to Potter's Field, where the gringo commander was waiting beside a plane whose motors were all warmed up, As Alejo climbed up the metal steps behind the brigadier's aide, he turned and told the gringo commander, "I shall return," beating Douglas MacArthur to the phrase by two months.

So that afternoon Alfonso and I did not go home to the palace, to the patio where the bronze faun pissed nonchalantly while I drilled BB's into him; to the unused suite of rooms above the ballroom where Alfonso and I played a kind of hide-and-seek, creeping through the smothered blackness of closed doors and boarded windows to growl terrifyingly at one another; to the attic where one morning I caught Alfonso playing with himself and where, after some shame and much complaining that I was too young, he taught me; to the bedroom where, as I was too big now to sleep with a light or seek asylum in the neutral embassy of Edilma's room, General Epifanio Mojón, his skin split and oozing from all those hours in sun and sea water, hulked in the shadows beside the window curtain; to the salon beside the Cabinet Room where, one night when an operatic thunderstorm extinguished all the electricity in Tinieblas and flung sheets of rain and lightning across the bay, a beautiful Peruvian woman whom my father held captive long enough for him to hurt and me to fall in love with played the guitar for us, holding its tawny neck against her ivory check and caressing its waist with alternate tenderness and passion, while the wind sang *saetas* and the candle flames danced *farucas* and great gouts of jealousy dripped from the curved rhythm to stain my face like sea spray. We went into exile at Uncle Erasmo's. Aunt Beatrix had no room for Edilma, but I sent her my Christmas money to build a chicken coop in her village in Remedios and missed her more than Alejo missed his ministers and his decrees and his purple, green, and yellow sash. I missed her especially when I was badly thrashed by a classmate whose mother I had mentioned in the high and palmy days before Alejo fell, but as she was gone there was no one to take pity on me, and the next afternoon I began lifting weights at the Y.M.C.A. in the Reservation.

Alejo went to Paraguay, where over the years he collected Egon and Gunther and Furetto. The gringo commander died six weeks later in a plane crash on his way to a command in the Aleutian Islands. The brigadier drowned when a U-boat torpedoed the ship carrying him to England. The major who looked at me across the avenue was roasted to death inside a similar tank at the Kasserine Pass. The brigadier's aide hanged himself with an electrical extension cord in Saint Elizabeth's hospital, where he had been committed screaming that he was an Alaskan wolf four weeks after the night when, somewhere over the Bolivian Andes, the full moon shone through one of the C-47's tiny windows and President Alejandro Sancudo ran amok, biting the captain so fiercely that two of his front teeth broke off in the former's collar bone.

15

"Aren't you hot?"

Alfonso pulls up beside me, then slides back, having given me a glimpse of the high-cut side vents and narrow pants of his stylish mohair. Always á la mode, Alfonso. Sends his tailor to the movies to copy Mastroianni's suits.

The sun glares, but has not yet succeeded in making itself unpleasant. And I like to bake until I'm a bit uncomfortable, the better to enjoy the cool downstairs. No way to explain this to Alfonso, who scarcely understands my swinesong. I shake my head, but he has already seized the chair, turning it to wheel me back inside.

His question was rhetorical anyway. Alfonso enjoys a natural immunity to the feelings of others. He can make a project of a person—man to be molded, woman to be nailed—making carefully controlled experiments to discover melting point and tensile strength, but normally he doesn't pay attention. He wants to talk, he feels warm, we will go inside. If I said, *Look, animal, I'm comfortable here; if you want to talk, sit down!* he would hang his head and say he's sorry, suddenly and dumbfoundedly aware, as though it just came over the AP teletype, that there are other people on earth besides himself.

"I'm sorry about that *Patria* thing, Kiki," he says over my shoulder as he trundles me along the hall. "Sons of whores don't respect anything. I'm beginning to understand why that hack Cepillo goes around with a pistol stuck in his belt. Someone's going to take a shot at him before this campaign's over, and he's too fat to miss. Apropos, I think you'd better keep an eye on that indian of yours."

Why call Jaime "that indian"?

"... a disaster. It's essential to represent Alejo to the gringos as a force for stability. No violence. And Cepillo's not worth dirtying hands on. Terrible thing for Elena, though. And you too, Kiki."

He wheels me around the corner and into the little study at the head of the stairs, leaves me in the middle while he closes the door and switches on the air conditioner. Then he sits down in the cane chair by the bookcase, looks at me with a sadness which is not becoming to him—Alfonso should be gay or harried, active in any case, not contemplative—presses the bridge of his nose with his left thumb and forefinger, smoothes his mustache, ending up with a tug at the little conquistador's beard he added a couple of years ago to strengthen his chin, makes something between a smile and a grimace and says, "Ah, ho! Kiki, hombre, why don't you and Elena get out of this shit?"

"If you want to converse, cal Marta."

"What?"

"If. You. Want. To. Converse. Call. Marta."

"No. I don't want her here. I'll talk, you listen," and he tells me to take Elena and go back to California. Take Marta and Jaime and Edilma too if I want. And the film crew. Evening plane to Mexico. Don't even stay for the rally."

He has a big spread—half the issue at least—all ready for this afternoon's *Informe Trópico:* how Pepe's henchman (mine really, but become Pepe's for campaign purposes) gunned me down in Bolívar Plaza four years ago today and how I've come back to Bolívar Plaza to lend my name and my sacrifice to the cause of democracy in Tinieblas. Sort of thing he can do better in a tabloid than in *Correo Matinal,* and it will hit the streets an hour or so before the rally. Picture of me being haltered with a medal at the 1952 Olympics. Picture of me carrying the flag into the Reservation in November 1964. Picture of Elena, the famous international artist who also believes in democracy in Tinieblas, a wonderfully efficient picture, taken at Hickory Hill the year before I met her, with a good profile of Jack and the back of Bobby's head. Both were very big in Tinieblas even while alive and, being dead, are now even bigger. Their names linked to mine in the text along with King and Mboya.

Sap of an editor wanted to mention Lumumba and Malcolm X, but Alfonso caught it. Small picture of Ñato, *The Pampered Assassin,* with a smaller one of Pepe opposite, *Did He Give the Order?* But before I can mention the spread, Alfonso says he can have it stopped. Better for me to be on the plane. I'd be taking a risk. My presence would increase the chance of violence.

"I know you've never cared about risks, but think of Elena. And if there's trouble, Pepe could use it to his advantage. Maybe persuade Puñete to stop being neutral. People are saying Alejo will make you a minister or ambassador to Washington, and that sounds more like the old Alejo than the new Alejo. We've all worked very hard inventing a new Alejo, Kiki, but nobody knows what he'll say this afternoon. He doesn't know himself. You shouldn't expose Elena. You shouldn't expose yourself. Ay, Kiki, carajo!" eyes glazed with older brother's sad, protective insolence, "I know how you must have felt with that *Patria* thing! Leave it, Kiki. You've been through enough."

I can turn my head fifteen degrees in both directions.

He nods. Pursed-lipped smile-grimace that makes him look like Uncle Erasmo. Gets out a cigarette—he wouldn't think of offering me one—and says, "I knew it. When have you ever listened to advice? Especially mine. I told you to watch out for Ñato years before he shot you, but you wouldn't listen."

Oh, Fonso. You told me to watch out for everybody. Watch out for Duncan. Watch out for Angela. Watch out for Tolete, and we had the best gun operation in Latin America, if not the world. You even told me to watch out for Elena, though you wouldn't admit it now. The only person you didn't tell me to watch out for was a Panagra stewardess you fixed me up with in 1950, and she gave me the crabs.

"Don't you care about Elena?"

"She. Gets. Worse. From. Gossip. Columnists."

"I'm not talking about that. There could be a mess here. If not today, tomorrow. The Guardia could step in. If Puñete doesn't double-cross us, the younger officers may throw him out. Five years ago he and Látigo got rid of Tolete."

I can smile by hauling back the left corner of my mouth. "Don't. Get. Scared. We'll. Win."

He stands and goes to the desk and stubs out his cigarette in the square ceramic ashtray and picks up the jade-handled paper knife which Olga, who liked giving me presents, bought for me to cut French books with, and scrapes under his left thumbnail. Never had dirt there in his life. Suppose a speck crept under by mistake, thinking it was someone else's thumb, the manicurist would deal with it. He goes every morning at eight to the Hotel El Opulento barbershop to be shaved, shined, trimmed, and manicured. Eye-surgeon's care exercised in snipping his beard and tweezing gray hairs from his crown. I see him holding a quarter-folded Miami *Herald* two feet off his port bow, unable to read for having to supervise the barber, the girl who ministers to his right hand, the Jamaican Negro at his feet.

"Maybe," he says without looking at me. "But if we get in, can we stay in? Alejo's been in three times and thrown out three times. To come this far he's had to neutralize the Guardia. To stay in he'll have to break it up, and the Guardia won't let him stay in long enough to do that. Maybe they'll be stupid. Puñete made a deal, maybe he'll keep it. Maybe he and the others will let Alejo get rid of them one at a time. But it doesn't look good for the long term." Pursed-lipped side glance. "You don't care about the long term, do you?"

I shake my head and he goes back to his nails.

"If they throw him out this time, before or after the election, we'll all go with him. You know that, don't you? It'll be worse than '52 this time. First jail, then exile."

He shifts the paper knife to his left hand and goes to work on his right thumb. He'll have to get to whatever he's got to say without help from me. Working on the middle finger now. Here it comes.

"Pepe's offered me the Social Security. Not for after he wins. Right now. I'll have it for sixteen weeks no matter how the election goes."

No need to explain the exciting things possible for the Director of Social Security. Fifty million inchados to manipulate, mortgages to distribute among eager builders, consignments of drugs to buy from competing salesmen. An active director can become secure in sixteen weeks.

"Should he win, the government will recondition the building and move the Ministry of Education into it."

How can Alfonso resist? His poor building! Put it up on Washington Avenue six years ago and named it Edificio Petrolero to get the Hirudo Oil Company to take the top two floors. The flag-riot mob thought it belonged to gringos and set it on fire. Gutted from roof to lobby, and the banks won't finance remodeling for fear of another riot. Worst thing is Alfonso has to drive by it every morning on the way to the paper.

"All I'd have to do is take the papers out of the campaign. Lots of foreign news in Correo and keep the tabloids full of stabbings and auto crashes. I suppose Pepe would make some capital out of Alejandro Sancudo's own son taking a post in the Fuertes Administration. I think he's got something for Nacho—a quiet deal with Nacho spending a little less without actually leaving the ticket. An insurance policy so that Nacho will be all right no matter who wins. That's the mark of a political genius in this country. Now what I think Pepe's ultimately after is getting me and Nacho to convince Lucho to go over with his TV station. Lucho's got too much money to be bought, and he's already been president, so it would have to be that farsighted men like Nacho and me think Pepe would be better for the country. That would take Alejo off TV. I began hearing rumors of this stuff yesterday morning, and Pepe sent Meco to me last night. I'm not going to do it, Kiki. I told Meco I'd think it over, but I'm not going to do it."

"You. Do. What. You. Want. Fonso."

"I'm not going to do it, Kiki. At least not before I talk it all over with Nacho. I don't think I'd do it anyway. How could I do it? But I mention it so that you know that all kinds of things might happen. That's why I say you ought to leave. Not even Alejo would blame you."

"You. Do. What. You. Want."

"Look, Kiki. What if Pepe turned Ñato over to Interpol?"

I can shake my head. "Ñato's. Mine."

"Coño, carajo! When are you going to stop fighting? You don't care about yourself, but what about the rest of us?"

Poor Alfonso. He doesn't mind betraying Alejo, but he doesn't want to betray me.

"You. Do. What. You. Want."

Which isn't a release. To release him I'd have to give up, stop fighting, leave the country.

"We all want Ñato punished. The surest way would be to make a deal with Pepe. Pepe might win, you know. Or Ñato could get away before Alejo's in control. I'm sure Pepe would make a deal. He's only keeping Ñato like a counter to be played at the right moment; Meco said as much last night. He said, 'The President sympathizes with the desires for personal vindication of certain members of the Sancudo family.' You can't expect him to bring Ñato to trial here. Ñato knows too much about everyone for that, you included. But if Pepe turned him over to Interpol, he'd spend at least fifteen years in a French jail." Alfonso holds the paper knife in both hands near his sternum and looks sideways down at me like a pitcher wondering what to throw. "But that isn't enough for you! You want to watch that indian torture him to death!"

Bravo, Fonso! Dumdum wedding and peritonitis honeymoon, because it's too messy to cut him up with a chain saw, and too quick too. I might strap a cage full of starved rats to his belly. No. Just one rat. A big, strong one, though lean of course. Tripe's a delicacy. Never cared for it myself, but I bet the rat would give Ñato three stars, gnawing his way to a gourmet dinner. Making me smile.

Alfonso's check twitches, as though he had a film-clip of my thoughts. Then he flips the paper knife onto the desk and covers his face with his hands. "It's all right," he says through them. "I don't blame you. Whatever you do to him it's too good."

He turns away, shoulders hunched. "Coño!" He drops his hands. "If the old hound had heard this conversation!" He turns around to smile at me, eyes swimming. "Making deals with Pepe Fuertes! In the middle of his last campaign!" Wide grin and sniffle. "He'd have an attack! And I'm supposed to be the good son, you the prodigal. You're the one who got thrown out of college. Who borrowed the presidential yacht to smuggle whiskey. Who laid the presidential girlfriend in the presidential bed. I'm the one who never gave him any trouble. Now I'm ready to sell him out and you're sticking with him."

"Not. For. Him. Fonso. For. Me."

"I know. But it's still funny." He shakes his head, still grinning. "God, what a lot of trouble you've given us all, Kiki. Me especially. How many times have I bailed you out, Kiki, one way or another? Remember the time you needed twenty-five hundred, in dollars, to pay off the Panamanian police? I had to sell a car. I know, I know. I'll never regret it. You always said that. Phone calls from Olga at three in the morning, 'Where's Kiki?' Holding her hand on nights when you were flying to Costaguana. When Erasmito broke his head, who took him to the hospital? Me. And now, when I've a chance to straighten everything out, you won't let me. You know I can't do it unless you leave." His grin dissolves and he looks down at my slippers. "I think the real reason I want you to leave is that I can't stand to see you like this."

He springs up and smacks his left palm with his right fist. Another big grin. "Remember when you wrestled the captain at Cambridge? I was a senior at Harvard; you must have been a sophomore at Yale. That beautiful gringo with his blond hair and his sportsmanlike smile. You put him into one hold after another, all the ones that hurt, letting him struggle out of one thing to get him in something worse. Everyone was booing you. I happened to be sitting next to his parents, and of course I didn't say you were my brother. When the ref warned you for choking him and let him rest for a minute, his father said to me, 'I'm surprised Yale admitted an animal like that.' Then you pinned him in a split scissors. What a degrading hold that is, legs spread and his asshole aimed at the gym skylight. Then you walked out of the gym and left him lying there."

"I. Remember." It was right after Easter vacation, and my mind was still scalding from the way Angela stood naked on the beach, laughing at the lump in my bathing suit.

"His name was McAndless or McAndrews or something. He was an officer of our class, vice president, I think. And that was his last bout. His farewell college try for dear old Harvard." This phrase in English, with Alfonso laughing hard enough to cry, well, laughing and crying a little anyway. "God, Kiki, you really gave it to him!" Then, suddenly, his face goes tragic. Plucks a handkerchief from his breast pocket—foulard pattern, same as his tie—and wipes his eyes. "Whatever you do is too good."

I nod.

He fidgets from one foot to the other. "Look, Kiki. I'm not going to make any deal with Pepe. Forget I mentioned it."

I nod.

"You need anything?"

I shake my head.

"Look, Kiki. I have to get to my office. Where do you . . ."

"Send. Me. Jaime."

"All right." He keeps staring tragically at me, as though he wants to pick me up in his arms. Life is simpler for me than for Alfonso.

"Look, Kiki. I'll see you this afternoon. Tell Elena hello for me when she gets up."

I nod, and he makes that pursed-lipped smile and steps by my chair, out of my field of vision.

16

Alfonso didn't notice me until that wrestling match. All the while we lived at Aunt Beatrix's and even after he left for Harvard, I was invisible. Even when my torpid elbow sent one of Aunt Beatrix's precious *objets*—a Lalique piece like an outsized ice cube with a draped Persephone imprisoned inside—smithering to the tile floor of the living room, she failed to see me and howled over my head at the poltergeist she believed to be to blame. Uncle Erasmo saw me once, one Saturday afternoon just before my fourteenth birthday when he was on his way to play chess at Don Felix Ardilla's house, but he took me for one of the street boys who prowl the better quarters of the capital seeking odd jobs and pressed a ten centavo piece into my hand, saying that he was taking his car but that I could wash it the following morning. My invisibility extended to my personal belongings, even to my food and silverware, so that no one had to endure the hallucination of forks levitating themselves to dump rice into thin air and guests could admire my Aunt Beatrix's Wedgwood plates, her Ming figurine, her Baccarat goblet (from the 1909 exposition) while I stood between them and the breakfront which sheltered them.

At first I believed that my Aunt Beatrix was unable to see me because her mind was totally occupied with the knowledge that she was an Anguila and, more than an Anguila, which was a great deal, an Anguila Ahumada, families more august and anointed than the Hapsburgs or the Hohenzollerns. Everyone knew that Ahumada females conceived parthenogenetically by dispensation of the Holy Ghost and that the Anguilas, instead of shitting like ordinary mortals, produced milk-white turds with a faint aroma of wild jasmine. And Pope Benedict XV, in respect for Aunt Beatrix's genealogy, had arranged for her soul to be raised into heaven even while her body remained on earth, thus insuring against a permanent taint from her union with Uncle Erasmo. She paraded her ancestors like saints on feast days. Each morning the gem-encrusted effigy of her father, Don Fermín Anguila, in his uniform of Knight of the Holy Sepulcher, was carried three times around the patio to the beat of a funereal drum and the swing of incense chasers, while Aunt Beatrix extolled his virtues for the edification of Uncle Erasmo and Alfonso. Her hysterical monotone was not aimed my way only because she couldn't see me, but Uncle Erasmo, who had made her brother President of the Republic, who had been President himself, who had earned a fortune at law and founded four newspapers, was so wary of it that he trembled lest the faintest spiral from his havana leak from his study to defile her forebears' shrine.

He couldn't see me because he was absorbed in his law practice and his newspapers and the intrigues attendant upon his becoming a justice of the Supreme Court. Or so I thought for a while, but what, then, was Alfonso's excuse? In the end I had to admit I had become invisible. This caused me anxiety at first; then I came to take a perverse pleasure in it, like a cockroach when the kitchen light goes off, as soon as I realized that I had not ceased to exist and would someday return dramatically to view.

The only place where my invisibility was not in force was the Reservation Y.M.C.A., a scarred brick building off Washington Avenue with a lobby full of ping-pong tables and a slimy indoor swimming pool and an auditorium in which six Unitarians assembled every Sunday at ten-thirty and a basketball court where poorly chaperoned dances were held on Friday nights and a wrestling room whose mildewed mats were soaked in the onionpungent scents of straining groins and armpits, whose random litter of barbells (the relics of four or five broken sets) was pitted by rust. Dick Angel, the retired master sergeant who was athletic director, saw me the moment I wandered in dragging my book bag. He seemed, in fact, to be waiting for me, holding a position of attention, fists braced against his hips, while suspended from the hand rings which hung from a beam near the ceiling.

"What you want, kid?"

"I want to be strong."

"You come to the right place, but stay off the mats with your street shoes."

Then he let go of the rings and floated down—white tennis shoes, white wool socks, white duck trousers, white undershirt with white cotton tufts of hair blossoming from the neck—to teach me how to exercise and weightlift and handbalance and box and wrestle. He taught me wrestling last, as though he knew that was what I would like best. I worked out with soldiers and marines on their way to Saipan and Tarawa and sailors back from Savo Island and the Coral Sea, anyone remotely near my weight, and had my first bout at fifteen with a merchant seaman who tried to bugger me in the showers. I took him down with a standing switch and tired him with a cross-body ride—scene off a Greek vase, one naked athlete on his knees, another snaked across his back from one leg to the opposite arm—and sprained his shoulder decisively with a chicken-wing lock; thank you, Dick, because I wasn't yet strong enough to break his arm. That night I materialized briefly to Alfonso while walking across his bedroom on my hands, but when I flipped over onto my feet to tell the story, he lost sight of me and went back to his homework. The next time he saw me was five years later in Cambridge.

Alfonso got his exercise dancing to boleros like "Flores Ne-gras" and "Bésame Mucho" on terraces hung with Japanese lanterns and shielded from the moonlight by mango trees, and also copulating with the maids Aunt Beatrix brought from the interior. Each spring she brought a new girl to train to wait at table, and each fall Alfonso sent the girl back to her village pregnant, though this was always brought off without Aunt Beatrix's knowledge and in collusion with Uncle Erasmo. The girl was given a little money and told to go home, while Aunt Beatrix grumbled about the sloth and ingratitude of the peasantry. Uncle Erasmo underwrote the sys-tem because it was annoying to his wife, safer than having Alfonso debauch girls of good family, and on the whole cheaper than send-ing him to a whorehouse. What with the boleros and the maids and his close collaborations with Uncle Erasmo, Alfonso so mas-tered the graces of society, the arts of love, and the ways of the world that by eighteen he was the most accomplished young fop in Tinieblas, a distinction he proved during the vacation between his freshman and sophomore years by becoming the second of three favored men to take the virginity of Irene Manta. The first was her father, Don Reynaldo Manta; the third was Nacho Hormiga, who married her. Irene and other girls of her class throughout Latin America were able, Venus-like, to renew their innocence through the skill and sympathy of a Buenos Aires surgeon who specialized in vulcanizing punctured pudenda. Alfonso destroyed one of his finest pieces of work and was so impressed he fell in love for the first and last time. My first intimation that Alfonso was in love came when I was awakened one very sultry night by the silence of the bedsprings in the maid's room below my own. I assumed Alfonso was sick, but found him singing through his shaving lather the next morning. I followed him into his room and learned (sec-ond sign) that he had been keeping a diary. He read aloud from it to himself while I stood invisible in the doorway: "Some virgins seem gifted by God with amatory skills a courtesan might envy. Ah, Irene, my Irene! So innocent and yet so wise!" Then he looked through me into the hallway, his face wreathed in an idiot's beatific grin (third signal), and sighed, "Puta, madre! Qué cosa más sabrosa!"

From that morning, nourished by the rays of love, Alfonso began to grow. Normally he was a couple inches short of six feet and slender, but by the Fourth of July three weeks later he was as tall and sturdy as the picked men of the Marine color guard who translated the Stars and Stripes from Fort Shafter to the Plaza Inchado. His chest broadened, his shoulders swelled, even his soul grew tumescent, overflowing in such profusion that wherever he walked men stared at him and women bit their lips in desire. He cultivated a pencil mustache, and when he took Irene to see his idol Errol Flynn as *El Halcón del Mar* he was mobbed in front of the Teatro Trópico by screaming adolescents who took him for the great man. Our cousin Raquel, Aunt Beatrix's immaculately conceived daughter, returned from finishing school in Washington with a diploma written in French and a Bolivian diplomat's son on a velvet leash, and the night of their wedding, which was the high point of Alfonso's love affair with Irene Manta, he stood six feet three inches tall and radiant as Lucifer. All six bridesmaids had orgasms when they danced with him, fluttering limply to the dance floor like wounded butterflies, while the Bolivian gnawed his leash in envy and Raquel prepared to spend her marriage haunted by longings for him. And when he took Irene in his arms and tangoed her off into the darkness at the back of the patio, Don Reynaldo Manta fainted from jealousy and came to weeping from the knowledge that his first daughter was forever lost to him while his second was only nine years old. Long after the last guest had departed and the orchestra had folded their music stands and packed their instruments, when the humid air was freshened by breezes from the gulf and the moon hung wan and sallow in a fading sky, I climbed to my room to find Alfonso lying there laved by a golden haze while Irene Manta knelt naked on the bed beside him, her lips sleepwalking across his abdomen. I slung a hammock on the upstairs screened porch and slept no more in my bed that summer, for when I went to it the next evening the sheets were still scalding to my touch.

Irene Manta was tall and slim like a young palm, as wild and lithe and ruttish as an otter, with golden eyes and lips like an unopened rose, and that slight separation between her two front teeth which the Arab sages knew as a mark of lasciviousness. She and Alfonso made love in her friend Orlando Logarto's studio and on the front seat of her cousin Tito Avispa's 1936 Packard coupe and on the moist fairways of the Club Campestre and standing up in a corner of the card room at the Club Mercantil while a dance was going on outside and in all the rooms of Aunt Beatrix's house, even in Aunt Beatrix's bed one afternoon while she and Irene's mother and two other ladies played mah-jongg in the living room, even in the bathroom, once in the tub and once on the toilet, Alfonso sitting and Irene straddled over him. They drove all the way to La Yegua to make love in the pastures, and that year the cows dropped triplets and an old stud bull who had been consigned to the slaughterhouse regained his powers and sired more calves than ever before. On the way back they stopped to make love in a drought-seared ricefield in Salinas Province, and that night the drought broke and it rained for forty days and the crops were saved.

But after my cousin Raquel's wedding, Irene's ardor cooled. She was accustomed, even at eighteen, to have men at her feet, and now Alfonso could have any woman in the country and was beginning to undervalue her. She knew without considering it, in the uterine wisdom of women given over to love, that it was either her or Alfonso, so she grew less avid and then began rejecting his advances, and in ten days Alfonso had shrunk back to his normal size. With this she saw that Alfonso was just an ordinary man and, besides, neither old nor rich enough to make a good husband, so she neglected him more and, as he started to whine and plead, went out with other men, principally Nacho Hormiga, though she did not go to bed with Nacho for the excellent reason that she wanted to marry him. Then Alfonso accused her of betraying him and threatened violence on himself, on her, on his rival or rivals, on the whole country, the entire world, and she laughed at him, a delicate laugh like the tinkling of ice cubes in a Cuba libre. As she laughed, Alfonso shriveled and shrunk, so that he became shorter than I was and thinner than I had been before I started working out and very pale, so pale it seemed that he might become invisible too. Still he continued to hope and plead until Irene told him publicly she did not love him.

This was at the funeral of Tito Avispa's Packard. Tito was ready to get a new car when the war started, but of course there were none to be had then, and for nearly two years after the Japanese surrendered no new cars arrived in Tinieblas, and all this time the Packard served faithfully, its tires accepting retread after retread while its fenders decayed and its grill tarnished in the rigors of our tropical climate. Then, when the new models finally came in on the Galactic Fruit steamers that summer of 1947, Tito's cousin Irene Manta began going out with Alfonso, who had no car, and begged the Packard. Its springs strained over potholed backroads and its cushions bore the buffets of love, yet it rolled on, uncomplaining, until Irene, after a particularly sloppy argument with Alfonso, drove it into a ditch. The broken axle could have been repaired, but Irene had no real need for the car now that she was seeing so much of Nacho Hormiga, who had bought my father's excellent Daimler after he went into exile, while Tito saw the wreck only as an excuse for a party. Thus the following announcement appeared, bordered in black, in all the newspapers:

DON ALBERTO AVISPA MANTA
IS GRIEVED TO ANNOUNCE THE PASSING
OF HIS BELOVED PACKARD COUPE,
WHICH WILL BE LAID TO REST AT THE FINCA "LA PERFECTA"
RÍO TIBIO, PROVINCE OF TINIEBLAS,
AT ELEVEN OF THE FORENOON, SATURDAY, 22ND JULY.

Tito's *finca* lay just past the Guardia Civil checkpoint to the north of the capital, and mourners began arriving there at around ten o'clock. Tito greeted them in the large thatch-roofed pavilion, behind which the departed lay in state, its body festooned with black crepe and its swooping swan radiator cap hung with a simple gardenia wreath. Besides five cases of Pirata Morgan White Tinieblas Rum, Coca-Cola, and two large cakes of ice, the pavilion contained a sixteen-piece Mexican mariachi band which was playing an engagement at the Hotel Excelsior that month. The day was overcast and muggy, and before the wake had been long in progress, a fine rain began to drool pathetically on the drinkers and dancers who could not squeeze under the pavilion's roof. It was an affair that straddled social frontiers. The best families had sent the generation born between 1915 and 1930, but the married men, no doubt by previous agreement, left their wives at home and brought their concubines, while the unmarried brought dates and fiancées who were very often the younger sisters of the wives left at home. The result of this experiment in democracy was to make the concubines feel respectable and the girls of good family thrillingly dissolute. Guchi Oruga left both his wife, who was Tito's sister, and his concubine, and brought two jello-breasted Dominican whores from a brothel called *Lo Que El Víento se Llevó,* the premier whorehouse of Central America until it was wrecked by a contingent of Puerto Rican soldiers returning from Korea six years later. The two were in great demand once the dancing started, especially as there were many young solo males like Alfonso, with whom Irene Manta had refused to come. She arrived with Nacho and another couple and was gayer than ever, flirting with everyone but Alfonso, who squatted under the weeping eaves, drinking straight rum from a paper cup and mooning out at the soggy meadow where Irene Manta danced barefoot in the warm rain.

Sometime before noon Tito had the mariachis play a fanfare, and Orlando Lagarto, who was expelled from a French seminary the year Tito bought the Packard, stepped out beside it with a soutane on over his bathing suit and carrying a large crucifix, and in a high, squeaky voice like that of Monseñor Irribarri, the Spanish Basque who was Archbishop of Tinieblas, began:

"In nomine Grouchi et Chici et Harpi, amen!" Then he spoke of the Packard's ample windows, out of which so many drunks had vomited, and its noble lines, by which so many streetwalkers had been captivated, and its generous seats, on which so many bastards had been sired, and its mighty engine, which had outdistanced so many Reservation MP's, and its firm and upright gearshift, which was an example to the young men of Tinieblas—all this to cheers and catcalls from men who had stripped off their shirts and in some cases their trousers and giggles from girls whose thin dresses were rain-plastered to their flesh and raucous toots from Tito's brother Meco who had taken a horn from one of the musicians. Then he turned and held the crucifix out before him and marched solemnly away toward the huge pit Tito had had dug, and all the men, all save Alfonso, who stayed inside the pavilion drinking, began pushing the Packard after him, with Tito steering with his right arm through the left window and the girls skipping alongside and the band trudging in the rear playing "La Golondrina," and when they had the car next to the pit, Orlando stood on the other side praying ("Hail Maisy, full of grease, the lard is with you . . ."), while they rocked it until it tipped over and crashed, roof down, into the ground. Then they covered it with empty rum bottles and a little dirt and trooped back to the pavilion.

As they returned, Alfonso slouched out into the rain and took Irene Manta by the arm and dragged her away from Nacho, though this looked in no way menacing for by this time he was no larger than she, and whined something to her, and she laughed and said, clearly, so that everyone nearby turned around, "But I don't love you."

Alfonso shrank three inches before everyone's eyes and sat down on the ground and stayed there, not bothering to wipe the rain from his eyes, so like it was to his tears, until Lino Piojo took him home. He was no bigger than a dwarf when he arrived, and he stayed in his room, not eating or sleeping or bathing or shaving or opening the invitation to the formal party at the Club Mercantil where Don Reynaldo Manta announced the engagement of his daughter Irene to Ignacio Hormiga. Irene danced at a number of parties in her honor, and then flew off to the Argentine to have her womb scraped clean of Alfonso's child and her hymen reconstructed for Nacho. On the day after the operation Alfonso ate the egg Aunt Beatrix sent up to him, and the next day he came down to dinner, and then he began growing again, so that by the time of Irene's and Nacho's wedding early in September he was his normal size, and that same night a whining of bedsprings in the maid's room certified his recovery. As I passed his room the next morning I saw him writing in his diary. He put down the pen and read aloud: "I have been in love. Once is enough." Then he looked through me into the hallway, his face gnarled by a sardonic smile, and sighed, "Puta, madre! Qué cosa más pendeja!"

As for me, three weeks after successfully defending my innocence against assault from the rear, I lost it in a face-to-face engagement. That was two years before Alfonso's nearly fatal seizure of love, the night of Hiroshima. There were several soldiers working out at the Y that day, men from a kind of commando unit which had fought in Europe and was refitting for the invasion of Japan, lean, pebble-eyed assassins who took desperate joy in the knowedge that they would all be dead before the year was out and whose only commerce with the world was in the hard currency of violence. Their workout was a free-for-all in which they aimed savage kicks at each other's testicles, rabbit-punched anyone whose back was turned, ganged up two and three against one (these alliances dissolving in gouges and chops as soon as the victim was subdued), stomped the kidneys of those who were down and bit the ankles of those still on their feet, pausing only to wipe blood from bashed noses and spit loose teeth into the corner near the weight rack, until they all lay piled and tangled in the center of the mat, groaning, cursing, and laughing. Then a sergeant from their outfit came in with the news that a hundred fucking thousand fucking Nips had been cre-fucking-mated with one fucking bomb and that the fucking bastards would fucking well throw in the fucking towel, the reaction to this being fifty-one percent relief and forty-nine percent resentment, their reprieve just outweighing the loss of all that horizontal snatch, and the ones who could still walk decided to go celebrate. One of them, with whom I had been practicing jujitsu throws before the free-for-all began, suggested that they take me along to interpret so that the greasers wouldn't cheat them, and we set off as soon as they had put on their boots, first on foot to the labyrinth of cantinas behind Washington Avenue, then by taxi to the Alameda, where my book bag was used as a football in an impromptu game of rough tackle and passed and punted to shreds and my books hurled through the yellow bug-clustered globes of park lamps and lofted into the trees, all with my complete approval though of course they didn't ask, while strollers hustled for their houses and a lone Civil Guard looked on in terror, and finally in three buggies out to whoresland. The buggies, which in better times carried family groups and sweethearts and tourists around the square park or perhaps all the way down to Cervantes Plaza on nights when there was a band concert, were commandeered and their drivers tossed down off the boxes and their skinny, carbuncled horses lashed in a kind of Roman chariot race out the Vía Venezuela, past swerved autos and gape-eyed citizens standing at bus stops, with the buggy in front of us hitting a pothole and careening, spilling its people out into the street, one soldier jumping up and lunging to cling to the lip of our buggy, hopping and trying to climb inside while the corporal who was driving flayed his shoulders with the buggywhip, until another man reached past me to shove a palm in his face and flip him back into the street, and the third buggy pulling alongside us, the two drivers whipping at each other and us passengers. That's how we came to *Lo Que el Viento se Llevó.*

Eighteen years later I had to remember that night as, lying in bed with Elena, I listened to her tell me how she'd been smoothly seduced by an army companion of her father's, who took her on an outing from her convent school near Udine, gave her lunch on a terrace in Trieste, brought her to his palazzo in Venice, and excised her girlhood with quick, surgical skill.

"And who seduced you, Kiki?"

"Lo Que el Viento se Llevó."

"What the wind blew away? Was she some tramp off the streets?"

"No," I laughed. "A whorehouse. That was the name of it. The Spanish name for the movie. Clark Gable and Vivian Leigh."

"Gone With the Wind."

"That's it."

The movie played in Tinieblas the week of my father's first inauguration, and the day after Don Horacio Ladilla saw it, he sent to Metro-Goldwyn-Mayer for the plans to Tara. He had the mansion duplicated on a swampy flat outside the capital and stocked it with women from all over the hemisphere, haughty *limeñas* who wore evening gowns and carried themselves like queens; witty *chilenas* with darting tongues; lithe, coffee-skinned *cariocas* whose samba churnings could wring love's libation from the most jaded client; blue-black *haitianas* who strutted the dance floor in a voodoo dream lolling bubbles of saliva over soft, swollen lips;

meek, sad-eyed *ticas*, submissive as tame heifers; statuesque *gringas* with platinum hair; savage-souled *mejicanas* with white teeth and flashing eyes; sullen *argentinas* who lounged like jaguars among the tables; and agile *cubanas*, tutored in arts unequaled since the sack of Rome. The ground floor contained the bar, which was sixty feet long and at which no women were allowed, and a huge ballroom with tables and a bandstand where a Cuban orchestra played till dawn. This room had no windows, only louvers high up near the ceiling, and its walls were decorated with an immense mural by Orlando Lagarto representing the interior of Noah's Ark the night before the rains stopped. Here the lion lay down with the lamb, and the elephant buggered the rhino who buggered the hippo who buggered the bull, and the ostrich fellated the prancing giraffe, and the alligator ravished the zebra, and the dromedary humped the tigress, and the peacock futtered the ewe, and the goat swived the gorilla, and the chimpanzee frigged the bear, and one of Noah's sons banged the orangutan while another was reamed by the wolf and a daughter-in-law was tongued by the antelope, and another blew the jackass, and the rest of his family writhed and grappled with each other and the odd animals in a combined collective incest-bestiality which hallucinated across the whole rear wall and formed the background for Noah himself, white-bearded and toothless, who jacked off above the bandstand, hopping on one foot. Upstairs a corridor tunneled back beneath cobwebbed rafters, its end obscured by the curvature of the earth, and on both sides were bedrooms with mirrored ceilings and revolving colored lights and speaking tubes which breathed in the rumba rhythms of the tireless musicians, and all night long the stairs creaked under couples rising to paradise in flesh and bone, while maracas chuckled the lewd Te Deum of "Mamá Inés" and the dancers swayed under a constellation of flaring orgasms.

Well, that night, after the buggy horses had staggered up to the columned portico, their mouths dripping blood and froth, my fine pack of murderers trooped inside, full of gross shouts and laughter and boasts of Apulian shrines defiled and Rhine maidens violated, but when they pushed their way in to the ballroom and saw the women waiting by the door and clustered at the tables and preening themselves beneath Lagarto's mural, they grew hushed and reverent, like ghostly janizaries arrived at the Muslim heaven, and bent to me whispering, "Get that one for me, Kiki," "Ask that there little girl if she'll sit with me." So I moved along the tables serving Cupid's office, while the women rumpled my hair and smeared my checks with lipstick and caressed my stomach with warm hands and pulled my face down into perfumed bosoms and the men gaped and rubbed their eyes as though afraid they might be dreaming it all back in the jails and chain gangs where they'd been recruited. The hulking corporal let himself be led away by a fragile mulata no older than myself, shuffling meekly after her while she tittered to her colleagues, and others followed with their partners, hanging their heads and mewing like tame beasts, until there was only me, an ape-shouldered Kansan with a knife scar under his eye and a pocket full of gold teeth he'd rifle-butted from the mouths of dead men, and a willowy Colombian girl, not from Baranquilla or some other coastal town but from a valley in the Andes where the Andalusian blood had remained unmixed with indian or negro, a doe-eyed girl with black hair down to her waist. My gringo asked me to tell her she reminded him of a Neapolitan girl he'd abandoned with child when the outfit was sent to Anzio, and when I translated, the girl stroked his check and said, "Malo, malo."

"What's she saying?"

"She says you're a bad boy."

He nodded, and tears rolled down his savaged check.

Then he said he didn't want the girl, that I should take her, and when I said I had no money, he fished up a wad of one-inchado notes and threw them on the table. I grabbed them and stood up, displaying my manhood clearly through my thin school trousers, and took the girl by the hand and said, "Vámanos!" in a voice that was meant to be as tough as the soldiers' but which came out squeaky, and she followed me without laughing, though she had to stop me at the window at the head of the stairs where one paid and retrieve the odd inchados after I threw all the money in. And in her room I tried to pretend I knew what I was doing, but as I knelt before the target, I had to ask how, and when she reached to guide me, I fired the whole clip into her hand. Then she made me lie down beside her and tell her how I'd got my muscles and what I was doing with those gringo soldiers, while she ran her fingers lightly over my chest and flanks, and if she were making fun of me I was going to rip the gold rings out of her ears as one of my jovial comrades had done to a cantina barmaid earlier in the evening, and what story could I concoct for my patron below so he wouldn't guess how futilely I'd dribbled away his money? But my body rearmed before my mind capitulated, and I lay on a great warm plain which rose beneath me and sucked me down, and when it swallowed me, I was free.

17

Alejo returned on the same plane which took Alfonso back to Harvard. As an expert in my own right on pre-dawn returns from exile, I assume he shuffled impatiently by the aircraft door, looking out through its bathysphere window at terminal lights captured in puddles on the tarmac, that when the door finally opened he felt the air of the savannas like an animal tongue on his face, like a sodden cape dropped across his shoulders, that he stepped out immediately, not smiling at the admirers who were not packed around the foot of the ramp, not blinking at the flashbulbs which did not explode below him, not waving at the multitude which was not cheering from the observation deck of the terminal, hurrying down to be reassured by Uncle Erasmo that his presence in his own country would not be disputed, that it had been cleared with President Gusano and Colonel Culata and the Ambassador of the United States. He was followed down the ramp by four citizens of the Republic of Paraguay: broad-shouldered Egon and narrow-hipped Gunther, former members of the marine detachment of the *Graf Spee;* Baldesare Furetto, former Italian Vice Consul at Punta del Este; and a round little man called Doktor Henker, former passenger on U-477 during its final voyage, from Kiel to the River Plate, in the late spring of 1945. The Paraguayans conversed in

German while waiting for the customs inspector to finish the game
of dominos he was playing with two corporals of the Guardia Civil.

Alejo had two gold front teeth and wore dark glasses. If the
last were intended as a disguise, they were inadequate.

"What happened to your teeth, Mr. President?" asked the customs inspector.

"I bit a gringo."

"Bite him again, Mr. President," the man said softly, thinking
Alejo spoke figuratively. "This time we'll help you."

"Do you see?" said Doktor Henker. "The stars are propitious."

Outside the customs shed Alfonso was waiting to embrace him.

"You are Alfonso, aren't you?" Alejo asked, pointing a finger
at him.

"Yes, Papá."

"You did not tell me you had a son," said Doktor Henker.

"I had forgotten."

"It must go into the chart. Young man, what was the day and
hour of your birth?"

They drove straight to La Yegua in Uncle Erasmo's state-owned
Cadillac with *Corte Suprema* on the plate. Armed ranch hands kept
the gate. Alejo and the Paraguayans stayed indoors. For five years
alejistas and anti-*alejistas* had variously boasted or warned that
Alejo had slipped ashore from a Japanese submarine, that he was
poised to cross the Ticamalan frontier with a thousand volunteers,
that he had air-freighted himself to the capital in a coffin or come
in by ship disguised as a nun. Now he was really back and nothing
happened. The government did not fall; the gringos did not inter-
vene. "He's given up," sighed the *alejistas*. "He's beaten," chuckled
the rest. But one by one the leaders of the Tinieblista Party were
summoned to Remedios. They were asked the date and hour of
their birth and given audience with the leader.

"I have come home," he told Dr. Fausto Maroma. "Next year
I shall be able to say, 'I have returned.'"

"Don't worry about the gringos," he said to Fidel Labrador,
the secretary of the Union of Tinieblan Reservation Employees.
"The gringos are learning who their true enemies are."

And when Gonzalo Garbanzo Maduro asked him point-blank

if he were going to run for president, he replied: "For the present I cultivate my coffee and my cattle. But I am destined to be President of the Republic twice more before I die."

These remarks were repeated, and old Tinieblists got their armbands out of mothballs. Meanwhile data was being collected on the precise moments of the discovery of Tinieblas, its declaration of independence, and the founding of its principal towns. Parish records were consulted for the birth dates of political figures and officers of the Civil Guard. Doktor Henker began casting horoscopes. The only modern political campaign conducted according to the science of astrology had begun.

Alejo announced his candidacy on November 28th, my seventeenth birthday and the seventeenth anniversary of his first taste of power. It was raining throughout the republic, but a patch of fair weather followed his car like a spotlight from La Yegua to the capital. The trip took sixteen hours, so crowded was the way with people. People stood in the mud beside the road and perched on the steel rafters of bridges and hung from the trees, waiting all day under the pelting rain, and in the towns people packed the post offices waiting for the phone to ring and the postmaster to shout, "He's just passed Palo Seco; he's coming now!" so they could run down to pack the highway crossroads, women holding newspapers over their heads and men with kids on their shoulders, and the clouds would part and the rain would break and the car would come in view and they would shout, "Arriba Tinieblas! Arriba Alejo!" and he would pass without looking either left or right, and as he disappeared down the road the clouds would fold in over the sun and the rain would hammer down on the still shouting people. At the guard post on the outskirts of the capital he got down from the car and mounted a white stallion owned by Don Belisario Oruga and rode through the poor quarters preceded by two men carrying torches, and when he entered Plaza Bolívar there were forty thousand people waiting for him.

"The stars are propitious," he said. "Destiny calls me to lead. Neither I nor the republic have any choice."

The stars were also propitious for Belisario Oruga as vice president. His and Alejo's candidacies were ratified by the Tinieblista Party in convention three days later. Alejo took over Oruga's man-

sion on Avenida Pizarro for his campaign headquarters, installing
Doktor Henker and Furetto and Dr. Fausto Maroma and Gonzalo
Garbanzo with him on the upper floor and removing all the pictures from the salons below to make room for horoscopes. These
were done in great detail and included every important man in
Tinieblas, particularly all the Tinieblista candidates for deputy, for
which bank balance and voter appeal were the usual qualifications.
Now the stars had also to be propitious. I saw the charts with my
own eyes, for I would mingle with the numerous visitors every afternoon after my workout. Doktor Henker paced nervously from
chart to chart in his black gown with gold symbols embroidered on
it, talking to himself in German and shouting orders in bad Spanish
to hangers-on, while Furetto sat sneering into the telephone, taking
reports from the wards and provinces and making notes in a Ren-
aissance script. The Italian was no scientist and preferred the precepts of Machiavelli to advice from the stars, but clever as he was
he could not overrule Doktor Henker at the strategy conferences.
These were held every night at nine when they were not on the
road, and, invisible as I was, I often remained for them.

"La Merced is unfavorable with Mars in Saturn," Doktor
Henker might say.

"Ma Signore Presidente!" Furetto holds his hands in front of
him as though weighing invisible tennis balls. "The committee is
expecting you."

"La Merced is unfavorable."

"It will be an insult, Signore Presidente; it will show contempt.
It is very clear in the *Discourses* that 'Contempt and insults engen-
der hatred against those who indulge in them.'"

"Didn't you hear Doktor Henker?"

"Signore Presidente!" The tennis balls become heavier. "Why
not a small speech. We have to pass through anyway."

"We will not pass through."

"Madre di Dio! We will have to go How far?" He looks to
Garbanzo.

"Two hundred miles."

"We will have to go two hundred miles to get from Otán to
Salinas without passing through La Merced." He lets the balls fall.

"Pay attention to Doktor Henker. He has killed more people than the bubonic plague."

Once Alejo saw me, standing under the huge horoscope of the Republic of Tinieblas.

"You are Kiki, aren't you?"

"Yes, Papá."

"You look like a man."

"Another son?" said Doktor Henker. And I believe he was going to ask me for the date and hour of my birth, but then both his and Alejo's gaze slid through me.

Now at that time Alejo was at the height of his strength and energy and, on Doktor Henker's advice, no longer drank or smoked or ate meat, so that he could campaign eighteen hours a day and make love to a different woman in every town where he slept and in every village where he took siesta. Wherever he was women came to him or, if they were too old to aspire to being selected, sent their daughters, and though Furetto never ceased quoting that "Women have been the cause of great dissensions and much ruin to states," Alejo took one after lunch and one after dinner the way a dyspeptic takes peppermints or bicarbonate of soda. From this sprang the rumor that he had lost a testicle and hence was sterile, for none of these women ever brought a child to be recognized, even after he was in the palace again, while by rights that campaign alone ought to have furnished me a hundred half-brothers and -sisters. This was used against him by his opponents, along with the accusations that he had had Furetto murder my mother and that Doktor Henker was Adolf Hitler with his mustache shaved and that if elected Alejo was going to castrate every negro in the country and feed their women to the sharks, but Alejo took no notice of these calumnies nor paid any attention to his opponents but spoke only of what the stars intended for Tinieblas, a school for this town, an agricultural bank for that province, new contracts for the oil and banana workers, and so forth. These were not promises he would try to fulfill if elected; they were part of the country's destiny, of which his election was the principal fact. Wherever he went, he inspired instant and intense love or hatred, so that by Christmas Tinieblas was completely divided into *alejistas*

and anti-*alejistas* without one neutral man, woman, or child from
Caribbean to Pacific, from the Ticamalan to the Costaguanan frontier. Men who had loathed each other all their lives, whose ancestors back to the days of the Spanish colony had been blood
enemies, who had exchanged the most bitter insults and unpardon-
able outrages, suddenly found themselves working together for
Alejo or fighting side by side against him, while husband and wife,
father and son, brother and brother cursed each other and slunk
snarling into opposing camps. So it was that nineteen political parties banded together behind the candidacy of Olmedo Avispa, Tito's
and Meco's father.

Olmedo Avispa had practiced law for forty years without ever
making an enemy. He was nominated first by the Conservative
Party, which had not yet split and which had put Lucho Gusano in
the palace. Then the Liberals nominated him, followed by the Liberal Nationalists, and the Socialists and the Authentic Socialists,
and the Independent Revolutionaries and the Revolutionary Inde-
pendents, and the Practical Utopians, and the United Anarchists,
and the Personal Opportunists, whose entire program was to get
Humberto Ladilla elected to the Chamber of Deputies and who
sold lottery chances on the government jobs in his patronage, and
the Radical Republicans, and the Peasant Laborites, and other parties whose names are forgotten now even by their founders, all
nineteen of them parties which have long since dissolved and whose
flag colors and zoological symbols have disappeared or passed to
other groups. That year they united to stop Alejandro Sancudo.
And besides those nineteen parties, the anti-*alejistas* had four newspapers and six radio stations, while the power lines to Radio
Tinieblista and the plant which printed Uncle Erasmo's papers,
lines maintained by the Compañía Tinieblina de Electricidad y Gas
(a subsidiary of the Yankee and Celestial Energy Corporation,
whose legal counsel was now the firm of Avispa y Abeja), kept
breaking down. Nor was it an accident, a regrettable misunder-
standing, that whenever Alejo's campaign caravan reached a guard
post it was detained for an hour or more. The Guardia Civil remembered Lieutenant Colonel Domingo Azote. But Alejo paid no
attention to this opposition and went on talking about the stars.

It was this trust in the stars which preserved his confidence, for all was not well. True, wherever he went the masses acclaimed him, and province after province reported that he would win a majority of the votes, but as the proverb says, "It's not who votes, it's who counts," and the arrangements for counting were not propitious. During the last week in March carpenters began putting up voting booths and tables in every ward of the capital and in the parishes of the towns and the squares of the villages, and every voting table was nine yards long because the arrangements for counting held that at six P.M. on election day the ballot boxes would be opened at the tables and the votes counted openly by representatives of all the parties who supported candidates for President. And while some of the parties supporting Olmedo Avispa were so small that they could hardly find enough representatives for all the voting tables, they were bona fide parties and entitled to be represented at the counting. So every voting table sat twenty people: one representative of the Tinieblista Party and nineteen representatives of the parties supporting Olmedo Avispa. And the Electoral Jury in the capital which checked the table counts and tallied the vote for the whole country was of the same composition, one representative from each party, with an administrative staff headed by Avispa's law partner Ernesto Abeja. President Luis Gusano, who aspired to the status of elder statesman, described the fairness of this system in a scholarly article written for him by the political officer of the United States Embassy in Tinieblas and published in *The New Republic,* and the Tinieblan Ambassador to the United Nations offered the plan to the General Assembly as a model for protecting minority rights in developing countries, but few Tinieblans were fooled. Yet when Gonzalo Garbanzo went to Alejo on behalf of all the provincial chiefs and told him that something would have to be done about the counting arrangements, Alejo merely looked to Doktor Henker and asked about the stars.

Doktor Henker untaped Olmedo Avispa's horoscope from the wall and carried it across the room to those of Alejo and the Republic of Tinieblas. I had to jump out of his way. He compared the three charts while Gonzalo stood clenching and unclenching his fists.

"The stars remain propitious," Doktor Henker said finally.

"Tu 'tás loco!" shouted Gonzalo. He slapped his forehead with the palm of his right hand. "It's nineteen to one at every table and nineteen to one on the Jury! Not counting the staff! What do the whore-stars know about that?"

Alejo held a finger up toward Gonzalo. "Pay attention to Doktor Henker."

"You pay attention to me, 'Lejo," screamed Gonzalo. It was the first time I ever heard anyone raise his voice to my father or call him by anything but a title, Engineer Sancudo or Mr. President. "This whoreson German has you all whored up with his whorestars! If you don't get rid of him, he'll whore us all!"

"Pay attention to Doktor Henker, Gonzalo. He invented Cyclone Five."

"Is he going to invent a cyclone to blow away the nineteen *avispistas* on the jury? What the whore has a cyclone to do with Tinieblan politics?"

"My career," said Doktor Henker in his phlegm-clogged spit-stained Spanish, "is the mirror image of Sir Isaac Newton's. You know who was Sir Isaac Newton? He went to Cambridge to test the judicial astrology and later turned to chemistry, then physics. I am doctor of physics from Leipzig. Later I study chemistry, then astrology, the most exact of all the sciences. Your matronym is Maduro, a Sephardic Jewish name, and if the Führer had listened to me, you would know very well what is Cyclone Five."

On election day a record number of Tinieblans went to the voting tables to put their ballots in the boxes and have their identity cards punched and their left wrists smeared with purple indelible ink, and there was no doubt but that most of them voted for Alejandro Sancudo, but when the polls closed and the Civil Guards made everyone move a decent distance back from the tables and the ballot boxes were opened, many irregularities were discovered. Ballots were found smudged, or slightly torn, or sometimes folded in quarters instead of in half. The party representatives had to decide whether or not to accept such ballots, and where it concerned Sancudo ballots—as in almost every case it did—the decision at every table in every ward and parish and village square was always the same: nineteen to one for rejection. Then the accepted ballots were counted and the count certified by the party representatives, and here again the result was the same throughout the republic: the Tinieblist representatives refused to certify the counts, except for the representative in the village of Baldosa in Selva Trópica province, who signed after the Civil Guard on duty at the table had pointed a rifle at his car and chambered a round and released the safety. Then the accepted ballots and the certified counts were locked back into the ballot boxes, and the rejected ballots were locked in other boxes, and all were sent to the Electoral jury in the capital. There the table counts were checked against the accepted ballots, but when these were examined, more irregularities were discovered and more Sancudo ballots had to be disqualified. Meanwhile the days passed and the populace waited eagerly for the results, *alejistas* claiming victory and denouncing the table counts as fraudulent, anti-*alejistas* claiming Alejo had been beaten and boasting gleefully about how many Sancudo ballots this or that table had managed to disqualify.

It took the Electoral jury ten days to rule on all the irregularities and complete the count. All this time they were locked in the Alcaldía with the telephones disconnected and a company of Civil Guards outside. No one was allowed in or out except the waiter from the Hotel Colón. Still there were rumors. Certain cynics alleged that the count was not being conducted fairly. The populace grew unquiet, and President Gusano took the precautions of declaring a state of siege, suspending constitutional guarantees and imposing a seven P.M. to five A.M. curfew. Then it was announced that Olmedo Avispa had defeated Alejandro Sancudo by some four thousand votes.

It was the greatest fraud in the history of Tinieblas, greater than the fraud of 1916 when sixty-six sealed ballot boxes disappeared as by enchantment en route from Salinas to the capital, greater even than the great frauds of 1920 and 1924 when men rose from the dead to vote for Heriberto Ladilla and fifteen thousand indians voted for him as one. The leaders of the Tinieblista Party begged Alejo to call for an uprising or at least a general strike. So many citizens had been robbed of their votes that the Gusano

Government would fall, they said, like a ripe papaya. Not even the Civil Guard could be counted on to support Avispa's inauguration. The men had been without leave for weeks and the officers were beginning to forget Lieutenant Colonel Domingo Azote and remember the splendid field gray uniforms Alejo had issued them during his administration. But Alejo conferred with Doktor Henker and then announced that the stars remained propitious and that he would go to La Yegua and await the call of destiny.

Olmedo Avispa received the presidential sash at eleven o'clock in the morning on the first of June and choked to death that same evening on a piece of filet mignon from his inaugural banquet. His vice president, Fernando Comején, was sworn in on the spot and struck dead by a coronary thrombosis before morning. The succession ought then to have passed to the Minister of Justice, but neither Avispa nor Comején had had time to name a cabinet. Nineteen men from nineteen parties claimed to have been promised the post by Avispa; another nineteen protested that they had been favored by Comején. Don Lorenzo Abeja, Ernesto's brother and an amateur of spiritism, offered to resolve the matter in consultation with Avispa's ghost, but was shouted down by the Chamber of Deputies, where the Tinieblista Party had gained a majority. This majority called for new elections and a caretaker government under Speaker Caballero. The Supreme Court, where Uncle Erasmo was in the minority, asked Colonel Culata to head a junta, but Culata refused.

"The politicians are as bad as the gringos," he told his deputy, Lieutenant Colonel Aiax Tolete. "They foul their pants, then ask us to clean it up."

Meanwhile the banks were closed, the government offices shut down, the shops boarded up, and the people ready to go into the streets, Civil Guard or no Civil Guard, the moment Alejo whispered.

Alejo said nothing. He didn't have to. Men who had spent fortunes to keep him out of the palace had begun to believe in fate.

"There's no way," said Ernesto Abeja to whoever would listen. "It's either God's will or a joke of the devil's, but that madman will be president whatever we do."

In the end it was decided that he should reconvene the Electoral jury and recount the votes. Twelve hours later the jury proclaimed that Alejandro Sancudo had won the election after all.

Alejo did not come to the capital to be inaugurated. He waited for the sash to be brought to him. So it was that the entire Chamber of Deputies and the Supreme Court and the Commandants of the Guardia Civil and the diplomatic corps and the foreign journalists drove to La Yegua in a motorcade that stretched seven miles, and assembled in the rain in the pasture across the highway from the house, and waited under their umbrellas until Alejo felt like coming out. He stepped from the porch into the saddle of a bay gelding and rode the fifty yards to where the President of the Supreme Court was waiting to swear him in. He took the oath on horseback and reached down for the sash and knotted it across his chest. Then he delivered the shortest inaugural address in Tinieblan history:

"I was chosen by the stars and am responsible to destiny. You can all go home now. I'll call you when I need you."

18

About fifteen months after Alejo took office, when I had already left for my sophomore year at college, an Argentine circus came to Tinieblas. I assume it was the usual display: the tattooed fire-eater, the clown with the trained pomeranian, the chubby woman in a spangled corset who stands upright on the crupper of a pacing percheron, the pimpish fellow in jodhpurs who cracks a whip and waves a pistol while a toothless lion squats on a stool and a mangy bear chugs around on a tricycle. There was also a tumbling act, two brothers and a sister who used a seesaw to catapult themselves up on each other's shoulders. When the impresario went to see Lalo Marañon, who was mayor of Ciudad Tinieblas, about a permit to pitch his tent on the vacant plot where El Opulento is now, he took the sister along. The next morning Lalo went early to the palace to tell President Sancudo that there was an Argentine acrobat in town who was the best whore in the Western Hemisphere, if not the entire world.

"She's more than a whore," he told Alejo. "She's a succubus." And he repeated this judgment for years, verbs changed to the past tense, long after the girl had left the country.

That's how Alejo found Angela. He summoned her to the palace that evening and bought her contract from the impresario the next day, giving the man five hundred inchados and twenty-four hours to get his circus over the border into Costaguana. Then he made Lalo Marañon consul in Macao, partly as a finder's fee—Lalo made his fortune there, selling Tinieblan passports and certifying phony bills of lading—and partly so there would be no one else in the country who had had her. Then he recruited four butch queers to guard her and packed her off to his villa at Medusa Beach.

Alejo had bought the beach and all the land around it from the state and had had the Ministry of Public Works run a road in from the highway, but he held the land and kept the road closed to the public, so that while today there are over a hundred houses and cottages set side-by-side along the strand and a casino and a surf club and riding stables and the beginnings of a golf course, in those days there was only Alejo's villa in a walled compound surrounded on three sides by scrub and wild coconut palms and on the fourth by the sea. Angela lived there with a maid and an old woman and the four sturdy sodomites. Alejo visited her every weekend and took her to the capital once a month for shopping and a dinner at the Hotel Excelsior. She dressed demurely for these excursions and might have passed for Alejo's niece or daughter, but at the villa she went naked. That's how I first saw her, dancing naked on the sand.

I went with Lino Piojo, in his speedboat, "to have a look around," and as the wind was offshore she didn't hear the motor when we came round the point and kept on dancing, a kind of adagio, to the slow rhythm of the surf. Then she saw us and stopped, and spread her legs, bumped her sex toward us, and clasped her hands over it, and then opened her arms in invitation, and I was crossbowed back into a fresher age when mermaids sang and nymphs came out of the sea to sport with mortals and sea demons took female form to drain men of their souls. I dived toward the shore, leaving Lino to idle the boat beyond the breakers, but when I reached shallow water and stood up to see her laughing at me, covering her breasts and sex in mock modesty, a man came through the villa gate carrying a submachine gun, and when I kept wading in, he fired a burst over my head. I stopped then, and Angela dropped her arms and said, "Why don't you shoot him?" to the guard, and then turned and walked in through the gate. I saw what looked like a tail hanging in the cleft of her buttocks, but I noted it without surprise and looked after her as in a dream, until the guard fired again, this time into the sand in front of me. Then I waded back into the surf and swam out to the boat.

"Didn't you tell him you were Alejo's son?" asked Lino.

"I don't think it would have mattered. She wanted him to shoot."

"Lorelei of the tropics," he laughed. Then: "God, Kiki, look at yourself!"

My chest and stomach and, when I looked inside my bathing suit, my groin were scored with leprous blotches.

Angela had yellow hair and pale gray eyes and pale golden skin and full breasts which stood out from her body and tiny white teeth, no bigger than milk teeth but pointed like those of an animal. She had firm arms and calves and lovely, firm palm-sized buttocks and a flexible tail the diameter of her middle finger and about twice as long. She was kept by my father and danced naked on the sand and laughed at me. After that day she danced on a movie screen stretched across the inside of my forehead and laughed through banks of speakers bolted inside my ears, and as time passed, she danced more wildly and laughed more tauntingly, and the blotches on my body grew redder and more disgusting. She danced and laughed while I wrestled the Harvard captain and when I punched my English instructor and got put on probation and during every fight I had the next summer in the alleys behind Washington Avenue. That summer I paced my dream of Angela like a rabid wolf. I slept into the afternoon each day, waking chalk-mouthed with hangover to the sound of her laughter. In my workouts I used more and more weight and spent hours smashing the heavy bag, for no one would box or wrestle with me, not after I snapped a soldier's wrist and then had to be pried off him. And with darkness, I would streel off to the cantinas, looking for trouble.

I lived with Alfonso, who had graduated and gone on the Foreign Ministry payroll with a fat salary. Actually he worked for Uncle Erasmo on the newspapers. He had an apartment in a new quarter and hung out at the Excelsior, stalking stewardesses in his Brooks tropicals. Now that he could see me, he tried to include me in his romps. He'd get calls from his regulars when they ricocheted up from Panama or down from Miami—could he get a date for Jean or Joan or Jane or June?—and sometimes I went. But those girls liked the hotel bar and good restaurants where they wouldn't get the trots, while I had no money and had to be careful about getting the lights out before disrobing. And no stewardess could slake my leech for Angela. That needed white rum and Reservation gringos to whack the piss out of and lava-quimmed street whores with jism on their panties and hair under their arms.

One night, in the Relax or Trópico, some loud cantina hazed with rum and violence, a wizened gringo pushed up next to me and stuck a herring-flavored finger in my face.

"Pussy," he announced.

"Yours?" I inquired.

He raised his chin and poked my chest with the finger. "You got a nice built," he said, "but don't mess with me. I'm a killer."

He was no taller than I and twenty pounds lighter. His left hand was in his pocket; his front teeth were AWOL from his grin. He wore a Hawaiian shirt and a baseball cap, and had DUNCAN, T.S. and a service number tattooed on the inside of his forearm.

"I'd kill a greaser as soon as a gook," he said. "Just smell that pussy."

I might have made a bad mistake, despite the knife I assumed was in his left hand, but a big soldier danced by with one of the bar girls, and Duncan reached between them and grabbed her box. The girl screamed and the soldier bellowed. Duncan drew out his left hand, and there was no knife nor even a hand but a pink stump which he drove into the soldier's throat. He flung both arms over the soldier's shoulders and climbed up on him and butted his nose with his forehead. Then he stumped him in the belly and kneed him in the groin and chopped him behind the ear as he fell.

"See?" he said, winking proudly at me. And he dissolved through the swinging doors to the tweet of MP whistles.

When I ran into him again a few nights later, he greeted me like an old friend. He asked me if I was as strong as I looked, and said he'd been looking for me to back me against an arm wrestler in the Cantina California who gave three-to-one odds to Tinieblans. I went along and won sixty inchados for him, though I had to show my Tinieblan identity card before he could collect.

"Any relation to the Sancudo who's President?" asked my opponent.

"His son."

"You think I'd back a crum?" sneered Duncan, seizing the bills. "Come on, kid. Let's get out of this gin mill."

He was a Marine sergeant who'd lost his hand on one of the islands. They kept him in the Corps because of his record and gave him assignments like sergeant of the stockade guard at Quantico and now steward of the naval officer's club in the Reservation. He would rather have been in Korea killing gooks. He taught me how to shoot—lovely gold Marine Corps .45 caliber match ammunition, which we blasted into the warm drizzle of Sunday afternoons at the Reservation Gun Club—making me hold and squeeze off timed fire while he lit matches under my nose and blew his old drill instructor's whistle in my ear. Also how to use a knife and a honed hacksaw blade which could be carried taped in the small of the back, and how to throw an ice pick, and how to kill a man without any of these instruments. Then he tested me against three Reservation punks—soldiers or civilians, I never knew—going up to their table at the Jardín Cortéz, a beer garden opposite Fort Shafter about five blocks up from the Politécnico, and saying, "This kid with me says the three of you is cocksuckers, and you can blow him or fight him outside in the lot." Then he sat on a car fender and watched me take the three, not even intervening when one broke off an antenna to whip me with, and when I'd finished chopping, twisting, and stomping, he took me inside and bought me a drink and said, "OK, kid. You're all right. Now let's make some money."

In three years Duncan had put aside forty-eight cases of Old Parr whiskey by adding bottles to the bills of private parties and a case or two whenever the admiral gave an official reception. There was so much smuggled whiskey in Tinieblas, he couldn't give it away, but he could get sixty dollars a case in Ticamala. For that he needed a boat and someone who could speak Spanish.

"Now, kid," he said, "I never asked you why you hang around gin mills when you could be over to the palace drinking champagne, or how come you're such a mean bastard, but I never seen you with much money, so maybe you'd like to make some. You get a boat, and we'll split fifty."

Now that was interesting, because only two days before I had realized that I could have Angela for money. Strange, perhaps, that this hadn't come to me earlier, as all the world knew she was a whore, but she was so special for me I had got the idea one had to be powerful or famous or at least not hideously blotched before one could put in a bid. Then I saw that the problem of Angela was financial.

That was at Medusa Beach again. Alejo treated Alfonso and me like dogs—Alfonso like a good dog who knew how to roll over and would fetch a stick, me like a mean dog who snarled when you went to pat him and wouldn't come to heel. He took us to the villa to show Alfonso a stretch of beach front which he was getting for being a good dog and me what I was missing out on by being a bad dog. He had Gunther blow the horn three times at the gate, perhaps as a signal for Angela to put some clothes on, and when we went down to the beach, she joined us, wearing a bikini. There were no familiarities between her and Alejo and no introductions. She gave me no sign of recognition, though my face burned and I could feel my blotches crimson when I imagined her tail tucked in between her hind cheeks. We picked our way across the point, where palms grew right down to the sea, Alejo stopping on the way to toss his jacket to Egon and open his shirt, revealing the purple wound on his throat. Then we came out on a crescent cove some three hundred yards long.

"Yours," he said to Alfonso. "You can sell it when my term is up, but if you hold it fifteen years, it will be worth a hundred thousand."

And Angela looked at Alfonso with interest, as though she had just discovered he was there.

Angela and Alfonso groped obscenely across my movie screen for a frame or two; then it struck me that it was the money which interested her. Alfonso had suddenly become a possible provider of what she wanted. I would do just as well. I simply had to pay her price.

At that moment I was too taken with Angela to generalize from her to other women, but I later found her to be perfectly representative. Any man, however blotched, could have any woman, however beautiful, if he paid her price. And if I stopped dwelling on my blotches, I would know the price, not by figuring it out but as a hunter knows how much to lead a running target. Some only wanted to be asked nicely; others, like Marta, wanted not to be asked. Olga wanted to be treated like a queen, while Elena wanted to be treated like an ordinary woman. Some wanted pleasure and some wanted suffering and some wanted tenderness and some wanted a firm hand. All wanted you to know what they wanted without their having to tell you. I once had a German girl who wanted to be hit. I only had her one night, for I never enjoyed that kind of love, but she came back to my hotel with me at four in the morning and then smirked and said she wouldn't, and the next thing I knew I had hit her in the face and she was down on her knees fumbling with my belt buckle. Her price had come to me. Well, that afternoon on the beach it came to me that Angela wanted money and that mine would be as good as anyone else's. So when Duncan made his proposition, I said I could get a boat.

The boat I had in mind was a scow-nosed Higgins landing craft about forty feet long which the gringos had given to the Civil Guard during Lucho Gusano's administration. Alejo had a cabin built on it and designated it the presidential yacht. He made Belisario Oruga take diplomats fishing on it from time to time. It was moored about a hundred yards off the end of the yacht-club pier, and it's a fine exercise in mental masturbation to recall strolling out on that pier five or six midnights later, after Duncan had procured a three-day pass and chatted with the second secretary of the Ticamalan Embassy, not being pushed in a wheelchair or babied in an indian's arms but padding along on my own power while a dance band wailed "Noche de Ronda" on the club terrace behind me and the lights from the bar shivered in the water on either side. Animated portrait of the vegetable as daring young man: he trips with tennis-shoed softness down the ramp to the float, extracts a sweat sock full of BB's from his hip pocket, knots a thong around the neck of the sock and ties it around his waist so it hangs dongishly against his left thigh, sits down on the edge of the float dipping his sneaker toes in the water, straightens his back and slides in. Soft gulp from the Pacific Ocean. He finds an oil drum with his feet, uncoils and burps back to the surface. Splashless breast stroke with his mind full of sharks. Just poke them on the snout and they swim away. Shout at them underwater. Bash them with a heel if they nuzzle up behind. Cowardly bullies every one, and you're perfectly safe if you have no cuts and aren't menstruating. Arm sweep and frog kick with his back swayed by the weight of the BB sock. Did one hundred yards in a minute five at Payne Whitney. Respectable time for freshman fitness tests. Salt water's more buoyant too, and no nasty chlorine in your hair. Sweep and glide, kick and glide.

He goes up the mooring line hand over hand until he can grasp the gunwale. See him there, that dark smudge against the white hull, swinging slowly back toward the stern, which the ebb tide has pulled out into the bay. The guard's dinghy is tied there, and he brushes it away with his feet, then rat-scrambles silently over the transom.

Sopping mound beside the engine housing. Breathing carefully through the mouth and fumbling with soggy leather knots. He creeps forward with the sock in his right hand. Through the windshield the club lights, street lamps, headlights along Avenida de la Bahía. All very distant. The guard sleeps face down, and the armed animal steadies himself against the slanted hull and bludgeons him behind the ear.

Wait, is this filthier or less filthy than shooting a man from behind? The guard's holster was beside his pillow; on the other hand he was fast asleep. He had never befriended me, but neither had he ever done me wrong. I have more leisure now to debate such questions. At the time I was alertly concerned for my own interests. In fact I was never concerned with morality until Ñato blasted me into the contemplative life. Let me note in my favor that when he rolled half over, I didn't automatically crunch him again but waited to see if the first blow was sufficient. It was. He flopped back on his face.

Then I carried him, more or less as Jaime carries me now, back to the stern and lowered him into the dinghy. I untied the painter and walked the skiff along to the bow and untied the Higgins' mooring line and knotted it to the dinghy painter and cast off. Then I let the tide suck the Higgins out into the channel where no one would hear me start the engine.

I steered around to the beach at Fort Shafter, the same beach where Palmiro Inchado's sailors had found his head. There was a little wharf used by sport fishermen, and Duncan was on it, sitting on a pile of whiskey cases surrounded by jerrycans full of gas. He'd had to make three trips in the officers' club panel truck and then walk back from the club to the beach, but though Alfonso had told me to watch out for him, he'd thought to bring dry clothes for me. We loaded and were fifty miles up the coast by dawn.

All day the boat ground over the long Pacific swells which rose and fell gently like the breasts of a sleeping woman, churning on under an egg-white sky between the low green coast and a line of rain squalls. When Duncan went down to sleep, I pushed the windshield up to feel the salt wind on my face and kicked off my sneakers to feel the boat's pulse with my toes, and when a squall caught us, I kept the cabin window open to feel the rain on my cheek and shoulder. The sea stopped breathing then and flattened under the rain, and the drum of rain on the cabin roof deadened the rumble of the engine, and a curtain of water the same color as the sea hung around the boat, so that even when I looked back over the whiskey cases at the wake humped behind the transom, I could get no sense of motion. There was nothing left anywhere beyond the boat. Time had reorganized along biblical rhythms, and the compass tried to swing to port. I held west-north-west for several weeks with the tachometer always at nineteen hundred revolutions, and at length one morning the rain lifted, and the coast reappeared exactly where it had been before.

As it grew warmer, I peeled off my shirt, and then my trousers, and began singing, all the songs I knew, and when Duncan staggered up from the bunks, his eyes stained with sleep, that's how he found me, standing in my shorts, singing into the wind.

"If you like it so much," he said, "maybe you don't want your share of the money."

I kept on singing, so he said: "Maybe we'll get caught."

I kept on singing.

"Well," said Duncan. "If we don't get caught and if I give you your share of the money, what are you going to do with it?"

"I'm going to buy my father's girlfriend and fuck her in his bed."

"It's too bad you're not American, kid. You're mean enough to be a Marine DI."

Duncan refilled the tank and sank the empty cans, and then I went down to the bunk where the guard had been sleeping when I sapped him behind the car, and as I lay there waiting for the engine to throb me to sleep, I didn't wonder if I had broken his head or worry about getting caught or even watch Angela dance on my movie screen. I simply felt alive.

Duncan called me when we were off Puerto Ospino. There was a hundred-mile shelf of purple cloud hung a thousand feet off the ocean to our left with a great fading splash of vermilion above it and gloom below. In three minutes the light was gone. We turned to starboard and fingered our way up the coast by starlight with me lying prone on the foredeck looking for breakers that might warn of rocks or shallows. "Why don't you sing now?" Duncan yelled when the wind came up. Then he stuffed his jacket to me under the windshield. Later he called, "There's a current here the navy doesn't know about. Either that or we missed the drop." And much later: "Four cans left. Think this thing'll run on whiskey?" The bow rose and slapped down jerkily. Sometimes the dark shadow of the coast forced toward us, and Duncan would turn away to port; sometimes it faded entirely, and he would swing back to starboard. In the long intervals when he did not speak I forgot him completely and lay there like part of the boat, the niggerhead against which my left flank was pressed, the cleat on which my right hand rested, while the water flapped beneath the blunt bow and the engine purred distantly.

When we saw the light it was almost behind us. Duncan had turned out to sea around a spur of coast, and when he turned back we saw there was not one spur but two, and the light was between them.

"Get back here," said Duncan.

He cut the throttle, and the wake rolled under us, lifting the boat forward. I waited, swaying, on my hands and knees, and then crawled back and dropped feet first through the cabin window. Duncan switched on the running lights.

Truck headlights carved a yellow tunnel through the darkness. Below it was a pier on wooden pilings with a man standing on the end of it holding a flashlight.

Duncan put the boat in neutral. "Back her in," he said. "If anything happens, come out fast."

He ducked down to the bunks and came back with an autoloading shotgun. He poked it under the windshield onto the bow and then climbed through the side window after it. He kneeled on the bow and leaned his chest against the windshield. I stood facing the stern with the gear lever in my right hand and a spoke of the wheel in my left. I pushed the lever and let the boat idle in toward the pier.

When we were twenty yards out, the man on the pier reached for our stern with the beam of his flashlight. "Es esa la mercancía?" he called. There was another man crouched beside him with a pistol in his right hand and his right elbow resting on his right knee.

"What's he saying?" hissed Duncan.

"He wants to know if that's the whiskey. There's another one. With a gun."

"I see him. Tell him what does he think it is. Tell him when we get in close to jump down and tie us on. Tell him not to fuck around. I got them both covered."

I put the boat in neutral and stepped out from under the cabin roof and translated what Duncan had said.

"Prefiero quedarme," said the man. "Cuando vengas mas cerca, te tiramos la soga. No tenga miedo, hermano. Somos buena gente."

"What's he saying?"

"He says he wants to stay on the dock. That they'll throw us a line. He says not to be scared, that they're nice guys."

"Sure," said Duncan. "We're all nice guys." He paused. The boat wallowed away to the left of the pier. "OK, kid. Do it like he says."

I put the boat in reverse and turned the wheel to the left and gunned the throttle. Then I cut it back and took the boat out of gear and climbed back on the whiskey cases into the flashlight beam, feeling the pistol eye stare down at me, and took the line a third man threw down from the pier. Then I hauled the boat in against the wooden pilings.

"Cut the engine," said Duncan. "We got to save gas. Tell him sixty bucks a case. You give him a case, he gives you the money."

That's how it was that first time, a moonless night lanced by truck headlights, a narrow cove between two points. It was low tide, and I had to lift each case to my shoulder and push it up onto the pier. One Ticamalan held the flashlight; another held the gun; the third opened the cases with a machete. When he'd counted to twelve, the man with the flashlight gave me three twenties. Duncan stood on the roof of the cabin, cradling his shotgun at the three Ticamalans.

Gunwale squeaking against wooden pilings, machete thrusting under cardboard flaps. There were mangrove thickets beside the pier and a patch of clear sky over the truck which I glanced at each time I raised up with a case. I stopped to breathe with a case on my shoulder—smells of mangrove mud, salt water, gasoline, my own sweat—and the man with the flashlight said, "Apúrate, hermano. Ya la noche s'está acabando."

"What's he saying?"

I pushed the case up onto the pier. "He says hurry up. The night's almost over."

"Ya fuckin' A," said Duncan. "Ya fuckin' A."

Three twenties in my pocket. Another case up onto the dock, and with each one I could feel the boat lighten. Bending and lifting smoothly while the pistol eye followed me.

And when the last case was up on the pier and the last twenties were stuffed in my pants, and when I'd started the engine and untied the line and run the boat out from the pier, the man with the flashlight cupped his left hand to his mouth and cried, "Adios, gringos de mierda!"

"He says, 'Goodbye, shitty gringos,'" I told Duncan. "I guess he thinks I'm a gringo, too."

"That's 'cause you're such a mean bastard, kid. Now let's see some of that money."

We ran back down the coast with a following wind and the current the navy didn't know about, and raised Puerto Ospino just after dawn and ran the boat in onto the beach and threw the anchor up on the sand and hiked back to town, Duncan carrying his shotgun wrapped in a poncho and me with the guard's revolver stuck in my pants and my shirt flapped over it. We had a meal there and a shave and caught the eight o'clock bus for the capital, dozing all the way past Córdoba, while the bus rattled between rain-soaked fields, through muddy pueblos mashed beneath gray clouds. It was after dark when we passed the road in to Medusa Beach. I nudged Duncan and called for the driver to let me out, and when the bus lurched away, there was no light nor any sound but the high wail of cicadas and the pounding of my heart.

I stumbled off through the scrub, bearing slowly to my right for two or three hundred yards, hitting the beach road well in from the guard post. It was seven miles to the villa, and I jogged most of the way, switching the revolver from one hand to the other. When I could hear the surf, I left the road and circled down to the beach. The wall around the villa had glass shards set in cement at the top of it, but there were only a couple of strands of barbed wire over the beach gate. I went in between the wire and the top of the gate, tearing my shoulder but no worse than Angela's fingernails did later. No dogs, because Alejo hated them, and the lights were out in the guards' cottage to the left of the villa.

The light from Angela's room flowed through the open French window across the terrace and seeped into the shallow end of the pool. Tango music moaned in the lulls between breakers. I went across the terrace with a roll of surf. The screen door was ajar. Angela lay naked on the bed with her hands clasped under her neck and her right elbow just touching the phonograph on the night table. I went in with the revolver in one hand and seventy-two twenty-dollar bills baseballed in the other.

"What do you want?" she asked, the boredom in her voice wilting my gun barrel.

"You!" said I, and threw the money over her.

She rubbed the money over her as if it were beauty cream. "Here I am."

I took her by the arm; my hand was shaking. "In his bed."

Angela smiled to herself and shook her arm from my melting grasp and brushed the bills from her body and rose and led me into the adjoining bedroom. There she turned and passed her hand before my face, and I sank onto the bed, unable to move or speak. She took the revolver out of my hand and laid it on the floor. Then she opened my shirt and drew off my shoes and trousers and played oboe scales on me till my teeth ground. She mounted me and knelt Kali-smiling and immobile, milking me slowly, while I tried to move and begged silently for her to kill me, and the rotting corpses under Alejo's bed shivered in their winding sheets and moaned for their turn, until she drew her lips back over her pointed teeth and whispered, "Now," and I flung my soul up into her.

She pinched me out and jumped off and danced back into her room, returning after a bit with the money to switch on the lamp and sit down, golden haunch beside my head and lithe tail twitching on the bed sheet. She stacked the bills between her knees, Jackson's eyes on her target, moving her lips with each one. Red blotches burned over all my body.

"You'd better go now," she said, folding the bills. "The guards."

I nodded and dressed quickly and slunk away.

I went to a corner of the villa wall and scooped out a hollow for my body in the sandy earth and lay there with beating heart while the tangos repeated themselves like an object set between two mirrors, their sad strains rhythmed by the beat of the surf. At length her light went out, I crept back to her door, listening for her breathing. When at last she slept, I stripped off my clothes and plunged for her. Then, as I spitted her, she began to change shape: swan, heifer, lioness, and sow, wriggling serpent, bucking mare, clawing panther, each transformation raising my blood, but I held on to myself through everything, until she saw defeat, fading back to woman, and I whispered, "Now," and she threw back her head, sobbing.

Later, she told me about Alejo's wound and much else, all I asked her, and we made love again, playfully, with affection. At dawn I left her sleeping hunched up like a little girl and stumbled out onto the terrace to dress. I was ten yards from the beach gate when one of the guards came out of the cottage and covered me with his submachine gun. He and his chums punched me around a little while the Guardia truck was coming to take me to jail in the capital, but I was too tired to care, and too happy, for all the blotches were gone from my body.

19

Jaime is full of apologies about his absence. Marta sent him to the pharmacy. Came to me the moment he got back and has his shoes on to prove it.

Bundles me up in his arms for the infant-lift to the ground floor. One step at a time, feeling with muffled toes. Nestles me in my spanking collapsible runabout and rolls me to the dining room.

A room I like. Massive colonial table with breakfront; heavy chairs whose carved backs rise above your head. Permanence and formality.

"All journalists are animals," says Marta, sipping milk tea. "Pancho Cepillo is a pig. Isn't that right, Kiki?"

Hearty good-mornings from the film-makers. Double-strength smiles for use with freaks and cripples. Sprayed my way as Jaime parks me at the head of the table.

"What kind of animal were you, Feel? When you were a journalist."

Phil flashes her a grin. "A wolf, I guess." Then to me: "Marta's been telling us about the filthy smear in *Patria* this morning. They hit pretty low here."

"In the States they'd say I was soft on communism. It's just a question of different values."

Marta translates my heehaws, then asks in Spanish if I want a Librium. I shake no. A cigarette would be nice, but it makes a poor spectacle. Have to have it held to my lips, like the moribund second lead in a war movie.

"Me estás bravo?" Feeling my face with soft eyes. Strange girl, scalds then soothes.

"No. I'm not angry."

"Different values, different styles," says Phil. "I guess it's all politics, but the style here seems more like quattrocento Italy than the States." He looks to Marta for approval and gets a bored stare. Sure sign they went to bed together last night. Her bitchiness varies directly with degree of intimacy. But if she smiled at him, I'd take that for a sure sign too. "I guess we'll have to soak up the mood."

Carl slurps up coffee; Sonny scoops up eggs. Phony Phil does all the talking. But why call him phony; because he humped Marta? Assistant director when Elena was Carlotta, Empress of Mexico, last summer, and sold her the idea of a TV documentary on our election. Expenses and a cut of the sales. With Elena narrating he ought to make money. Probably knows what he's doing and is no phonier than anyone else.

"I'd like to look around today, until the rally of course. Can I borrow Marta?"

Borrowed her last night, didn't you? Off the plane forty minutes, and you had her out on the town. Or were you already screwing her in Los Angeles? "Up. To. Her."

He looks across, eyes raised hopefully. Good-looking fellow with his youthful grin and silky beard. Probably went down on her with it last night and was disappointed by her reaction. Could have told him Marta doesn't like tricks. Now she shrugs why not, and he grins happily. Perhaps she'll take to that grin and marry him, and they'll have babies and fights and infidelities. In short, live like other people. Better for her I suppose than tending a plant.

"But if you could manage a few questions first . . . I'd like to get some things straight."

Worried look from Marta. "Te cansarás."

"No. I won't get tired. What tires me is being a cripple when inside I feel as normal as him. Come here and help me. Tell him I'll answer anything he wants."

"Ya, Kiki." She tells him and pulls her big chair next to mine.

Phil plucks a ballpoint from Carl's shirt pocket and takes a notebook from his own. "The Alliance is your father and the Coalition is President Fuertes. Right?"

Nod.

"Your father was deposed from the presidency twice, and then he decided to stay in retirement and pass the baton to you. Okay?"

Another nod, for the viewers needn't know that the stars had informed him it would be a bad year.

"Then you were shot while campaigning. Like Robert Kennedy."

"Mine was a bit botched. We're poor on quality control here."

Marta translates like a professional interpreter, not putting it into third person, simply repeating my words.

"And now your father has come out of retirement to end the corruption of the Fuertes regime and redress the injustice of your, er, injury."

Bravo! Much better than that Alejo wants to get in once more before he dies. And Elena will recite it with conviction.

"Now, according to *Economist,* this Alliance is built around the Tinieblista Party but includes parties directed by men who helped depose your father in 1953."

"'52."

"Yes. I'm sorry. That these men are supporting your father and financing him. Why?"

"It goes back to the last election." Marta leans in, because I lose control as I raise volume. "Four years ago Pepe Fuertes had nothing to run on but his dead brother León." Lifting the words. Pushing them up to Marta like cases of whiskey. "During the campaign he accused both me and the other candidate, Felíx Grillo, of that assassination, which, by the way, I had nothing to do with. Being out of the country. And accustomed to settling, differences face to face."

No odd looks from Marta. Translates as I tell it, making up for this morning's nastiness.

"Who did shoot León Fuertes?"

"Not shot, blown up. Plastic wired to his car. He drove his own car, like Janio Quadros. To save state funds and show he was a man of the people. No one knows who did it. Probably a foreigner. Since Tinieblans, as you see, are sloppy assassins. As for who ordered it, or paid for it, that too's a mystery. There are numerous candidates. You're not important in Tinieblas if you haven't been accused, or at least suspected. I believe it was some people from Miami. Who were running the casinos here, along with other ventures. León threw them out. But maybe it wasn't them. There are always people who want the President dead. Tinieblas is no more civilized than the United States."

"Touché."

People who grin too much come to look like hyenas. Blimpish confidence of healthy gringo interviewing greaseball basketcase; when it's punctured, giggles whistle out. Marta may sift some suffering into his life. Make an artist of him. "But as I say, Pepe had nothing else to run on. A clever dentist with a clubbed foot. Yet he wanted to be President. The Tinieblan vice. Being León Fuertes's brother wasn't even enough to get him the Progresista Party nomination. León founded it, but Carlitos Gavilán helped build it. So Pepe made a deal with Carlitos. He said, 'Let me run this year, and we'll milk the Fuertes name and win, and you can be President in four years.' That's how he got the nomination. But he needed more. Because while the Progresistas were the best organized, thanks to Carlitos, the Tinieblistas were the biggest. Always were and still are. And I was quite popular. As a defender of Tinieblan sovereignty."

"In the flag riots, right?"

"All over the world nations fly their flags on their territory. One takes that for granted. Except here. When I carried the Tinieblan flag onto a portion of Tinieblan territory known as the Reservation, United States citizens started a riot."

"There seem to be two sides to that story."

"Naturally. A right one and a wrong one. We had best get back to Pepe." Phil would like to argue. He's made himself an expert by studying the back issues of *Time*. "Pepe needed more. So he approached Ignacio Hormiga. Who controls the Reformista Party.

Don't let the name confuse you. Nacho doesn't want to reform anything. He has too much money for that. Pepe made a deal with Nacho. He said, 'Support me now, and I'll win, and in four years I'll support you.' That's how Pepe got the Reformista nomination. But he wanted more. So he approached Luis Felipe Gusano. Who was President from 1944 to 1948. And who controls the Movimiento Civilista Conservador, the Civil Conservative Movement. And who owns a TV station. Pepe made a deal with Lucho. He said, 'Support me now, and I'll win, and in four years I'll support the candidate of your choice.' That's how Pepe got the nomination of three parties and campaign funds and a TV station. By promising the same thing to three different people. Dáme agua, Martita."

"Wait!" says Phil as she gets up. "This is terrific!"

"Kiki wants water."

"There's water here." He swings the pitcher over.

"Fool." She turns away toward the kitchen to get one of my glass straws.

"I'm sorry. Are you sick?"

I shake my head. And concentrate to keep it from flopping. Not sick, just helpless, and perhaps I ought to thank you for forgetting it. Sonny and Carl don't enjoy looking at me, especially when Marta hunches near my lips to collect my whispers, but Phil shows no disgust. Either totally insensitive and thus unable to imagine himself in my place, or so sensitive he identifies and treats me as a human being.

"What do you think of that story?" He turns to Carl, who tries to lounge against the upright chair back. "Terrific, huh?"

"Sounds like Arnie Schicksal."

"Right!" He turns back to me. "You know Schicksal. You know how he got his start? He moved into an empty office at Magnetic without anyone knowing he was there and started calling up stars. He called up Gregory Peck and said he had Ava Gardner and John Wayne and Lana Turner for a film, and would Peck like to be in it too. Then he called up Wayne and Gardner and told them he had Peck. Then he called . . ."

He tells me who Schicksal called while Marta pours me water

and puts the straw in the glass and holds it for me to sip. Child's gift of enthusiasm, and as an artist he naturally admires successful con men.

"... every star in Hollywood, and the picture grossed fourteen million. But this Fuertes has him beat."

"He's a thief," says Marta.

"Of course he's a thief. But it's a terrific story."

"Phil wishes he were a thief," says Sonny. He is a short, skinny fellow with large ears and a pointed face. Carl calls him Superrat. "When we were in the Army, he had a plan for robbing the Fort Ord payroll. Then he didn't have the guts to do it and made it into a movie script." He lights a cigarette, throws the match into his empty coffec cup.

"Dáme un cigarillo, Marta."

"No debes fumar."

"Y tú no debes joder tanto."

She takes a Galoise from the silver cup on the breakfront and lights it with the silver Ronson and holds it to my lips. Sweet blue smoke and slight dizziness. Two puffs are enough.

"So Fuertes stole three political parties and a TV station."

I would have won anyway."

So he had you shot."

I shake my head. Because if Pepe had arranged for Ñato to shoot me, he would have arranged for someone to shoot Ñato. And Ñato didn't need Pepe's encouragement. And the radio report said I'd been wounded in the shoulder—Alfonso fixed that—and when Pepe heard it down in Selva Trópica, he bet Carlitos Gavilán a case of whiskey I'd set it up, and had myself knicked in the shoulder to win a few more votes.

"Fuertes wasn't behind it?"

"The French have a saying, Feel." Marta is furious. "It goes, 'One doesn't speak of rope in the hanged man's house.'"

"It's all right, Marta. Let him ask what he wants; you just translate. Do you think that if no one mentions it, it will go away?"

"Él solo piensa en su preciosa películas!"

"Of course he's thinking of his movie. Trying to find the hero and the villain, make reality fit together like a work of art. That's his business. If he's any kind of a man he won't forget his business just because he went to bed with you last night."

"Maricón de mierda!" And goes on in Spanish: "You have to throw that up to me! You told me yourself to go out with him, and what I do with my body's my own business! If you have to be jealous, go scold your wife!"

Even gringos understand that tone. Carl gets up and strolls to the living room. Sonny follows. "Look," says Phil, "if I said something wrong . . ."

Hard for Marta to stop once she gets started. "I suppose I ought to burn myself like a Hindu woman because you're impotent! Yes, I went to bed with him! Yes, and I liked it! More than with you, with all your he-man crap!"

Ought to translate that for Phil. With a gloss on the perils of *machismo*.

"Look," he says, "maybe we ought to . . ."

Sponge up her hate with steady stare. Whom does she hate more, herself or me? The way to stop her is never to let her know when she's hit a nerve. "Can we go on now?"

"If he's tactless, why do you defend him?"

"Can we go on?"

She looks away. "Why not! I'm only a machine!"

"Then tell him Pepe had nothing to do with my getting shot. That it was a personal matter."

She does; and I go on to tell how Carlitos went to Pepe last fall and asked for Pepe's endorsement; and how, when it came out in the papers the next morning, Nacho gave Alfonso the story of how Pepe's cement company was overcharging AID, and Lucho's TV station ran Donald Duck cartoons during Pepe's press conference; and how Pepe tried to save the situation by withdrawing his endorsement from Carlitos and announcing he would seek a second term, telling Carlitos and Nacho that if they didn't support him they would lose the ministries they held—there being seven months left of Pepe's term, which meant a lot in graft and patronage—and telling Lucho that if he did support him, Lucho's son-in-law Bertito Alacrán could keep his ministry or be vice president, whichever he liked best; and how Lucho reminded Pepe that it was unconstitu-

tional for a President to succeed himself; and how Pepe reminded
Lucho of the amendment to the contrary which Alejo had pushed
through before he was thrown out of office for the second time in
1952, and which no one had bothered to repeal; and how Carlitos
and Nacho and Lucho, all of whom (as *Economist* correctly
pointed out) had helped throw Alejo out, drove all the way to Otán
in Nacho's bulletproof Lincoln to offer to help put him back in;
and how Alejo accepted, getting clear commitments from all three
as to how much cash they would put into the campaign and giving
only the delphic assurance that once he returned to power everyone
in Tinieblas would get what he deserved; and how Pepe threw Carlitos and Nacho and Bertito and all their friends and relatives and
supporters out of the government, thirty-seven hundred people
purged in three weeks, from senior civil servants down to porters
and charwomen, and distributed the vacant jobs where they would
get him the most votes; and how Carlitos formed the Partido Soberano Revolucionario and took about a third of the Progresistas into
the Alliance with Alejo; and how Pepe made up the difference with
Reformistas and Civilistas who couldn't stomach a deal with Alejo,
so that both Alliance and Coalition are composed of people who
have hated each other all their lives. I push mushy grunts to Marta,
and she translates them to Phil in a flat voice, and he makes notes,
neither grinning nor exclaiming "Terrific!" And when I say, "That's
all," he says, "Thank you, Mr. Sancudo, Marta," nodding to both
of us and looking his age. "I'll be outside."

"Agua." Sounds like a choked dog.

She holds the glass for me. "How do you feel?"

Water gone tepid. I nod for her to put it down. "Tired. It was
fun at the start. He's a good audience. I could see him casting it all
for a wide-screen movie. Afterward it wasn't fun."

"Kiki . . ."

"Wait. It was my fault. I shouldn't have said anything. The living ought to live."

"You're not . . ."

"Wait. It's right for you to go to bed with a man who pleases
you."

"Is it right for Elena too?"

"Yes. You're both widows. It's right for me to be jealous too. But not for me to show it."

"I didn't mean what I said about enjoying him more. I only said that to hurt you."

"No one can remember either pleasure or pain. You can remember having felt them, but not how they felt. On balance that's a benefit."

"I can remember feeling whole, and I haven't felt it since the last time you made love to me."

Thank you, Marta.

"He doesn't mean anything to me, Kiki. You're the only one who's ever meant anything to me. Before I had to share you with Elena and God knows how many other women. Let's go away, Kiki. Let's go away from here, and I'll take care of you, and you won't have to share me with anyone."

Shake my head.

"You'll never change, will you?"

"I've changed, Marta. I've had to learn. But I don't want to learn too much. I don't want to learn how to like being a cripple, for example. Or how to forgive my enemies. Or how to live in the passive voice."

"You don't want me to take care of you?"

"Of course I do. I want everything." Make my smile. "That's another thing I don't want to learn: how to stop wanting."

"Well." She shrugs. "What do you want now?"

"I want you to smile."

"How?"

"I do it by pulling back the corner of my mouth. See?"

"I'll have to practice. What else do you want?"

"I want you to go out with those gringos and help them make their movie."

"You don't want me to read to you?"

Shake my head. "You go out. Send me Jaime. I'll have him push me out to the patio. And then I'll talk to Elena when she gets up. You can read to me this afternoon. You can read me the *Count of Monte Cristo*. The last part. When he gets Danglars."

"And what does he do after he kills Danglars, Kiki?"

"He has a girl, Marta. Don't you remember? He has a girl, and they just sail away."

20

I sit in my chair, my eyes half-closed against the glare off the swimming pool, my hands packed in my lap, my shoulders caped by the shadow of the pink umbrella which sprouts through the aluminum table beside me. Otilio crouches barefoot at the back of the patio, an old pair of tuxedo pants rolled below his knees, an old dress shirt flapping his butt, pruning the grass near the fence. Three swicks, four, with his machete, and he shuffles to the right without straightening up. He keeps the yard as well-groomed as Alfonso's beard, all neat and orderly like my current life. Easy in this dry season, but I prefer June, when the grass leaps up overnight around fallen mangoes and the plant garden along the kitchen wall is a jungle of fronds.

Jaime squats doglike in the shade of sere mango leaves. I used to wonder how our people can wait that way, hour after hour. I would see them along the sun- or rain-swept highway, waiting, inert as the trees they leaned against, for a bus I'd passed a hundred miles back, or on the straight-backed benches of public waiting rooms, waiting all day for their names to be called while surly clerks lounged behind the glass partitions, flirting with secretaries who filed and polished their nails, and I would wonder what they did with their minds while their lives seeped into eternity. How can they wait like that while I have to have action? They must have a switch that shuts their minds down, or puts them on a standby circuit.

Now, of course, I have to wait, but my mind isn't circuited for it. My mind keeps chewing at full power, and if left unprogrammed gives off frightful blares and screeches, woof-tweets of rage and terror that flash adrenal signals toward my dead nerves. Which signals go unanswered, clog the circuits, feedback causing more noise, until everything explodes in the gray static of convulsion. And that can kill me. I've had two; another one could kill.

At first I took pills and spent my days being read or TVed to. My reward for learning to move my left index finger was a remote-control switch to my hospital room TV, and I stayed full of pills and kept Marta nearby. But it's enough, more than enough, to be dependent for the tending of my body, so I learned to handle my mind. It needs exercise, or it'll hoof me to death, yet it can't be let loose to roam unguided. I take it on well-planned expeditions into the future and long jaunts over the past. These are perfectly safe, so long as I don't let the reins drop.

Before my assassination I was never conscious of my mind as an alien and destructive force. I could always find some action. Even in prison one can exercise—I don't mean a few sit-ups but real exercise, where you push yourself against pain or hunt rats. The exception is the coffins, each one two feet high, two feet wide, six feet long. After the flag riots they put one of Canino's communists, a black called Tonio, into one of the coffins, and when they took him out two or three days later, his forehead was all scraped and welted from being beaten against the ceiling. He wasn't trying to kill himself, just to calm his anxiety with unconsciousness. I was never in one, though it might have been good training for the way I am now.

Still, as long as you're not in one of the coffins, there are ways to keep busy. Massaging your armpits and kidneys, for example. That's what you do on the first day, for everyone gets a beating upon admission. They call or drag you out of the truck and walk or rifle-butt you up the stairs. In the guard room to the right of the door they take your name, prints, and picture, your belt, shoelaces, and keys. Then they shove you down three flights of stone steps, perhaps even prod you a bit, for it's hard to move quickly without shoelaces, to the Sala de Interrogaciones. Along the way you pass the coffins, or their two-foot-square steel doors. The lower ones are almost flush with the floor, the upper ones almost flush with the ceiling, which isn't high down there. Six rows of two; some people call them the ovens. The walls of the Sala de Interrogaciones are streaked with mildew; the floor slopes toward the center of the room where there is a sump drain. You stand over the drain with your arms above your head while the guards who brought you beat you in the armpits and on the kidneys with their truncheons. There's very little sadism in this. Sometimes a little anger, if the guards know and dislike you, but everyone gets a beating to calm him down and make him less of a bother. It helps to make a little noise. You certainly shouldn't curse the guards, but if you yelp a little they'll know they're getting through to you and will quit all the sooner. In 1952 they beat Egon unconscious because he wouldn't cry out, and on my first visit they might have done the same to me, for I didn't know enough to satisfy them with a squeal or two. But although Alejo had told the prison commandant to show me no favors, the guards who did the truncheoning didn't have their hearts in it. If Alejo changed his mind, it would be their turn, so they didn't beat me beyond the call of duty. In any case, if you aren't defiant or excessively stoical, they beat you only hard enough to give your urine a rich, resinous tint. Then they escort, prod, or drag you upstairs to a cell.

There are three levels of cells, two above ground and one below. Common criminals are kept on the upper levels; I was put below with the politicals. This because there was no charge against me and because rumor—started no doubt by the villa guards— already had it that my offense was one of *lèse-authorité*, to wit: banging the President's girl friend. It is impossible to imagine how quickly news circulates in that prison or how deftly the false is separated from the true. So, after the flag riots, when I had been in prison for weeks, I learned all the details of the plot which General Látigo was preparing in the greatest secrecy against General Puñete, a plot of which Puñete was entirely ignorant before I warned him and in which he refused to believe until I recited his itinerary for an inspection of the Civil Guard barracks in Córdoba, where Látigo intended to have him arrested and hanged. Rumor floats along the corridors and drips from the cell walls, so that even while the guards were thwacking my kidneys, the whole prison knew that Alejo's son was inside for disputing the preeminence of the presidential prong. Yet what is common knowledge even to an unfortunate buried two floors underground in one of the coffins never seeps out into the city. Alfonso learned of my escapade two weeks later when I told him. Certainly Lazarillo Aguda, the nosiest of journalists, had no inkling of it until he was locked up, for he couldn't have picked a less propitious moment to publish his doggerel.

> The ladies all enjoy it,
>   Although it's rather small;
> A girl can't get in trouble at
>   The Presidential Ball.

The lower cells have two-by-three-foot windows high up against their ceilings, which are just above the level of the Civil Guard Compound in which the prison sits. These windows allow a kind of twilight to grope down into the cells, and also serve as impromptu latrines for whichever guardias find themselves in a bladder-draining mood when near the prison, so that the lower cells breathe out a sharp ammoniacal reek and, while cooler than the ones above, are generally considered less comfortable. They are five paces long and three paces wide and have sleeping facilities for fifteen men, that is three tiers of steel slabs two feet wide by six feet long hung by chains from the walls, six slabs on each long wall and three on the wall near the window. The top slab on the window wall is usually the last one filled. In 1952 I shared one of these cells with Gunther, Egon, Furetto, and twenty-one other human beings, and we used the slabs in shifts, all but the top one under the window. This we gave to Egon, who had been beaten too badly to mind being pissed on. There were two thousand political prisoners then during the weeks after Alejo fell from power, and they amnestied criminals to make room.

It is a tribute, on the other hand, to Alejo's second administration that when I made my first sojourn in the prison the lower cells were almost empty. A dozen or so communists rotted placidly, three to a cell, to ease the sleep of the American Ambassador and keep up Alejo's credit with Washington. A Dutch zionist, who had been snooping after Doktor Henker, sighed through a leisurely deportation process. The four Cormillo brothers—unregenerate anti-*alejistas* who had persisted, even after friendly warnings, in distributing mimeographed sheets which denounced Alejo as a war criminal, assassin, and morphiamaniac—shared a corner cell, palatial accommodations arranged by Major Dorindo Azote, who allowed them razor blades and a domino set, who got their food parcels to them unopened, and who saw to it that the guardias relieved themselves into other prisoners' windows. The rest of the cells were empty, except for three set aside for the homos dredged in during the vice squad's weekly raids.

On certain nights, the guardias who cared to were allowed to come down and use these men, and we other prisoners would hear the smack of boots on stone, the loud, self-conscious laughter, the titters and squeals, the high-pitched giggles of mixed fear and desire, "Not me, darling, I'm having my period," the shouts and the screams and the sobbing, and I would imagine the faggots fluttering like starlings around their cells, in and out of the flashlight beams, and the guardia ape-grinning as he held a kneeling queer by the ears, and the boy whimpering with his face pressed against a steel slab while love drilled into him like a jackhammer, and I would feel the shadowed violence and smell the pain and lust. My sex would stiffen and my stomach turn. My mind would drag me through the walls into those other cells, where for a moment I would rut with the guards and whimper with the faggots and stand spread-legged in the doorway with Duncan's shotgun, blasting them all to blood and sperm and shit. Then I would get up to hunt rats, feeling my way to the door while Lazarillo Agudo hawked juicily and snorted, "Animals!"

And even now last night's feast is bleeding into the slop pails and fresh meat is being basted in the Sala de Interrogaciones. Even now in this sun-shot mid-morning a frieze of women is carved along the compound wall, bent ancients with greasy shawls over their foreheads, vacant-eyed mothers with infants at their breasts, firm-haunched girls who bite their lips at the guards' wisecracks, each with a paper bag full of tenderness for some beast inside. Right this moment one of them is being let through the gate and up the steps to the prison guardroom. She waits before the desk while the sergeant tears the bag half open and lifts out the paper plate and spreads the waxed paper with his index fingers. Hmmph! Chicken rice. He spies a piece of breast and forks it into his mouth with his thumb and forefinger. Hmmph! Spits gristle into the wastebasket. Pokes his middle finger into the rice and stirs slowly, pushing grains off into the paper. Nods seriously. Bunches the food in both hands and drops it back into the bag. Then he flicks his hand as though shooing flies, and the woman takes the bag and carries it outside to a cart filled with similar bags, squashed and torn, with the names smeared, the tenderness squeezed out. Even now the prison sits there, turning out its quota of suffering and debasement.

I didn't think about things like that then. What happened to others was their problem. I saw prison as a personal test and as proof I'd done something notable. When they put the handcuffs on me, especially when they began beating me, I knew I'd reached Alejo. The harder they hit me, the more he was hurt, and I was proud of myself, even later when Lazarillo explained that the smart prisoner made a little noise for the guards and told me that, as I'd been able to walk out of the Sala de Interrogaciones, I'd been pampered with only a run-of-the-mill beating. It was as if the prison had been built and the police organized all for my benefit, though I didn't realize until later what a service Alejo was doing me without intending to. Every stress that doesn't crush you makes you stronger, and those two weeks in jail were a final exam in the course I'd been taking with Duncan and Angela.

I didn't know it would be two weeks, of course. No magistrate came to interrogate me; no judge told me what my penance would be. I didn't know if they'd connected me with the stolen Higgins boat, but I assumed they hadn't, for the blackjacked guard would have entitled me to a full-dress beating. I had no news of the world outside the prison until they put Lazarillo in with me, and what he told me was disappointing, for none of it concerned me. Nor could I keep my spirits up with the prisoner's common fantasy of frantic family effort to get me out. It was my family who had put me in. At the same time, however, I knew Alejo wouldn't have me killed or maimed or locked up forever. Family ties are sacred in our culture, and it would be bad politics for him to do me calculated permanent harm. There was always the danger that the guards would try beating me without putting handcuffs on me first and that I'd lose my temper and kill one of them, but that was part of the test prison offered me. So I had no more fear than was easily controllable and hence invigorating, the kind of fear you feel at the top of a ski run or when first soloing a plane. It was a different story five years ago when Dimitri Látigo was in power and I had to worry about being shot while attempting to escape.

Snap me that first morning squidging my laceless tennis shoes down the prison corridor with my manacled hands shading my crotch and a guard's billy club nudging my shoulder, the freest man in Central America, responsible only to myself. Inside the cell they loosed my wrists, and the turnkey came in with a wooden bowl full of water and a wooden spoon and a big chunk of cold, greasy cornbread—I'd missed the daily meal—and when he bolted the thick wooden door, I stuck the spoon in my pocket and drank half the water and put the bowl and the bread on the top left-hand slab nearest the door and climbed up on the middle slab and laid one hand under my head and clasped the other in my aching armpit and hunched onto my right side to ease my aching kidneys and fell asleep. I woke a few hours later with a bad ache in my right kidney and got down to spray Valdepeñas into my slop pail and ate half the bread and drank the rest of the water and then went back to sleep, on my left side this time. Some hours later I rubbed my shoulder against a tickle on my check and sent a roach tripping down my lower lip and over my elbow and came awake so skewered in terror that my heart stopped beating. It was tomb-dark and clammy, like the bottom of a crypt three days after your burial, and one moment it seemed the opposite wall was just beyond my chin and the next that there were no walls at all, only a limitless darkness. I settled this by poking my hand out over the edge of my slab and rolling my face against the cold stone behind me. Then I breathed through my mouth until pain and hunger brought the world back to me. I raised up on my elbow and reached to the slab above me for my chunk of cornbread and put my fingers onto fuzzed nervous life. I drew my hand back so fast I wrenched my shoulder and lay twitching again while my mind flashbulbed rats the size of dachshunds trotting across the slab above me. Dozens of them, and a thousand million roaches swarming the walls, and huge furry spiders stalking across the ceiling and swaying down toward me on nylon ropes, and snakes and slugs writhing beneath me, but that was better than the way I am now, yes, a hundred times better, because I could swing down to the floor despite the snakes and step to the center of my cell, even though at the center of my cell the floor dropped away a thousand feet to a bottomless cesspool, and do knee-bends until my thighs screamed, and then flop forward into push-ups, flushing the toads and scorpions from my brain, and then get up, rubbing my armpits and kneading my kidneys, to take possession of my cell, three short steps right to the door, then palming along the wall to the first slabs, circumnavigating and claiming. Then I found the cubic inch of cornbread my rat had abandoned and set it down near the corner by the door and waited, squatting motionless in the total womb-coffin dark, while my mind felt around the contours of the cell like radar. Then after about five thousand heartbeats I got an instinctogram straight from the mid-Pleistocene: fat rat sniffing through gnaw-hole at base of door. I could feel him coming for the bread, poking his nose, brushing his side hairs against the wall. I held my hand absolutely still and relaxed, waited while a roach scudded over my ankle between my pants cuff and my sneaker, and when rat-flank touched my fingers and rat-nose probed my wrist, I swept him up, as a bear scoops fish from a river, and flicked him against the opposite wall of the cell. Oh, I thought, as I heard him thud the wall and then one of the slabs, all that talk about you in psychology class, but you're not so fucking smart.

He was the only rat I killed that night. I found the bait, spun almost to the other wall, and went back on stand, but before another rat came, weak, weary light began seeping through the high window, and after it the splatter of some guardia's urine. Later there was a turnkey with a garbage can on a low-wheeled trolley, and I emptied my slops and dropped the rat in after them. He came back a good while later with the same trolley and a similar, if not the same, garbage can, filled with bacon-globbed lentil mush and covered with a tray full of cornbread. I got three chunks and a ladle full of the mush. Later on he came back with water. That was all.

I massaged my kidneys and armpits and walked around the

cell on my hands and did some serious exercise—my main worry
was that I'd get out of shape—and got some sleep, for I meant to
hunt all night. The one available diversion which I didn't take
advantage of was thought. Oh, I daydreamed myself a hard-on
remembering Angela and bent it down with a hundred sit-ups, but
I didn't sort out my life. Six meters underground and with no one
to distract me I might have drawn up a working map of the world
and located myself on it. I might have found Alejo's place on it,
and my dead mother's, and Alfonso's and seen how they stood to
me. I might even then have plotted a course for myself. Other men
have passed prison time that way; some do it even when at liberty.
But I didn't have the inclination, and prison didn't teach it to me.
Prison taught me only that I was free. It took Professor Espino to
teach me the other.

One midnight almost three years ago, as I lay in my hospital
bed, I realized that I had survived but would not recover, and I
began for the first time to examine my life. I was watching a movie
on TV, a gangster film. The hero was brave, energetic, talented,
one who might—as his mother and sweetheart told him—have
made his mark in any legitimate field, yet he set himself against
society, and while he had made himself powerful and free, he was
clearly destined to die like a dog. The appeal of such movies is, of
course, that they enable people to suck a little danger and freedom
into their lives without actually risking anything. The violence in
them doesn't breed violence. It calms most people down, giving
them their necessary modest ration of excitement so that when they
leave the theater or turn off their sets they may continue to lead
placid lives. There are some people, though, who have a greater
appetite for danger and freedom than can be satisfied by movies,
and as I was lying there in that California hospital—which was
really more of a sanitarium, out in the hills, with its drug addicts
and alcoholics and psychosomatic invalids as well as medical cases
like me—all alone (for I couldn't stand the night nurse wheezing in
the chair) late at night, watching this gangster hone his ego on the
world around him, I realized I had never had any purpose in my life
except to satisfy my appetite for action, for contest involving risk.
When I wasn't where the action was, I felt dull and mean and

blotchy. When I could find action, I felt alive. Alejo has an appetite for having people kiss his butt, in other words for power, so he convinced himself he could save Tinieblas and went into politics. I went into politics because it was the biggest action available to me at the time. Before that I'd had other kinds, going from one to another without any plan. It wasn't a bad way to live; it was the right way for me. I knew it had been right because I hadn't had to think about it. That night in the hospital I had to think because there was no action left in survival—I'd done it, except for learning how to ride my mind so well it would never buck me into another convulsion—and the action of recovery was rigged against me. Now I've found some action again, but in the two years I was without it, from that night in the hospital until Alejo announced his candidacy, I developed the habit of contemplation.

I didn't have to develop it in prison because I saw prison as a contest. Kiki against Kiki. Kiki was afraid of vermin, so Kiki went down in the verminous dark and hunted them. That was the way to live. Jump in over your head, don't sit on the edge contemplating. I even argued this point with Lazarillo when he joined me. He was self-taught and had read a great deal, in English as well as Spanish, but his bible was *Quixote*. He had great slices of it deepfrozen in his memory and was quite willing to serve them to me, even when I was trying to sleep, garnished with tidbits from the author's life. He considered Cervantes the greatest man who had ever lived, and went on about him until I got annoyed.

"Some people live life and other people write about it," I told him. "Some people make love and others play with themselves."

"Cervantes practiced arms as well as letters. He was wounded at Lepanto."

"I went to school, Lazarillo. He lived for a while; then he gave up life for literature."

"And created a universe!"

"Because he didn't know what to do with the real one. It's like the painter who gets a naked woman up to his studio, and instead of screwing her he paints her picture."

"Sometimes he does both."

"Why? Isn't the one enough?"

"When Miguel de Cervantes y Saavedra was in the Royal jail at Seville," said Lazarillo, getting down off his slab and taking his stand in the center of the cell, holding up his pants with both hands, "a worse place than this, 'the seat of all discomfort and the home of every melancholy sound,' he began writing the *Quixote*. I suppose he ought to have chased rats!"

"When he was in prison in Algiers, he made three attempts to escape."

"Four attempts!"

"Four then. Well, he should have tried to escape from the jail in Seville. And no doubt he would have tried, but he was already so old and tired and worn out that he hadn't the energy to have adventures but only enough to imagine some. As for rat-hunting, it's just as difficult as inventing fantasies. I don't think my father will keep me here too long, but if I'm not released inside a month, I'll see about escaping myself. Meanwhile, I stay in shape."

"Rat-hunting and the *Quixote*!" He snorted and bulled his neck. Pugnacious little fellow with no lack of balls, or he wouldn't have been in jail, and he'd been quite friendly, saying straight off that if Alejo Sancudo had put me in prison, I couldn't be all bad. I thought he was going to come over and hit me. "I suppose that you agree with your father's great friend Adolfo Hitler that books ought to be burned!"

"Keep calm, Lazarcito. Why get so worked up? You'll give yourself a stroke. I've nothing against books, or Cervantes either. It's just that life is short, so the people with balls live it. Don Quixote was a greater man than Cervantes. He took his lance and got out on the highway. And I'm going to stop this jabber and take my workout."

And you, Lazarillo, you snorted, "Animal!" and went back to your slab, without ever trying to teach me that when Cervantes took up his pen he engaged himself in a contest involving risk, a contest with the powers of disorder at the risk of his sanity. You didn't think of that, and besides I wouldn't have accepted it. No one ever learns anything until he has to, and I was three months shy of my twenty-first birthday and in as good shape as when I took the gold one at Helsinki. My wrestling weight was one fifty-seven, of which not an ounce was fat, and I could lift twice that over my head and walk on my hands better than most men walk on their feet. I was five feet nine inches tall, which is tall enough in this country, and if I wasn't pretty like Alfonso, I wasn't ugly either, despite my cauliflowered ear. No one mocked or slighted me, and while no one loved me either I didn't care. I could digest that prison lentil slop and sleep sweetly on a cold steel slab. What need had I of the contemplative life?

That's how I left prison, tough inside and with a bright glaze all over me. I was already planning my escape when they released me. I'd badgered Lazarillo into climbing onto the top slab under the window and taking me on his shoulders so I could test the piss-stained bars. They were firm, so I began to figure ways to get past the guard room and over the compound wall once I'd jumped the turnkey and the guard who accompanied him. Instead, an officer came for us one evening and took us upstairs to the common criminals' showers and let us bathe and shave and gave us clothes picked up at our homes. Then they handcuffed us and took us out to the airport in a patrol wagon.

Alfonso was there, along with Lazarillo's wife, with my suitcase and my birthright: a ticket to Miami.

"What did you do, Kiki? He says you're not his son, that Mama deceived him and got you with a Jew."

"I'm his son all right. That's what bothers him most. And never mind what I did. You're better off not knowing."

"I'd say it had something to do with Angela," he said, smiling at me in admiration. "He sold her day before yesterday."

"What!"

"He sold her. The president of Hirudo Oil was through here, and Papá had him out to the villa and sold Angela to him for five thousand dollars. They left for Texas yesterday on the gringo's plane. Oh, he told me to tell you this ticket is the last thing he's giving you."

"Whatever I want from him I'll take. But you've got to loan me a thousand. Don't whine. I know you've got it. It's for my tuition, Fonso. I'll pay you back by Christmas. You'll never regret it."

"I regret it already. I only have fifty on me."

"Then hand it over and send me the rest in New Haven. Stuff it in my shirt. They're calling the plane."

They took the handcuffs off us at the emigration counter while tourists glanced nervously at the desperadoes who were sharing their flight. The propellers were already turning, brushing spray from pools of rainwater on the tarmac, but the pilot couldn't be in too big a hurry for me. When we took off, I didn't crane my neck for a last look at my native city. I sat self-contained as a bullet, soaring off into my manhood.

21

Elena's hand on the side of my neck. "Buon, giorno, caro."

She comes round the table and sits down in the aluminum chair, hunches it in out of the sun. "Were you sleeping?"

"No. Inventing the past. Sleep well?"

She nods, smiling. "Many dreams of you."

I believe her. Didn't I imagine those dreams? And with women I have always believed what's most convenient. If one said she loved me, well, of course she did. That I was best, of course. If another said she loved X, or that Y was exciting, or Z the man of her life, it was so much bluff to salve her pride or bruise my confidence. I wasn't fooled by that. True, in Manhattan once I woke and reached for the girl who was with me, and she shuddered and wiggled gratefully into my arms and nuzzled her sleeping face against my throat and sighed, "Oh, Peter!" and that put me off. There was no doubting the sincerity of that sigh. The little bitch was dreaming of Peter, thought she was with Peter, some pencil-shanked, calf-faced *Playboy* reader named Peter, and why should I go to her party with Peter's invitation? But then I thought, well, these girls are young, and they get confused, but she'll know the difference before I'm through. And in the morning when I asked her—she was sitting on the toilet top with a towel wrapped around her and another turbaned over her hair, watching me shave, because when they're starting out they love "intimate" things like that—when I asked her, "Who's Peter?" since I was still just a bit annoyed, and added, "Have to watch that sleep-talking when you're married," and when she blushed and said, "He's this boy I'm engaged to, but it's going to be hard to appreciate him now," I believed her. On the other hand, when Olga told me she'd been unfaithful, I couldn't believe her, though she was a very pretty woman, only twenty-six, with a million good reasons for betraying me. I had as hard a time believing her as Europe had believing Copernicus.

So I believe Elena. And even the futile fool, who suspects his wife of assignations with shoe clerks and grinds her ecstasy to sobs with a "Who are you thinking of?" while he makes love to her, might believe Elena, whose purpose on earth, after all, is to make people believe in marvelous things, for she delivers that lovely line, "Many dreams of you," with a smile so full of sadness and gaiety and love of life as to make it universal law. Then it becomes a case of the relative superiority of possible universes. In the small, dark, messy universe described by *La Patria*, a coffin-shaped universe bungled together out of soft lumps of dog shit scraped from people's shoes, I am an impotent, cuckold cripple, while in the luminous and orderly universe described by Elena's smile, I am a man whom lovely women dream of.

"I thought your dreams belonged to Schicksal?"

"No, caro. Only my soul belongs to Schicksal, who sends you his love, by the way. In one dream you were a gladiator."

"And you were Aphrodisia, Queen of the Sybarites."

"No, no," she laughs. "It was a dream, not a Schicksal picture. I was Elena Ravici, very young, your daughter's age, riding on the trolley in Trieste with my friend Magda and you got on. I guess it was a little like the movie. You had on that fox skin, with the nose sticking out over your forehead. And a *cache-sexe* the color of dried blood, and sandals, and you held your sword in front of you. Oh, you were beautiful, so strong, and they were all afraid of you. Magda whispered, 'Te va uccidere!' but I said, 'No, Magda, ha venuto prendere la mia virginitá.'"

"And did I take it?"

"No. The dream finished there. It faded on you holding your sword, and I felt very calm and happy. Later on I dreamed more, and we made love."

"This morning?"

"Yes. Did you dream it too?"

Shake my head. "I imagined you dreaming it. Was I still a gladiator?"

"No. But it was wonderful like that first time."

Neira emerges from behind me and sets down a tray with coffee, butter, and rolls.

"Ci ricordi?"

Nod. I can remember it all before she takes one sip. I was working out in a gym off Alcalá when Schicksal came in with Dennis Housman and Shelly Barb and his interpreter and his secretary and his guide. León Fuertes had made me Ambassador to Spain, and the only thing I liked about it was that there was someone to wrestle with, a gringo who'd just missed Melbourne in 1956 and who'd stayed in shape since by weight-lifting. We were working out, or beginning to, inching around the mat trying to take each other down, and the gringo, whose name was Custer like the general or Koestler like the writer, who lived in Madrid doing no one knew what, locked up with me, his temple against mine, and whispered, "Some movie people just came in, let's show them some greco-roman throws." We started hurling each other around, grunting like hippos and slapping the mat when we fell, bouncing up with fearful snarls and grimaces, and Schicksal started screaming, "Tell them to stop! Tell them to stop before they hurt themselves!" His interpreter rushed onto the mat pleading, "Esperen, señores, el señor productor quiere hablar con ustedes," and Custer pushed me back and seized the interpreter and lifted him over his head, roaring horribly as though he was going to dash him to the mat. Then he seemed to come to his senses and smiled and set the interpreter down slowly and said, "Forgive me, little brother. I have no qualm with thee." Then he roared again and charged me, and I threw him back into a corner of the mat, where he fell with a tremendous slap and lay as though dead.

"See what you've done!" screamed Schicksal. "You let him get hurt! Oh my God, Dennis, must I do everything myself? I ask for gladiators, and they send me gigolos, so I send Shelly for gladiators, and he brings me drag queens, so I have to go looking for gladiators myself, and when I find two, this moron lets the best one get hurt. Oh my God!"

"I believe he's only a bit stunned."

"Stunned?" Schicksal rubbed his forehead. "Oh my God!"

"And I rather prefer the other one myself."

"You do?" Schicksal turned to the interpreter. "You. Moron. Whatever your name is, tell that fellow to come over here. You like him, huh?"

"Well, he's all right. They're both all right, I suppose. Have to see them in costume, of course."

Schicksal looked at me. He was a round little man with kinky red hair and flabby hands with red hairs on the knuckles. He poked my pectorals like someone inspecting a steer. "Real muscles. Ask him if he'd like to be in the movies. Tell him if he looks okay in costume, we'll give him ten thousand pesetas a week."

"Fifteen," said Custer, who since no one was paying attention to him, had got up and come over. This was about two hundred and fifty dollars.

"Oh my God!" screamed Schicksal. "Right away they want to be stars. What's gotten into these people, Dennis? I remember when this was a nice, simple country where you could make a picture without going over the budget. Now it's gouge, gouge, gouge. Spain is ruined, Dennis. Bronstein and Spiegel have ruined Spain."

During this lament I turned and walked away, because I was a fully accredited member of the diplomatic corps not some gym bum, and I didn't like to be poked, and the farther I get from Tinieblas, the more patriotic I become and the less I care for gringos like Schicksal, who could keep his movie and his gladiators. But when Schicksal saw me go, he screamed, "All right, all right, tell him it's all right, we'll give him fifteen, you too [to Custer], we'll give you both fifteen, if the test's okay," and Custer whispered, "Don't get pissed off, Kiki, this'll be fun," so we became gladiators.

Schicksal was making *Dorieus the Spartan,* with Chip Trill and Monique Mandragore and Elena Delfi and Sir Osmond de Vere and a large chunk of the Spanish population. He'd built three Greek cities south of Madrid and already begun filming when he decided he needed gladiators. Schicksal is the kind of executive who puts

together an excellent organization, hiring top talent and giving it
free rein, and then, when things are purring along smoothly, plunges
spasmodically into the operation, disrupting everything. There were
no gladiators in the book he'd bought or the script he'd had written
or, according to his Danish historical consultant, in the ancient city
of Sybaris, but Schicksal had to have some. As Housman tells it, he
drove out from Madrid one morning, watched a couple of takes,
screamed for everyone to stop, and called a conference.

"There's something missing," he said.

"Vulgarity," said the Irish playwright who'd written the script.

"No," said Schicksal thoughtfully. "Decadence. We need gladiators. Shelly, tell that Spanish actors' union to send me some
gladiators."

Then he began to spin things out of his head, glancing over his
shoulder at his secretary to make sure she was getting it all down.
He keeps relays of secretaries to take down everything he says.

"Chip, you'll be gladiator."

"He's supposed to be a Spartan prince," sneered the Irishman.
"The son of King Anaxandrides and rightful heir to the throne."

"So he's a Spartan prince who's been captured by pirates and
sold to a Sybarite slave dealer who forces him to become a gladiator. My God! Do I have to write this thing, too? You're a gladiator,
Chip, and after the banquet scene Elena's restless. You're restless,
Elena. What you want is a little schtup, but Ozzy's out goosing
slave boys, so you send for gladiators, and they bring in eight or ten
and you have them strip and pick two, Chip and some other guy,
and make them fight, while you lie on a couch getting your rocks
off. Got that, Dennis? They fight naked, except for helmets."

"Arnie, I'll have to check that with my agent," said Trill. "I
don't know about flashing my ass across the silver screen."

"Don't be ridiculous! It'll be the biggest thing since Lamarr in
Ecstasy! Then you kill this other gladiator, Chip, and by this time
Elena's creaming all over the place, and she makes a play for you.
You dip your hands in the other guy's blood, Elena, and smear it
down across Chip's chest."

"Are you sure you don't want me to drink a little? Like a
vampire?"

"That's it, honey! After you smear him with blood, you kiss his chest and get some on your face and then kneel like you're going down on him. First you resist her, Chip. You remember Monique back in Croton, but then Elena gets to you, and you throw her a hump."

Then he didn't like the gladiators the union sent or the ones Shelly Barb found, so he went gladiator-hunting in Madrid and came back with me and Custer and a Brazilian negro who played soccer-football for the Atlético and two Basque jai alai players. Meanwhile the Dane, very melancholy by this time, went detail-hunting in Herodotus, flushing out ideas for our nationalities and costumes. Felix, the football, became a leopard-skinned Ethiopian; Custer, an Assyrian with bronze helmet and iron-studded club. One Basque was a Persian with a jacket of aluminum fish scales; the other, a Scythian with pointed hat and battle-ax. Trill had his horsehair-crested helmet, his round shield, and his spear, while I was Olorus the Thracian—so the gladiator-master presented me to Queen Aphrodisia—with my foxy headdress, my light shield, and my short, thick sword. That's how I looked when I first saw Elena, surrounded by klieg lights and cameras in the lost city of Sybaris.

Elena's reddish-brown hair was dyed black for that picture to contrast her with Monique Mandragore. She is taller than she looks on the screen and more slender, and with her gold-brooched robe and mask of molten depravity, she was every inch Queen of the Sybarites. Like all true artists, Elena has no fixed personality. She is too sensitive to the accidents and possibilities of life to let herself petrify into one person. Instead she keeps an intricately carved rosewood chest full of the materials of humanity—passions, cravings, sentiments, philosophies—and from these, with great care and imagination, she constructs her roles. Which, once fitted and sewn on, transform her utterly-lusty queen or, as now, facing me over her breakfast tray, faithful lover. And her sorcery is such that anyone playing a scene opposite her is transformed as well. She murmurs, "Ci ricordi?" with that sad, gay smile, and I know she remembers and has been faithful, and more, much more, that I am still the kind of man such a woman is faithful to. So that day out-

side Madrid, as she was the queen, I was a barbarian warrior, ready
to kill or die for her.

The magic of Elena's creations lies partly in their unity and
order and economy—not one glance or mannerism, however beautiful it might be in itself, that isn't necessary—and partly in the way
they fit, so once she has prepared one, whether for the camera or
for what is called real life she doesn't lightly strip it off, which
would mean tearing hidden seams. She wears it until she's tired of
it or, in the case of movie parts, until the picture's finished. The
roles she created for our private life were always pleasant to play
opposite: variously wise, generous, demanding, passionate, and
clever but always proud and loving, aiding, testing, and comforting
the adventurer. But it was sometimes annoying to be with her when
she was working. I visited her in Rome while Aldo Marchese was
directing her in his Strindberg movie, and flew back to Paris after
two days of sneers, smirks, and insults, for which I received profuse
telephonic apologies and an assent that it was best for me not to see
her until that film was done. So after our day's work in Sybaris—
a dozen rehearsals and as many takes of the scenelet, three minutes
long in the movie, where the gladiators were brought in—she
remained Aphrodisia, a passionate queen whose ennui demanded
that she be treated like the most ordinary woman for an hour
or two.

Now despite what my friend Custer had said, I was not enjoying my film career, mainly because I had been without action for
too long and felt flabby-souled and blotchy and wasn't enjoying
anything. The movie set, which might have seemed a magic realm
where toads were kissed into princes, was to me an encampment of
phonies, a pasteboard slum full of trulls and cowards with no more
relation to the heroic and marvelous than Schicksal to the King of
the Maccabees. While Custer wore his spiked Assyrian helmet
proudly even when motorcycling to and from Madrid, I felt self-
conscious. Picked as Trill's opponent and put to rehearsing with
him, I was at first listless, then, when chided by Housman, furious.
"You're supposed to be fighting for your life, old man," and I
stepped inside Trill's spear and belabored his shield till it looked
like a washboard. He gave the part to Custer then, and I was just

as glad. It was ridiculous for me to be killed, even in a movie, by a dimple-kneed pretty boy with capped teeth and shaved armpits who had never been in a real fight in his life.

But when Elena appeared, all was transformed. We were gladiators and she the queen and the set a fabled city, despite gum-chewing technicians and hovering makeup men and a jungle of electronic gear. I was confident of my sword, which I thrust out toward her again and again as the slave master presented me, and hoped, with that illusion of freedom and possibility which animates our lives in the face of all intimations that the script is already written, the queen would choose me as her champion, while again and again she appraised me, looked away with regal contempt, then glanced back in questioning desire. And when Housman called the final cut, I went up to her and asked her out as one asks an attractive shop girl or a girl met casually on some resort beach, and she shrugged with an air of "Your invitation's presumptuous if not insulting, and I never do such things, but since I've nothing better planned . . ." And said she'd pick me up in forty minutes on the highway south of the set.

She was half an hour late and gave me just three seconds to jump from my car to hers, a sleek Italian sedan which she drove at terrific speed, though I'm sure she could hardly see for her dark glasses.

"Where are we going?" she asked after a while, and I told her to keep on. I stopped her at a *posada* past Toledo on the Andalusia road, where she gave herself to me with the kind of abandon Schicksal hoped to get from her in her scene with Trill, enjoying and pleasuring me wonderfully without ever relinquishing her role of queen who had decided to be a woman for a while with a slave whom she allowed briefly to be a man. Sometime after midnight, while I was sleeping, she rose, and dressed, and drove away, leaving me to wake pierced by wild regret and longing.

Next day on the set we neither spoke nor gave any sign of recognition, for a queen's dalliance with a slave is not prolonged past sunup, but at the first rehearsal of the scene where Aphrodisia inspects the gladiators stripped, as she ran her hand across my chest, it became instantly clear to fellow players, cameramen, script girl, director, and host of gaping extras that Olorus the Thracian had a bone on. Elena acknowledged this proof of affection with a smile so sweet and humorous that I remembered my Roman school days and, while the crowd squawked and tittered, recited:

> Amor, ch'a nullo amato amar perdona,
>> Mi prese del costui piacer si forte
>> Che, come vedi, ancor non m'abbandona.

> (Love, which no loved one will from loving free,
>> Seized me so strongly with its sweet delight
>> That, as you see, it still remains with me.)

She looked at me with new interest and said, "Bravo!" and I was about to whisper, "Tonight," when I decided that it had been quite perfect, queen and slave, star and bit player, and recalled all the things I'd spoiled grabbing for second helpings. Much later Elena told me she'd had the same feeling. That day we spoke no more.

That afternoon Felix, the Basques, and I were paid off and sent back to the twentieth century, but four weeks later, when all Queen Aphrodisiac's scenes had been filmed and Elena was about to leave for Italy, I met her at some countess's cocktail party. The social gap between us had vanished, I having risen from slave to diplomat, she having fallen from despot to actress, and we soon realized that what had appeared a self-contained lyric was, in fact, the invocation to a longer poem.

We went to Italy. She had another film to make and there was nothing at my embassy which couldn't be left to a clerk. But while we were waiting to change planes at Milan and, fatigued by our journey, we sat in the airport restaurant, sipping unwanted aperitifs and drawing back into ourselves after the excess of intimacy, the almost forced exposure of body and soul common to the first days of a love affair, I glanced toward a table by the door and saw my mother dipping into a silver pillbox for some saccharin for her tea. It was like one of those dreams in which a long-forgotten schoolmate, still in short pants and cap, comes dribbling a soccer ball across the lawn of a house built just last year and, without noticing your business suit and thinning hair, calls you out to play, for my mother dropped the pills into her cup and looked up at me with the same weary stare with which she would greet me when the maid reported that I'd refused to eat or been pestering Alfonso. Then, just before the cock crowed and she changed back into a perfectly commonplace European gentlewoman, she saw Elena, and she smiled.

"Can you spare a day?" I asked Elena. "I'd like to go to Como."

"Yes," she said. "Let's go. The lake is lovely."

"I wasn't thinking of the lake. My mother died in a sanitarium there. If you'd rather go on to Rome . . ."

"No. I'd rather go with you."

And I went out to ransom our bags from the airline and hire a car.

We slept that night at Como and found the sanitarium the next day. No one remembered my mother. I saw her records and her grave, a plain stone with her dates, 17 Luglio 1904–14 Febbraio 1941, among a dozen equally plain stones in a hedged plot inside the hospital grounds. No dreams, no spirits, but in the car riding back to Milan, Elena said, with her eyes turned away toward the countryside beyond the driver's window:

"It's strange. My father was killed in Libya the same day that your mother . . . and I dreamed of him last night. I didn't see him, of course, because I can't remember how he looked, but I dreamed that he was with us and that he liked you."

I felt a shiver and was silent for a moment. Then I told Elena what I had seen in the airport the afternoon before.

We had the blessing of two honored ghosts. My divorce wasn't valid in Italy, but the frontier was less than an hour away, and we were married by a Swiss judge that same evening.

22

Elena sets down her cup with a sigh of delight. "What wonderful coffee your father grows! Now I know I'm in Tinieblas again."

"You still like it here?"

"You know I loved it before I saw it because it's your country. And when you brought me here, I loved it . . ."

My modest fatherland revealed itself a labyrinth of histrionic treats, a place where life itself was a festival of movies, all with yummy parts for Miss D.—the problem comedy where she shone as light-bringer and emissary of European culture; the technicolor transplant of *La Chartreuse de Parme,* with Miss Delfi as a tropical Sanseverina, guiding her lover along the corridors of power; that gripping melodrama *Coup!* in which her role mushroomed marvelously from the early frames, till, Tosca-like, the luscious diva pleaded for the life and liberty of her unworthy mate; and, of course, the role of her life, the one she never got to play, First Lady, which would have surpassed the celebrated performance of Miss Grace Kelly, since Tinieblas is a real country (with starving peasants and evil exploiters whom La Delfi would inspire her Prince to feed and crush respectively), not a papier-mâché enclave, a casino with side streets, from which strife and suffering are prophylactically shut out.

". . . always love it, though last night, when we passed the hospital, suddenly I hated it. I remembered all those people sweating, shouting, and pushing, and General Puñete's bodyguards pushing with their machine guns, and the men who were supposed to be your friends whispering politics while the doctors were taking bullets out of you. Oh!" She clasps her arms over her breasts and looks into the pool. "How I hated this country, and hated you for making me come back!"

"I don't make you."

"I know, caro. You have to do this, with me or without me, and I help you out of love, not constraint. And the secret of marriage is to understand what the other person really has to do and then help him do it. These things are clear on a sunny morning, and that this will always be your country and I shouldn't hate it."

"You can hate it if you want. It's a shitty little country."

Elena looks at me with concern. "How have you been, Kiki? Last night Marta said you've been depressed."

"It's Marta who's depressed. Not me. Keeps hounding me to leave. Alfonso, too. Are you going to start?"

"Would you like me to, Kiki? So you can prove you're as stubborn as ever?"

"No it gets tiring. Tell me something."

And she begins about the movie she's just finished, which is terrible and will make lots of money, and continues to the others she has to make on her contract to Schicksal, flashing scorn at the trite scripts, making deft little épée cuts at her fellow players, gifting me conversation *Life* would pay five figures for, but she has closed down the universe of her smile by mentioning the hospital, or I have smashed it by imagining she saw Tinieblas as a movie set and me as a supporting actor, or it has simply collapsed, as universes do all the time, in a series of descending diminished sevenths:

1.   *On a sun-shot tropic mid-morning Elena Delfi, a gifted and beautiful actress, sat beside the swimming pool of a fine house, chatting with her husband—a man who, in the course of an adventurous career, had been cruelly disabled but who remained the one true love of her life.*

2.   *Confident that she had charmed more difficult audiences, Elena Delfi concealed her pity—the only emotion she could now feel for the man she once had loved—and set herself to entertaining her invalid husband.*

3.   *After a sound sleep and an extensive toilette, Miss Delfi found it penitentially boring to play a short scene as Florence Nightingale to her paralytic husband.*

4.   *La belle Hélène raised her brilliant green eyes to admire the fine, twelve-point set of antlers she had generously furnished her once proud, now crippled husband.*

5.   *Elena crossed her legs, remembering with joy the pulsing life that had thrust between them hardly a day before, and averted her eyes from the wasted vegetable to whom she was married.*

6.   *Doña Elena regarded the slobbering, sweat-streaked gelding in the wheelchair and, without interrupting her tinkle of small-talk, asked herself how much longer she would be able to endure the disgusting fiction of their marriage.*

7.   *Sex goddess Elena Delfi spent half an hour this morning amusing her basketcase hubby. Since she gave up a week of French tongue jobs to be by his side, it seems true love's not dead after all.*

"You're not listening, are you, Kiki?"

"Yes, I am." Pick my chin off my chest. "I'm listening to everything you're not saying."

"I'm sorry, caro, I don't understand."

"Never mind," because I won't say I'm listening to you tell me about your guest on the set, about the soft-voiced, sleepy-eyed muff artist who slurped your hot clam broth and made you squeal, or about having to whore your talent, having to spill your grace on hollow roles in shallow pictures to keep this sack of sallow flesh and dead nerves in dreams of revenge, or about how you can't divorce me because you feel sorry for me. Sorry for me! When never once did anyone, not Schicksal, nor Kennedy when we met him in San José, nor any bitch scandal writer or faggot actor, even for one second think, much less breathe, that I was the great movie star's kept boy or pampered plaything. No, I was a man, everyone saw that, and worthy of you or any other woman, living on the top wire with no net below, and now I have to listen to you feel sorry for me!

"What is it, caro?"

"Nothing. Never mind," because I won't tell you what I'm listening to you not say. I won't make cutting remarks the way I did with Marta and Marta did with me. I won't inform you that you are a whore and a hypocrite, no matter how clear that seems at this moment, any more than I'll announce that I'm a cripple, though that's precisely what I am and nothing more, a flabby, shabby, used-up cripple with a voice like hyenas coughing and shriveled little dried-up nuts and a little soft wilted prick like a plucked tulip. I won't say any of it out loud because I will not live in a tabloid universe. Nor a medical report universe nor a group therapy universe. Not with you, Elena. I was wrong to say anything to Marta, but it wasn't fatal because Marta believes in facing what social workers call reality. But never with you, Elena, because you and I are different. We make our own reality, and the day I say such things to you, we won't be able to any more, and I'll have Jaime put me in the garbage.

"Are you all right?"

"Yes. I felt bad for a minute. Now I'm all right. But let's go inside. Call Jaime."

"I'll take you, caro." And she dabs her lips with her napkin and smiles her lovely smile and comes and turns me back toward the house while Jaime rises to trail us in, doglike.

23

Elena pushes me up the half-inch rise between the dark gray tiles of the terrace and the light gray tiles of the *sala*. "Where shall we go, Kiki?"

"Library."

She wheels me left through the door and up to the card table where, with Marta moving the pieces, I give Alfonso his regular Sunday chess thrashing.

"Turn on the air conditioner, please," and to Jaime who stands in the doorway: "Traiga *La Patria*. Y diga a Edilma que me sirva comida aquí."

"Sí, Kiki."

"I'm going to eat. Will you feed me?"

"Of course, caro. I'd forgotten all about Phil and the others." (Elena knows I won't eat at the table with outsiders present.) "Where are they?"

"Out with Marta. Seeing the city. He hasn't asked, but tell him no filming in the house. I do freak shows for the elections, not here. He can take our picture at the rally."

"All right." She brings a chair up beside me. "But he's a sensitive boy. I doubt if he'd even suggest it."

"Nothing's sacred to an artist with a project or a lover with his pecker up."

"Or a politician anytime."

"Correct. But apropos of lovers, does he want to marry Marta?"

"You know about them?"

"I only know they went to bed together last night."

"And, very paternally, you want to know if his intentions are honorable."

I say nothing.

"Does it bother you that she has a lover?"

"Of course it bothers me. And pleases me too, if she enjoys him. I care for Marta. So it pleases and bothers me too."

Elena nods, smiling. "I used to feel something like that. Though you're more bothered than pleased, while I was usually more pleased than bothered. You were always so full of life whenever you had a new girl. More loving too, a better lover. And I would enjoy the girl through you. That's the closest I've come to making love with women, but I suppose we all have at least a little appetite for that sort of thing. And you were bound to have other women anyway, weren't you, Kiki? It was annoying at times, but a one-woman man is ridiculous. With Marta I was never really bothered until your campaign when she knew so much more about the politics here than I did and could help you with it and was closer to you than I was. I think if you'd been elected I'd have made you get rid of her. Now everything's different, and you need her."

Shake my head. "I don't need anything. She helps me live. I want her to stay. But I don't need her. I want lots of things. But I don't need anything. I'm not pretending. Or playing tough. I'm stating fact. Ñato stole a lot from me, but I get by. I do without. I still know how to want. But I haven't learned how to need."

"Not even me?"

"Not even you. I love you, Elena. I want you to dream about me. And smile at me. But I don't need you. I'm not trying to hurt you. I don't mean you're not valuable. You are. You're a very valuable woman. And the pity is"—make my smile—"I can't make full use of you any more. When you smile at me, I feel . . . not crippled. And that's valuable. I want to keep it. I want to keep you. But if I can't, I'll do without."

Jaime comes in and puts *La Patria,* folded, on the table in front of me and goes out and shuts the door.

"And if I had a lover? Like Marta?"

"We'll get to that in a minute. Now we're talking about her. Does Phil want to marry her?"

"Yes. He even spoke to me about it. He was sleeping with her in Los Angeles, you know."

"I didn't know. I was never sensitive to that. Though last night I felt it would be natural for them to go out together. Maybe it's a faculty that's developing since my murder."

"Sensitivity to other people?"

"If you will. Does Marta want to marry him?"

"I think she would marry him if it weren't for you, Kiki. I think you ought to let her."

"What do you mean, 'let'? I'm not stopping her! She can marry tomorrow If she wants, and I'll wish her luck."

"You don't tell her to go."

"Why should I? She can stay if she wants. I want her to stay. She helps me live."

"What do you give her?"

"I don't know. Ask her. I must give her something, or she wouldn't stay. It could be that she loves me."

"Or feels sorry for you."

"No, Elena. She doesn't feel sorry for me. She's told me that. And I wouldn't allow it. Not from you either, by the way. It wouldn't work. Sometimes, for a minute, I think maybe you feel sorry for me. Then it passes. As long as I act correctly you won't feel sorry for me. You can feel sorry for what happened. To me and all of us. That it was a bad break. But you can't feel sorry for me. Unless I act badly. And if that happens . . . well, there's a cure for that."

"So you'd keep Marta with you?"

"If she wants to stay. I'll keep whatever I can keep and get whatever I can get."

"The same as always."

"Exactly the same. Inside I'm exactly the same."

"Without giving anything."

"I give what I give. I never thought about it before. Lately I've thought about it. And it seems I must give something. I saved Jaime's life, but that's not why he serves me. Before he served me because it made life interesting. There must still be something of that, or he'd leave. I don't need him either. Though it would be hard without him. I don't beg or whine. He doesn't feel sorry for me. He knows how I lived, how I still live. That when you live that way, what happened to me isn't surprising. A bad break, yes. A bad break that Ñato didn't kill me with his first shot. Or miss me completely. Or give me a minor wound. Or a stupid mistake on my part. To underestimate him. But not something surprising, something absurd. Not like an insurance man paralyzing himself by slipping in the bathtub. So I must give Jaime something. And Marta. And you."

"You don't understand devotion, do you, Kiki?" She looks away.

"Of course I understand it. That's what I give you. All of you. Someone to be devoted to. And memories."

"And if that isn't enough?" Eyebrows raised and light smile. Perfectly calm, as though we were speculating about the weather, not my life or death, and that's why I love you, Elena, because you always tested me and keep testing me now, just as though I were still whole. Woman is a safe harbor, but also a test. "If that isn't enough?"

"Too bad for me. Open the paper." She spreads it on the table. "Can you read it?"

"Nuovi corni per Kiki," she translates.

"All right. Inside it talks about you and some Frenchman. I'm not going to discuss it with you. It's beneath discussion. Just the kind of filth they print in this country."

"And in Italy and in England and in the States."

"Yes. I show it to you for two reasons. First, so that you will know what people are reading about you and me this morning."

"It explains the look Edilma gave me."

At which Edilma comes in with my lunch, a bowl of what we call *huacho* and the Italians *risotto,* white bread to mush in it, fruit, and ice water with my glass straw. She doesn't look at Elena, who lifts the paper so she can set down the tray.

"Te doy la comida?"

"La señora me la dará, gracias."

And Edilma goes out, still without a glance at Elena.

"She makes me feel very welcome, your Edilma."

"I'm sorry, Elena. She's old. And very simple. And devoted."

"To the master."

"I'll say something to her later. But the second reason for showing you the paper. Is by way of telling you. That I know that what I give you may not be enough."

"It is, Kiki."

"Good. I believe you. But you asked me a question. About if you had a lover."

"We were talking about Marta going to bed with Phil, and you said it bothered you, and I felt jealous."

"All right. That pleases me. You being jealous. Now."

"I was always jealous, caro, but I'm just as strong as you are. I certainly wouldn't let it get the better of me. You were going to have your little adventures. Had you ever preferred one of them to me, it would simply have meant that I'd been wrong about you, that you had no taste, and I would have left you. But I was always jealous."

"Good. But you asked a question. And will get an answer. Which is that you're free. Like a widow. If you remain faithful, it's from devotion, like a widow. And for memories. But you're different from Marta."

"Because I'm your wife?"

"No. Because you're my woman. I can give Marta to Phil. For a night. Or to marry him if she wants. And wish her luck. But not you. I can't give you. So if you were to have a lover, I wouldn't see you again. That's not a threat. As a threat it's ridiculous. It's a statement. An answer to your question. You're free. But if a widow takes a new man, she shouldn't be hanging around her dead husband's tomb."

"I can do without too, Kiki."

"Good. It's for you to decide. But I'm glad you decide that way. Sometimes I think you should have love. That I should tell you, 'Take a man.' But as soon as I think it, I know it would be wrong. I can't tell you that. It wouldn't be me. And you probably wouldn't like it."

"No, Kiki, I wouldn't. Don't ever tell me that."

"I won't. It's a bad break for both of us. Eh, Elena?"

"Yes, caro. But you and I don't have to talk about these things. Come," she says, smiling, "let me give you your rice."

24

Restful to be fed. Pleasures of infancy with a kind *mamá* spooning me warm rice and smiling at my coos and gurgles. And my mind has been such a good dog, not fouling the rug after all, I must let it out again. To sniff the past. So many exciting odors sprayed about, and in a ramble clocked at thought-speed whole seasons can be inhaled between swallows. Romps so merrily when unleashed. From soggy flesh which must be fed the same kind of pap now being reverently prepared for Alejo. By a dozen women in a dozen towns, for he can't chew meat either any more, and who knows where or when he might feel hungry along the way back to power? Prayerful fingers stirring in the lentils. Grace and blessings conferred on the happy hamlet where he deigns to eat. And he's coming! Jesus promised to come a second time and hasn't kept it yet, but Alejo Sancudo has already risen twice and is going to make it three.

When he came to power the second time, Tinieblas lay before him breathless, like a naked girl, expecting rape or romance. What followed was a conjugal domesticity equally poor in agonies and orgasms. It seemed that Alejo had decided to settle down. It was enough to be tucked in with the country; he didn't have to make it moan or twitch. Of course, he reconstituted the entire civil service, removing opponents, installing *tinieblistas,* and canceled all government contracts, redistributing them among his friends, and petitioned the President of the United States for revision of the Reservation treaty, and served notice on Hirudo Oil and Galactic Fruit and Yankee and Celestial Energy that Tinieblas would have to have a share of their profits, but he allowed employees to beg and contractors to bribe him, and made no objection when the President of the United States waited seven thoughtful months before replying that treaty revision was awkward at the moment, and, in the case of the foreign companies, settled for nominal contributions to his Panamanian bank in lieu of larger payments to the Tinieblan treasury. In short, he acted like any other president, so that it appeared he had decided to adapt to custom and tradition rather than make the country over in his own image.

True, several months after his inauguration he began to act bizarrely. When the new university campus, a work begun under Lucho Gusano, was dedicated, Alejo gave one of the buildings to Doktor Henker, making ours the only university in the world with a faculty of astrology. Then he proposed a law requiring couples to submit horoscopes with their applications for marriage licenses.

He was applauded when, on the first anniversary of his inauguration, he told the Chamber of Deputies that Tinieblas was not destined to remain a rest room and a brothel for foreign troops and
that he would take steps to compel the foreigner to cease defiling
Tinieblan sovereignty, but the steps he took were to send to Haiti
for a wax effigy of Harry Truman and a technician to instruct
Tinieblans in its manipulation. Word of this leaked out, along with
rumors that the same Haitian had been seen in Tinieblas at the time
of the sudden deaths of Olmedo Avispa and Fernando Comején.
People began to talk about the old Alejo and to fear or hope for a
return to the heady days of his first administration, yet before anything actually happened, Lalo Marañon told Alejo about Angela.
The new mood dissolved, the horoscope law was tabled in the
chamber, the Haitian was sent home. Hopes and fears went unre-
alized; there were no uniforms, no reprisals, no decrees. And in the
two years Angela was with him Alejo grew steadily more mellow,
so that Lazarillo Agudo could write: "The forces of evolution are
irresistible. Even Don Alejo progresses, from whoring after strange
gods to gadding after strange whores."

There is a gland in him that drips acid on his brain, distorting
his perceptions until the world mirrors his own chaos and the monsters of his mind, but Angela drained his evil humors and pumped
the pus from his soul. All week long the death-smelling distillations
seeped higher around his cortex, but now he had Angela to bleed
them away. No other woman had served this need, but Angela had
the knack of transformation and could flesh his fantasies, incar-
nating all the objects of his hate and terror for him to subjugate
and defile. Through Angela he committed necrophiliac pollution
on his father's body, so fearsome once but now pruned of manhood. Or she became a black man, the embodiment of his own
negroid genes, whose lips he forced and fouled. She was the
Tinieblan people, squirming and whinnying under him, so why put
them in uniform? And why torment a man with voodoo pins when
you can sodomize him in fantasy the weekend long? And then,
flushed pure of poison, he would lie in the thickening twilight of
afternoons notched by the roll of surf and the cries of sea birds,
with Angela beside him, now a daughter, listening in cuddled rev-

erence to stories of his youth, now a mother, scolding him gently and drawing him, warm with shame, into the safety of her body.

But once she was gone—and it was a lucky thing for both of us that she'd been milking his venom sacks for two years, for it was dangerous to slight him in any way, while we'd given him a ringing swipe where it hurt most—once she was gone, he had no choice but to stage his dreams in public with the country as supporting cast and audience. The nightmares she'd been sopping up then burst on Tinieblas with greater force than in 1940, for everyone had begun to think of him as just another president. His supporters were fat and torpid from three years gobbling at the public trough. His opponents were complacent: things hadn't been so bad, and his term would be up in nine months. Before anyone realized, he turned the country upside down.

His first step was to get the entire Guardia Civil to swear personal loyalty to him. Colonel Tolete—Culata had retired—sent the officers to him one by one. Dr. Maroma gave them the oath—"I swear on my honor as an officer, my faith as a Christian, and my dignity as a man, to uphold the authority and defend the person of Engineer Alejandro Sancudo Montes, President of the independent and sovereign Republic of Tinieblas by the will of the people and the design of the stars"—while Alejo sat behind his desk and Furetto stood in a corner of the office, scrutinizing the swearers for signs of insincerity. Then Dr. Maroma and Furetto went to the barracks, and to every town of the interior, administering a similar oath to the men. The forty officers and four hundred guardias who wavered, grimaced, or twitched, along with Major Dorindo Azote, who refused point-blank to swear, saying that an officer's oath to uphold the constitution was sufficient, were organized into a battalion and sent to Korea, supposedly because Tinieblas had supported the United Nations resolution to aid that country and restore world peace.

"We are a small nation," Alejo said, speaking at the naval docks in the Reservation when the battalion sailed on a gringo troopship, "but a valiant one. The nations of the world respect only blood, and so"—here he looked at Major Dorindo Azote, who stood in his gringo steel helmet in front of the color guard at the head of the troops—"let our blood be shed. I say to Señor Trygve Lie, set our flag alongside those of the nations who sacrifice for liberty, and to Generalísimo MacArthur, place our soldiers in the vanguard where they can die like men."

He had no need to swear the Secret Police to allegiance, for he had made Gonzalo Garbanzo the Inspector General, and Gonzalo had reconstituted the organization completely, firing or retiring the former agents and replacing them with men loyal to him. Alejo, in his dotage with Angela, had given no such order, but Gonzalo was a prudent man who preferred friends to enemies and sycophants to friends. There were only two hundred men in the Secreta, but they were all Tinieblista Party members, who owed their salaries and their surplus gringo .45's and their surplus gringo staff cars (with POLICÍA SECRETA stenciled in yellow on the front doors) and their opportunities for shaking down small businessmen to Gonzalo. But the firemen were made to swear, and the chief, who had been appointed by Lucho Gusano after attending a Boston course in fire prevention and control, was replaced with Fecundo Llamas, who made his name burning ballots during the 1940 elections.

Yet while Alejo drew in the reins, he dug in the spurs. The Tinieblista Party had organized student, worker, peasant, and intellectual groups during the 1948 campaign and, after the election, had allowed them to wither. Alejo now reactivated these groups, each under a chairman named by him, and gave them money to hold national convention, and had them select delegates to a Tinieblist People's Congress. The Congress met in the Legislative Palace, empty now that the deputies were out of session, and promptly began to debate national policy in the most vociferous manner imaginable, denouncing the classes not represented for having exploited the people and sold the national birthright to the gringos and even criticizing the Sancudo Administration for not dealing firmly with these abuses. The president of the Congress was Eugenio Lobo, son of the president deposed through gringo pressure in 1917. Alejo "suggested" him to the delegates on the opening day of the Congress, and they elected him unanimously. Lobo was a humpbacked dwarf with a huge head and glasses like the bottoms of Coca-Cola bottles, who had degrees from at least four universities and was a professor of sociology. He made no attempt to restrain the passions of the delegates, who invariably began by affirming their ignoble origin and current squalor, as if these were marks of particular distinction, and ended by fixing blame for all the country's woes on a few prominent families referred to as *Los Bichos*—The Bugs. Some held that *Los Bichos* were congenital betrayers and predators; others, among them Dr. Lobo, believed they had merely surrendered to the irresistible seductions of the gringos. All were allowed ample use of the floor, and it was only when a delegate's voice or virulence was exhausted that Dr. Lobo would beat on the podium with his *curriculum vitae*, which he carried with him wherever he went, rolled up in a bamboo rod, to recognize a new speaker. Besides controlling the debate, Lobo named and directed a shadow cabinet, which proposed final solutions for every problem of Tinieblan life, and these schemes, along with the invective of the delegates, were sloshed across the front pages of all the newspapers and spewed by radio into every crevice of the land.

The result was a turmoil such as Tinieblas had not witnessed in ten years, though now the conflict was drawn on class, not racial, lines. So great was the excitement over the Congress that now, six months before an election, no one was interested in the crane's dance of prospective candidates or the manipulations of the party chiefs. The opposition bosses accused Alejo of having organized the Congress for just this reason, condemned him, as politicians will, for risking the country's stability for political profit, and warned him that the Congress was a monster which might destroy its own creator. Even his own party was disturbed. Vice President Belisario Oruga, one of the few *bichos* in the Tinieblista Party, was the first to warn Alejo about the Congress.

"I'm sure you had a good reason for calling it," he said, "but it's getting out of hand. They're attacking property."

And Alejo, who was a man of property himself, nodded gravely and assured Don Belisario that he was following the situation carefully.

Francisco Caballero, the Speaker of the Chamber of Deputies, was more perceptive, but made the mistake of being too familiar:

"One parliament is enough for any reasonable country, Señor Presidente. If you want to stir up trouble, we can do it."

"What makes you think Tinieblas is a reasonable country?" Alejo replied. "I intend to call the deputies into special session; all in good time. Until then, go home."

The ministers whom the Congress attacked and the men angling for the Tinieblista Party nomination for 1952 were similarly worried and resentful, but Alejo either turned their objections aside or ignored them. None knew that the substance of every Congress speech, even of the attacks on the government, was composed in the palace by Alejo and Furetto and then transmitted secretly to Dr. Lobo for distribution to the scheduled speakers of the day. None dreamed that he was preparing a *coup d'état* against his own regime.

All through the fall the Congress squawked and shouted, sowing dissension and harvesting discontent. As the delegates' vocal cords grew weak, Dr. Lobo instituted a new practice, forming the Commission on Social Abuses, which held public hearings, inviting members of the lower classes to testify on the iniquities of *Los Bichos*. Everyone knew that Reynaldo Manta had an empire of firetrap tenements, stocked with rats and roaches and never repaired; that Fernando Anguila used child labor in his shoe factory; that Orlando Alacrán exercised *droit de seigneur* over every peasant girl on his copra plantations, but now their names were mentioned in public without genuflection and their way of life considered as social abuse. These hearings were followed by those of the Commission on Political Abuses, during which the graft of ministers and deputies was exposed. Such scandals were nothing new, but it was amazing to hear them aired while the men involved were still in power. The accusing finger of Dr. Lobo, who was getting his information straight from the palace, reached higher and higher into the Sancudo Administration, until people wondered breathlessly whether Alejo himself was going to be exposed, but while the Commission was considering a contract in which Belisario Oruga sold beef to the Guardia Civil for five inchados the pound, its hearings were suddenly suspended to allow the Congress to take up a more exciting matter.

Some two months before the Congress was called, there was a momentous trial in the Reservation. A Tinieblan gardener was accused of raping a gringo wife. What had happened was that the gardener had been troweling away at the wife for months when one morning the husband came home for lunch a little early. When he came up the stairs calling for his sandwiches, she began howling "Rape!" The gardener didn't wait to put on his clothes, which he'd disposed of neatly, socks in his shoes, pants creased over the back of a chair, shirt on a hanger in the bathroom, but dived through the window buck naked. The husband grabbed a shotgun and lamed him as he went across the lawn. He was then charged with trespassing, breaking and entering, burglary, assault, assault with intent to rape, rape, and resisting arrest, tried in a military court, convicted on all counts but the last, and sentenced to one term of six months, one term of a year, three terms of twenty years, and one term of life, the terms to run consecutively. The case caused a furor in Tinieblas, especially when the gardener's counsel, a young second lieutenant, declined to question the woman on the ground that it would only subject her to unnecessary emotional stress. Now a Tinieblan girl came forward claiming to have been raped by this very Lieutenant. The Foreign Ministry requested his extradition from the Reservation and was told he had been transferred to Korea and could not be recalled. At this Dr. Lobo declared that the Congress would try him *in absentia.*

Hearings and debate were suspended, the Legislative Palace vacated, and the Congress convened in the Olympic Gymnasium. Chairs were set up on the basketball court for the delegates, who formed the jury, Dr. Lobo, who presided, and the accused, who wasn't there. More than fifteen hundred spectators were admitted each day free of charge, though many sold their places for as much as five inchados to people who didn't care to stand in the huge lines that began forming at dawn. They cheered wildly for the delegates, for the complaining witness, and the prosecutor, Licentiate Crecencio Galán, who was himself a member of the Congress, and Dr. Lobo, who sat on a dais between the flags of Tinieblas and the Tinieblista Party and had a Chinese gong to beat on for order, and they whistled, booed, and cursed the defense counsel, Dr. Inocencio Listín, who was a member of the Chamber of Deputies and a chess crony of Furetto's, the cleverest criminal lawyer in the republic in the opinion of Uncle Erasmo himself. Dr. Listín fought every step of the way, so much so that it was widely, though falsely, believed that the United States Government was paying him ten thousand dollars to defend the lieutenant, badgering witnesses mercilessly, interrupting the prosecutor constantly with objections, leering salaciously at the complaining witness and asking her to admit that gringos were superior lovers, that she'd enjoyed it, that if anyone was raped—which he very much doubted—it was the Lieutenant, so that a cordon of Civil Guards had to protect him whenever he entered or left the building. Then, when the prosecution had presented its case—which took ten days, what with medical experts and huge color diagrams of male and female sexual organs and life-sized mannequins which were manipulated to show exactly how the rape had been committed—Dr. Listín moved that the indictment be thrown out on the grounds that the alleged rape had taken place in the Reservation. Here Dr. Lobo rose on his little soda-straw legs to his full three-and-a-half feet and beat furiously on his gong and fined Dr. Listín a thousand inchados for contempt of Congress and country, since the Reservation was part of Tinieblas, now, in the past, and for all eternity, and declared that, as President of a Congress that represented the Tinieblan people, he was expanding the case, that, concurrently with the absent lieutenant, the Congress would try the United States of America for rape of the Republic of Tinieblas.

That afternoon a new personage was present at the trial. This was a drunken drifter called Fulo (Blondie) Montalvo, the bastard son of a gringo soldier and a Tinieblan woman, a tall, gaunt fellow whose hair had actually been red, not blond, and was now mostly white, who was dressed up like Tío Sam in a red, white, and blue cutaway and cardboard top hat. He was marched in from the gymnasium dressing rooms by two guardias to the hoots and jeers of the spectators—which he answered with his right hand held high above his head, middle finger extended—and took his seat between Dr. Listín and the empty chair reserved for the lieutenant. Dr. Lobo then read the indictment, which specified ten counts of rape, Dr. Lobo admitting that the United States had raped Tinieblas on many more occasions, but since God Almighty had been satisfied with ten points, the people of Tinieblas would not exceed that number:

"*FIRST, that the United States*"—here, and at this point in the reading of the other counts, Dr. Lobo pointed his bamboo rod accusingly at Fulo Montalvo, who would stick out his tongue, or thumb his nose, or slap the crotch of his right elbow with his left hand, or simply blow air flatulently through his lips, while the spectators hissed and booed and Dr. Lobo gonged for silence—"*that the United States violated the Republic of Tinieblas, conspiring with Monseñor Jesús Llorente in the murder of General Feliciano Luna and tricking the people into an unjust peace;*

"*SECOND, that the United States violated the Republic of Tinieblas, bribing President Ildefonso Cornudo into signing an unjust treaty;*

"*THIRD, that the United States violated the Republic of Tinieblas, forcing, by threat of naval and marine attack upon a defenseless city and People, the Tinieblan Assembly into ratifying that unjust treaty;*

"*FOURTH, that the United States violated the Republic of Tinieblas, sending armed marines into the Tinieblan capital to reinstale Modesto Gusano after he had been overthrown by the Tinieblan people;*

"*FIFTH, that the United States, in the person of the Galactic Fruit Company, violated the Republic of Tinieblas, corrupting President Modesto Gusano into granting piratical concessions;*

"*SIXTH, that the United States, in the person of the Copperhead Mining Company, violated the Republic of Tinieblas, corrupting President Ascanio Pícaro into granting piratical concessions;*

"*SEVENTH, that the United States violated the Republic of Tinieblas, forcing, by threat of military and economic reprisals, the deposition of the Constitutional President of the Republic, Don Eudemio Lobo;*

"*EIGHTH, that the United States, in the person of the Hirudo Oil Company, violated the Republic of Tinieblas, corrupting President Heriberto Ladilla into granting piratical concessions;*

"*NINTH, that the United States violated the Republic of Tinieblas by armed invasion, deposing the Constitutional President of the Republic, Engineer Alejandro Sancudo;*

"*TENTH, that the United States, in the persons of the Yankee and Celestial Energy Corporation and the First Secretary of the United States Embassy, violated the Republic of Tinieblas by interfering in the elections of 1948 and aiding Tinieblans in the commission of electoral fraud.*

"These, then, are ten specific counts," said Dr. Lobo. "A thousand others might be brought, but we are content to try the accused for just these ten. How do you plead?"

Fulo Montalvo got to his feet, stuck his thumbs in his ears and waggled his fingers, and shouted, "No speeky fuckin' Spanish!"

At this a roar of protest broke from the spectators as if to lift the roof off the gymnasium and explode its walls, and Fulo pranced around the basketball court like a bullfighter touring the ring, stopping at each corner to sweep his cardboard hat off his head and bow deeply, each time drawing more abuse from the crowd, so that it was ten minutes before Dr. Lobo and the guardias could restore order. Then, Dr. Lobo fined Fulo ten thousand inchados for contempt and asked again how he would plead.

"Your Honor," said Dr. Listín, "my client pleads 'Not Guilty.' And if you, your Honor, and this distinguished Congress, will hear the grounds for this plea, I think you will withdraw the indictment and save us all a good deal of time and breath."

"Proceed."

"Well, Mr. President and members of the Tinieblist People's Congress, as any lawyer knows—and there are many lawyers here, including, I believe, yourself, Mr. President, for unless I am mistaken, among your many illustrious degrees is one from the School of Law of Columbia University—as any lawyer knows, the crime of rape is composed of two elements, penetration and lack of consent, both of which elements must be present," Dr. Listín emphasized the word "must" by pointing his finger at the basketball net over Dr. Lobo's head, "must be present if it is to be said that a rape has occurred. If either one of these two elements is absent, there is no *corpus delicti,* no crime, no rape. Is that not so, Mr. President?"

"That is so, Doctor. Proceed."

"Well, Mr. President and members of the Congress, my client readily admits penetration. One might say"—here Dr. Listín began snickering—"one might say that my client has penetrated—if I may be permitted a small vulgarity—up to the short hairs into the fair and fragrant body of our land."

Here Dr. Listín was interrupted by such screeches, catcalls, and hoots that Dr. Lobo had to order the squad of guardias ranged at parade rest behind his dais to fire a volley through the gymnasium roof before order could be restored. Then he reminded Dr. Listín that he had already been fined a thousand inchados and his client ten thousand for contempt and advised him that the Congress permitted no vulgarities and warned him that he, Dr. Lobo, would not hesitate to fine anyone a million inchados if such a fine were necessary to preserve the dignity of the proceeding. Then he bade him to proceed.

"Well, Mr. President and members of the Congress, my client admits penetration. But that is only one of the elements of rape. The other element is lack of consent, lack of consent. And this element has not been present. No, Mr. President. No, no, ladies and gentlemen, distinguished members of the Congress. No. No. No. There was no rape because Tinieblas consented. Monseñor Llorente consented to the conspiracy; President Cornudo consented to the bribe; Ramiro Aguado and the Assembly consented to the treaty; Modesto Gusano consented to be reinstated by the marines; he and Ascanio Pícaro and Hildebrando Ladilla consented to the seductions of the foreign companies; the leaders of the Liberal Party consented to the deposition of Eudemio Lobo; the Civil Guard consented to the invasion of 1942; Luis Gusano and the leaders of the nineteen parties consented to the interference into the 1948 elections. On every occasion you have cited, Mr. President, the Republic of Tinieblas, in the person of its leaders, consented to the penetrations of my client. Not only consented, but shook its ass and humped right along!"

Here pandemonium broke forth again, but when the uproar subsided Dr. Lobo did not fine Dr. Listín for contempt but spoke thoughtfully to him in his high-pitched, though grating voice:

"Your line of argument has merit, Doctor. It comes close to proving itself, for your brilliant reasoning is another example of how your client finds clever Tinieblans to serve his contemptible ends. We cannot, however, sustain you to the extent of dismissing the indictment. You admit penetration but deny lack of consent, but in this regard we must consider the republic a maid unwise in the ways of the world and the leaders you have mentioned, her unscrupulous guardians. It is nonetheless rape when a trusting waif, too innocent to realize the consequences of her actions, is lured by her own guardians into the lecher's greasy embrace. We rule, therefore, that a *prima facie* case of rape exists, and you and Dr. Galán will have to convince the Congress of your client's innocence or guilt. Still, your argument has merit; it may prevail. At the least it compels me to widen the indictment. The guardians too must answer for whatever part they took in the alleged crime. True, most of the men you mentioned are dead, but they must be seen as representatives of the class that spawned them. We, therefore, rule that *Los Bichos* will stand trial alongside your client as accessories before, during, and after the fact in this crime of rape of the republic. In order, then, to bring this new accused before the people's justice, we hold this trial recessed until ten o'clock tomorrow morning."

Now, on the morning of this most momentous day, Alejo, who along with Furetto, had composed the entire scenario of what took place in the gymnasium and had even passed personally on Fulo Montalvo's outfit and short speech, went to his villa at Medusa Beach for a bit of rest. Before he left he had two interviews. The first, which took place at two A.M., was with Juan de Arco Soplón, president of the Tinieblist Student Phalanx, who was smuggled in and out of the palace disguised as a woman. This caused no suspicion, in fact even calmed some of the more worried members of the government, for Alejo had now been some three months without the company of Angela or any other female. Alejo told Soplón that he had decided to liberate Tinieblas once and for all from the gringos and *Los Bichos* and ordered the Phalanx to organize a student protest march through the Miramar quarter, where the American Embassy and the homes of many prominent families were located, the following evening. In the morning he sent for Vice President Oruga and put the government and the country in his care. He told Oruga that he was fed up with the Congress and alarmed by the direction it was taking. Colonel Tolete had orders to execute

Oruga's commands. In the event of any disruption of public order or any threat to continued good relations with the United States, Oruga was to act with the utmost vigor and decision. Then he left for the beach, along with Furetto and Doktor Henker and Egon and Gunther, all of whom were now naturalized Tinieblans. The papers carried the news that President Sancudo was at his villa and Belisario Oruga in the palace.

Even before the trial recessed, students began gathering on the University campus and in the quadrangle of the Instituto Politéc-nico; and at five they marched, the one group coming down the Vía México past the newly laid foundation of El Opulento, the other passing through the Plaza Bolívar and out Avenida de la Bahía, about three thousand students eleven years old and up, along with laborers, hoodlums, and bums collected on the way. The students carried placards denouncing gringos and *Bichos* in terms familiar since the opening of the Congress and pocketfuls of coarsely ground black pepper to throw in the nostrils of the Civil Guard's horses, and those who came from the University picked up a good deal of rubble from the hotel construction site. Neither group had gone more than a block before Colonel Tolete called Oruga for orders on what to do about them.

The American Ambassador was in the palace when the call came through, making an energetic protest about the afternoon session of the trial and demanding that the Tinieblan Government put a stop to the slanderous proceedings of the Congress and (since the Student Phalanx was riddled with spies for gringo intelligence agencies, the military Metaphysical Police Command and the civil-ian Committee for Research and Penetration and the Ambassador thus knew all about the march before it got started) warning Vice President Oruga that the United States would tolerate no insult to its flag, no injury to its citizens, and no damage to its property. Oruga had got Alejo by phone when the Ambassador presented himself at the palace and was admonished not to disturb the pres-idential repose over trivialities. We can imagine Alejo grinning past the mouthpiece at Furetto.

"Don't be afraid, Orguita. It's only the Ambassador. What would you do if they sent troops? Tell him that it would be easier for us to deal with the Congress if President Truman would consent to revising the treaty. Give him all the assurances you want, but if he gets snotty, remind him we've sent troops to Korea. And be a man. I might as well have stayed in the capital if you're going to call me about every little thing."

But Oruga lacked Alejo's talent for abusing diplomats, and now, when Tolete's call came through, he saw a chance to end an unpleasant interview.

"Colonel Tolete with a minor problem," he said, holding his palm over the telephone. "Which nonetheless requires my attention. I shall arrange for you to see the President when he returns."

"If it's about the student demonstration, you may be interested in knowing that it's headed for my Embassy."

"Are you sure?" asked Oruga, whose own house was on the next block.

And when the Ambassador nodded, Oruga remembered Alejo's parting orders, saw a chance to impress the gringos, and told Tolete to keep the marchers out of Miramar with all necessary force.

Hence, the sort of shabby cops-and-students brawl which gave us latins a reputation for irresponsibility until the same amusements grew modish in Paris and New York. A guardia broke his shoulder when pitched from a sneezing gelding; a dozen adolescents were saber-flatted into the accident room at San Bruno Hospital; a dozen more were jailed; and cars were overturned, lawns trampled, windows smashed, and an American flag ritually cremated. Mild, as such things go nowadays; primitive; a Model T of a protest clash, underpowered, innocent of such ornaments as molotov bombs and vomit gases, most modest in property damage and looting, too frail and fleeting to produce a single death or permanent maiming, but a beginning, something to build on, and altogether sufficient for Alejo's needs.

He stormed back that night, the sirens of his motorcycle escort wailing all the way to the capital, and called the Chamber into special session. He demanded and received emergency power—state of siege, suspension of guarantees—to deal with the unrest fomented by the Congress. Then he went to the Congress and congratulated the delegates. He apologized for the torpor of his administration. "Three years a somnambulist, I called this Congress in an inspired dream. 'Thank you for waking me, for rousing me to the agonies and aspirations of the people." He praised the students for leading the country in justified protest and condemned Oruga for depriving the people of their constitutional right to demonstrate. He criticized only the burning of the flag: "An unseemly and empty gesture, no matter how strongly motivated. True vindication will come only when we have put our own house in order. First we must purge the fatherland of the poisons which corrupt it from within; then we shall win justice from the foreigner. Perhaps I am not worthy to lead you to these goals; for I have been your president for three years and done nothing. But now I have bathed myself in the will of the people and emerged revitalized. I promise you I shall sleep no more."

With this he returned to the Chamber and asked the Deputies for a law permitting him to succeed himself. "The people," he said, "would be robbed of their franchise if they were not allowed to choose from among all Tinieblans the man they wished to lead them." And when the Chamber did not respond immediately but began to debate the question, led by the opposition deputies and those *tinieblistas* who had themselves hoped for the nomination, he had the doors sealed and the building surrounded by troops. "They can debate all they want," he told Francisco Caballero by phone, "but they will neither leave the building nor eat one grain of rice until they bring me the law I want." And since he had the guards smuggle food to the deputies who were supporting him, their number grew with each approaching mealtime. He had his law in three days and immediately announced his candidacy for reelection. Then he dissolved the Chamber, and sent Belisario Oruga to Japan as Ambassador, and fired all his ministers and appointed Dr. Lobo's shadow cabinet in their place, and told the Congress they had served the fatherland and could now go home, and settled down to govern in the way he enjoyed most, by decree.

The first decree established the People's Tribunal for Economic, Social, and Political justice, with Dr. Eugenio Lobo as Chief justice. This court was to try Tinieblans for the kind of offenses discovered by the Congress's Commissions on Social and Political Abuses and for the newly named crime of Sale of the National Birthright. A section of this decree read, somewhat biblically, that *"the People's Justice shall visit the crimes of the father upon the children unto the third and fourth generation,"* so that one of the first indictments prepared was against Nacho Hormiga, whose maternal great-grandfather, Hildebrando Ladilla, had run off with the national treasury and whose maternal grandfather, Heriberto Ladilla, had granted concessions to Hirudo Oil, while the indictment against Lucho Gusano cited not only his own collusion with the gringos, but that of his father Modesto. It was now clear that Alejo meant to finish with what some people called *Los Bichos* and others the *Oligarchy* and others the *Club Mercantil* Group—that is, the long-established, wealthy, prominent families, most of them descendant from creoles come out from Spain during the colonial period, who had run things in Tinieblas since the days of Simón Mocoso. But the gringos couldn't call him a communist, for he had sent troops to Korea, and the Guardia had no call to move against him, first because its dissident elements were the troops sent and second because he promised Tolete to use the fines collected from the *Bichos* to double the Guardia's pay, and though there were many middle and even lower-class Tinieblans suspicious of Alejo's motives and ashamed of his tactics and afraid of his success, the masses were enchanted, not so much by the prospect of their own rise as by the spectacle of the *Bichos'* fall. People began to refer to Alejo as the Fumigator, while his intended victims started acting like roaches when the DDT powder hits, rushing about frenetically trying to get themselves and their money out of the country. But Alejo's second decree froze the bank accounts and canceled the passports of everyone whose indictment was being considered and ordered the People's Tribunal to begin trying offenders by January fifteenth.

Now if Alejo had managed to try, convict, and punish even one of the *Bichos*, then probably we would have had a real revolution, which would have run its course, as in Cuba, or been halted by gringo intervention, as in Guatemala, and since the machinery of the Tribunal was already in motion, all he had to do was to let events take their course. But that was just the thing he was incapable of doing. He was enjoying himself too much whipping events along, and besides, he had been so successful that he was convinced he could do anything

he cared to. He didn't care to run for reelection. The opposition parties were so disorganized they hadn't even named candidates, but it
was a bore to go campaigning when he could be issuing decrees. And
he didn't care to have a Chamber of Deputies, which might prove re-
calcitrant and have to be sealed up in the Legislative Palace again, or
a Supreme Court, whose president, his own brother Erasmo, who
had married a *Bicho,* was pestering him about the constitutionality of
his decrees. So on the day after the feast of the Epiphany he issued his
third decree, which abolished the Constitution, and with it the Chamber and the Court and all political parties, even his own, and proclaimed himself, Alejandro Sancudo Montes, Perpetual Guardian of
the Tinieblan State and People for the duration of his natural life.

Alejo's perpetual guardianship lasted thirty-eight hours, from
eleven A.M. on January eighth, when he proclaimed it, till one A.M.
on the tenth, when he sneaked out of the palace. His fall was preceded by one of the rarer political phenomena, a middle-class strike
and protest demonstration and was engineered by two young
lawyers, León Fuertes and Carlos Gavilán. Fuertes had an ideolog-
ical antipathy to Alejo. He had been studying in Paris when the
Germans invaded and had served first in the French Army and then
in the Maquis and finally with the Free French under Juin. "I
fought the Nazis in France and Italy," he liked to say, "why
shouldn't I fight them here?" I think he also felt that if Alejo took
all the power in the country, there would never be any for him, but
if you dig too deeply into motives, especially in politics, everyone
turns out to be a son of a bitch. Fuertes was friendly with Aiax
Tolete, who, since he had never fought anywhere, was fascinated with
war and never tired of reconstructing the Battle of Monte Cassino,
where León had been both wounded and decorated, so while Carlitos
organized the demonstration, León neutralized the Guard.

He went to the barracks, a short, stocky man full of energy in
repose like a stick of dynamite, very spruce in the white suit everyone wore those days, with the roseate of the Legion d'Honneur in
his buttonhole, jaunty as on a social call with an inquiry after the
crippled kid of the sergeant at the gate and a joke for Captain Dimitri Látigo, Tolete's aide-de-camp. Oh, León was a charming man,
and he had natural authority, so that even before he became pow-

erful, one felt favored by a word from him or a twinkle from his brown eyes, but once he was in Tolete's office, he put charm away, for he was a killer at heart like every man who seriously seeks power.

"It's time," he said, "that Engineer Sancudo returned to private life."

"I took an oath to support him," said Tolete.

"You took an oath to the constitution first."

At that moment—it was shortly after noon—Tolete's phone rang. It was Alejo, ordering the arrest of León Fuertes and Carlos Gavilán and the posting of troops in key points in the city. Tolete repeated the message to León when he put down the phone.

"You can arrest me," said León. "It won't break up our friendship. In a few days you'll be downstairs too."

"Only if I listen to you."

"No," said León. "Only if you don't."

One evening after a session of the San José Conference, John Kennedy remarked that both he and Khrushchev had the same problem in persuading their generals to give up nuclear tests, and León said that any man in authority could give a soldier orders but only a genius could make one think. Probably he was remembering his conversation with Tolete.

"You could throw Alejo out, couldn't you?" he asked Tolete.

"Of course. If I didn't mind breaking my oath and killing a few people."

"Well, if you know it, don't you think he does? And don't you think it bothers him? You must have realized by now that he can't bear for anyone else to have any power. Especially not the power to throw him out. He has abolished the constitution and the Chamber and the Court. Don't you think he will next abolish the Guard?"

"How the devil can he do that, León? We have all the guns."

"He can issue a fourth decree, renaming the Guard the People's Militia and giving command to the sergeants. Of course, it wouldn't work because the Tinieblan Civil Guard is different from every other military force in the world, because in the Tinieblan Civil Guard the sergeants love their officers. You have two choices, Aiax. Either admit I'm right today and help me get rid of him, or admit I'm right next week when they put you downstairs."

"And if I admit you're right . . ."

"You don't have to do anything. Just order all your men into the barracks and pay them."

Now the Guard, like all government employees, is paid on the first and fifteenth of every month, so the eighth was no payday. But January eighth, 1952, was different because Lucho Gusano and Nacho Hormiga had raised a fund among *Los Bichos* (who, by the way, were reimbursed with interest from the public treasury before the year was out) to pay the Guard an extra time. So instead of following Alejo's orders, Tolete called his men, even the traffic cops at school crossings, back to the barracks and confined them there, and León went back to his office.

Now for thirty-six hours no guardia was seen on the streets of the capital, but there was no looting or disorder, for Carlitos had organized committees of vigilance. Moreover, all the shops were boarded up and their owners in the streets with placards that read *Abajo Alejo*. The entire middle class was in the streets, kids and women too, parading peacefully and cheerfully, with only the doctors and nurses putting in their turns at the hospitals, and while the government offices remained open the afternoon of the eighth, they too were closed the next day. Nor were there any disorders, for it was as though everyone in the country had spontaneously decided that he had had enough of Alejo. The third decree had something offensive to everyone. The politicians, even the *tinieblistas,* were naturally against it, while many of the people who mistrusted politicians had a vague affection for the constitution. And the masses hated to give up elections, which meant barbecues and block parties and free drink and cash handouts at the polls, besides the ritual excitement and competition that sport provides in northern countries. That's the rational explanation, but perhaps Alejo was right that Tinieblas isn't a reasonable country, and the people who had been with him now abandoned him, like one of Homer's gods abandoning a hero, for no particular reason except that his time was up.

Nor was there much he could do about it, for as soon as León Fuertes neutralized the Civil Guard, the Yankee and Celestial Energy Corporation rerouted the palace telephones, so that whenever Alejo or Furetto or Doktor Henker picked up a phone, they got an operator who said, "Abajo Alejo," and hung up. When he looked out over the Plaza Inchado, he saw a frieze of *Abajo Alejo* placards, and on the other side of the palace, out in the bay, all the men with pleasure boats turned out with the same signs, and Tito Avispa even hired a skywriter to scrawl *Abajo Alejo* across the cloudless heavens from dawn to dusk on the ninth. At first the demonstrators were wary, but when it was clear nothing would happen to them, they became confident, even gay, whole families together marching under the homemade signs, and on the evening of the ninth there was dancing in every square in the capital. No move was made to oust Alejo from the palace. The demonstrators stayed at the edge of the Plaza Inchado, ready to duck back up Avenida Bolívar if shooting started, and the boats maneuvered out of rifle shot from the palace, but Alejo could hear the singing and the shouting, and the placards were like a million moth wings beating at his lips. First he said he would leave the palace only as a corpse, and if the demonstrators had stormed the place, probably he would have died bravely, but when they did nothing and when he realized that no one in the country could or would listen to him, his nerve broke, and at one in the morning on the tenth he and the former Paraguayans sneaked out through a secret passage dug by General Epifanio Mojón which led under a corner of the plaza to the Alcaldía. Gunther jumped the wires on a sedan parked behind that building, and they set out through the jubilant streets for La Yegua and the Ticamalan border.

It was past three when they cleared Córdoba.

"The road is better now," said Gunther.

"I built this section during my first administration," said Alejo with the weary rage of resentment.

"The Führer built roads," mused Doktor Henker. "Ach, such roads!"

At the far end of Salinas Province oil derricks stretched steel cobwebs across the dawn.

"If only we had had more oil," said Doktor Henker. "Oil is the blood of the modern state."

The morning sun baked them through the scrub hills of La Merced.

"This country is no good," said Furetto, gazing through the window.

Alejo had his eyes closed behind his dark glasses. "It's not the country," he snarled, "it's the people."

An attendant recognized them when they stopped for gas at the first town in Remedios. He called the Guardia Civil in Angostura; they called Tolete in the capital. Alejo and his companions were arrested just outside Angostura. By noon he was on his way to jail in the capital, handcuffed, ankle-manacled, blindfolded, and gagged, in a closed truck with two guardias pointing shotguns at him.

25

At the same time they were expelling Alejo from the Tinieblan presidency, I was deposed from Yale.

This was largely Alejo's fault, for he only partially disinherited me, giving me no money but passing me his tendency to push luck past the brink. I would never have made a scholar, but I knew the value of education and would have emerged as respectably degreed as Alfonso if I hadn't been forced to live by my wits. First I needed money to live and pay my debt; then things were going so well I thought I'd build up a little capital for the future. In the end I was risking for the sake of risk, and besides, the influence of the gringo business-worldview had made me greedy. Like Alejo I went too far, and my luck ran out on me.

Alfonso's bank draft arrived in New Haven a few hours after I did, but it barely sufficed to pay one term's tuition. I had decided (in Tinieblas Airport) to support myself and repay Alfonso by gambling and calculated that I needed three thousand—a thousand for Alfonso, a thousand for spring term tuition and books, and a thousand to live on. There was that much and more at the Law School, where a pot-limit, table-stakes five-dollar-ante poker game was celebrated every night, but I needed a stake and therefore took a job as Spanish stand-in for Astor Dupont Pelf.

Pelf, who was related to a stock exchange of plutocrats and got an allowance of two thousand a month, had one obligation in life: to graduate from Yale as had every one of his male ancestors back to Isaiah Pelf, who had roomed with Nathan Hale. Upon receipt of a bona fide Yale B.A., Pelf's daddy would provide a seat on the New York Exchange and Pelf's mommy a bloc of chemical shares. Pelf's problems would then be over, for while he was inept at academic subjects, he had a lively business sense. "An executive doesn't clog his brain with details," he would say in his Groton baa. "He hires experts." And he applied this principle to his studies.

Pelf's English themes were written by an assistant professor at Boston College, who received the topic by telephone and sent the finished work by special messenger. A Sperry-Rand physicist drove up from Bridgeport twice a term to take Pelf's science examinations. Since his major was economics, he had three of the brighter graduate students on his payroll as consultants and met with them for brunch in a private room at Mory's every Monday morning to plan his posture in class. For Spanish, where there were daily recitations and spot quizzes, he needed a full-time impersonator, someone who would show up at every class as Astor Pelf. His first appointee, a music major from Bolivia, had performed brilliantly for almost two years and had virtually fulfilled Pelf's language requirement when he hanged himself from a shower spout during Easter vacation. Pelf was forced to drop the course and find a new stand-in to complete the last semester. I applied for the post and was appointed, after assuring Pelf that since wrestling season didn't start until spring term, my athletic celebrity wouldn't interfere. The pay was four hundred dollars, plus a clothing allowance, for no one answering to the name of Astor Pelf could be seen in anything but a J. Press suit, a pastel button-down, a rep tie, and white buckskins. I managed to get two hundred in cash as a retainer before Pelf, clasping my forearm with his right hand and patting my back with his left, eased me out of his rooms while I experienced the mixed pangs of wonder and contempt common to lackeys of Yankee imperialism.

Then I went to the registrar to arrange my own program (no classes before eleven or on Saturday), and to the gym for a nerve-calming workout (rings and parallel bars, no wrestling, though there were sparrers available, or bag punching, for I wanted to conserve every nip of aggression for the poker game), and to my college dining hall for a light supper (the last meal I ever ate there, though food was included in the tuition bill), and, just forty-eight hours after Lazarillo and I had been yelped out of our cell, over (at a careful stroll under elms still leafed with summer) to the Law School.

The Law School poker game was performed in the rooms of two New York Jews named Fox and Lyon who now hold posts in the United States Justice Department, Lyon as Deputy Attorney General and Fox as Librarian at Leavenworth. They played in partnership, alternating in and out of the game as one grew tired or the other felt lucky. Fox wore a green eye-shade and when dealing stud liked to call the cards as they fell, announcing pairs and triplets and warning of possible flushes and straights. Lyon, on the other hand, had none of this finesse. He addressed everyone, including his partner, as schmuck, and his only comments as dealer were snarls like, "How many cards, schmuck?" or "High schmuck bets." Both were excellent, players, Fox a virtuoso of the sucker bet, Lyon a thunderclap sandbagger, and they made a generous living at the felt-topped hexagonal table they had brought with them from the Bronx two years before. This came from the fish, undergraduates with large allowances, who swam up from the residential colleges each evening looking more for excitement than gain. Fox angled them delicately, complimenting them on their fine clothes and sporting spirit, throwing them a few small pots until the right hand came up. Then he would reel in his fish, murmuring, "Bad luck." Lyon's technique was different. "You shouldn't play in this game, schmuck," he would say. "You're a fish, and you're going to lose," and the fellow would get angry and decide to show that smart-ass New York kike who was a fish, and he'd lose just as Lyon said. "Bad luck," Fox would say when a fish tapped out and hunched pitifully in his chair, wondering what to tell daddy. "You're a fish, schmuck," Lyon would say, raking in the pot. "How do you expect to win?" And as soon as his next check came, the fish would wiggle back.

There were other players who were not fish: Mike Qualm, who played goalie on the soccer, hockey, and lacrosse teams, and who was so used to having hard objects hurtling at him that he had the best poker face at the table; John Barker, who put himself through four years of college and three of med school playing cards, and who had his bridge pigeons and his gin pigeons and his minor league poker pigeons secreted throughout the university. Barker milked his pigeons every afternoon and evening and would drop in on the Law School game one or two midnights a week to lose a hundred or win two hundred as his luck decreed. And others whose faces dissolved in an incense-haze of tobacco smoke, whose voices alternated in the service ("I bet." "I raise." "I call." "I fold."), while the elm leaves burst golden, and then withered and fell, and were shoveled across the Old Campus by October wind and sogged to compost by November rain and buried by December snow.

I had played in this game three times my sophomore year and had each time lost every cent I had on me and would have lost more if Fox had been willing to accept my paper. Each time he shook his thin Dachau-gray face sadly and gazed with compassion out of pogrom-stained eyes and shrugged his persecuted shoulders and held up his palms with their beef-red stigmata of Roman spikes, while his partner growled: "Tough shit, schmuck; we don't take markers from little fish," and the other players fidgeted in their chairs, and the man waiting for my seat recounted his stake and edged in behind me. And each time I hung my head and slunk away with neon blotches creeping up from under my collar and down across my wrists. Back in my room I would replay every pot—the strong hands where I scared everyone out with an idiot-screamed pot bet and won only antes; the weak hands where I called and called, waiting for a card not even I believed would come; the mocking hands where I folded only to see my card flash down into the next man's hand; the futile hands where I stayed to keep some smug winner "honest"; and the hideous second-best hand which tapped me out when, suckered like the fish I was, I pushed the whole, helpless remnant of my stake into the pot (which I was already spending on a glorious foray to New York, where I would meet Angela and reduce her to gibbers of joy in a posh suite at the Pierre), only to learn what everyone else had suspected, that Fox had four of a kind all the way, not the flush I thought he filled with his slimy one-card draw, and that my lovely pat full house was worthless. Then I would

imagine what those gringos thought of me: stupid greaseball, mus-
clebound spic; and my shame would spread until I had to jump up
and walk around in the icy darkness chanting my credo: "I am Kiki
Sancudo. I can wipe the wrestling mat with any man my weight in
the Western Hemisphere." And when gray dawn scraped against
the lead-glassed, gothic-arched little window over my bed, I would
fall into a swirling half-sleep where I seized long gooey kisses from
Angela to find her transformed into Fox while my father sneered at
me and called me schmuck.

So after the third time, I gave it up, not permanently, for I was
never the sort of person who could admit his limitations, who could
say, "I'm not a good poker player, so I won't play poker." No, I
gave it up for the year, vowing to go back reborn from little fish to
shark and tap them all out, Fox and Lyon and Barker and Qualm,
to humiliate them publicly and pin them down the way I did
wrestling opponents. I missed the game, the marvelous manufactures intensity of life which gambling gave more generously than
love, for the body tires, or wrestling, as there were only a dozen odd
matches plus the Eastern Championships (which I won) and the
New York Invitationals (which I won) and the Nationals (which I
missed, since, thanks to Fox and Lyon, I couldn't afford to go to
Oklahoma). The game gave tension and release, and action and satisfaction, every night from dusk till dawn, and there was always
another deal if you could meet the ante. I missed it and yearned to
creep back, "Just to watch a few hands," but I had always been a
proud bastard, am proud even now, sitting up like a Westminster
show terrier to gulp my mush, and wouldn't go back till I was ready.

No plans were made to hasten the hour of return and revindica-
tion. I didn't buy Jacoby's treatise or study game theory and the laws
of probability. I even, once back in Tinieblas for summer vacation, succeeded in forgetting my three trips to the cleaner's, except for certain
dark nights of the soul when, with a blossom of shame (the master
card for this emotion was punched on a Roman street corner in 1939
when I crashed my Black Prince two-wheeler into a fashionably
dressed matron, slicing her shin with my fender and knocking her
into an oily puddle) I was catapulted from some Tinieblan cantina to
the merry old Fox and Lyon, where, for the millionth time, I cravenly

folded what turned out to be the winning hand. Then, that midnight at the airport, so recently squeezed from prison back into the world, it came to me that my minnowhood was over. More, an inner voice said the stars were propitious. I might go back to the game, not only to fulfill my vow but to support myself. I never thought, not even for an instant, of acting out the wan gringo myth of working one's way through college, not because I'm lazy—I am, in fact, quite the reverse, a restless man to whom inactivity is torture—but because work, by definition, is dull. In the mesh-windowed van going out to the airport I considered joining the American Marines or the French Foreign Legion, there being two moderately exciting wars in progress (I favored the one in Indochina, where the women are good looking), but when the guard on duty at the airport clicked his heels (a fossilized memory of when the Guardia wore *feldgrau*), and saluted the officer herding Lazarillo and me, I realized that a soldier pays more than I cared to in freedom for the luxurious legal right to shoot people and be shot at by them. So that fall I campaigned neither in the Red River Delta nor in the mountains northwest of Seoul, but on a green felt hexagon in a sitting room on the second floor of the Yale Law School dormitory, flanked by a Castro convertible day-bed, which a man who lived downstairs had bet on a pair of aces and lost to Fox's two small pair, and impartially observed by the sullen negro in a framed reproduction of Winslow Homer's *Gulf Stream*.

"The little fish is back," said Lyon, as I sat down opposite him in the only empty chair. He peeked at his hole card and, as the bet came round to him, flipped the six he had showing. "Go home, schmuck. A fish like you stinks up the game."

With that Qualm came in. "No room?"

"How much you got, schmuck?" Lyon yawned at me. The Jack of Diamonds swished by him toward the player on his left.

"Two hundred." I counted Pelf's retainer on the felt in front of me and handed it to him over the pot.

"Ten minutes," he said to Qualm. He fingered ten white, five reds, and five blues from the merry-go-round chip holder, making four stacks of five, then two of ten. "This fish's seat will be open in ten minutes."

I fixed Lyon with a stare resembling that of the gloomy King of

Sceptres. The dealer's hand celebrated a double royal wedding in Swords and Cups, and its owner swooped for the pot. In a nearby room Marlene Dietrich was falling in love again. Jack Diamond's late employer rolled his chips into a tricolor sausage and asked if we were playing or not, and Lyon availed himself of this pretext to glance away. He tumbled the two stacks toward me. "Take your chips, schmuck." Then he gathered the cards and began riffling them with pudgy thumbs.

White chips flopped in the center of the table. The winner of the last pot cut the deck into three equal layers and watched Lyon reassemble them in reverse order. Cards came round. I got a pair of tens back to back. The player on my left showed an ace. Lyon, a king; the sausage man, another ten.

"Ten dollars," said the ace, bloodying the pot.

I called. The next man folded a four. The last pot's winner stayed with a seven. Lyon called. His neighbor drew his hole card off the table, rubbed it along his chest, cupped it below his nose, then slapped it down and closed his ten. Pot right. More cards.

The ace got a king, I an ace, the seven a queen, Lyon a nine.

"Ten dollars," said the ace-king.

I raised thirty, hoping the others would suspect me of an ace in the hole. The queen-seven folded. Lyon called. So did the ace-king.

Jack. Seven. Nine.

Lyon checked his pair of nines, and the ace-king-jack bet fifty.

Raise or fold, I thought and called the bet. I was too poor to raise and too loyal to my tens to fold them.

"How much you got left, schmuck?" Lyon asked me.

"Ninety-five dollars."

"Then that's what I'm raising." He stacked seven blues and one white, derricked them over the pot, and dropped them in.

"Sandbagger," said the ace-king-jack and called.

Pair of aces or pair of kings or pair of jacks or possible straight. What did it matter to me when Lyon had three nines. In fact I could see the nine of hearts crushed face-down under Lyon's right fist. I could see the number and spot right through the back of the card. Strange. A case for the parapsychology lab, but no good now. Why didn't I look before?

I looked to my right and saw the faggot jack of diamonds lying on his stomach under the newly arrived jack of clubs. Amazing, but again too late. Miss Dietrich was buying drinks for the boys in the back room, and I started to fold my cards. Wait. What about a glance at the deck?

It lay throttled in Lyon's left hand. The top card, if my insight was twenty-twenty, was the deuce of spades, of no use to anyone, but underneath, yes, a black ten, the fourth ten, the ten of spades!

"Are you calling or folding, schmuck?"

But I wasn't listening to either Lyon or Marlene. I was peering through the deuce of spades and the ten of spades to see if Lyon's next card would be a nine or a king. No, it was a six. Wait. Did I read it right side up? To be safe I counted the spots. A six all right. No help at all.

"I call." It was worth ninety-five dollars to find out if I was seer or madman.

Deuce. Ten. Six. As prophesied. I confess to no surprise, though I was hugely pleased with my courage. More people would enjoy the revels of second sight if they had the guts to trust its readings. I was also somewhat greedily disappointed that I had no chips to sandbag Lyon with when he bet into what he surely assumed was two pair, aces and tens. As it was, I could only wait as Lyon bet fifty in hope of scooping a side pot from the man on my right. The latter folded, Lyon withdrew his fifty, and I discovered my third ten.

"So you drew out on me, schmuck," said Lyon. "Keep playing like that and you'll be tapped out in no time."

I nodded meekly and sheep-dogged in the chips. Six hundred twenty-five dollars, two hundred of it mine. Two hundred twelve point five percent on my money and cash to bump with if my gift remained.

"What about that, schmuck?" he said to Fox, who circled the table nervously, like the sharks in Homer's painting. "The fish drew out the fourth ten."

"Are you cooling off?"

"No, schmuck. Go in and study." And he cut the cards to the next man.

All that night, indeed for the rest of the year, I was able to scan people's holdings through the backs of the cards and to read down through the red- and blue-fanned decks of Bicycles as though they were transparent My view was so piercing and complete that I picked up my hole card only for form's sake and, in draw, developed the habit, a sort of trademark, of flicking away a bad hand without even lifting the cards.

"Aren't you going to look at them?" one of my kibitzers would plead, for I attracted kibitzers the way a great surgeon attracts med students—day-beds full of tapped-out fishes who hoped to learn my game, several statistics majors who were writing theses and term papers on the way I drove loopholes through the laws of probability, non-poker-playing celebrities who were looking for thrills, men like Theron Whippet, the legendary scatback, who ran back five Dartmouth punts for touchdowns that year, and Gil Haddock, who while still in prep school had won three backstroke gold medals at the London Olympics, and Joel Quarter, then editor of the *Record* and later, of course, a famous screen writer (he came out of a catatonic trance to babble about my poker playing when, two years ago, he saw me being wheeled through the rose garden of the Fasholt Clinic), and Schwartztrauber, the sociologist and author, the most popular lecturer at Yale, who was later in Kennedy's cabinet, and De Botte, the fencing captain, and De Botte's girls: all these people came to kibitz Sancudo that autumn—"Aren't you even going to look?"

And I would shrug and sneer down at the mismatched quintet of low hearts and spades which showed their anonymous backs to everyone else and say, "Doesn't feel like the hand."

But this was during the great days when I'd mastered my gift. That first night I was only just learning how to use it and played a profitable but inelegant game, winning far too many small pots and losing two rather large ones. On one of these I was so eager to force my right-hand opponent out and thus get a queen to fill my straight it never occurred to me that, if my left-hand opponent also dropped, Qualm, who had by this time found a seat, would fill his flush. I bet the pot, sent both opponents scurrying and wound up second-best, just like a fish. On the other I dealt myself four diamonds and a heart, divined that, whether or not Lyon kept a kicker to his triplet kings, he would not improve, while I, all other players having dropped, would get my fifth diamond, called his hundred, drew one card, and, blinded by second sight, threw away not my worthless heart but one of my precious diamonds. He checked to me; I bet two hundred. He winced, wavered, and finally called. He took my blunder for an almost expert bluff, refrained from calling me schmuck as he pulled in the pot with still shaking fingers, and later on saw several big bets at which he might otherwise have folded. The hand gave me a valuable reputation as a sometime bluffer and, in the end, made me more money than it had cost, but, as I hadn't engineered it, I couldn't take much pride in it. Meanwhile I won so many pots, both big and small, that people began to think I was cheating. In view of my biceps no one ventured to accuse me outright, but Lyon sent Fox trotting to Liggett's for new cards and ten eagle eyes watched my every cut, deal, and shuffle.

In time I learned how to exploit my talent, how to fold a winning hand when the pot was small, or when I had no prospects of my own, how to stay in and draw two cards so a loser on my left would fill his straight and win a little money. Something for everyone. Everyone should get a nice hand now and again, win a pot for himself, so he doesn't lose heart, so he'll send his soldiers— platoons of stalwart reds, crack blue battalions—trudging bravely into my set-piece double envelopments. I learned, in short, not only how to flesh my visions, how to incarnate the words whispered to me by the god of thieves, but how to do so with panache. That first night I played a deplorably sloppy game.

All was redeemed, however, on the final hand, final because it put the Lyon-Fox combine temporarily out of business, though it was then long after midnight and time for anyone who planned to show up for the first classes of the term to quit. Hours had passed since Marlene, after waiting under the lamppost for several bilingual choruses, had strutted off to bed. Two players had tapped out. Barker had come, lost his hundred, and gone. I stood some fifteen hundred to the good. Lyon, Qualm, and the one other remaining player were losing heavily, and Fox, after many unheeded pleas for Lyon's seat, had slunk into his den. Qualm had the deck and called draw. Antes went up; cards fluttered down. I read the three opposing hands as they filled up on the table: eight, nine, ten, jack of hearts, and a black three for Lyon; a low pair for the next man; three aces for Qualm. Then I picked up my own hand: kings of clubs and diamonds, tens of clubs and spades and a nine of clubs—not an exciting holding, considering what Qualm and Lyon had, but when I peered into the deck I saw that if Lyon drew one card (as, of course, he had to) and the next man dropped (which could be arranged), Cherubim would sing on radiant heights while Kiki marched triumphant into the Holy City.

Lyon could not open his possible straight flush no matter how much he would have liked to. The next man's pair were below jacks. I opened for the pot, which was twenty dollars. Qualm looked again at his three aces and raised fifty; Lyon called; the next man folded. Since my affairs were now being managed by friendly Fate, I simply saw Qualm's raise and tooted the pitch pipe to the angelic choir. Lyon dismissed his nasty tray and welcomed the lovely Queen of Hearts, filling his straight flush. I plucked the red king and spade ten out of my hand and placed them carefully under the pot in case a broken foe later wailed to see my openers.

"Two cards, please." A winner can afford good manners, and the Queen and Jack of Maces, who had been nestling illicitly together under the blushing heart queen, tripped into my hand.

For Qualm, who forever after was known as the Third Man, there was a fourth ace. A brisk round of betting now ensued.

The first bet fell to me as original opener, and I matched the pot, which held two hundred thirty dollars. Qualm, who liked round numbers, saw that and raised two seventy. "Five hundred to you, Lyon."

Lyon, who could scarcely believe his hand, much less the heady sums bet into it, had only six-hundred-odd dollars in front of him.

"I'll see that, schmuck. And raise one hundred forty. And my car."

"Make, model, and year," demanded Qualm, who had won a car on four aces the spring before.

"A nineteen fifty-one Hippogriff, schmuck. Four-door sedan. Black with white sidewalls and red slipcovers and hydromatic drive. Forty-five hundred miles on the clock. It's worth two thousand."

"The pot's only sixteen hundred."

"Sixteen hundred then."

"I'd allow sixteen hundred for calling," said Qualm. "But for raising purposes a car like that is worth no more than a thousand."

They wrangled heatedly. Neither asked my opinion, but, as the car would soon be mine, I was content to let the two losers enjoy negotiating its value. Qualm was adamant. A thousand and no more. In the end Lyon, with the odds a million to one in his favor that he would be driving the car to football games all season, yielded. Time was then called while he fished up the keys and registration, endorsed the latter, and flung both into the pot.

I was just able to call, and how Lyon glowed as I shoved my stacks forward. Qualm would have raised if Lyon and I had had anything left worth winning. He pushed in most of his chips and completed his call with fifty-dollar bills from his pocket.

"Straight-flush, schmucks!" howled Lyon, fanning his cards on the table. "Queen high!"

"Good draw," said Qualm manfully, tapping the table.

"King high," I sighed, spreading my cards. "Where's the car parked?"

Lyon slapped his neck where the Amazon blowgunner had hit him with a curare dart. The poison brings instant paralysis.

I didn't go to bed until after the banks had opened and I'd wired Alfonso his thousand. First I took Lyon's Hippogriff out on the Merritt Parkway to get the feel of it, easing up to the speed limit as dawn spread west over the Atlantic, running on, seventy, eighty, ninety, past the exit signs of towns where a million blind men were saluting alarm clocks, and out of time altogether into a golden dream.

26

"Bright college years, with pleasures rife, the shortest, gladdest years of life." So goes the song; I have no call to argue. Many of my contemporaries found those years a swindle. They had debts to pay and daddies to placate; they were puzzled by professors and re-jected by girls. And these annoyances seemed great burdens. But, in that fall of 1951 at least, I slid lightly over the surface of life from one easy pleasure to another.

My father had disinherited me; I owed him nothing. Each night, Monday through Thursday, I took a golden egg home from the Law School. Just one moderately large golden egg, for I didn't want the poor bird to strain and cackle. In my classes the same gift that served me at the poker table gave me test questions even as the professors thought them up. I scarcely needed this advantage, for I was studying history—the one commodity with which my fatherland is bountifully supplied—and read the texts with pleas-ure. And the first weekend of the term, when my gleaming Hip-pogriff whisked me to Poughkeepsie, a beautiful girl, the daughter of a millionaire, fell in love with me, inevitably as the sun comes up or autumn trees turn gold. She fell into my hand before I reached for her, and I enjoyed her as I enjoyed all the other lovely things which had obviously been created for my pleasure.

It was the only placid period in my life, and it lasted about six weeks. I had to mispronounce a few words in Pelf's Spanish class and make one or two spelling errors on each quiz to suspend the instructor's disbelief. I had to tolerate a certain eminence of schol-arship who tried to wring the wonder and fantasy out of European history and stuff in scientific cause and effect. I had to leave Fox and Lyon enough fishmeal to stay alive on. I had to moderate my workouts lest I be overtrained when wrestling season started. I had to exercise a little care with Karen between the 7th and 20th of the month. Those were my problems, all so easy to solve; against them I had money, love, and campus fame. All of which I threw away because I cannot bear tranquility.

Boredom struck, with all its fury, one afternoon in mid-October while I was making love to Karen at an inn in Balling, New York. There had been warning symptoms, but I paid no atten-tion to them, brief spasms of unmotivated wrath which I dismissed as one dismisses the headache and unquiet sleep which are later identified as the advance guard of a joint-cracking grippe. There was the almost irrepressible urge to hurl a cashmere sweater Karen brought me out the window when, one rainy Friday morning, she drove all the way from Vassar to tiptoe into my room, kiss me awake, and lay the rich gift on my pillow. Or the desire to throttle Fox—my hand actually leaped half way across the table—the night he pitched me a fat pot, folding three kings to one of my most transparent bluffs. I would have that kind of attack and then forget about it, for in those days I didn't spend time examining my life. Then that afternoon . . . I was driving Karen home from a football weekend, and we stopped at an inn run by a Frenchwoman, who took a fine gallic pleasure in renting us a room for the cocktail hour and feeding us later on. The sheets were cool and smooth. It was the week before the leaves fell, and a nippy breeze played among them just beyond our window. Boeuf bourguignon was simmering downstairs, and Karen was a lovely girl. So warm and loving. All the security of wealth and none of its snobbishness. Eager to please and yet not sloppy. No fawning, no gushed endearments. Gentle glances like a flower turning toward the sun, and a soft sigh each time I entered her. Off at the first stroke of the baton. Little grace notes added to the adagio, and a smiling look up at the maestro to see if he approves. Andante, allegro, presto. Flourish and flick shoots her into her cadenza, but as I waited for her to finish—there would be flute divertissements for me *tout de suite*—I felt I couldn't bear it any longer, this being loved along with the surfeit of other blessings, all too easy and no fun any more, and by God I'll put a little life into things, I'll just pull away and leave her dangling. Then that seemed too passive and too kind, and I dug my thumbs into her armpits and held her shoulders down and stabbed through her pleasure, but instead of feeling wounded or frightened or betrayed, oh no, she mistook my anger for desire, for ungovernable love, and cried out in joy and threw her head back, and even as I polluted her, gasped, "Yes, Kiki! Oh, yes, Kiki, give me your baby. Oh, Kiki, thank you!"

That was it. She had everything, and I had nothing. She had the joy of loving and the pain of loving and the excitement of risking everything for love and all kinds of hope and worry over whether she was pregnant; in short, she was alive and I was bored. She would go on loving me no matter what, and even if she stopped, if

I beat it out of her, what did it matter to me? Oh, I liked her. How could I help liking her? and I was happy for her that she was enjoying life and feeling it deeply, but I didn't care if she loved me or if she was pregnant or if I ever saw her again. There were plenty more as good or better I could have as effortlessly as I'd had her. That was it: the damned ease of everything was taking the taste out of life.

We didn't stay to dinner. It was all I could do to nod and grin at her on the short drive to Poughkeepsie, for I didn't want to hurt her; I didn't care about her that much. I left her at her dormitory, glowing with love, and sped straight to New York City, where I spent the week. I played at a famous bridge club for tremendous stakes. I scarcely knew the game, and the place was seeded with experts who had written books and devised systems, but no game is very difficult when you can see everyone's cards, and besides I was lucky, and I won more money than I knew how to spend. I visited an after-hours spot in a brownstone on West 72nd, an elegant place with a band and gaming tables and a heated swimming pool with naked whores of all sexes splashing in it. The roulette ball hopped dutifully after my chips wherever I flung them, till I grew sick of winning and rented one of the little mermen because I'd never done that and wasn't sure I could. I drilled him smoothly, but neither enjoyed him very much nor had any strong feelings of disgust, so the next night I bought a Puerto Rican girl, green eyes and café-crème skin, to see if I could make her come. And when this proved easier than I'd expected, I took her dancing to see if I could have her for nothing. And when I found I could, I asked her to take care of a couple of men I'd met at the bridge club to see if she'd do that for me. And she said she didn't mind, to send them over to her apartment, and one of them had such a good time he gave her a fifty-dollar bill, and Linda—her name was Linda— handed it to me as soon as I walked in that night. Then I got tired of New York and decided to go back to New Haven for the football game, and Linda cried and begged me to take her with me and said she wasn't lazy like a lot of girls and would keep me well, so I put her in the car along with her two suitcases and the stuffed panda some john had bought her at the Latin Quarter and zipped her across the state line and set her up in an apartment opposite Cotton Mather College and began sending her customers, and pretty soon she was earning me three or four hundred a week.

After that week in New York I began sleeping more and more, until I was averaging about fourteen hours a day, and of course going, less and less to class, even cutting Pelf's Spanish class, attendance at which I considered a debt of honor, and missing my workouts. I devoted my waking hours to business, that is gambling and vice, playing poker at the Law School and fishing fresh whores from New York. Soon I had the campus bracketed, north, south, east, and west, and while I relied solely on word-of-mouth advertising, my merchandise was high in quality and the demand for it intense, so the girls worked day and night, and the money rolled in. And as I made my rounds, Linda on Monday afternoon; Monika, my blond Valkyrie, on Tuesdays; on Wednesdays, sweet San Antone Annie; on Thursdays Brooklyn Faye; collecting the receipts, passing back rent and laundry money and a bit for food and frills, and of course ladling affection freely, I felt, as successful businessmen are wont, that I was not merely turning a profit but serving the world as well. Here I'd lifted my girls out of foul bars and whorehouses and set them down in puritan New England where they need fear neither disease nor degenerates but consorted only with the clean-limbed sons of the best families in America. As for my customers, I felt a perfect Dr. Schweitzer to those benighted college boys, for blue balls was epidemic in New Haven in those days, and many was the lad whose sanity I saved of a Sunday evening when the little tease who'd tortured him all weekend tripped back to Smith or Bryn Mawr.

The richer I grew selling love the less I wanted it myself, and it became something of a chore to service each of my girls one afternoon a week. I couldn't have them grow so horny they'd start enjoying the customers, for then they'd get picky or fall in love or even run out on me. Withal I slept more and more and ceased exercising entirely and gained twelve to fifteen pounds a week, so that I celebrated my twenty-first birthday by sleeping round the clock, and when I weighed myself the next day, I couldn't see past my gut to read the numbers and had to call Andy Smart, who lived on the same floor.

"Two oh six," he said. "Going to wrestle heavyweight next term?"

I had to smile at this, for my waddle to the bathroom had set me panting, and what did I need wrestling for when I was clearing over a thousand a week on poker and the girls?

It got so I just couldn't get up for Pelf's class, and finally I went to him and asked to break our contract, refunding all pay and allowances and offering him an indemnity of five hundred dollars. He pouted and said he'd taken me for a more reliable man, adding that if I was going to walk out on him in the middle of the term I might at least have the decency to hang myself like my predecessor. Then he asked how I'd grown so flush so fast, and as I felt I owed him some explanation, I told him about my good luck in cards and love. He was fascinated by the girls, two of whom he'd visited thinking they worked freelance, and he immediately forgot all about his Spanish class and clapped me on the back.

"By George, you've got a head for business there's hope for South America yet if there are enough fellows like you!" And he proposed I take him as a partner and expand.

"I see one of those big trailers—no, two of them—each with three girls inside, one parked at Princeton and another shuttling between Williams and Dartmouth. Ten girls in all with the four you've got here, and we'll rotate them to give the clients fresh meat each month."

I said if we made it that businesslike, we'd have to pay the girls, and he began to lecture me on modern business methods, saying that no one exploited workers any more since it was simpler to corrupt them.

"We'll pay the girls a straight salary," he proposed, "and give them retirement benefits and medical care and a profit-sharing, plan, and once we've developed a market, we'll raise prices and pass the costs on to the consumer."

It sounded logical, and he was ready to put up the cash for the trailers, so I agreed and took a week off in New York to do some recruiting, and we were open for business in Princeton and Williamstown the first week in January when the students returned from vacation.

Pelf was also intrigued by my poker success, though I didn't tell him exactly how I worked it, and said that if there was that much money being gambled, Yale ought to have a casino. He got on the phone and in twenty minutes found a couple of seniors who were short of funds and had a large suite of rooms in Jay Gould College. We bought a roulette wheel and a dice table and opened the next week, with our seniors dressed up in tuxedos running the tables and a Jap exchange student in a white jacket serving drinks.

Now, a day or two after I returned from New York with Linda, Karen called me wondering where I'd been and why I hadn't called, asking if I'd been sick and saying she'd been afraid I'd had an accident. I didn't bother to invent anything; people often tell the truth out of laziness when, with a little effort, they might concoct a decent lie. I told her she was a lovely girl, but I didn't enjoy being with her any more. This was incomprehensible to her, of course. We'd been so happy, she pointed out, only the week before. She begged me to tell her what she'd done and promised never to do it again. Or what hadn't she done, and promised to learn how to do it. Sobs rolled along the phone lines like breakers. Foaming unpleasantly around Kiki's ears. I hung the phone on my index finger a forearm northeast of my ear, admiring her capacity for suffering and envying her the intensity of the moment. Which never came to me any more, not even when the pot was counted in four figures or one of my stable mares was treating me to prances not practiced with the customers. The swells subsided little by little. Soft drizzle of tears which I blotted with the receiver. And with a knuckle nudged a sympathetic drop of ennui from the outlying corner of my left eye.

Next came a letter, blue paper, and bluer ink, which I didn't fully read since her handwriting was cramped. Skipped from love to love as across a rivulet and slipped it back in its discreetly scented pale blue envelope. And held it between thumb and middle finger before my nose in hope of feeling a Proustian shudder or a Pavlovian flow of juice. And then dropped it in the swing-topped waste can at Yale Station.

Then, just before or after my birthday, another call:

"I'd like to see you," in a dry-eyed voice.

"I'm rather busy."

"I'm rather pregnant."

"Are you sure?"

She was. The level-headed girl had consulted Drs. Frog and Rabbit directly she found things amiss. Slightly annoying, as I'd considered the Karen file closed and had a full business day before me, but an executive must treat problems as challenges, and I agreed to meet her in Balling, at the scene of the crime.

She didn't recognize me at once, I was so fat. "Oh, Kiki," she said when she was installed at my table. "I'm six weeks pregnant, and you look six months." It's good breeding that gives them the stiff upper-lip. Centuries of money and deep knee-bends with the White Man's Burden up.

"You're taking it very well."

"I was certain I was pregnant the moment I felt you come. And I'm beginning to get over you. You never loved me, did you?"

"I never said so, Karen. Of course I liked you. I still like you."

"Of course." She bit her lip. The Frenchwoman brought Karen a martini and me a filthy look. "What a tepid word, 'like.' You're not capable of love, are you?"

I sipped my whiskey.

"I loved you so much. What I got was the echo bouncing off you. You really aren't capable of loving."

"I don't know, Karen. I suppose I've never tried."

"Oh, Kiki. It's not something you try. It's something you do or you don't."

"My brother was in love once. It didn't work out."

"Oh, God!"

She raised her drink in both hands and drank a third of it, a wave of auburn hair splashing her left wrist. The Frenchwoman sat behind the zinc bar, cooing at a fresh pair of lovers who were drinking Pernod out of season. If the interview ended soon, and I drove at top speed, I might be in New Haven in time to play a few hands.

"Well," she said, "I didn't ask you all the way over here to discuss love. I mean, I'd be glad to, but you don't seem to be interested. I wondered what you might want to do about our baby. I'll make the decision, but I'd like to have your opinion."

"Have it out, Karen."

She made a little smile. "I was sure you'd say that. As a matter of fact it's what I'd decided myself."

"It's the logical thing. Why mess up your life. Look, Karen." I reached for her hand, but she drew it back. "I'm sorry about it. I should have been more careful."

"No, Kiki. That's the one thing you did right. That's the one moment you loved me. At least you wanted me. You couldn't wait."

I nodded. I'd done her enough damage without telling her the truth.

"Well," she said. "Since you were so good at putting it in, maybe you know something about having it out. I mean I can see you've been in this situation before, probably dozens of times, but it's the first time for me, so maybe you could recommend me to your abortionist."

"I don't have one, Karen. But I'll find one. I'll let you know in a couple of days."

"I'm sorry, Kiki. I promised myself not to get hysterical. It's not your fault. You're a wonderful boy, Kiki, though I wish you hadn't gotten so fat. Perfectly wonderful, except you can't love. It's not your fault."

Well, I did get back to New Haven before the poker game finished, and I managed to win a sizable sum from a fellow named Sharp who had graduated from the Medical School the June before and was now interning at Grace-New Haven. I was kind enough to accept his IOU and then buy him coffee and something to eat, not at the Waldorf Cafeteria where all the cardplayers went but at the White Tower, several blocks from the campus. The conversation got round to abortion, a logical enough subject to discuss with a young doctor, Sancudo admiring the courage of young women who risked their lives in such operations, Sharp maintaining that there was no need for risk, that the problems of abortion were legal not medical, that the operation was as safe as plucking a splinter, provided the surgeon was competent and the patient in good health and the circumstances sanitary. Ah, said Sancudo, a competent surgeon; one would certainly want a mature man with decades of experience. Bullshit, rejoined Sharp; he himself had already brought numerous infants into the world and could whisk a fetus out of it as smoothly as any man in America. Very well, conceded Sancudo, you could. You're a graduate of an excellent school and an intern at an excellent hospital. But would a man with such qualifications take the risk? Even with the most robust of patients scarcely six weeks pregnant, even under discreet and sanitary conditions, even if he were in debt and an interested third party were willing to tear up his IOU and pay him, say, three hundred dollars?

He didn't waver, and I liked that. One either goes straight or cuts corners. God doesn't think a bit better of you for wavering, and neither does anyone else. Sharp simply said he would need three fifty, but that he would furnish the instruments, and Grace-New Haven, the drugs.

Linda was going to change apartments and had a nice, clean place picked out. I told her not to move her clothes in for a few days and drove Karen over that weekend. She'd had her hair done, no doubt to make as attractive as possible a corpse, but she neither sniffed nor picked her nail polish on the long, silent drive from Poughkeepsie. Some men like soft, clinging women who have to be protected, and I'll admit their company is pleasant enough while things go well, but I prefer associating with the brave ones who can stand up to crisis. That day Karen treated me like a chauffeur, ignoring my feeble probes at conversation and then making me wait downstairs in the car. I had my purple Tinieblan passport tucked over my heart and gross rolls of hundreds in all my pockets, and while Sharp scraped the makings of my first child I planned the dash to Idlewild. But Karen reappeared in an hour or so, groggy from pentathlon but still self-possessed, and curled up in the far corner of the seat.

"Did it hurt?" I asked when we were a little ways out of the city.

"Oh, no," she answered without opening her eyes. "No more than the first time we made love. It was easy. All so easy."

So when I began my partnership with Pelf and was beginning to think like a top-flight gringo businessman, I recalled how easy it was and considered all the fine young women who were having their lives garbled by footloose sperm cells or unplugged by haphazard quacks with dirt under their fingernails. (Two or three classmates had already asked me, as a man who knew his way around, if I knew how they might help a roommate's girl—always a roommate's girl—out of a little trouble.) I invited Sharp and Pelf to steaks at Mory's and proposed we open a clinic. Both agreed that such an institution might serve a humanitarian need as well as turn a profit, and, effectively, we rented a house on a quiet street above the Engineering School and put in an operating table and a sterilizer and a comfy bed for convalescents and a stock of supplies and began nodding thoughtfully to queries on behalf of roommates' girls and were admitting patients by the start of Christmas vacation.

I took two weeks in Miami, stuffing my paunch with gourmet food and sunning it at a poolside cabana. It had been some time since I'd any real desire for a woman, but the cabana boy, who was about my age but hardly as successful a hustler, kept pestering me, so one afternoon when I was particularly bored I had him send something up to my room. The girl was good-looking and well-trained, but though she worked over me conscientiously for forty minutes, nothing happened. Well, what did it matter when I was partner in three successful businesses and, besides, was picking four or five winners a day at Hialeah?

It was in Miami too that I lost my gift. I had had a warning. At the Law School, just before vacation, there was a draw hand when I saw the top card was the six of hearts, so I broke a pair of aces to pull in the flush. I glanced at my hand only for form's sake and glimpsed a red six and bet the pot and was called by one fish.

"Flush!" said I, spreading my hand, but the red six was the six of diamonds.

But that fish was so used to losing he didn't even look; he threw his hand down and left me the pot. So what did it matter if I'd mistaken a diamond for a heart? I'd won the pot, hadn't I?

Then that day in Miami I was playing gin beside the pool for twenty-five or fifty cents a point, and I dealt the cards and checked my hand and looked over to see what my opponent was holding, and I couldn't see anything. Just the backs of the cards with a blonde and a beach ball and the name of the hotel in gothic script. I rubbed my eyes and looked again. Nothing. I looked at the deck and couldn't see the top card either. Just that stupid slut, when once I'd been able to read each card right to the bottom. Struck stone-blind in the midst of a triple gin game, and I'd thrown my opponent a hand or two lest he think me a cheat. I played on, hoping my gift would come back. It didn't. It never did. Still, I had a great run of luck and won a lot of money. So what did it matter? Whatever I did came out right just because I was doing it.

Back I went to New Haven, fat and torpid, stewed in money and oozing greed at every pore, delighted with myself though I'd lost my gift and needed sixteen hours of sleep a night and puffed when I climbed one flight of stairs and couldn't have put my pecker up for Marilyn Monroe. On the first day of class we held a board meeting, Pelf, Sharp, and I, in a conference room at the Taft Hotel. Pad and pencil at each place, iced water and glasses, sheafs of deposit slips and bundles of receipts. The casino was bringing in three hundred a week above what we paid the seniors and the Jap. The trailers were operating at capacity in Princeton and Williamstown. Nineteen young college ladies had spent abortive vacations on Hillhouse Drive, and the clinic was soundly in the black. Pelf suggested we put two more trailers into New England and send one south to the University of Virginia. Sharp said he'd like to fly out to Ann Arbor and establish a clinic for Big Ten coeds. Both proposals carried, and we adjourned after toasting ourselves in champagne.

Off to collect from Linda, thankful she was on salary now, and I found a squad car parked outside her door. Sheer coincidence of course, but I decided to come back later. In my postbox a card from the Dean, who wished to see me immediately. Back to my room to slip on a more conservative necktie, and Smart told me a Mr. Tallon from the Internal Revenue Service had been by to see me and would return at three. So instead of changing my tie I removed a stone from the fireplace and plucked out my money. Bills in all my pockets and the big ones wadded in my jockey shorts. Passport, health certificate, and down the stairs, into the arms of two large men in wide-brimmed fedoras.

"Where's Sancudo live, Fatso?"

"Sancudo . . ." I mused. "Sancudo . . ."

"Here. He looks like this."

Creased press photo from the New York *Times*. Outstanding wrestler of the 1951 Metropolitan Championships, a trim, hard-muscled bruiser who bore no resemblance to bloat-bellied, triple-chinned me.

"Ah. Sancudo. Top floor, all the way to your left."

They tramped upward without a grunt of thanks for helpful Fatso, who suppressed an urge to foul his bill-stuffed drawers and mushed out across the icy quad. And through the side gate where a constable, blue of lips and overcoat, was guarding my Hippogriff. And past him over a snow mound to hail a cab.

"How would you like to drive me to Hartford?" because they must have the train and bus stations under surveillance. As in the films I watched last year, before I became a businessman. Aided no doubt by finks culled from my poker victims. Or Linda's clients. Or Sharp's patients. "For fifty dollars."

He eyed me through the rear-view mirror; cop eyed me from beside my car. Driver nodded and cab slithered forward across the ice and I fled north, like poor Eliza, away from the baying blood-hounds, leaving my books and my rich suits of tweed and flannel and my faithful sedan and my share of the assets of three flourish-ing enterprises and my partners and my associates and my employ-ees and my customers, by cab to Hartford and by bus to Boston and by train to Montreal. Where I sat in the airport waiting room reading the New York *Daily News*—YALE MEN STUDY SEXOLOGY, ECONOMICS; USE BOTH—until a nonstop flight left for Panama. Where I emptied my underwear into a safe-deposit box and caught a flight for Ciudad Tinieblas. Where the terminal was decked with *Abajo Alejo* signs and I was seized by four guardias and handcuffed and shoved into the same van that had taken me out to the airport four months before and driven to the prison and beaten by the same guards, less inhibited now but on the other hand more arm-weary, and dragged to the same cell, now crammed with friends and relatives, and locked securely in.

27

"The thing would be," says Phil, "to have more cameras."

He sits on Elena's left, Sonny on her right, Carl next to Phil, Marta next to Sonny, and Kiki here at his end, on his rollaway throne.

Steaming delights orbit the centerpiece: rice with shaved coconut, lean Tinieblan beef cut in strips and seethed in onion and tomato, curried shrimps, buttered sprouts, yucca, yam, maize, fried plantain. to be spooned onto English bone plates rimmed with gamboling blue griffins; and attacked with heavy, florentine-chased sterling; and washed down with the contents of cut crystal goblets; in a room louvered from the one o'clock glare and breezed by a sea-breath shown in from the *sala*.

"We have a camera in the car behind the candidate, but we could use one in the crowd and one on the roof of the Excelsior. And one in a helicopter. I wish we could afford a helicopter."

"So you could direct it all from up in the sky," says Marta. "Like God."

"That's how Frankenheimer did *Grand Prix*. And this is a race too, isn't it?"

"We're doing a documentary, not a feature," says Carl.

"And you're not Frankenheimer," adds Sonny.

"I'm better than Frankenheimer," Phil says smiling. "It's just that I'm the only one who knows it. And there's a great feature in this campaign, in your father's career, Mr. Sancudo."

"*The Last Hurrah* with rum instead of whiskey. *All the King's Men* with chile instead of grits." Marta translates.

"No. I wouldn't want to make another soap opera. Or another morality play. What I mean is, I don't believe in lovable old warriors, and Lord Acton's cliché has been dramatized to death already."

"Acton was inaccurate." Sounds like a dog retching. "Power doesn't corrupt. The desire for power corrupts. When the private itch seeks a public fingernail. When you first guess the body politic might be a good lay. You're already soiled. And that goes for every-one. Including honest backwoods lawyers like Willie Stark. Or Abraham Lincoln, for that matter."

"For you too, Kiki?" asks Marta after she translates, and I nod.

"What about the man who wants to do something for his country or for the people?" asks Phil. "Who isn't thinking of him-self?"

"He's grafted his personal urges onto the mass." Wait for Marta to translate, and Phil tries to say something, sitting up like a bright child, mouthbound shrimp detained two inches above his plate. Blue eyes glisten as he tries to shine, but I belch on softly. Still able to command a conversation. Authority intact at all gath-erings, and I won't give it up. "Your man may not be thinking of himself consciously. Your true politician has a hard time seeing where he leaves off and the people begin."

"Well, what about the man who has power forced on him?"

"Usually the result of years of quiet maneuvering. Only looks like he's being forced. But assume it's true. A man who doesn't want power has it forced on him. He'd be a poor leader. It's like making love: if you don't enjoy it, you're not much good at it."

Marta leans to wipe my chin with her napkin and goes on translating. Elena smiles across at me. Phil nods intensely. Carl and Sonny eat.

"And the more you enjoy it, the more you want it. Is that it?" asks Phil.

"Enjoy it, or can't live without it. A politician is a man, driven toward power, by inner whips. There are two kinds. Those who know the whips are there, and those who don't. I'm not sure which king is best. Or worst."

"I should think," says Elena, taking a sip of wine, "that the man who knows himself would be best. Don't you think so, Marta?"

"I agree with Kiki: they're all bastards."

"A politician operates." Sounds like a hog feeding. "By ration-alizing his private powerlust. In terms of the public good. Too much self-knowledge. Can work against him. Compare. A man can seduce a woman. More efficiently. And more pleasantly for them both. When he's not too conscious. Of all the subtle ways. She reminds him of. His mother."

"Do you want some water?" asks Elena.

Nod, and she rings the silver bell for Edilma.

Vein beating at the side of my nose, and I'm too short of breath to say that one might imagine a man conscious of ambition yet unaware of a secret urge to do good, to help his country and the people. And then, when power is almost in his grasp, he begins to realize that power isn't what he cares about. And because of this he commits an error, which costs him . . . In short, that a man may be destroyed by a noble motive. That grace corrupts as well. But there's no need to bring it up, or ask Phil if he thinks it would make a good plot for a movie. And probably I had no secret urge. Probably I'd merely brainwashed myself with my own speeches. And yet, perhaps that's how people grow, some people anyway. By saying things first and then coming to believe them.

Edilma holds the water. Eyes turn away in fake nonchalance. Tall glass with two cubes floating. Short breaths between sips, and lean my head against her old turkey talon. Ache in my neck. So much effort to make my body do a simple thing like chat at the lunch table. Mind as strong as ever. Dynamo in a rotten shack. Bust it apart someday.

". . . atmosphere of an election here," Phil is saying. "That's what I'd like to capture. So much surface brilliance masking darkness beneath. I mean, the purpose of an election is to stylize the struggle for power, to sublimate violence into words and votes. But here it seems to work the other way."

"In the States, too," says Sonny.

"Yes. I suppose so. We need a cinema Shakespeare to make history-movies of the last few administrations. Then maybe we'd understand what happened. But Shakespeare did it too, didn't he? I mean he went to foreign countries like Denmark and Rome to dramatize political themes. So a film about an election here could have relevance in the States."

"We hope you can achieve that in the documentary, Phil," says Elena.

"Of course. But the more I see and hear," he looks to me,

"about Tinieblas, the more I wish I could do a full treatment. And be free to arrange things. The trouble with documentaries is that reality is more or less meaningless. The only way to make sense of it is by inventing. Hell, Shakespeare even rearranged English history."

"Do you see yourself as a modern Shakespeare, Feel?"

"Well, the movies are still waiting for a Shakespeare. Though Bergman has a claim. And the form isn't much older than the English theater was when Shakespeare showed up. I'm not trying to be pretentious, Marta. Why not aim high? And Shakespeare would have gone crazy with a movie camera."

"If he'd been able to afford a helicopter."

"OK. OK. But there's tremendous communication in visual imagery. I mean, you can say a terrific amount about the level and extent of political participation just by showing those kids in T-shirts with the candidates' pictures stenciled on them. And the faces of the people. We saw some wonderful faces this morning."

"Did you do any filming?" asks Elena.

"I got the President," says Carl.

"He almost got you," Sonny says. "We were down on the main drag, Miss Delfi, when about thirty cops on Harleys came by at fifty miles an hour with all their sirens blowing, leading a Caddy limousine, and this jerk jumps out in the middle of the street and starts shooting film. They would have run him over if I hadn't pulled him back on the sidewalk by his belt."

"That's going to be a great sequence," says Carl. "All those cycles filling up the street, and the glare on the cops' sunglasses. We could run it in slow motion and open the picture with it."

"Starring Peter Fonda," says Phil. *Easy Rider South.*"

"You wait'll you see it."

"It did give a terrific impression of power," Phil tells Elena. "Those eyeless faces, and all those machines blaring along to take one little man to an appointment. It communicated power like a tank."

"Kiki walked." She smiles at me over the centerpiece. "Didn't you, Kiki?"

Nod.

"I don't get it."

"On the day he was hurt, when he went to speak in the plaza, he went on foot."

"You. Went. Too."

"Yes. I went too. Through the crowds and the heat. It took us over an hour, Phil, but it was better than an air-conditioned car and a motorcycle escort. You know, if one were to do a feature film here, the best subject would be Kiki. It's better than anything anyone could write."

"Yes!" says Phil, seizing the idea. "We could center on the, uh, day you mentioned and flash back over the whole career."

"Aren't you sick of movies with flashbacks?"

"You're right, Marta. Better to sketch in the past with dialogue. We could use a foreign reporter covering the campaign."

"Or a director making a film of it. An intense young gringo with a bushy beard who doesn't know anything about politics here and has to have it all explained to him. And the movie would be about the impact of the campaign on him."

"No, Marta. It has tremendous drama. A young candidate in a violent country. Simultaneous working out of individual and collective destines. And structured like a bullfight with everything rushing toward the moment of truth in the afternoon." He looks at me and returns from his movie world. "Excuse me for discussing it, uh, you in those terms, but . . ."

"An artist always considers experience as potential art. That's it, isn't it, Feel? Do you have the talent to go with that attitude?"

"It might be all right as art. As personal experience it could use touching up." Marta translates.

"What would you change, Kiki?" asks Elena.

Change Ñato. Make him a better shot. A good way on a good day.

"Would you decide not to run?" she goes on. "Or change what you said?"

"I'd hire a stand-in. Every candidate should have one."

"Can we talk about something else?" says Marta when she's finished translating.

"What's the program for this afternoon?"

"The rally's at six. Which means somewhat later."

"You have siestas here, don't you?" asks Sonny.

"I'm going to take a walk around," says Phil. "Want to come, Carl?"

"Is that an order?"

"We slept late. The way to do this documentary, Mr. Sancudo, is to shoot plenty of film and compose afterwards. We don't know how the campaign will turn out or what might occur during it or what might turn out to be good background footage. In a city like this we might find good stuff anywhere."

"That's right, Feel. Three blocks from here is the street where they blew up León Fuertes, which is less than half a mile from the square where they shot Kiki. And there's the tree where they hanged General Luna and the palace where Alejo shot Colonel Azote. In the States you'd have to fly thousands of miles between locations like that, but we have them concentrated within walking distance of the good hotels."

"I. Was. Going. To. Make. Marta. Director. Of. Tourism."

Which gets a laugh, and Elena starts the bowls revolving again.

"Yes," muses Phil, helping himself to more meat. "It's better than a film script. You were an Olympic winner, weren't you?"

Nod.

"It was almost a disaster, Phil," says Elena. "Kiki was the only Tinieblan entered in the Games, and the Finns hadn't bothered to get a Tinieblan flag. When he made the finals, they panicked; there were no Tinieblan flags in Helsinki. Finally the Americans stepped in and flew a flag in from Paris in time for the ceremony. Which was nice of them, since he'd beaten the American wrestler, but not so nice, because the Russians were bringing a flag from Leningrad by rail."

"Was that the flag—I mean the one we flew in from Paris—was that the flag you paraded through the Reservation?"

Shake my head. "Too good. You can do that in your movie."

"There never was a president anywhere who was an Olympic medalist."

"The King of Greece won a medal sailing," says Carl.

"It's not the same," argues Phil. "Sailing's a different kind of sport. Wrestling's one of the original Olympic sports. 'A victor in the Games.'"

He nods thoughtfully, thinking of ironies, restructuring his masterpiece to give the star some wheelchair scenes. Happy problem of selecting from a superfluity of juicy incident, whereas I must be thrifty, composing my today and my tomorrow on a low budget. No wide-screen melodrama, no technicolor swashbuckling, no hairbreadth scapes, unless from a convulsion, and there's small romance in that. No high pageant of state affairs, no filter-lensed tableaux of lyric love, no battles, no revolutions, no elegant soirées from which the principals withdraw to intrigue in an alcove. No music, except perhaps a fugue in minor key, unceasing variations on a somber theme. No gaudy lights, no brilliant costumes, no rare, exotic sets. Only a drab revenge play cast on the torn screen of my mind. But nicely planned for impact and economy. And adequate to keep me occupied. For I've become an artist too, Phil, by circumstance if not by inclination, and I trust I'll be able to communicate to my small public. I'm sure he'll get my message.

Or are you gauging me as a rival, Phil, computing what chance you'd have with Marta if I were whole? And not linking the result? Poor Phil, you've got it wrong. I'm more competition now than in my prime. She wouldn't have felt guilty if you'd come after her then, and I was always able to find room for new girls and say goodbye to the ones who left. I can hear you reassuring yourself: "I've got my gift, my insight, to match his life of action." Take all the comfort in it that you want; I won't deflate you by mentioning the insights shown to me by Professors Pain and Paralysis. Take her and get out. Make your documentary and take Marta, and Elena too, and get out, and let me make my own movie. Let me make my little horror film for Ñato.

"Well," says Carl, "if we're going to go . . ."

"Never mind," says Phil. "I'll go alone. I just want to get the feel of the city. I'll get more out of it alone."

That's right, Phil, go alone. Walk along the sea wall toward the docks. Feel the heat. Watch the people. Stop a pushcart man and eat shaved ice with fruit syrup poured over it, or get a beer at some cantina. Listen to the music from radios turned up too loud in tenement rooms hung above garbaged alleys. And political announcements you won't understand screamed by earnest fools. Smell the dirt and smeared baby sweat on chocolate-colored urchins. Aim your insight through unpainted walls at undershirted men on rumpled cots and women with cotton bathrobes clasped to flaccid breasts. Buy lottery, like everybody else, out of the trays of limbless cripples and hollow-eyed black crones—*You dreamed of Satan? play number fifteen*—and guard the tickets like a pardon that may he signed on Sunday. Walk, walk along the sidestreets with your shoulder brushed against the wall to snatch a little shade. Lounge in a doorway and watch the narrow sidewalks fill up with people hurrying back to work. Sit in the little park behind the Alcaldía and have your shoes shined, a boy to each shoe, while bent old men in torn white suits play checkers, chattering like monkeys. Breathe our air. Soak in the city through your pores, and when it's dark go marinate yourself in the cheap perfume of cantina barmaids and the body smells of moon-hipped negresses who sell themselves for fifty cents against the limestone wall of the cemetery and in the breath of twelve-year-old whores waiting in taxi cabs along Bolivar Avenue. And think yourself the brother of such a girl, or, if that's too hard, a merchant sailor who's missed his ship and had his papers stolen. Wander the streets, and in the hour before dawn you may begin to taste the killer's terror and the murdered man's despair.

"Who'll have coffee?" asks Elena, which is my signal, for there's no reason why my guests should have to watch me being carried upstairs.

"Now?" asks Marta. I nod, and she goes to get Jaime. He backs me out of the dining room, and the conversation bubbles in around my empty place.

"How is it, Kiki?" he asks over my shoulder.

"Tired, brother. Lift me easy."

"Sure, Kiki."

He parks the chair beside the stairs and comes around to get me. Flat-faced grin. Not embarrassment, just happy to be able to do something for me. Right arm thrust under my thighs, left clasping my back, he bends and heaves me up, pushes the chair out of his way with his foot. Jounces me against his chest and plods upward. Reliable as a Sherpa for these climbs, and if I asked he'd carry me up Everest. Gentle too, considering my dead weight. I can't put an arm around his neck to take the pressure off his forearms. Want him just as tender with Ñato when he carries him inside. Seventeen steps, and I rise like a soul in Purgatory.

Cool and dark in my room, curtains drawn and air turned on by Neira while I ate. Lays me softly on my bed, feet toward the pillow, and takes off my shoes and socks, pulls off my trousers and shorts. On to the bathroom. Now that I have some control over my sphincters there is pleasure in relaxing them. More mental than physical, but I list it along with coffee in the morning and the alcohol rub I let Marta perform on some evenings. Jaime removes my shirt while I sit, then wings me, naked, back to bed and tucks me in.

"Anything more, Kiki?"

"No, brother. Yes. Take a drive by Ñato's. Park in front. Let him see the car. But if there's a guardia, just drive by."

"To help him enjoy his siesta?"

"That's right. So he'll enjoy it as much as I do mine."

"How is he going to die, Kiki? Like Garza or like Memo?"

"I'm thinking about it, Jaime. I'll tell you."

He nods, and turns, and, as he goes out, Elena comes in.

And locks the door, and opens her silk dress and lets it fall around her feet, and kicks it away and with it her soft suede shoes, and unhooks her brassiere and drops it forward, and brushes down her half slip and panties, and, pale and golden, slips into bed beside me.

"Do you mind, Kiki?"

"No. It's lovely. I just wish I could pull my weight. If it were you who was paralyzed, there'd be less of a problem."

Soft hand on my chest. "I wanted to be with you." Soft kiss against my scarred neck.

"Don't you find it a little morbid? Like nuzzling a corpse?"

"No, Kiki. Don't think like that. Or make me leave."

"I won't. I'm getting soft. The times I wouldn't let you. Be with me like this. It was because I like to pull my own weight. But I'm getting soft. And you just want to show me some affection. It isn't pity or perversion. You still care for me. And want to show affection."

"That's right." And she kisses my mouth, so sweet it aches. Sea spray trickling my cheek, and she kisses it away. "Gia, caro."

"Sorry. See why I shouldn't let you? See how it gets me?" Brushes my eyes with her lips. "It isn't weakness, Kiki."

"No. I guess not. But I have to keep control."

"Give in, Kiki. Give in." And she holds me to her lovely breasts.

Where it would be nice to stay forever, sniffling quietly. While she licks my scars with kind fingers. And thinks what? God knows. That I'm the child we waited too long to have? Or a warrior to give repose? Who is she now? No matter, as vague fingers creep along my flank to play among my dead flowers. Dead, dead, and I mourn them sobbing.

Which brings a kind of peace, after all, once it passes. Ride with the current for a while at last and let it draw me down to a dark grotto where there are no monsters. Soft and warm here. Close and protective. Salt-moist and safe.

And, holding me, she carries my hand to her like a child. Not lustful, just to have me there. And let me taste the warm yolk of life again. Which can't be synthesized or faked.

"It's not so bad, Elena."

'No, Kiki."

"I've learned some things."

"Yes, Kiki."

"And there are still good things, aren't there?"

"Yes, Kiki. Yes."

Soft and warm here. Safe and sea-moist. Melting into sleep.

28

Mito and I walk hand in hand across the bridge, the silver-painted, steel-girdered, one-lane bridge that reaches forty yards over the river at La Yegua. Mito is still only seven, still frail with

all his ribs showing and his shoulder blades pushing out like wings,
yet I am my full age, thirty-nine, and no longer paralyzed. No time
to puzzle this through, for the asphalt is hot under our bare feet,
and we begin to trot, Mito holding my two little fingers, toward the
far end of the bridge, where a cloud of purple and yellow butterflies
floats through the wild acacias. He's going to swim the river today
without a life preserver, and I'll scull backward in front of him to
keep his fear down. We'll start under the bridge and let the current
help us toward the shallows below the house, because it's some-
thing I promised him long ago when he was also seven but I not yet
thirty. And broke the promise to make some trip or slay in the cap-
ital with some girl, and has choked voice told me on the telephone
he wanted to make the swim with me, not Jaime. But all that's
wiped away now, and he's waited for me.

"And after you swim the river," I tell him, "we'll take Mamá
and Olguita to the fair in Angostura."

"Can I ride in front, Papi?"

"Of course. Men in front, women in back."

And he looks up at me with Olga's timid smile.

Dry wind rolling off the pastures to flick our suits. A hundred
yards upstream to our right, two peons on horseback are fording
a dozen dusty cows, and the beasts stand thigh-deep, lapping the
cool water. Be in it soon, Mito and I, yet the far end of the bridge
recedes before us.

And now we are no longer on the bridge above the river but in
the bottom of a jungled trail, and the butterflies are no longer but-
terflies but brown mosquitoes, and not ahead, all around us, and
we are no longer running because the ground sucks at our feet, and
no wind blows, and it is all sticky heat and the sweet-foul smell of
decay, and we are nowhere near La Yegua but on Fangosa Island.

Two or three days after I was put back in prison, three or four
days after Alejo fell from power, a leash of guards, led by Lieutenant
Narses Puñete, the assistant warden, and accompanied by the newly
liberated Dutch zionist, sniffed through our cell for Doktor Henker
and, finally, made us file out into the corridor one by one, even
Egon, whom Gunther had to lift down from his slab, while they

checked our faces against a photo marked "BEWEISMITTEL #4140, NÜRNBURG," and, still not finding him, searched all the other cells and even the coffins. Then the arresting officer was summoned from Angostura, and when he maintained that Doktor Henker had not been in the car with Alejo, that there had been Gunther and Egon in front, Alejo and Furetto in back, and with them only a large black poodle with yellow eyes who had bounded across Alejo's lap and out the car window, Colonel Aiax Tolete issued orders that all *alejistas* would remain confined until after the elections.

These were being organized under the stewardship of Belisario Oruga, whom León Fuertes, who was sensitive to constitutional niceties, had urged to return to Tinieblas and assume the presidential sash. Whether much urging was actually necessary is doubtful. Oruga was a Tinieblan after all, and your legitimate Tinieblan seeks the Presidential Palace as water does its own level. More, this charter member of Acción Dinámica who had had a brother wounded in the coup of November, 1930, this Captain General of the Vanguardia Tinieblina and founder of the Tinieblista Party, was finally disenchanted with Alejo.

"He played me for a sucker," Oruga remarked to Uncle Erasmo. "And to think I loaned him Babieca, whom no man but me had ever rode, for his triumphant entry into the city."

The nineteen opposition parties sprang up fully armed from the earth where Alejo had planted them, and in the space of two weeks León and Carlitos Gavilán organized a new one, the Progresista, and announced their candidacies for deputy and declared their support for the Liberal Party's nominee, Pacífico Pastor Alemán. Only the Tinieblista Party, most of whose leaders were in jail, remained inactive, while all candidates campaigned on the platform of democracy for Tinieblas and a complete political gelding for Alejandro Sancudo. León and Carlitos proposed he be tried for *lèse-constitutionalité;* Father Benigno Pan de Dulce, running for councilman on the Conservative ticket, favored prosecution under a seventeenth-century witchcraft statute devised by the Holy Inquisition; all agreed he should be firmly chastised.

Colonel Tolete's decision to detain all *alejistas* no doubt contributed to the tranquility of the elections, but it posed certain logistical problems which had clearly never occurred to the architect of La Bondadosa Prison. Besides Alejo's family, close advisers, and conspicuous sycophants, Tolete had jailed all the important members of the Tinieblista Party, including twenty-seven deputies and three hundred forty-two councilmen, ward leaders, and bosses, all the delegates to the Tinieblist People's Congress, the members of the Commissions on Social and Political Abuses, persons remarked cheering with particular enthusiasm at the gymnasium trial, most of the students involved in the Miramar demonstration, and the entire complement of the Policia Secreta, so that every cell, except the one where Alejo languished incommunicado, was filled to bursting and prisoners were asking to be put in the coffins to get some elbow room. Thus as election day was still months away it was decided to send the excess prisoners to the penal colony on Fangosa Island. The leading agitators of the Congress, the most refractory of the students, and the toughest of Gonzalo Garbanzo's secret policemen were culled from their cells for shipment.

In normal times only the most demonic criminals were sent to Fangosa, for the climate of the place was such that few inmates ever remained a burden to the state for long. In fact judge Arquimedes Malsano—known for his witty remarks when passing sentence—was wont to amuse convicted murderers with the smiled whisper, "I'm giving you the shortest sentence in Tinieblan law: life on Fangosa," and it was a rare fellow indeed who was not free of all earthly durance within a year or two. But when Puñete's guards came for Gunther and Egon, I asked to be taken too.

"You're crazy, Kiki!" said Puñete when they brought me to his office. He'd been a class ahead of me at the Politécnico and a fellow officer of Young Patriots. "If the guards hit you on the head the night you were brought in, I'll have them restricted. You don't want to go to Fangosa."

"Yes, I do. I have to get back in shape, and there's no room in here to work out."

"Look, Kiki. We know you didn't get along with your father. We just have to keep you inside for form. In a day or two, when we've shipped these pigs out, I'll speak to the colonel and get you a soft spot."

"That's the trouble. Things have been too soft. If you don't want to send me now, how would you feel if I knocked out a couple of your front teeth?"

So he shrugged and had me handcuffed to one of the students and shoved onto a truck.

We went in convoy, five U.S. Army surplus six-by-six trucks, forty prisoners to a truck, through Tinieblas and Salinas and Tuquetá Provinces to the port of Bastidas, where we were loaded on an LST which the U.S. Navy had given to the Guardia during Lucho Gusano's Administration, and then southeast along the coast, which we couldn't see since it was after dark when we boarded. But in the morning there was the low green hedge of jungle stretched away to our right and the sun, glazed by sickly clouds, and the sea, oily and metallic, smoothing the wake a hundred feet astern, so that without the throbbing of the engines we might have thought the ship bolted to the bottom. In mid-afternoon a green blot appeared on the horizon ahead of us. It grew prodigiously, and in twenty minutes we could make out mangrove thickets growing down to the water's edge and a flotilla of sharks swimming in single file clockwise around the island a few hundred yards offshore. We fell in with them and chugged around toward the south end of the island. The bulbous north end was umbrellaed in gigantic clouds, which, every five minutes or so, let down tons of rain like a celestial interrogator training a high-pressure hose on an already unconscious victim. Then the sun would burn through, raising great wraiths of steam from the expiring jungle. It was like being translated back into a carboniferous age, when the planet was swathed in plant life and not yet so tame as to permit the habitation of men and beasts.

On the south end of the island was a high bluff graced with palms and laved by an Atlantic breeze that cooled the air and swept the midges and mosquitoes toward the invisible coast. Here no rain fell, except perhaps a fragrant shower at dawn, and here the guards lived, and the homosexuals, for anyone who would renounce his manhood was pardoned from the dank swamp to the north and given light work, tending the maize and yucca which, along with fish, made up the diet of the colony. Here also, atop a towering cliff, was the house of the governor, who had been appointed by

Ramiro Aguado in 1912 and reappointed ever since and who now, four decades later, was polishing the ninth volume of his great treatise on *Sexual Inversion: Key to the Purification of the Criminal Soul.* But we didn't climb the bluff. We waited on the sand where the LST dropped her ramp until our heads were counted and our names taken and our irons removed. Then they marched us along a narrowing path north into the swampland.

As we moved toward the interior of the island, a fetid breath rose about us, magnifying the odor of our sweating bodies and the pervasive ambiance of decay. Soon we were among huge twisted trees, whose branches, twined with vines and brambles, reached out to drop new sets of roots into the quivering earth and whose top leaves filtered the light, admitting hot rain and the softer fall of bloated leeches. No birdsong here, nor any sound save the panting of our lungs and the greasy smack of mud sucking at our footwear. After we had marched about nine miles, we came upon a clearing, all stinking mud and pools of stagnant water, with a double circle of huts squatting around a kitchen tent where a congregation of ulcered skeletons were queuing up to eat. Here we got maize mush in wooden bowls and one or two tiny pieces of fish, and here we slept on mud-soaked straw to the D-minor hum of mosquitoes, and at dawn we went to work on the road.

The road ran in a circle, five miles in radius, around the camp. We had crossed it along our march, without noticing anything, however, for that section of it was badly overgrown. It overgrew, in fact, much faster than it was built, though, as it led nowhere and there were no vehicles to drive on it, this was hardly a disadvantage. A practiced eye might note where secondary growth revealed the route along which long-dead prisoners had hacked and heaved, but as it took a year for the work gangs, laboring only with machetes, to make one revolution, there was never any chance of its being finished. A number of paint-blazed trails led to it from the camp like spokes of an immense wheel, and each morning we were marched out along one of these to sweat all day, hewing away trees and roots, dragging off fallen logs, feeling, if not actually seeing the jungle seep in behind us to obliterate the progress we had made the day before.

No effort was made to keep us in the camp at night. At sundown the guards departed for their barracks and their handmaidens, and anyone who cared to might wander off into the jungle. The man not present for work simply did not eat. There were those—new arrivals—who talked of making rafts and of escape, while old hands nodded with wan smiles. Egon and Gunther thought of this at once, and every night for weeks they slunk away to a part of the shore where they were building a raft of branches lashed together with vines. But when they launched it, it sank like stone, as did the second craft they made, and a third, until one evening they complained of their bad luck, and a wasted parricide, then on the fourth and last year of his life sentence, remarked with a gap-toothed grin, that, though he'd hunted for months, he'd never found a stick of wood from that island which would float. At night the long-term convicts, some no older than myself, though they looked already aged, told us how so-and-so had gone mad and tried to swim for mainland, or how someone else had turned upon a fellow prisoner, or a guard, and killed him with his machete, to be rifle-butted to death on the spot and buried in the mud, and such stories seemed at first fantastical, for the men around me looked so beaten down under the endless rain in that foul heat that they seemed incapable of that much defiance. Yet each man there was holding on to his integrity with an iron grip, for he had but to wink to be lifted from that hell to what appeared at times a kind of paradise.

On one Saturday each month work ceased at noon, and we were marched back to camp and made to tidy up as best we could, and then, an hour or two before dusk, marched south out of the swamp. Halfway up the bluff there was a terrace with a large pavilion where we were allowed to sit and were given a kind of liquor made from coconut milk. And in the fresh glow of early evening the homosexuals came down to entertain us, dressed like women and perfumed and painted. A thin, mocha-skinned negro in an evening gown sang love songs to us, accompanying himself on a guitar, and in between his songs a phonograph played the old boleros, and soft, feline inverts led men out to dance or nestled on their laps to lick their bearded checks. "Why go back to the swamp," they asked us softly, "when you can stay here with us? Why choose death over love?" And each month there were men who wandered out into the darkness with these synthetic women, and these men were never with us on our long night march back to camp, but the next month would be found, barely recognizable, among the queers. And all were so gentle and submissive that it was hard to believe that they had once been men, violent men who had murdered and robbed and maimed.

Yet there were many who remained in the swamp, who, in effect, chose death, for most men weakened quickly and took fever, and those unable to work received no food. It was impossible to predict who would resist. On my first visit to the pavilion I was shown a famous bandit, author of many cold-blooded murders, who had been converted after only two weeks on Fangosa, while the senior member of our road gang, who had served nine years when I arrived, was a printer's helper who had killed his young wife, more or less accidentally in a fit of rage, and was really not a criminal at all. Our group was exceptional in that we were political prisoners who could expect to be released in a few months, yet nearly a quarter of our number converted. We would be sitting at the pavilion, listening to the music, and some fellow would whisper, "I'm going to get a little piece of that bugger over there, just to see if my tool still works," and he would slink off with his partner, not to be seen for another month, when we would find him mincing about the pavilion in a kimono or sarong. Those who used the homosexuals invariable joined them. Some said that they knew pleasures it was impossible to abandon once one had tasted them; and others, when the prospective convert was drained, guards would rape the self-respect out of him; and others, that the true seduction was a day or two off from road work in the swamp, which vacation would be extended subtly until the fellow was ready to do anything rather than return. And, of course, everyone knew there was no need to suffer and die in that swamp, that all one had to do was change sex to gain a long life of comparative luxury, so that a fair portion of the converts were not seduced at all but came stumbling out of their huts into the morning rain to beg the guards to take them up the hill.

Yet many stayed, sullen or blaspheming, bitten by insects, made crazy by the heat, while their flesh turned yellow-green with rot and their bodies shook with fever and the road inched endlessly into the jungle, drawing its tail up after it like a snake; and I, of course, stayed with them. But of all those on the island only I, besides the governor, was there of my own will; he in service to the science of criminology and his own private madness, I in search of a physical challenge to return me to myself, and while others dropped fainting in the mud or simply wasted like lumps of lard melting in a skillet, I thrived. No insects bit me. No leeches battened between my toes. They smelled bad blood before they tasted it and went to feed on riper victims. The fat of a too easy life dropped off me in great gouts; my arms grew hard again swinging a machete and hauling logs. And while others twitched in agued nightmare on their damp straw, I slept soundly and woke fresh to each dawn.

The great complaint, that our work was pointless, that the jungle lapped up our road faster than we built it, that there was no use for the road anyway, that it led nowhere, did not affect me. I might have been happier in some northern gym with a set of barbells and a school of clever wrestling sparrers, but the road was good enough, it served. I might have learned then that no road leads anywhere, that nothing is ever accomplished, that disorder always grows faster than we can beat it back, that no project is valuable except for the exercise we get working at it. Fangosa might have taught me that before Ñato did. Some men learned and despaired; others learned and kept on working. But I still wasn't ready to learn. I cast my mind ahead to the Olympics, not to the triple pillar where ribboned victors drink the crowd's applause, but to the feel of some proud champion weakening in my grasp. I sucked strength from the swamp and grew lean and dangerous. And harvested pride from sterile marshes. And nursed a stern contempt for the guards, for the inverts on the hill, for prisoners who shirked or whimpered or anguished for dead friends or distant families, for those who fell behind on march or fainted in the mangroves, even for those who died stoically (since death announced weakness), and, specially, for everyone who sheltered on the terra firma of an easy life, avoiding hardship, fleeing pain and risk, crouching their shriveled souls into a place of safety. And when I left Fangosa, I took that contempt with me. I took it out of the swamp, marching with Gunther and Egon at the very tail of the column, for it turned our stomachs to see the feeble push and shove that others made to get a place in front; and onto the LST (returning loaded for the first time, though not full, for men had died and the converts had chosen to stay in their earthly paradise); and to the capital, and to Panama, where I emptied my safe deposit box, and on to Helsinki, and kept it fifteen years, till the people of Tinieblas leached it from me.

Fangosa Island, with Mito. We march through the jungle, two figures in an endless file of stumbling prisoners dissolving before and behind us in the steamy gloom of the trail.

"Is it much farther, Papi?" Mito looks up at me with his timid, trusting smile, but I cannot answer, for my mouth is full of dead moths.

Now we sit on the sandy mud, and a guard, a chocolate-skinned cholo, shirtless with a shiny, hairless chest, comes to take Mito up the hill.

"I don't want to go, Papi!"

I look up at the guard with the cold stare I've seen men wilt at, but he isn't afraid of me. He drags Mito to his feet. I try to rise, but I am paralyzed. Mito whimpers and presses his face against the guard's bare chest.

I say, "I'm sorry, Mito," but it comes out pig grunts, and Mito goes off holding the guard's hand.

I lie alone and naked, face-down in that filthy swamp, while fat brown crabs crawl over me. But now I can raise my head, and a tunnel opens before me through the jungle, a dark tunnel under arched trees draped with vines and moist hangings, and at the end of it bright sky, and the foaming, pounding sea, and my eyes are full of tears of deliverance, and I cry, "Mito! Mito! My journey to the sea!"

29

I am playing tennis on the grass court within the compound of the British Embassy residence. A white-jacketed butler comes to the base line with a pasteboard invitation on a silver tray. But not an invitation, though it is elegantly engraved and has my name scripted on it in violet ink:

DR. MALCOLM LOVEJOY, M.D., F.R.C.S.

HAS THE HONOR TO CERTIFY THAT

MR. *César E. Sancudo M.*

HAS BEEN COMPLETELY AND PERMANENTLY CURED

OF GONOCOCCAL INFECTION

I take the card, and it splits in two layers. On the second, a cramped scrawl warns that the bearer is suffering from acute, infectious, incurable tertiary syphilis.

"Why bring me this?" I ask the butler. "I had this dream years ago.

"Pardon me, sir. I just hand them around, sir."

"Well, who sent it?"

"Mr. Espino, sir. He said it's for your birthday."

My twenty-second birthday, the day I met faithful Ñato.

I had been tumbling around Europe for three months with a gymnast from the French team, a fine, healthy girl whom I took like a nerve tonic on nights before important matches at Helsinki. She had the idea of us putting together a nightclub act, had cluttered up her mind with full-color posters of the two of us, me in dancer's tights and my Olympic gold medal, she with her sweetmeats bulging from a tricolor bikini. I recall a practice session at Cannes, she balanced on one hand on my head while I strolled the sand reading a newspaper. Admiring gapes from the beachmasters, but I couldn't get interested in it, and all we did besides exercise was make contortive love in hotel rooms. Every two weeks or so I'd grow bored and tell her to meet me the following Thursday in the station at Brussels or at such-and-such hotel (I'd get a name from *Guide Michelin*) in Lausanne. She was always waiting. Like most Frenchwomen she took an intense, simian joy in grooming black-heads from my temples, and she chattered—fine for tuning my French but on the whole annoying—and though reasonably tough would sniffle when I translated her Neruda's lines:

> I like you when you're silent
> because it's as if you weren't here.

At length I got fed up with myself for being with her, told her I'd meet her in Vienna, and went instead to Athens. I sometimes imagine her still lingering in the *Bahnhof* (completely reconstructed save for the bench she sits on), keeping a shrewd gallic eye on her disintegrating suitcase, while two decades paunch beneath her chin and she waits for a long-extinct Kiki to come handspringing across the marble into her arms.

So on the eve of my birthday I took my boredom on the streetcar to Piraeus and joined the human sewage that sloshes through port cities and, like a style of interior decoration, gives all dockside bars the same look: the dipsomaniacal Swedish first officer who peers blue-eyed into a tumbler of gin; the hairy-armed Bremen oiler with brace of whores fumbling at the blutworst in his trousers; the gringo white-hat with his billfold tucked in the waistband of his arrogantly tight pants. I drank from bar to bar among such types and sometime after midnight got to a place called the John Bull and entered the men's room.

The first thing I saw was a gringo sailor standing by the urinal —a stretch of tiled wall with a drain and a pipe which dripped a little water—with his heel on a purple Tinieblan passport. At the far end two other sailors, big burly louts, one with red hair clipped *en brosse,* the other with a high, sweeping wave built up over his forehead, had hammerlocks on a flat-nosed fellow in a sharkskin suit. The nose bled into the toilet bowl, toward which the sailors were bending Sharkskin's head. They weren't pushing hard, more enjoying Sharkskin's anticipation, for the bowl brimmed with the kind of droppings one could expect from the clientele of a busy if not fastidious bar in a country where the staples are greasy lamb and ripe olives.

"Take it easy," Sharkskin was saying. "You're hurting me. Don't put my face in there, you shitty gringos. I'll kill you all! Give me a chance. We'll go to the bank in the morning." On he went, whining, cursing, threatening, pleading, and promising, while the red-haired sailor cooed, "In you go," and the others giggled.

That's how I first saw Ñato, aimed head first for the toilet in a bar in Piraeus, Greece.

"Go piss outside," the small gringo told me. "This place is *occupato.*"

I hesitated for a moment, making what turned out to be a big decision. I didn't mind if Sharkskin got his face dunked in the crapper; no doubt he thoroughly deserved it. I felt no sentimental yearnings over our common nationality, nor any animosity against the gringos. It was none of my concern. On the other hand I was bored, and the odds made the situation potentially exciting. I'd lost my gift for second sight and couldn't put the deal correctly: that I'd be buying some years of laughs and a certain comradeship at the cost of pain and paralysis. So I chose excitement.

Captain B. H. Liddell Hart advises that, when campaigning against a coalition, one should knock out the weakest ally first. I rabbit-punched the little gringo into the urinal.

"What's going on!" yelled Wavy Hair, letting go of Ñato.

I stepped forward and kicked him with my right foot in the side of the knee. His leg crumpled and he went to the floor on one elbow. I stepped back and leaned some of my weight on the sink and kicked him with my left foot in the side of the head. Red Hair threw Ñato at me and came across Wavy Hair's body and hit me on the check with a left. He weighed fifty pounds more than I did, and if he hadn't been off balance he'd have knocked me out. I stumbled to the wall, and Ñato tried to make it out the door, but Red Hair grabbed his coattail and slung him back toward the toilet. That gave me a chance to chop his neck, but I was dizzy and it didn't hurt him much. So he began to stalk me like Joe Louis, plod, plod, with his left hand out, watching my eyes, while I stepped around, wiggling fingers in his face, waiting for my head to clear and him to commit himself, but there wasn't much room in there and I was worried he might corner me.

Was Ñato any help? Not him. First I saw him cowering in a corner, and then, when I came around again, he was trying to get through the vent over the toilet, and then, as I tried to get past the sink without tripping over Wavy Hair, he came scuttling on all fours along the wall toward the door. Red Hair reached to stomp his ankle and turned too far. Stab to the throat, chop under the nose, and another between the eyes. He went down and out.

The small gringo began elbowing up from the urinal, but I waved him back with a finger. The two big ones slept side by side near the sink. I gazed at them with the kind of warmth which, ten years later, would come to me when I'd peek in at Mito and Olguita after a midnight prowl, smiled into the mirror at the fine purple star Red Hair's ring had chiseled on my cheekbone, plucked Ñato's passport from the tiles, and skipped out the door.

I caught up to Ñato as he limped around the corner, holding a handkerchief to his snout. Didn't he want to say thanks?

"Sure, sure. Thanks a lot. But I'm in a hurry."

Didn't he have time to buy me a drink?

"Sure, sure. But not in there."

Didn't he want to go back for his passport?

He searched himself frantically. It was all right. I had his passport.

He followed me across the street into another bar. He sat down, blew his nose carefully, checked the handkerchief for fresh blood, then gave me a grin so insincere it had a kind of reverse-twist honesty.

"Look, man, I'd like to buy you a drink, but I have no money."

That was all right. I would buy. I ordered us rum and cokes.

"You really know how to fight!"

I nodded.

"It's necessary in a stinking place like this."

Nod.

"The people here aren't human."

I shook my head.

He launched into a long complaint on the inhumanity of gringo

sailors, how he'd done those three a favor, selling a few cases of ciga-
rettes for them without making one drachma for himself, and how
they'd accused him of cheating them and bloodied his nose and would
certainly have put his face in the toilet if it hadn't been for me. I let him
go on, listening without word or movement, wondering if he'd have
an explanation for not helping out in the fight, thinking how much his
facial muscles must hurt from so much grinning. Finally his grin faded.

"What do you want?"

"Nothing."

"Nothing?"

"Nothing."

He finished his drink and set the glass on the table. I hadn't
touched mine.

"Look, I don't have any money. You won't get anything out
of it."

"That's all right."

"Then why?"

"Why what?"

"Why'd you help me out? Why'd you fight those three sailors?"

"I felt like it."

"That's all?"

I nodded.

He fidgeted on his chair. He looked around the barroom. He
kept glancing at the door. He wanted his passport, but he didn't
dare ask for it.

"Don't you want your drink?"

"You have it." I pushed it over.

"All right! All right!" He grabbed it and drank half.

Suddenly I felt sorry for him and took out his passport and my
own and slapped them against my palm. "I'm Tinieblan too."

"Ah, ho! That's it! You're Tinieblan too!"

I nodded.

"That's it! That's it!"

I opened his passport. "'Jesús Maria Espino Amaro.'"

"They call me Ñato."

I flipped him mine. He opened and read: "'César Enrique Sancudo Maldonado.'"

"They call me Kiki."

"Ah, ho! Alejo's son! No wonder! No wonder the way you kicked that gringo! And we have the same birthday, not just the day but the year too."

I looked down and saw it was true and that we had the same height and weight, the same color eyes and hair.

"Ah, ho! And me without money to buy you a present. You gave me one. You saved my neck, and I can't buy you a present. I can't even buy you a drink." He grimaced in despair and finished mine. "But wait, brother. You like girls, don't you? How could Alejo's son not like girls? I'm going to get you a girl like you never had before. Only fifteen, and does things you wouldn't believe. Even speaks Spanish, so you won't feel lonely."

"How much?"

"How much? Why ask how much? She's a present! I'm giving her to you, brother. You can stay all night, all week if you like. You're going to think you're in heaven. Look, brother, you can't say no. Come on."

I didn't think she'd justify the way he smacked his lips and flicked his fingers, but it would have been too cruel to say no. And what else did I have to do at three in the morning in Piraeus, now that I'd rounded the bars and had a good fight and toyed all I cared to with a cowardly buffoon who shared my birthday? I let him lead me through a maze of alleys, while he whined about the cold and praised my birthday present, to a tenement built in the days of Pericles, and up four flights to a door, which, after much pounding, opened just wide enough for me to see two big eyes blinking at the level of my sternum.

"I bring you my brother," Ñato said signorially. "Treat him well." Then he slapped me affectionately on the neck. "All week, if you like," he said. Then he scampered down the stairs.

Ñato's present came up to my shoulder and was so thin she looked more like twelve than fifteen. She tried to smile as I entered, but her huge eyes had had little practice at it. Her room was like a painter's studio: the steep roof formed one wall and was gashed by a skylight whose several missing panes let in the salt wind from the harbor. A candle flickering in a niche above the bed writhed our shades onto the empty hallway.

The girl closed the door behind me and pulled her robe about her. "Will your worship take drink?"

"Who taught you Spanish?" I asked, thinking it must have been some mad Cervantophile like Lazarillo Agudo.

"My parents. Will your worship take drink?"

I shook my head. I must have frowned as well.

"Does your worship find me displeasing?"

What with the cold, and her so frail, and that crazy language, I wasn't much for love, but then I thought: The son of a bitch was right, I haven't had one like this before, and I smiled and drew her toward the bed.

"Wait. Let me take your worship's clothes."

So I waited while she took my jacket and hung it on a chair beside the door, and knelt and untied my shoes and took them off, and opened my trousers, all very respectfully, like the damsels who wait on knights in the old romances, but not without affection, and when I was naked she led me to the bed and dropped her robe and slipped in beside me. You could see every rib on that girl, but her body was warm, and, young as she was, she had wise fingers.

"Your worship is wounded." She brushed the bruise on my cheek.

"What's this 'your worship' business?"

"That's how we speak. My people are Sephardic, from Salonika. My ancestors left Málaga four centuries ago, but we still speak Spanish." All this while touching me.

"Sixteenth-century Spanish."

She knelt beside me. "I suppose so. But your worship did not come here to talk."

"No."

She blew out the candle and bent to me. Timid minnows swam from a sun-warmed sea to nibble at my thighs and belly. Eels wriggled along my flanks. A soft bivalve closed over me. My muscles melted. The cables of my mind parted, and it fell upward into an oval darkness.

Then I got a message like I'd had in prison hunting rats, one I didn't want to answer. Something was wrong, but I didn't want to be bothered. I wanted to enjoy the marine life, for now a firmer mollusk was peristalting me inside it. But the warning grew so strong I got angry, and without thinking I heaved the girl off me, tumbling her to the floor, and came over the foot of the bed, my sex jibing like a sloop boom, and ran two steps and raised my bare foot and slammed the door on Ñato Espino's shoulders as he crawled out into the hall.

I dragged him back by the collar and lifted him under the arms and shook him, flapping his forehead against the wall. He whined, "Ay, ay, ay," but made no resistance, so after eight or ten shakes I let him drop.

"Light!" standing with my foot on his spine. There was a scuffling by the bed, and the girl lit the candle.

I stood there with my wang pointed at his nape like a dowsing rod; then I reached under him and took my wallet and passport out of his jacket pocket. I tossed them on the chair which held my clothes and pushed the door shut and turned to the girl, who sat cross-legged on the bed with her wrists crossed over her Brillo pad.

"The drink you offered me was drugged, wasn't it? He brings you sailors, doesn't he? And you drug them, and he creeps in and robs them, and then he throws them down the stairs."

Ñato began whimpering and I swung my heel back into his ass. "That's it, isn't it?"

She nodded.

I grabbed my pants and pulled them on and stuffed my wallet and passport into a pocket. Just get out of there, and find another woman, and then go back to Athens and sleep, but I was too angry. I picked Ñato up and slung him onto a chair under the skylight.

"You turd!" Slapped his face. "I saved your life, and you try to rob me!"

"What could I do? I need the money."

Slapped his face. "Need it!" Backhand. "How many poor pubic hairs have you taken with this dodge?" Stroking medium force, forehand, backhand, forehand, backhand, forehand.

"One," when I'd stopped. "Only one. Only one stinking time. Forty stinking drachmas," blubbering down his chin. "Not even fifteen dollars, and it costs two hundred to get home."

"I'm weeping."

"Sure. You don't care. You don't care what happens to me. You didn't fight those sailors for my sake. You did it for fun, because you 'felt like it.'"

"So you try to rob me."

"I have to live."

"No you don't." I dragged him to his feet. "I can throw you out the skylight."

"Go ahead." He hung limp on my hands. "Go ahead and kill me. Is that what you 'feel like' now?"

I let him drop back into the chair. "You're not worth the effort." I turned to put on my shirt.

"I didn't ask you to help me. I'm stuck in this filthy, stinking hole, and I can't get home, and the gringos beat me, but I didn't bother you. But you pushed in anyway, the great fighter, the big macho. And stuffed with money, all you Sancudos. It's the big crooks who don't get caught. I never had your chances. I never had a father to steal for me. I have to steal myself, and you tempted me. And you owe it to me anyway. It's your fault I'm an orphan."

"My fault!"

"Well, your father's. The morning I was born my father went down to the cantina to celebrate, and some coffee peons came in yelling revolution and macheted him to death."

"While he was crawling out the door, no doubt."

"It's a big joke to you, but your father was to blame, and you owe me for it."

"I owe you another kick in the ass."

"I don't count what you did to the sailors. You did that for fun. And what good was the drink you bought me? One stinking drink! You didn't ask what I was doing in this filthy, stinking place. You didn't offer to help me get home." Sniveling up at me, the victim, the innocent. "And when I said I'd get you a girl, you, the big macho, assumed it would be for love."

"You said it was a present." Why was I arguing, with this clown?

"Did you expect me to ask for money like a pimp? You won't even leave a man his dignity. You should have left me with the gringos. I didn't expect anything good from them, but you're Tinieblan, you should have some feeling. But you only care about yourself. I get you a girl who does everything, a girl worth a hundred drachmas, but the way you are you'd stay all week and not even leave ten or twenty, so I came for my share. Not even my share! Who knows what your family owes me? How much is a father worth? You, strong man, tell me that: how much for a father who would have taken care of me and given me education? But you didn't give me anything or even promise, so I came for my share and you nearly broke my back and hit my head against the wall and kicked me like a dog. I'd have been better off with the gringos. But if I had your luck, and you had mine, I wouldn't treat you the way you treat me."

"Oh, shut up!" bending to tie my shoe with my joint aching from unrequited love. Four in the morning, and all the whores tucked away, and who knew if I'd get a taxi back to Athens or even find my way out of those alleys?

"I wouldn't treat a dog like that. I wouldn't hit you. I wouldn't leave you to rot in a place like this. I wouldn't do that to someone from my own country. I didn't grow up in the palace or go to good schools or have a father to give me everything, but I had a mother to teach me how to treat people. Yes, and the decencies of a Christian! We're poor, but we're human! You can't treat us like dogs forever! You'll see!" Someday things won't be so easy! and then you'll . . ."

"Shut up!" raising my hand, and he stopped, cringing like a kicked mongrel. "Here's thirty drachmas. Get out and don't come back!"

"You think . . ."

I took him by the lapels and lifted him and shook him till his teeth rattled. "Can't you hear? I said out! And if you try one trick, I'll throw you through the skylight!"

I let him go, and he bent to scoop the money. "The girl's worth fifty," half mumbling with his head turned away, and I thought: Should I break his arm? Shaking him's no good, but if I snap his arm at the elbow, maybe he'll understand. "Out," I said wearily. "Out." And he shuffled out the door.

I closed it behind him and set a chair against it. Then I pushed off my shoes and walked to the bed unbuttoning my shirt. The girl hadn't moved. I kicked off my trousers and lay down, and she nodded and knelt and blew out the candle.

And who knocked on the door next day, while I lay with my head under the covers and the girl spooned against my back? Who brushed the door respectfully with his knuckles and then rapped louder and finally called, "Come and open, don't sleep all day"? Who danced in to stand under the skylight in the Mediterranean winter sun with a fat box in one hand and a flat box in the other? Who grinned like a kid caught playing with himself in the shower and said, "Happy birthday, Kiki"? Yes, yes, Ñato Espino.

His cheeks were puffed and he had a huge hickey on his forehead, but he'd spruced himself up with a clean shirt and a shoeshine. "Sleep well? Ah, ho, I'll say you did! Not much meat on her," slapping the girl's rump and she slouched by on her way around the screen that hid the sink and the bidet pan, "but she knows her trade. I didn't lie, did I? What she doesn't do hasn't been invented. Here, take your present. And you," calling to the girl, "when you've rinsed that thing out, come arrange the cake."

Yes, yes, he'd brought a cake, less than a handspan in diameter, but a cake nonetheless, and in his pocket two tiny candles. I blew them out sitting up in bed, while he sang "Cumpleaños Feliz," then I lit them again and sang for him. Then we cut the cake in thirds and breakfasted off it. How could I be angry?

My present was an incredibly cheap necktie which Ñato insisted on windsor-knotting round my bare throat. In the midst of this operation he looked at me, eyes brimmed with liquid vulnerability, and asked, "You forgive me, don't you, Kiki?" How could I bear a grudge?

Five minutes later, as I was spraying at the sink, it struck me that I'd never had a friend, or ever been a friend in all my life. "You don't like this place, eh, Ñato?" I called over the screen.

"No, Kiki. This place stinks."

"Why'd you come then?"

"Well, Kiki, I was steward on a Panamanian flag boat, and I had an argument with the purser, and he fired me."

"Caught you stealing."

"Oh, no, Kiki, nothing like that. He was queer, you see, and when I wouldn't have anything to do with him, he got me fired."

"Of course."

"Then I couldn't get another ship and had to sell my seaman's papers."

"And now you want to go home."

"Yes, Kiki. That's why, you know, last night, I . . . There's a freighter sailing tomorrow for La Guaira and Veracruz with a cargo stop at Bastidas. The passage costs two hundred dollars."

"Well, it's time to get you your present."

And when I was dressed, we went down to Lloyd-Triestino and bought two passages.

Four days out I was seized with a steaming, Near East clap. There was no doctor on board, and by the time we reached Venezuela the bug had galloped up into my prostate gland, where it lurked for months, gobbling wonder drugs like bonbons and spewing out pain and foul drippings.

"That's the trouble with young whores," Ñato commiserated. "They don't know how to take care of themselves."

"And you!" I howled, shaking myself after my tenth fiery piss of the morning. "What are you so philosophical about? You must be riddled with it!"

"Not me, Kiki. I'm the careful type. I know those young whores. I let her fool with me a few times—she wasn't bad at it— but I never put my prick in her."

"Take the card back. I've had this dream before, years ago."

But the butler is gone, the tennis court is gone, and I lie paralyzed in a hospital bed while Dr. Fasholt shakes his head and sighs and mutters, "Incurable."

30

I drive along a city street late at night. Two iguana-like lizards are coupling beneath a streetlamp, a large male trying to penetrate a smaller female, who cries like a human child. I stop my car and say to a policeman, a New York policeman, "That's rape, isn't it?"

He agrees, and we attack the male iguana. I try to club him with a stick, but he escapes. Then I see him covering the female. I worry him with my stick, and he turns his head toward me fiercely without interrupting his thrusts. I continue to prod him until suddenly he breaks off and comes for me. Now he has human form but is still an iguana, naked, hairless, very smooth. He points to my chest and explains my human circulatory system to another iguana whom I cannot see. My chest is made of transparent plastic, and all my veins and arteries, my pumping heart, are visible. I call, "Officer," and the policeman rushes up and strikes the iguana with his revolver butt, felling him.

"La rabia," says the Policeman, using, for some reason, the Spanish word for rage or rabies. "It was la rabia."

On April Fool's day, 1952, a flunked philosophy student named Vacio disguised himself as a priest and got close enough to the inaugural parade of Apolonio Varón, President of the Republic of Costaguana, to blow Varón, three aides, several bystanders, and himself to meatballs with a nitro bomb. Because Vacio was rumored to he a leftist, conservatives went into the streets to protest. They were joined by liberals, who took Vacio's cassock for bona fide. There followed six days of bloodletting in the streets of Chuchaganga, culminating in the dictatorship of General Dionisio Huevas Pandilla. Thus began the decade of Costaguanan civil strife known as *la rabia.*

The Costaguanans, unlike their infinitely more civilized Tinieblan neighbors, are a violent lot, much given to killing, maiming, raping, and plundering each other, but during *la rabia* they outdid themselves, abandoning peaceful drudge entirely for racy games of murder and thus placing grave demands on the manufacturers and suppliers of weapons. Fortunately the Korean War was crunching toward stalemate and industrialists in New England, Brussels, and Prague were alert to the emergence of fresh markets. General Huevas never wanted for the instruments of repression, and a number of hardy and imaginative entrepreneurs came forward to furnish the instruments of rebellion (or revenge, or recreation) to those cash-bearing Costaguanans who did not care for the general or who, free of political obsessions, saw in the turmoil of the times a chance to even old scores or enjoy new amusements. (Among these last was the so-called *corbata,* or "necktie," practiced largely, but not exclusively, on the passengers of busses held up on rural highways, which involved slicing the throat with razor or well-honed knife and pulling the tongue through so that it blobbed like a garish and truncated cravat, and which became so fashionable that at least a dozen backland warlords called themselves "El Corbatero.") So *la rabia* proceeded with reasonable technological efficiency and petered out not from any lack of arms but rather from an increasing shortage of Costaguanans to bear them.

Besides feelings of satisfaction in helping Costaguanans exercise their national bent, the gun business also generated profit. Most of this went to the big companies who supplied General Huevas, directly through cash sales or indirectly through the United States foreign aid program, but a substantial dribble remained for the independent merchant who was willing to risk capital, freedom, and skin to distribute death evenly about the country. Profit and risk attracted me, but risk more than profit, the hope of rekindling the glow I'd felt on board the Higgins boat with Duncan, and I took my friend Ñato Espino as a minor partner, though all he could put up was companionship and guffaw-spawning attempts to justify our enterprise morally.

"Well, Kiki," he said when I told him what I'd heard about the demand for weapons across the border from Selva Trópica. "Those animals are going to kill each other no matter what we do. If we don't sell them guns, someone else will. And the common man has to defend himself. It isn't right that General Huevas should have all the guns."

"Jerk!" laughing. "We'll get shot if we're caught and make money if we aren't, and right and wrong has nothing to do with it."

"That's fine for you, Kiki. You don't believe in those things. But my mother taught me . . ."

"To be a hypocrite!"

"Make fun if you like, Kiki, but I'm more decent than you think."

This is my room at the Pensión Pizarro, some weeks after we returned to Tinieblas. We landed at Bastidas on the last day of 1952, which was also the last day of Alejo's impeachment. The Chamber voted articles against him the day they convened, between the inauguration of Pastor Alemán and a resolution to recall the Korea battalion, and as my previous return had come on the day of his arrest, this latest one fell on the day of his conviction.

Alejo's enemies had, of course, to do something about him; he was more than just another political opponent whom one could hope to defeat or buy off. Some foreign observers, however, considered it superfluous to impeach a President who had already been deposed, jailed, and succeeded, and suggested that it would be more rational—if Alejo had to be judged and muzzled—to try him in a normal court. But genius always operates irrationally, or rather according to a higher reason of its own, and it was genius, in the person of Humberto Ladilla, that conceived the impeachment. The Tinieblan Constitution provides that the Chamber may, on the vote of two-thirds of its full membership, establish itself as a tribunal for the impeachment of public officials, and that the impeached, if convicted, must pay the costs of the proceedings; and as Shakespeare wrung fantastic music out of the blind blunderings of history, so Ladilla turned these trite articles into a fount of cash. If the Chamber became a court, he argued, then deputies would be transformed into judges—no ordinary judges either, judges at least the equal of justices of the Supreme Court, and the salary of a Supreme Court justice was seventeen hundred inchados a month. More, judges needed clerks and secretaries, and courts must have bailiffs and stenographers and clerks and secretaries of its own, and these were responsible posts which called for decent salaries and which, by the way, might well be filled by people close to the deputies, as it was perfectly possible for a deputy to have a nephew learned in the law or a protégée who knew shorthand. And a court had to proceed deliberately, especially in so serious a matter as the impeachment of a president, so all appointments, and their salaries, could be expected to continue for many months—at no cost to the republic either, since who could doubt that Alejo was guilty and would be convicted? Thus the Chamber voted unanimously to impeach and proceeded with great industry, sparing no expense, to hire staff and make investigations and draft charges and prepare briefs.

Meanwhile Alejo prowled his cage, alone with his thoughts and the matinal excretions of Major Azote. The prison emptied after Pastor Alemán's inauguration to fill again, its upper floors at least, with common criminals. Alfonso emerged badly shaken—all day and in his dreams he heard his telephone ringing, ringing; the plaintive mewings of the stewardesses who'd rung in vain while he was inside—and went back to Harvard for a law degree. Furetto went to Argentina where he had relatives; Gonzalo Garbanzo, to live with a daughter in Miami. So Alejo had not even the comfort of feeling his durance shared, and his only contact with the world came in brief visits with his defense counsel, Uncle Erasmo, who had been elbowed off the Supreme Court and whose newspapers had been padlocked pending conclusion of the impeachment. True, one morning as he unzipped before Alejo's window, Major Dorindo Azote was sure he heard the deposed chief magistrate conversing warmly with someone who spoke Spanish in gluey teutonic snorts, but when the major repantsed and bent to investigate, all he could see in the cell, besides Alejo, was a plump gray rat, who looked up at him contemptuously for a moment before waddling out through a gnaw-hole in the door. The only logical explanation was that Alejo had gone round the bend at last and was not merely talking to himself—a common affliction among prisoners in solitary confinement—but orchestrating other voices out of his memory and pain.

The trial of Alejandro Sancudo opened on December 10th with the Chamber newly redecorated for the occasion and the deputies gowned in black silk robes made to measure by a London tailor. Preparations had lasted more than six months, and Ladilla predicted that it would take at least another six to hear the case, given each deputy's right to cross-examine witnesses. What with the sale of gallery seats and of commercial time during radio coverage, there was good prospect of making the impeachment the leading industry of Tinieblas. Half a day was consumed in calling the roll of the tribunal, the clerk pausing after each name while the radio touted soap flakes and Cortez Beer to an attentive nation, and Alejo, wedged between two guards, licked flecks of foam from bared canines. Another four days went in reading the charges, during which more sponsors were rounded up and Ladilla made downpayment on a villa at Antibes. But on the afternoon of the fifth day, when Alejo was asked to plead, Uncle Erasmo said simply, "Nolo contendere." All Ladilla could do was order two weeks' recess to consider sentence (and finish out the month). On the last day of the year Alejo was found guilty, sentenced to one year in prison (suspended, since he had already spent eleven months and twenty days in La Bondadosa) and ordered to pay costs, which amounted to just under three-quarters of a million inchados.

The figure caused a certain preening of buzzard feathers in Tinieblan financial circles: the coffee *finca*, La Yegua, and Medusa Beach might be available at bargain prices. But Alejo paid with a draft on his Panamanian bank and left at once for Europe. During a plane change at San Juan he found himself face to face with León Fuertes in a waiting room for in-transit passengers, and León, who was not fainthearted and who alone among the deputies had given his judge's salary to San Bruno Hospital (arguing that it was one thing to bleed Alejo, another to gorge oneself), offered his hand. Alejo stared for a moment—the year in prison had begun the transformation of his face into a death's-head—then took the hand. "Yes, young man," glaring with bronze eyes. "You are audacious. And interested in power, not in money. But for you I would still be President. But I bear you no enmity. I will be President again. Not even the Chamber of Deputies can alter destiny. And you too deserve a better fatherland. You too have an interesting fate."

Then he turned and stepped through the to-planes door into two decades of political obscurity.

Which left me the only member of my family actively engaged in the struggle for existence—or, rather, actively in search of a struggle which would give me the sensation of being alive. I was offered several jobs on the strength of my name and my medal, but I never considered working for wages, or working at all in the sense most men conceive it, and was set on investing my cash and energies in some enterprise which would bring a high return in excitement. So as the price of death was rising in Costaguana and the merchandising of it not offensive to my partner's moral sense, I went into the gun trade.

Ñato and I scrounged a modest first shipment in Tinieblas: a dozen M-1 rifles, their stocks scuffed by tepid-veined conscripts with "Better Bored Than Gored" signs in their hearts, from an ordnance warrant officer with a talent for cooking inventories; six thousand rounds of .30 caliber ammunition, armor-piercing, tracer and ball, which I saw advertised on the Reservation Gun Club bulletin board and which the owner, a blubber-jowled naval dockcrane operator, the kind of gringo who doesn't feel potent without an arsenal in his closet, was getting rid of after having stocked up on the new, noncorrosive stuff; four spanking M-2 carbines of the type lofted in one hand by the handsome young Irish American infantry captain who rallied an invisible platoon in the recruiting poster in front of Fort Shafter Post Headquarters—these, complete with banana-shaped magazines and two khaki-colored metal boxes of ammunition, from two khaki-colored stevedores; odd pieces brought back as souvenirs by members of the Korea battalion: a Russian burp gun which looked as though it might fire the carbine round; a 7.65 mm. Czech pistol, suitable for an Italian staff colonel to wear (in a patent-leather holster raked to the left of his paunch) when visiting his mistress; half a dozen serviceable Colt .45's, the cleanest of which I kept for myself; and a cobra-lovely Luger such as in nobler times and climes might have been left, along with a silver flask of brandy, on the table in front of an officer who had betrayed the code. All of which we packed in a crate and a U.S. Navy footlocker, and loaded in a Jeep which I bought at quartermaster auction, and covered with a tarpaulin, and trucked (since it was dry season and a Jeep could make it) over the *cordillera* and through three river fords to Sombras in Selva Trópica Province. Where we found Jaime heel-squatting by the bow of a Seahorsed *cayuco*, watching the ocher river slap beneath houses perched on cranes' legs on the steep bank.

He occupied the same place in his society as I did in mine: rebellious son of a notable chieftain. He'd had advantages. His father, who ruled a tribe that lived down between the Costaguanan border and the Caribbean, had taught him how to operate the official *cayuco* and its official outboard motor—though not how to swim, for swimming in those rivers is best left to the candiru, a kind of eel which will worm up a man's penis and lodge there with spines. Then Jaime quarreled with his father and stole the canoe and went off to the provincial capital to make his fortune. All of which I learned later. At the time he merely looked reliable and nodded when I asked, waving my hand vaguely toward the east, if he would take me "over there."

I left Ñato to watch our goods and went off with Jaime in search of customers. All day we slid along rivers the color of pus, past huge trees that clawed to wasted banks and mud flats strewn with dreaming crocodiles. I lay against a thwart, my head throbbing with the motor, too poached in somnolence to shake the flies from my forearms, and sometimes the banks pressed in so that we moved as in a tunnel under branches choked with gaudy feathers and great oval insect nests, and sometimes they spread back to leave us isolated as on the sea. Toward noon the stream grew viscous, and bright golden salamanders raced across the surface by our bows. We moved now with the current, now against it, and for a time a company of point-bearded phantoms in breastplates and curved helmets kept pace with us along the left-hand bank, hacking the vines with rapiers and sinking to their stockinged thighs in the gray muck. Then at dusk the water cleared. We heard the rush of rapids above us. Three uniformed bundles floated by us in the bubbly current, two face down with elbows wired, one face up with wagging pink necktie. And we stuttered round a bend to a landing where four merry lads were swinging a fourth bundle out into the stream.

That town was called Golconda. A mulatto named Cérbero Entrañas, who gave himself the title of colonel, had seized it that same afternoon, imprisoning the mayor and butchering the four-man garrison. He was my first customer, and when Jaime and I returned two days later with Ñato and the guns, he paid in gold pieces dug up from under the mayor's house (he'd spent the intervening hours convincing the mayor to tell him exactly where to dig) and tested the bulk of his purchase at once, ordering the townspeople assembled and the mayor tied to a large tree that grew above the bank and twelve disciples arranged in two ranks one kneeling, one standing, so that the rifles of the front rank all but brushed the mayor's fluttering chest, and convincing the mayor's son, a boy of twelve, to give the command to fire. And when the volley burst, splitting the sky above Golconda and snuffing the monkey chatter in the trees across the river, Ñato Espino retched, and then grinned his grin, and said, "That's justice, that's revolution," and I felt the left side of my face go hard and numb to feeling as though calcified.

Our immediate success sent us traveling. To Galveston, where we bought lever-action Winchester .30-30's (always a popular model south of the Rio Bravo, though somewhat bruising to the shoulder), a hundred of them and two unsinkable fiberglass boats. We opened the watertight compartments in the hulls and packed the rifles snug inside and sealed the fiberglass and shipped the boats to ourselves in Bastidas and claimed them at the customs shed and sailed them down the coast, Jaime in one, Ñato and I in the other, and up a river into Costaguana. To Havana, where the government was letting Springfields go dirt cheap. The gringos had replaced them with semiautomatic Garands, but they were unquestionably lethal and easy to operate as well, and we found a pilot who was willing to fly them and Ñato and me from Camagüey to a field in Jaime's father's territory. Jaime was back in favor by then—his share of Colonel Cérbero Entrañas' gold coins dangled about the plump neck of the most prominent of his several stepmothers—and his father gave us a feast and six giggling twelve-year-olds with conical breasts and rings in their noses before we took the guns over to Costaguana in our now sinkable boats. to Guadeloupe for some charming French-made Walther auto-loading pistols, a luxury item whose workmanship seduced me, which we imported smoothly enough thanks to an imaginative packaging job—they came in football-sized, cellophaned boxes labeled "Ma Griffe"—but had the devil's time selling at a decent profit. To Curaçao for a gross of Belgian Browning rifles, which sluiced through Tinieblan customs as dental drills, lubricated by a juicy bribe to the Bastidas port captain. To Guatemala, where we purchased Czech machine pistols from the private stock of the lately deposed President Jacobo

Arbenz. To Managua and Kingston and Port-au-Prince, wherever we could find things that went bang and caused trouble.

These we dragged up the Costaguanan rivers past floating islets of baled corpses and cindered villages haloed with buzzards, through regions ravaged alternately by outlaw bands and government columns where balloon-bellied children fed on dirt; and delivered them to those who craved them most. To Autólico Caco, another self-commissioned colonel, who held a town called Esperanzas and took tribute from the copra planters; to Bronteo Culón, "El Corbatero Negro," whose men churned like locusts through the ricelands of the Hermosura Basin; to Polifemo Caganza, a one-eyed ex-shepherd whose people, men, women, and children lived in caves at the headwaters of the Rio Manso, a cattle thief and occasional bank robber who could eat a whole calf at one sitting and who, they said, kept no woman for himself but made love to his mare instead; to Calixto Merdona, "El Corbatero Rubio," who left a prosperous provincial law practice when his student son was tortured to death in Chuchaganga Police Headquarters and who had a nail keg full of what looked like marbles and turned out to be the eyes of government soldiers. All these men fought General Huevas and, at times, each other and ruled their countrysides, collecting taxes and administering swift justice, and all were good customers, for during *la rabia* a Costaguanan's life depended on his weapon, and his place in the world on how many followers he could arm. They paid in gold, more often in greenbacks, at times in Costaguanan lunas, for I would take these too, at a slashing discount, if my buyer had nothing else, and with each shipment I grew harder. The sensation I experienced in Golconda when Cérbero Entrañas had the mayor shot reproduced itself in other parts of my body, and on examination I realized that a hornlike substance was spreading beneath my skin. It was thin enough to let a little feeling pass, supple enough to let me move without impediment, but infinitely hard, harder than glass and, more, unshatterable. It spread like a rash yet remained unnoticeable to others, creeping down my cheek and across half my neck to stop at my collarbone, appearing next on my abdomen and, within the course of one afternoon, flashing across my loins and down my right leg to my ankle. On the day we delivered two cases of Sten guns to Polifemo Caganza, the secretions began collecting on the inside of my left forearm, and during the night of carousing that followed, they seeped up my arm, across my shoulders, and over the right side of my face. It continued that way, a new outbreak with each trip into Costaguana, and before the year was out, I was sheathed from crown to toe.

I thought first of seeing a doctor, but I had never been examined or received treatment, not even as a child, and the idea of being poked and fingered by some grave, pretentious fool with manicured nails and a Latin diploma repelled me. My condition, whatever it was, caused me no inconvenience. No, once I became accustomed to the slight numbness, I enjoyed it. That was the way to be, I thought, hard as some prehistoric saurian, immune to the tame nips of newer species, and baked in danger. I left no minute's gap for the wedge of boredom and blotchiness. I poured my profits into larger shipments, always looking to risk my entire stake, and with each shipment risking prison in Tinieblas and death in Costaguana. Why not be hard? One had to be alert for government patrols and rival traders. One had to deal with ruthless men. And there was the discomfort of heat and rain and insects, the alien indifference of the jungle, the palpable ambiance of violent death, to keep one's lips sweet with the flavor of living. When I wasn't angling for guns in foreign cities, I was threading them into Tinieblas or sweating them up those rivers, as fully immersed in life as a panther.

Late in November we came to Golconda again, with the rain pelting so hard we had to bail, so heavy we had to rope the boats together lest we lose each other. It lifted just as we turned the bend to Golconda landing where our man was waiting for us, a Costaguanan nicknamed Memo whose full name I never knew. He'd come over to us one afternoon while we were eating in a cantina in Esperanzas, knowing our calling, for we weren't ashamed of it. He was tall and well-made, an educated man, traveled. He said he knew Tinieblas, a magnificent country, and Ciudad Tinieblas, a charming capital, elegant yet not stiff like Lima, say, or Bogotá, and finally that, if we didn't mind mixing business with our rice and fried beans, he was in the market for cartridges, delivery at

Golconda. Cérbero Entrañas was dead, forty-four bullet wounds and his thumbs chopped off to compare with print records in Chuchaganga, but Memo said that a new band was moving through in the wake of the troops. The leader, a friend of his, was cagey, afraid of spies; Memo would purchase for him.

He had fine table manners, this Memo, which he displayed for us on a slice of grilled beef, taking an ivory-handled clasp knife from his side pocket and carving the whole portion into neat parallelograms before closing the blade and forking the morsels carefully into his mouth. Sprucely dressed too, compared to the cantina's other customers, ourselves included, in a fresh brown shirt, sleeves buttoned over imperially slim wrists, and tight brown trousers stretched over the tops of well-buffed brown boots. And he was refined where it came to personal protection. He had a little .25 caliber Beretta which he carried in his hip pocket swaddled in fawn-colored chamois. He showed it to us during the course of our chat, and though it seemed light, almost frivolous, for the life-style then in vogue in Costaguana, I had to admit it was a lovely little pistol. More, he offered a most attractive price for .30-06 and .30-30 cartridges, items we could lay our hands on easily enough. His friend meant to do some serious pillaging when the rains lifted and was willing to pay well for dependable ammunition. Hollow-point bullets in hunting loads, Memo specified; the sort of round which left an exemplary exit wound. "'Pour encourager les autres,'" he quoted, patting the corners of his mouth with a folded linen handkerchief. How many rounds would his friend take? Why, as many as we could transport In one trip, of course. His friend didn't care to linger near Golconda. So we agreed to meet Memo there on such-and-such day.

He was waiting above the landing when we turned the bend. He'd rigged a little lean-to by tacking one side of a rubber ground sheet to the big tree where Cérbero Entrañas had had the mayor shot, and I suppose he'd sat there most of the afternoon, waiting for us. Reading, for when the whole thing was over I found a little leather-bound, vellum-paper copy of Unamuno's essays stuck back where the rubber met the ground. I suppose he heard our outboards and finished a paragraph and tucked his book away and rose just as we came in view. He waved but didn't come down to meet us. Stood stretching as we ran our boats up on the pebbles.

"Trouble?"

"The whore rain," Ñato called back, getting out of the bow of my boat to lug it a little higher up.

Memo took a couple of steps down toward us, then smiled and called, "Excuse me," and went back to urinate against the big tree. He stood there, legs apart, and I breathed the way you do after a long trip and took off my wet shirt and spread it on a case of cartridge boxes and swung my bare feet over the gunwale into the shallow water and waded out and up toward him.

"Stop there." He had his pistol out, gunhand extended toward my chest, left hand in his hip pocket as on a target range. I hadn't seen him move. First he was pissing; then he had us covered. "Put your hands on your heads."

I stopped. Not because I'd decided to. The stare of that little eye stopped me like a firm hand against my chest. I didn't raise my hands, though I suppose Jaime and Ñato did, for Memo said, "You too, Kiki." In the second that followed I was aware of the bullet scars on the big tree, whose leaves were sponging up the last rays of sunlight, and a parrot squawk across the river behind me, and the after-rain freshness of the forest which seemed gathered in a drop of water pendant from a twig above Memo's shoulder. Then I pushed my chest against the pistol stare, and the eye blinked fire.

Four blinks and four pops while other things were happening. My .45 rose from the waistband of my pants and floated upward. The hammer came back, the safety went down, and as the barrel passed Memo's chin on the rise, as it reached his lips, which were beginning to open in wonder, just as I began to feel the four stings on my breast, my pistol fired. Memo's head flew back, dragging his shoulders and trunk back onto his lean-to, flinging his gun arm up so that his fifth shot carried well above my head and his sixth straight up through the branches to shake a little shower on him from the rain-glossed leaves.

The sun went down then, and when I'd breathed and eased the hammer forward and clicked the safety up, I went down to my boat and put on my wet shirt, so neither Jaime nor Ñato noticed the four hornet bites in a cross around my left nipple or the four flattened slugs lying in the mud near where my feet had been. The sting marks went away in a week or so, but I kept the smiling glow of calm and power which came to me as I let my pistol rise on its own impetus and drive a widening tunnel through the roof of that man's mouth and out the back of his head.

I am in the Roman apartment where we lived thirty-odd years ago when Alejo was ambassador. The unconscious iguana has been carried to my mother's room, unoccupied now that she's away. But I am fully-grown and married. To Olga? To Elena? To Marta? To some composite woman who feels sorry for the iguana and has put the radio on for him. No matter, for his elbows are bound tight with baling wire. I enter the room to punish and torture him. I can't see him but can hear him rustling about. Perhaps he is not bound. Perhaps his hands are merely tied in front. He will be dangerous, able to defend himself. He comes for me from behind a chair, still in human form, not bound at all, and I am paralyzed. He begins to eat me, tearing my genitals away with pointed teeth. No pain, but the horrid anguish of mutilation. He rips flesh from my inner thigh and looks up, munching, his dull reptile eyes scanning me contentedly. Between bites he reminds me that it wasn't the woman who set him free; it was I myself.

31

Deathmusty shroud of cobwebbed dreamterrors which I strain at wearily. Afternoon sun bores at the green curtains. Air conditioner whooshes dully. My bed, my room, my house. Mito is safe at school. Iguanaman is back in Monsterholm, and I am happily returned to a reality where I am merely paralyzed, not gobbled alive.

Sopped in sweat. Wifely Elena has tiptoed off, drawing the covers up under my chin, and I've no way to throw them back. The buzzer has wandered from beneath my left hand. Intrepid explorations along, the full half-inch range of my middle finger, then I abandon the hunt and repose like Dr. Livingstone to await discovery and rescue.

And recover from my scare. Siesta dreams run a bit wilder than those at night, but today's were excessive. Nice to be with Mito at La Yegua though. And I enjoyed my vision of the sea. Marvelous expansive feeling; peace and fulfillment to balance that horrid fear.

I never dreamed before, or if I did I was never conscious of it. And I dealt with waking fears by diving into them, so I never got pinned down in abject quivering. Action's the antidote if you can manage it. A Costaguanan captain whom Bronteo Culón ordered shot insisted on commanding his firing squad. Stood on the lip of his grave and bellowed the orders in a parade-ground roar. By the time he got to "Fire," his pants were soaked dark from thigh to knee, and there was some discussion afterward, while the next man was being brought out as to whether or not he'd been a coward. The consensus was not to condemn his heart for his bladder's insubordination. He'd stayed on his feet, after all, and kept control of his vocal chords. The dark stain took something from the dignity of his raised chin, but his voice didn't break and he spaced the orders evenly. No doubt he'd commanded firing squads before. Surely the practice helped. But, on balance, he'd managed to translate fear into orderly action.

In contrast I performed shamefully in my last dream, calling a policeman to protect me from Iguanaman, fearing he might not be bound, dragging the soul of a cripple into a world where, for a moment at least, I was sound. Which is the mirror image of what I try to do waking: face a world where I am paralyzed with the responses of a healthy beast of prey.

That's what I was at twenty-three, a robust predator, a masterpiece of natural selection cased in horn and crafted for the jungles that I prowled. Then I caught love like malaria, or developed it like blood cancer, or declined into it like dementia praecox, and languished for four years, and never fully recovered since the disease crumbled the armor round my heart and left it vulnerable to human feeling. Without which weakness I'd be prowling still. At least I see a connection between my love for Olga and the conversion which possessed me during my campaign. Maybe it's just the fool's gold which will trick a novice prospector who pans for meaning in his life—what else have I to do while trapped here like a bug in amber?—but I don't think I'd have denied Ñato his big chance if I'd never suffered love. So should I curse Olga or thank her?

Olga Luciérnaga Tristealegre was Queen of the Club Mercantil at Carnival in 1954 and rode in on the poop of a Persian pleasure barge under a canopy of purple velvet. She was attended by twenty Saracen knights with scimitars and spiked helmets and twenty slave girls in gossamer silk trousers and gold breast plates, while her father, Don Edmundo Luciérnaga, sat enthroned beside her like Harun al-Rashid. A doctor in the etiology of love might decide whether I was stricken at that moment or whether I infected myself later on with I-love-yours spread in hope of getting her to bed. In any case, within a week I was mortally afflicted, incapable of cogent thought, forgetful of my business, and useless to myself and everyone else, except headwaiters, shopkeepers, and florists. And, worst of all, I was delighted with my state.

In all the world there were never two people so mismatched as Olga and I. She was lovely and delicate, like one of the magnificent butterflies which grace our forests for a few days after the rains and which the indians call Flowers of the Wind. She played Chopin and Schumann, bending in the swollen gloom of evening while slow rhythms rippled her dark hair. She painted in watercolor, grave children wreathed in garlands, and wrote verses in the romantic style of Gustavo Adolfo Bequer. Withal, she feared and hated violence, and not simply violence—which was a thing so foreign to her life as to be mainly an abstraction to her—but any roughness, any harsh word or brusqueness of behavior. And I was a death-seller, a killer by proxy and, lately, by my own hand. Olga heard violence chuckle in my throat, felt violence balled in my shoulders when she danced with me, tasted violence on my lips when I kissed her, saw violence in my eyes when she drew her lips away. My violent gaiety sang out on street corners while passers-by gaped; my violent generosity swept bucketfuls of anemones into her arms; my violent declarations—"I love you, Olga. Do you understand? I love you!"—rasped her ears like threats. And so she fled, and so I pursued.

I abandoned my affairs to remain near her. I sought out an old negro woman renowned for her skill at concocting love spells and potions, and for a month was at pains to bring her locks of Olga's hair, nail parings, and scraps of her clothing. And when this magic failed, I disguised myself as a man of Olga's liking, a docile man who followed her about like a tame leopard, mewing softly and bending liquid eyes, a gentle man who brought her one rose instead of three dozen, a steady man, strong yet not violent. I paid her court, I hovered in attendance, and, treating her as though the Carnival had never ended and she were still a queen, I won her to me.

On the evening of our wedding, at the very instant I took Olga for the first time, a great clap of thunder split the sky above the city. We scarcely heard it then, but later on we both remembered.

32

Many years later, at the Paris première of Weber's *Faust*, I had to remember the remote evening when I promised Olga I would make her happy. It was late on our wedding night, and the world was still quite simple, being composed of two chests and three mouths and located in the center of an equally simple universe, our lately virgin double bed.

"I'm afraid, Kiki."

"Of what?" holding her gently.

"Of being married. Of you. Of everything."

"Don't be afraid," as if that softly kissed command compelled obedience. "I love you," as if that were an infallible incantation.

"I'll make you happy."

I had to remember that moment when I watched Mephistopheles make his pitch to Faust. I wasn't pleased with the movie. I considered movies—and all art, for that matter—grossly inferior substitutes for life and went freely only to the ones Elena played in, while this movie was the child of a posturing, lizard-smiled Teuton who not only had been one of Elena's early loves (a minor annoyance) but who spoke condescendingly to me in the lobby. I knew the Faust story only by hearsay and, having small German, was condemned to bifocal glimpses at the French subtitles, but despite all these impediments the bargain scene caught my interest. Mephistopheles romped in wearing the kind of gown you can still see on student street-singers in Madrid. He looked ages younger and worlds healthier than fusty Faust (played priggishly by Weber), directed his spirit scene with great panache, and got so charmed by his own spectaculars, so conned by his own enthusiasm, that he made a poor deal. He promised to make Faust happy. He would get Faust's soul when, and only when, Faust acknowledged the promise fulfilled. After that I watched sympathetically as poor Mephisto, stupid Mephisto, overconfident Mephisto wracked his brain and sapped his powers trying to make Faust happy. He tried everything, even raised the dead, yet Faust remained depressed. Only through trickery did he at last get Faust to confess a moment's happiness—one could hardly say he'd kept his promise or triumphed or made a smart bargain—and at the end of the movie Faust saved his soul anyway. All Mephisto's energy and art served for nothing. By the end he was too exhausted even to feel bitter.

It might have been the story of my marriage to Olga, the early years anyway. When I promised to make her happy, it didn't seem a particularly difficult task. I loved her; I married her; I gave her my name. I planned to be faithful to her and, since other women no longer attracted me, saw no reason why I couldn't keep planning. I had plenty of money and no project in my life beyond her. Of course I'd make her happy. How could she fail to be happy when I, Kiki Sancudo, loved her to distraction? And to make sure, I went back to my negress witch and bought a small steel noose which fitted around my testicles and was arranged to tighten, reminding me of my promise, when Olga was unhappy. Olga didn't demand this, though other women bought such nooses and slipped them on their husbands while they slept. I volunteered it, and Olga didn't even have to pull: the noose tightened magically whenever she whimpered or otherwise expressed unhappiness.

Olga didn't want to be separated from me, even for a few days, so I retired completely from the gun trade. I didn't think twice about it, for it is wondrous the way a man can alter his life-style when his testicles are in a steel noose. Even before the noose tightened, I realized I didn't want to be separated from Olga either and that I was weary of those trips to Costaguana. Ñato hadn't the stomach for solo trade in arms and switched to drugs, mainly cocaine from Peru; Jaime returned to his tribe and founded a harem. We made a farewell safari through the rattier dockside cantinas from which I returned quite late to Queen Olga's reproaches: I knew she couldn't sleep when I was absent; I'd promised to make her happy, and instead I'd hurt her. My little steel noose tightened perceptibly, but, being drunk, I fought against it. I read her, in a voice that may have waked a few light-sleeping neighbors, from the masculine bill of rights, a broad statute which has been repealed in many parts of North America and Europe but which retains the force of Holy Writ south of the Rio Grande. She grew sad, the noose tightened, and I, feeling its bite, shouted louder. When Olga began to cry, the noose jerked tight. Blind with pain, I begged forgiveness. A certain space of agony endured before she stopped sniffling and embraced me, but at that instant the noose went slack. I swept her into my arms and told her not to worry, I'd take care of her. And so I did. And so I did.

Olga didn't want to stay in Tinieblas, so we went to Europe. Again, even before the noose grew tight I decided that I ought to finish my education, take a degree, and establish myself in a respectable profession. My Yale record would be available to American universities, and so I had better go to Europe, which just happened to be Olga's preference.

Olga didn't like planes, so we went by boat, Galactic Fruit steamer to New York, French Line to Le Havre. I realized suddenly that I too craved the leisured luxury of ocean travel, that my caged beast's anguish on the voyage from Piraeus had sprung from having only Ñato for company, that Olga was right: I ought to learn to relax. I realized this before the noose even twitched. I must confess to a certain glee when a marvelous tempest engulfed us off Newfoundland. It tossed the giant liner like a nut and emptied deck and dining room of all but the hardiest. Up on the spray-swept sundeck, plunged in the shrieking wind, I forgot the soft trappings of the salons and could recall the stress of life. Olga was cruelly sick, of course, but it wasn't my fault and there was nothing I could do about it, and so my noose stayed slack.

On the second day, as I was working my way like an alpinist along the felt-covered ropes strung about the first-class lobby, a tremendous wave caught the ship broadside and hurled it almost on its beam. I was flung off my hold against a corner of the purser's desk. Nothing grave, but the blow hurt more than Memo's bullets, and later, when I was changing in our stateroom, I noticed a great blue bruise spread all across my left shoulder. It was then that I realized that the inner sheath secreted during my trade in Costaguana had melted and that I was, if anything, softer than before. That's Olga's fault, I thought resentfully, but I didn't add my complaints to her sufferings. I had a promise to honor.

I wanted to honor it. I performed heroic labors even without my noose's proddings, as when Olga had Mito by Caesarean and I took a double room at Geneva Hospital and stayed with her night and day for a week. But often, either from negligence or perversity, I would muff a detail. Sometimes I lingered after class; sometimes I taunted her about her fears. Then she would suffer and my noose would pinch. An apology and some affection would soothe her suffering and slacken my noose. As time passed, however, she developed a resistance to this treatment, needed larger doses, took longer to respond. And I didn't always apply it immediately. Often I raged against my noose, though I knew very well this only made it tighter. Sometimes it drew narrow as a needle's eye before I yielded to the pain; sometimes I forgot the pain entirely in my fury. At such moments I could cause a lot of damage. I recall an oak bedroom door which I reduced to toothpicks when Olga sought shelter behind it during one of my fits. Once or twice, to my eternal shame, I hit her—not hard, not with my full strength, but that's small defense. Usually I merely terrified her by destroying the unwary objects that strayed into my path or by injuring myself. I found that pummeling my temples distracted me from the noose's torture and brought a transitory peace, and during the first years of my marriage I took more punishment than in all my wrestling career. Later, of course, my head would echo the noose's torments, and I would feel remorse, but a man can't be held responsible for the wild things he may do when there's a steel noose around his testicles. And what right had I to complain about it? I'd put it there myself.

I wore the noose three years nine months and twenty days, not because I was unable to remove it (though removing it was difficult, for the flesh grew around it, covering it completely), but because wearing it transformed marriage into a contest involving risk. I hadn't lost my appetite for action, I'd merely pushed it down. It popped up again right away and started munching on my marriage. My task was to make Olga happy; Olga herself was the opponent who made the game difficult and, hence, worth playing; the noose provided the vital element of risk: when I failed, I suffered. Olga didn't urge me to take the noose off, for it gave her a measure of control, but there were many times when she was willing to quit entirely. She wanted to be protected, and whatever peace I might weave about her in the morning I was likely to unravel into fear at night. Even while she was carrying Mito she said she wanted to leave me. That was after the First Battle of Geneva, which left our apartment ravaged as by Goths. What did she mean, leave me? I shook my bruised head and eyed the wounded furniture. Why would she want to leave? What amazes me now is that I persuaded her to stay. Olga said later that I did so out of stubbornness, and I imagine that was part of it. And vanity: Kiki Sancudo wasn't the sort whose wife walked out on him. And devotion to the game, which was my only source of action. And fascination with Olga as a woman and as a challenge. My love for her was compounded of these elements, and if I wasn't clever enough to make her happy, I was at least strong enough to make her stay. Even if it killed us. No matter how much we both suffered.

The Second Battle of Geneva (there were numerous intermediate skirmishes) took place the following spring with little Mito as terrified civilian spectator. Again Olga wanted to leave; again I persuaded her to stay. I proposed a fresh start, a change of scene, and we left Geneva (without my taking any exams) for Padua. En route we fought the Battle of the Milan-Verona Road, in which I won another Pyrrhic victory, quelling Olga's reproaches by pushing our Citroën past ninety and nearly destroying us all. But why recall these horrors? Our life was knitted out of pain and fear and anger. And love. The stout yarn of mottled love bound us and our dark emotions together.

It is good exercise for me to conjure the ghosts of peaceful evenings in the richly hung, high-ceilinged flat which an impoverished count carved from his palazzo. Sleet scourges the windowpane. Olga and Mito are asleep, he cocooned in soft blankets, she bunched beside me, her face cleansed of fear and sadness, and I have put aside my law text to nibble in Guicciardini. I close my eyes and roll a savory nougat of treachery and violence around in my mind. Tomorrow Olga and I will go back to grinding our unmatched hearts against each other, but for the moment all is serene while I nurse myself on the adventures of historical personages. The zoo panther recalls his jungle in the butchered meat thrown into his cage; dissolves the bars in dreams of future kills; is briefly absolved from paranoid pacing and the urge to maul his keeper.

Or let me recall the mornings of Olga's visits to Dr. Demenzella, for just two years after our first meeting she found an escape route along the knife-edge of hysteria into psychoanalysis. Five mornings a week she would lug a haversack full of dreams, anxieties, fantasies, phobias (and a few choice walking nightmares composed, directed, produced, and starred-in by Kiki Sancudo) up four flights of stairs (she was scared of elevators now) and unpack for the great Ferenczi's brilliant pupil. Meanwhile I minded Mito. That, and paying Il Dottore's immense fees, kept my noose just slack enough to bear. When it was too cold or rainy for the park, we went to the Scrovegni Chapel, where I sat him on my shoulders and taught him the Jesus story from Giotto's frescos. Madman with child stalks beneath the genius-spangled walls, his mind arrowing across the piazza to where his wife is cataloguing his bestialities to a total stranger, but Mito gives me therapy. Little Mito (a year old at the time of Olga's breakdown, almost three when we left Padua) clutches my hair in fat fists and asks why did they kill Him, papi, and papi, who wasn't wise enough yet to finger His two errors—a) He confused two things best kept separate: seizing power and adhering to principle; b) He was careless in his choice of associates—gains relief from his frenzy by parroting some priest-talk about His wanting to sacrifice Himself to rid the rest of us of sin. So now I close my eyes and feel Mito's heels thump against my chest, hear him speak sweetly and trustfully to the savage who so often terrorized him and mami. And I can see one panel, a scene no more remarked than any other then but clearly drawn on my closed eyelids now: the torches flared above the milling mob, the peering faces and the upraised spears, the doomed prince and the squat, lump-buttocked clown who clasps his shoulder, meets his tired gaze, and lifts plump lying lips for a gross kiss.

After about six months of visits to Dr. Demenzella, Olga began to respond. One by one she shed her phobias. Her anxiety seizures came less frequently. She grew less fearful and could spend whole afternoons alone. At the same pace I grew ill. One spring morning as I walked Mito through the park I found myself reluctant to approach a flower patch strafed by some azure butterflies. A week later, on an outing to Venice, a tourist tossed some pigeon feed at my feet, and when wings flapped about me, I screamed in terror and fled into St. Mark's cowering there until Olga, who came in with Mito in her arms, assured me that the birds were gone. A letter from Alfonso announced that Gunther was feared to have contracted leprosy, and by nightfall I was convinced I'd been infected by touching the letter, a delusion which persisted even after another letter came saying that, happily, all the tests on Gunther had proved negative. I could not bear open windows or closed rooms. I had the persistent sensation of having fouled myself and took to scrubbing my hands with alcohol. I had greater and greater difficulty sleeping, culminating in Holy Week of 1957 when I stayed awake from Palm to Easter Sunday and had hideous hallucinations of fat brown bears in coveralls bearing effigies of St. Joseph through the halls of our flat. Olga was not merely recovering from her symptoms; she was passing them to me. Still she grew no happier but rather blamed me for all her past sufferings, even for the fears she'd had before I met her. Along with all my new torments, I still had the pinchings of the noose.

Olga urged me to visit one of Dr. Demenzella's colleagues,

citing her own success with analysis. I answered that it worked for her because she had faith in it; for me it would be no better than voodoo or acupuncture, merely a waste of time. Besides, I had never sought help before, and no one was going to probe into my psyche.

No, no, the thing was to get Olga away from Il Signor Dottore; then those symptoms would go back where they belonged.

She refused to leave. She berated me for even suggesting that she break her analysis before it was completed, and the bite of the noose forced me to incredible frenzies. I was no longer relieved by beating myself with my fists and took to using glass ashtrays and a small bronze bust of Mussolini which the count had left tucked in the top of a closet. I considered flight but dismissed this as cowardice. Worse, I still loved Olga. I loved Mito. I was prepared to love Olguita, then about the size and shape of a goldfish. I had to save us all. I had to lead us out of Italy into Tinieblas.

And so, on the evening of my twenty-seventh birthday, I took off the noose. We had to leave: the thought of leaving made Olga suffer; her suffering tightened the noose; its pain made me incapable of action; so at last I took it off. I bought a pair of wire cutters and a surgeon's knife. I locked myself in the bathroom and disinfected tools and jewels with alcohol. Biting my tongue, I slit the skin which had grown over the noose, gouged the pliers under it, and sliced the steel. Then I gripped one end with the pliers and tore it from me. Blind with pain I emptied the alcohol bottle into my wound, bound myself with gauze, pulled on my shorts, and staggered into the bedroom to announce that we were leaving. All Olga's sobs and reproaches failed to move me. In fact it was rather pleasant to listen to them, for from habit I expected the noose to tighten, and now the noose was gone. My sole concession, made freely, for I did what I did in self-defense not sadism, was that we would not fly. Two days later we drove to Genoa and went aboard the *Dante Alighieri* bound through the Panama for Valparaíso.

33

There is no record of how long it took Samson's hair to grow out, but within four months after I cut the noose I had recouped four years of marriage. On the day I returned to Tinieblas, Ñato Espino showed me a photo of myself taken just before my wedding, and I looked up from the fellow in the picture and saw his alcoholic uncle in the mirror on Ñato's dresser. This uncle pressed his fist to his twitching right cheek and resolved to take the cure of action. I wasn't strong enough to plunge straight in. I had to go gingerly, dipping my big toe, wading to my ankles, so I accepted Ñato's offer of a marijuana venture in Panama.

My nerves were bad. My hand shook when I handed my passport to the immigration agent at the airport. I felt as though I had *contrabandista* branded on my forehead. I was so jumpy that the police had me three days after I arrived. But the marvel of civilized countries is that people can be bribed, and while I was waiting for Alfonso's bank draft to reach a certain officer of the Panamanian police—waiting in the Circle Modelo in Panama City, where, as a common criminal, I had luxuries (a cell above ground, an hour a day of sun on the prison yard clean-up detail) unknown to Tinieblan political prisoners—I had a chance to think. I realized I was no better than Ñato had been when I ran into him in Piraeus: a cheap peddler, incompetent to boot. That wasn't right for me, so when I was released I left the capital, where I'd been buying up grass to sell to a Greek freighter captain, and went up past Penonomé and rented twenty acres of *llano* from a small rancher and planted it in the highest grade red pot. I bought a horse and spent my days outdoors. I found a *chola* girl and let her and appetite wean me from my addiction to Olga. There wasn't any real risk, nothing like Costaguana, but Penonomé served for a convalescence. When I rode through my marijuana field with the sun hot on my face, I felt as though I'd come back from the dead. And when, after my crop was harvested and baled I drove it down to the

Canal Zone and onto a pier crawling with gringo customs agents, and put it on the Greek captain's manifest as cattle feed, and watched it swing, bale after bale, up onto the ship, I knew I was ready for better things again.

Which meant Costaguana, where *la rabia* was now at its height. I'd hit on a way of handling big shipments which I couldn't have conceived four years before when I wasn't a serious fellow with a family to support, and when I returned to Tinieblas with my marijuana profits, I explained it to Colonel Aiax Tolete, Commandant of the Civil Guard. The Guard was the duly constituted armed force of an independent sovereign state. It could buy all the weapons it wanted right from the factories without a squeak from the United States Munitions Control Board or its counterparts in other manufacturing countries. It could import those weapons by the shipload without a glance from Tinieblan customs. And its commandant could see to it that the airport guards looked the other way when those weapons were loaded onto transport planes and flown off to the south. If Tolete would provide cover in Tinieblas, I would take all the risks in Costaguana. As he was a reasonable man, he could not turn down the offer, and we inaugurated our partnership three weeks later with a shipment of six thousand carbines.

During the next three years the Tinieblan Civil Guard bought more small arms and ammunition than the Bundeswehr, and I ran an airlift into Costaguana that kept me on the wing five nights a week. I took Jaime back with me and found a pilot named Garza who owned a 1932 vintage Boeing which looked like a sanforized B-17. When he destroyed his plane and himself trying to get back to Selva Trópica on one engine, mashed his lower body in the wreck and took all night to scream his way to death, I walked home on a broken ankle and Jaime's arm and bought a DC-3 which I learned to fly myself. Within a year I'd also bought this house and La Yegua. The only thing that was missing was the armor sheath under my skin, but it never grew back, perhaps because I was not totally immersed in violence. I kept a fingerhold on love through Olga and Mito and Olguita.

For Olga the world was ash-gray with loneliness while I was

away and napalm-orange with migraine when I was at home. She recovered all her old symptoms and found frightening new ones— an urge to take a knife to Mito and the unquenchable conviction that she would smother Olguita in her crib. On nights when I was away she had Edilma lock her in her room. Often I would wake late in the afternoon to find her crouched by the side of my bed like an orphaned kitten, yearning to be petted, but this same thirst for affection made her dependent on me and bred in her the addict's hatred for the pusher who at once supplies and withholds the needed drug. If we were together for an hour we would fight, long sterile duels in which Olga's weapons were shrieks and insults, mine cold sarcasm and disdain. Then we'd make up in bed, not peace but armistice, for the physical bond lasted till the very end, and though she resented me and I had other women, we never lost our taste for each other. She hated herself for enjoying me, and as I slept, sated and defenseless, beside her, she would wipe off love's glow like a stain and bathe in dreams of violence. She watched herself glide toward me to blind me or slice off my penis and then, as my blood spouted in the bed, throw down her knife in horror not that she'd maimed me but that now I would leave her. And for this knowledge that she needed me despite all longing to be free, she loathed herself the more.

I gave her very little of myself. When I wasn't flying to Costaguana, I was answering some other woman's message or romping with Ñato. It is hard to believe now how close we were. He didn't travel anymore but worked for the newly established Tinieblan subsidiary of the gringo crime conglomerate, running a narcotics clearing-house and angling to be made manager of the syndicate-run El Opulento casino, and he would collect me at the air strip at dawn or honk for me at the house on evenings I wasn't flying and lead me on a round of pleasures in which he seemed to care more for my amusement than his own. He arranged touching little surprises for me: a pair of matched thoroughbred New Orleans call girls whom he sent prancing into my bedroom one afternoon when he knew Olga and the kids were at La Yegua; a thirtieth birthday party for me at La Amapola (the plushest nightclub in Tinieblas, which he took over entirely for the occasion), complete with a

pistol-shaped piñata full of silver half-inchado coins and a huge
cake in the form of a relief map of Costaguana with our river wan-
derings traced in pink icing. He assisted me in the pranks I felt compelled to play. We kidnapped Alfonso one midnight, hiding our
faces behind horror masks, brandishing unloaded pistols, speaking
only English. We muscled him into a borrowed car and told him we
were going to kill him, Kiki Sancudo, for double-crossing the syndicate. Alfonso kept whining that he wasn't Kiki, he was his
brother but had nothing to do with him, and when at last we took
our masks off, he was too relieved to be angry. We burglarized the
apartment where Nacho Hormiga kept his Ticamalan girlfriend
and stole the movies he'd bragged of taking of the two of them
with a remote-control camera. Then we bribed the projectionist at
the Teatro Capitolio to splice clips of the spicier positions into the
newsreel. Ñato and I were inseparable in everything but cocaine,
which he sniffed moderately but which I would never fool with.
He wasn't my best friend, he was my only friend, all the while I
flew to Costaguana.

The end of these flights coincided with León Fuertes' campaign
for the presidency. General Huevas died and his successors, a civilian junta, promised a return to democracy. The demand for
weapons dropped, which was just as well, for León opposed the
arms trade. He didn't mind dealing with a former trader, however,
and when I offered to support him, he took me on his team and
gave me to understand I'd have a place in his cabinet. The Sancudo
name was worth votes, after all, and people remembered my Olympic
victory, and, besides, I had money to contribute. So, toward the end
of 1961 I stopped flying to Costaguana. As a consequence—or so I
thought—things went better between me and Olga. She smiled
more often, reproached me less, laughed more gaily at our parties,
embraced me more warmly, felt her headaches less, and generally
gave me cause to hope the years of strife were ending.

I had my girls of course. Olga suspected and tried desperately
both to prove I had them and to believe I did not. Now she was less
suspicious, and when she did touch on the theme of infidelity, she
was no longer bitter but rather chided playfully about a Latin
American institution which I can recommended to the city planners

of the temperate zones: I mean the particularly convenient kind of house of assignation of which Tinieblas has about a dozen—the names range from intimate, "Mi Alcobita [My Little Nook]," to patriotic, "La Tinieblina"—spaced along the airport road. One drives with one's companion through a plain cementblock façade and finds a long one-story structure broken by carports, some covered by steel curtains, others (or, hopefully, at least one) empty. One pulls one's car inside, reaches out through the car window for the button that drops the curtain, and presses. One dismounts and feeds three inchados through the waist-high slot in the front wall. One waits for the unseen attendant to press another button, and, lo, a door swings open on an air-conditioned bedroom with adjoining bath, with a room-service telephone and a coin-fed music box—discretion, privacy, all modern comfort, lease renewable every hour-and-a-half if one has the time, the strength, the inclination, and another three inchados.

These places, called "pushbuttons," generated their own mythology. Olga glossed wittily on the rumor that Lino and Marina Piojo spent Carnival Monday at a different pushbutton each year in memory of the days when she was married to Hunfredo Ladilla and he to Andrea Comején and they would take El Opulento box lunches to a pushbutton every noon, struggling through traffic with Marina collapsed across the front seat, her kerchiefed head hidden in Lino's lap. Or Olga would warn, half seriously, that I would end up like Curro Avispa who, the story went, patronized the pushbuttons so constantly that, in accord with Pavlov's findings, he got an erection each time he rang a doorbell. I would say that was very funny, but I didn't go to pushbuttons, and Olga would smile ruefully and say, "Of course, of course."

In truth I only went to one, a place called El Segundo Círculo, which was the plushest of the lot, and the very fact I went there proved me a reasonably faithful husband, for I might have kept a woman outright as most Tinieblans do, or maintained a garçonnière as Alfonso did. I was scarcely adulterous at all for a Tinieblan. I scrupulously avoided the young women Olga had for tea or played canasta with, and I did no active chasing. I merely answered the messages ladies sent, picked up the gauntlets thrown. And not all of these, for I was a busy man. Still, I went to the Second Circle often enough for the outside attendant, the one who raised the steel curtain when you were through, to know my car, a Farinata sport coupe, the only one of its kind in the country.

One dry-season evening when I had stopped going to Costaguana and was helping out on León's campaign, the wife of the French Second Secretary (an École Normale graduate three or four years younger than I with whom I played tennis now and then) smiled so prettily at me across Irene Hormiga's living room that I had no choice but to make a rendezvous with her for the following afternoon. We had a charming bout of leapfrog, phoned for drinks—they pass them through a cut in the wall, the waiter lifting a slat on his side and setting in the drinks, you lifting the slat on yours and leaving the cash—chatted about her husband (whose failings I ascribed to youth and gently excused, for if you're younger than a lady's husband, she may be pleased by jealousy, but if you're older, avuncular concern works best), took a double shower, got randy soaping each other and played a rematch, had to pay another three inchados (the waiter's knock caught us in harness, but he retired discreetly at my grunted "Later"), showered again (she first this time, then I), and dressed leisurely, so that it was already dark when the attendant pulled the curtain up behind my car. He called, and when I went to him, he said, "Excuse me, sir, but your companion forgot this the other day," and slipped a ring into my hand. I dropped it in my pocket, took my friend to where she'd left her car, and hurried home for dinner.

Six hours later as I lay propped against my triangular green pillow reading Fouché's *Mémoires*—the French were on my mind that day, after all—with the air conditioner whirring cozily and Olga asleep in the other bed (we'd gone back to sharing a bedroom, the one Elena uses now; that's how kind and loving our marriage had become), I remembered the ring. If Olga checked the pockets of my suit before sending it to the cleaners, I'd have to think up a story, so I got up stealthily and tiptoed to the closet and recovered the ring to hide it in my study. Olga woke up and asked what was wrong; I grunted and nipped into the bathroom. Door locked, light on, seat down; whose ring is this anyway? I opened my fist to find a Florentine silver band chased with sprawled cupids, quite similar to the ring I'd bought Olga six years before in Italy, so similar in fact it might have been that very ring. Thieving wops mass-produce a ring, then sell it as antique for thirty thousand lire! I couldn't remember any of my little friends wearing one like it, but, of course, it might have spilled from a dress pocket. I shifted my bare butt on the toilet seat and peered inside at a minutely carved inscription: "O/Q Siempre Insieme."

Now that was odd. I'd had the jeweler scrape that same inscription in the ring I'd bought Olga. Surely life was marvelous, full of weird replays and bizarre coincidence. Our initials, Olga's and mine, were not unique; "Siempre Insieme" had to be a common ring inscription. But for the same inscription to occur on two identical rings, for those rings to rendezvous four thousand miles from the land of their origin, surely that was marvelous. I imagined a young gringo named Quentin, a Marine lieutenant, say, attached to the Sixth Fleet, bustling into a jeweler's shop for a trinket to please his Neapolitan sweetheart Octavia. He glances about and settles for a ring like I'd bought Olga, and when the jeweler asks if he wants it engraved, says, "Yeah, our initials, 'O/Q,' and 'Always Together.'" He marries the girl and is transferred to Tinieblas, where Octavia betrays him (with the Second Secretary of the French Embassy—let coincidence be infectious). She drops her ring in the Second Circle, and since it's a busy night, the maid doesn't sweep the room but simply throws on new sheets for the next visitor (me). The ring is found after I leave and given to the attendant, who assumes it belongs to my companion and gives it to me the next time, I stop by. Interlinked net of incandescent coincidence which proved life as inventive as Scheherazade.

All the same, and though I much prefer miracles to logic, I stood up and clasped the ring in my fist and went out into the bedroom.

"Find me a sleeping pill," to dozing Olga.

"On the night table," mumbled.

"I don't know which is which."

She fumbles with ringless fingers among the flasks and bottles. "Here."

Off to her former bedroom, where she still kept her clothes, her shoes, her dressing table, and, yes, in the bottom drawer, her jewelry box. I found her wedding ring—God knew why it wasn't on her finger—the cameo that had belonged to her grandmother, her class ring from the Instituto de la Virgen Santísima, the emerald I'd given her the year before and which she refused to wear because the money that bought it was somehow soiled, but not the cupid-gamboled silver band. Which wasn't that strange, really, since it was being bent into an oval in my left fist.

Very well, but life remained wonderful. The maid, the sulky little bitch from Bastidas whom Olga had insisted on bringing into my home, though she was no kin to Edilma, had palmed the ring. And given it as a love token to the lout who mauled her in the Alameda on her nights off. He, of course, had pawned it instantly, in the big shop off Bolivar Avenue. There it was glimpsed by Colonel Wiggler's daughter Mona on one of the shopping sorties she was making daily during her midterm vacation from Finch. Mona bought it and put it in her purse and had it there the Tuesday evening before when she made eyes at me along the bar at the Fort Shafter Officers' Club. It was no more than a yard away from me during our top-down, moonlight cruise in my flashy Farinata, and later it rolled out onto the floor of room six at the Second Circle when she groped in panic for the pill she'd forgotten to take that morning. And that was why the ring was now neither on Olga's finger nor in her jewelry box but mashed flat in my left fist.

I tried to pry the ring back into shape with an eyebrow pencil. It stayed badly bent, and I threw it into the box. I wasn't completely happy with my latest account of the ring's travels, but the only other one I could think of was even more fantastic. I'd accompanied León to Otán the weekend before, taking Jaime and the Cranston, leaving my coupe for Olga. It was conceivable—as a hypothesis it was just conceivable—that she'd taken it to the Second Circle. With her lover (what a disgusting term!) driving. With the pinky-dicked, bloat-scrotumed, slimy-assed son of a whore driving my car, so that the attendant (who despite being mired in loose fucking up to his eyebrows retained some faith in womankind) took him for me. But no. It was conceivable in theory but impossible in fact. Olga couldn't be unfaithful to me.

She was sitting up in bed with her lamp on when I reentered our bedroom. "Are you nervous about something, Kiki?"

"No."

"You've got a face like an ogre."

"It's the face God gave me," complain to Him."

"Something's bothering you. Want to tell me about it?"

"No." I got into bed.

"Well." She sat with her knees up under the blanket and her hands folded calmly in her lap. "There's something I want to tell you."

"Let's go to sleep," putting out my lamp.

"No. I have to tell you now. I've been unfaithful to you."

"For the love of God, Olga, it's after one in the morning. Do we have to play these games now?"

"It's not a game, Kiki." I half-opened my eyes to see her slide a wary glance at me. "It's true. I've been unfaithful to you."

"Don't say that any more, Olga. Let's go to sleep."

"No, Kiki, it's true. I've been to bed with another man. I have a lover."

"Don't use that word."

"You're supposed to demand to know his name, and I, of course, won't tell you. It doesn't matter. You don't even know him."

"I don't believe a word of it."

"You don't want to believe it."

"Of course I don't want to believe it. Do I look like some kind of masochist who's always spying on his wife, who's dying to catch her humping his best friend so he can suffer? I don't want to believe it, and I don't believe it, and it isn't true."

"It is true, Kiki, though he's not a friend of yours. He's just a man, He's been after me for months, and I didn't think I could do it, but I did finally and it worked out fine. You can check if you want. We went out Saturday night while you were in Otán. We took your car because his . . . well, because his might have been

recognized, and went to a pushbutton. I've heard about pushbuttons and talked about them, and now I've finally been to one. It
was called the Second Circle. I didn't know you could have drinks
there. Music too. Someone in one of the other rooms kept playing
Mexican songs. I thought it might be you, Kiki. Did you sneak back
Saturday night, Kiki? Wouldn't that have been funny if you were in
the next room with one of your little whores?"

During which speech I got out of bed and put on my shorts.
For some reason it was suddenly embarrassing to be naked in front
of Olga. Also I felt like being on my feet.

"Why don't you say something, Kiki? It's very important. I've
been to bed with another man. I didn't think I could do it, but I did.
Then I thought it was only because you were away, so I saw him
again today, and it was perfectly all right. And I was terrified you
might find out, but you don't pay enough attention to me to find
out something like that, and you don't think enough of me to
believe it. Then, just now, I decided to tell you, because it's dirty
to be doing things behind your back. What are you going to do,
Kiki? Are you going to kill me?"

"I can see I won't get any sleep here tonight."

"You're so cool, Kiki. I supposed you didn't love me enough to
be jealous, but I thought your vanity would be hurt."

I wasn't cool, I was numb. What Olga had said didn't seem to
relate to me. I considered it as a problem involving two people I
knew slightly. I'd always thought I loved Olga, but if she'd opened
herself to another man . . . I couldn't love her then, could I? It
wasn't reasonable for a man to love a woman who betrayed him.
Some men could do that, but it wasn't the sort of thing I did. As for
my vanity, it couldn't really be damaged by the actions of a whore,
and if Olga had spread herself for another man, she had to be a
whore. When I recall that moment—the scene took place twelve
yards from here; Mito was asleep in this very bed—I marvel at the
way I was able to separate things. The French diplomat's wife, with
whom I'd made love twice that afternoon, wasn't a whore. She was
a perfectly normal young woman who'd been attracted to me and
had a small adventure. Olga, on the other hand, had to be a whore,
for though she was my wife, she'd opened her legs and let another

man put his prong in her. If she'd done that, she was a whore, whom I could neither love nor be injured by.

"Oh, Kiki, I hope I haven't hurt you. I had to find out. The man doesn't mean anything to me, Kiki, but I was happy when he came after me because it seemed I might be a human being again. I had to find out. I was so scared, but it was all right. I hope I haven't hurt you, but I had to tell you. I think it's dirty the way some women fool their husbands. And I had to tell you so you'd know I was a free person again. Don't look at me like that, Kiki. Please tell me what you're going to do."

"I'm going out." I got out the suit I'd worn that afternoon from the closet and draped it on my bed. "I won't be back till tomorrow." I put on the pants and took a sport shirt from the drawer. "Then tomorrow you'll tell me the truth, that you've made this whole business up to get a reaction from me." I got a fresh pair of socks and found my shoes under the chair. "And I'll never bother you about it. I won't even think about it. Except if, next year, say, we want to laugh about it."

"But it is true, Kiki. It's true, and you've got to accept it."

"Tomorrow you'll tell me the truth."

I checked into El Opulento, but I didn't feel like sleeping and had left my book at home, so I went up to the casino and played twenty-one, betting the minimum each hand, until the place closed. Then I chatted with the assistant manager for a while, and finally, about five, I went to sleep. I didn't sleep well and woke before ten. I didn't feel like having breakfast and went straight home. But when I got there, Olga and Mito and Olguita and all their clothes were gone.

34

"Kiki?" Marta pecks in. "Are you asleep?"

"No. Waiting. The buzzer's slipped. What time is it?"

"Almost four." Comes in warily, lips pursed.

"What's wrong?"

"Colonel Gatillo just called. The Guard has Jaime."

"Why?"

"Oh, Kiki, you know why. They arrested him outside Ñato's. Can't you wait till after the election?"

"Is Gatillo on the phone?"

"No. He said to call him back."

"Then put my clothes on me. Get me into my chair. Wait. Call Elena and go get Otilio."

"What are you going to do, Kiki?"

"Whatever's necessary. Do as I say."

A cop guides Jaime, handcuffed, into the guard room at head-quarters. Sergeant loafing by the door grins and says something about indians; laughs at his joke and pokes his club between Jaime's buttocks. Jaime twists his shoulder out of the cop's grip and slams sergeant with clasped hands. Loops the cuffs over the sergeant's head and jerks against his throat. Cop cracks Jaime above the ear with his club; Jaime grunts and rams his knee into the sergeant's back for purchase. Slow-motion club blows explode on Jaime's head as the sergeant's knees buckle. Guardias converge on central group in great slow-motion bounds. Officer rises slow motion from behind his desk, opens the flap of his holster, draws his pistol, thumbs the safety forward, aims . . .

"Are you all right, Kiki?" Elena at the foot of my bed.

"Jaime's in trouble. Put my clothes on me."

"You shouldn't get exci . . ."

"Don't give me advice. Do as I say. Shorts and pants."

She gets a pair of shorts from the dresser and strips back the bedclothes. Works the shorts up my legs. Marta comes in, Otilio in the doorway behind her.

"Help Elena."

They tug the shorts under my butt, bunch in my baubles. Intent glances at each other as Elena rolls the legs of my trousers. Slips them over my feet. Heave-ho, like a pair of mortician's aides with a corpse who's late for his funeral.

"Get me in my chair. You hold it, Marta. Otilio will lift along with Elena. Let's go."

"If you fall, Kiki . . ."

"Don't worry about it, Elena. Pretend you're starring for Hitchcock and have to get rid of a body. Move!"

Up and in. Otilio lifts, Elena guides, Marta holds. Scrape my back on the wicker, but that's no matter. *Two guardias are dragging Jaime down the stone steps to the Sala de Interrogaciones. Each holds a foot, and his head bumps stickily from step to step.*

"Roll me to the study, Elena. Marta, take the phone downstairs and get me Gatillo. Stay on to translate. Come on!" *Two guardias stand by Jaime's feet while an officer pisses on his face to revive him.*

Elena holds the library phone to my mouth and ear. *In Guardia Headquarters the light is blinking on Flaco Gatillo's private wire. Three flights below a stocky guardia sways on his left leg and hicks Jaime's head like a football. An eye blossoms from its socket, and the officer shouts, "Goal!"*

"Colonel Gatillo."

He flashes on the backs of my closed eyelids, leaning forward with his belly pressed against the desk, clutching the receiver to a bulging check. Imprisoned within the blubbery colonel is a slim lieutenant who used to wait on the fringe of the grass strip beyond the Reservation, wait in the dawn twilight for me to swing in from Costaguana. He would wave with his right hand—his left was handcuffed to a bank satchel—and then lope over like a borzoi to let me stuff Tolete's share into the bag.

"Señor César Sancudo will speak with you, Colonel," says Marta. "I will interpret anything you can't understand."

"Flaco."

"Yes, Kiki. Want to hear about Jaime?"

"Yes."

"Ñato spotted him parked outside his house and called a friend of his here, Captain Acha. Acha sent an unmarked car and four men. They arrested Jaime, who was armed. One of them drove your car here; it's parked in the lot outside. Acha ordered Jaime held for loitering in case Ñato wants to prefer assault charges."

"What. Assault?"

"Threatening or menacing is an assault."

"What about shooting a man in the back?"

"What?"

"Señor Sancudo wishes to know whether shooting a man in the back is also considered assault."

"Look, Kiki, I can't do anything about that. You know Ñato was charged with attempted murder and released on bail, and the order from the top is not to bother him. You know that, Kiki.'

"How's Jaime?"

"He's all right, Kiki. Acha wasn't sure of the charge, so they didn't take him downstairs right away. When I heard about it, they had him handcuffed to a bench in the guard room. I told Acha to leave him there. I figured you'd want to bail him out."

"No bail, Flaco. Let him go."

"What?"

"Señor Sancudo suggests that instead of his posting bail you release the prisoner, Colonel."

"He's been charged, Kiki. I'll get the bail set at fifty inchados. What's fifty inchados? That way it'll all be normal."

"That way it'll be the same as Ñato. Forty thousand people saw Ñato shoot me down, and he's been free on bail for four years. So free he can have Jaime locked up for nothing. So free the Guardia jumps all over to do him favors. And now you're going to do me a big favor and let me bail Jaime out. No, Flaco. The charges against Jaime are shit! He has a permit for his gun, and he can park anywhere he feels like. You're going to tear up those charges, Flaco, and let Jaime go. Not because it's the nice thing to do. Not even because it's the right thing to do. But because it's the smart thing to do." All of which Marta translates faithfully.

"Would you threaten an old friend, Kiki?"

"No. I just think you've got more political sense than Captain Acha."

"What?"

"Señor Sancudo believes you better able than Captain Acha to predict the result of the forthcoming election."

"Ha, ha. Is that what you said, Kiki? All right. I'll let him go. But not because I need election insurance. It brings back my youth to hear you. Putting the screws on, just like before. I'm not scared of you, Kiki, but I do have a good memory."

"For the happy days when you were Aiax's bagman?"

"What?"

"Señor Sancudo asks if you particularly recall the period in which you and Colonel Tolete were associated in . . ."

"Sure I remember, but that doesn't scare me either. I remember you, Kiki. You treated me all right. I'll let your boy go."

"Thanks, Flaco."

"Does it hurt to say it, Kiki?"

"No. Thanks."

"I know how you feel, Kiki. I like to scare people too. But it's not so bad to be helped out of friendship. I'll send you your boy."

Nod for Elena to put down the phone.

"Do you want the rest of your clothes, Kiki? Otilio's brought them."

Nod.

"Are you all right?"

Nod. "A little tired."

"You were worried about Jaime, weren't you, caro?" She slips the right sleeve over my wrist, lifts my left hand and puts it through the other sleeve, then tucks the shirt between my back and the chair.

Nod. "If they'd touched him, he'd have fought. That would have been bad."

"I was afraid you'd go down there." Buttoning my shirt.

"I would have. But you needn't have been afraid. Nothing's going to happen to me, Elena. Don't you see that? Oh, some night I'll vomit in my sleep and choke on it, but I won't die in action. It's Jaime who takes all the risks now."

"A convulsion?" She kneels to pull on my socks.

"You're right! I might have had a fit down there. They'd have been stuck then, by God! Alfonso would accuse General Puñete of murdering me on Pepe's orders, and everyone would believe it. Even Pepe would believe it if the story ran long enough. There was that chance, wasn't there?"

"Do you want to die, Kiki?" Keeps her eyes on my shoelaces.

"Marta asked me that this morning. The answer is no. But just being alive isn't enough. I want to feel alive. Can you understand that?"

"Yes, caro."

"Marta can't. But if women weren't different, no one would want more than one. Send her up to me, will you? She said she'd read to me. And Jaime when he comes. And, Elena . . ." She turns back from the door. "Thanks for before. For the siesta. It was lovely."

"Prego, carissimo," smiling. And adds without the slightest sarcasm, "It's the woman who must feel grateful after she's been in bed with a real man."

35

"Are you happy, Kiki?" Marta smiles bitterly from the doorway. "Are you happy now?" She's good in a crisis: does what's necessary and saves her needle for afterward. "Now everyone will say that Kiki's still a big macho."

"I'm happy Jaime's out. Thanks for helping. If we hadn't gotten him out, he might have been badly hurt, even killed."

"And whose fault would it have been?"

"That wouldn't have made much difference."

"It would have been your fault, Kiki."

"And Jaime's. For getting caught."

"Your fault, Kiki. You sent him to Ñato's. Couldn't you wait till after the election?"

"I only sent him to remind Ñato we're still around. Jaime wasn't going to hurt him."

"That comes later."

Nod.

Looks down at her feet. "I won't stay for that, Kiki. I'm leaving tomorrow."

"When'd you decide that?"

"Just now. I was going to wait till Phil finished his film, but now I'm leaving tomorrow. If you come too, I'll stay with you. And take care of you."

"And if I don't?"

"Phil wants to marry me."

"Do you want to marry him?"

"It's a solution. I won't stay here. I won't stay for more violence. Will you come, Kiki? Will you leave with me tomorrow?"

Shake my head.

"It means so much to you, killing Ñato?"

Nod.

"Or I mean so little. You don't care if I go or stay, do you?"

"I care, Marta."

"Not enough. I can't compete with Ñato. That I love you and am willing to spend my life taking care of you can't rival the pleasure of seeing a man killed. Is it such fun, Kiki, killing people?"

"I can't have him sit there, Marta. I can't have him sit there safe in his house after what he's done to me. Here I am with my life smashed, and there he is, able to call his friend Acha and have Jaime arrested and maybe beaten and killed. Should I forgive him, Marta? Here I am, and do you know what Ñato's doing? Ñato's shaving. He shaves in the afternoon so his face will be smooth for his girlfriends. When he's finished shaving, his mother will bring him a cup of coffee, a demitasse of strong black coffee with three spoonfuls of sugar. He'll drink that, and at five he'll go collect some little typist or salesgirl. On the way to wherever he takes her, he'll buy an evening paper, because Ñato doesn't like to make love. What he likes is to have a girl fondle him while he reads the newspaper and smokes a joint. And here I am, Marta. Here I am. Here I am. Here I am.

"Well, I won't have it. It can't go on. He has to die. Would you rather I forgave him, Marta? Do you want him to go on enjoying life after what he's done to us? Isn't he your enemy too?"

Stares at me for a moment, ready to cry, then fires grief to fury. "Oh, how I hate you, Kiki! Oh, God, how I hate you! All your life has been violence and death, and you've fouled me with it. I thought once you were changing, but you changed right back, back to the side of death. How many have you killed, Kiki? How many did you and your guns kill in Costaguana? How many died because of you in the flag riot? I never loved Ñato, but I loved you, Kiki, and all you want is killing. Oh, God, I hate you, Kiki! And I'm glad you're paralyzed. I'm glad you can't kill any more. You have to have someone do it for you. It's what you deserve, Kiki. It's what you asked for! I'm glad! I'm glad!"

And she runs out with her hands over her face.

36

Counting the volumes that flank my unplucked Dumas. No Monte Cristo today, but in a few minutes Jaime will be here to tell me if he saw Ñato. And at six I'll go to the rally. And tomorrow Marta will leave me, then Elena in a week or two, and I'll be trapped in my mind, sewn up in a sack full of rodents, buried alive with roaches nesting in my mouth and scorpions stalking across my eyeballs.

Better count the books. Marta's too generous. Embraces the error decried by Tolstoy and his neighbor Toynbee, giving the individual too much influence on history. The Costaguanans had no trouble getting arms while I was in Europe with Olga. Would have killed each other with teeth and fingernails in any case, as Ñato pointed out. Though he sought to justify the gun business morally, whereas I merely wish to avoid the cult of personality, blah, blah, blah, but I have to think of something. For example, I never anticipated a riot or even hoped for one. Never dreamed the gringos would be so helpful. I was only looking for a little excitement, and the gringos were so helpful I wound up in the palace, for half an hour anyway.

Defending national sovereignty. The issue was there, but only the students had done more than talk about it. Doctors of education would fly down from Ann Arbor and Chapel Hill with AID contracts and flasks of Kaopectate to click their tongues over the failure of Latin America's universities; the student uprising hadn't caught on yet in the States. We were used to it, having had rollicking good riots over things like cracked toilets at the Politécnico, so no one was surprised at the students' rage when Bonifacio Aguado (who had been León's vice president) refused to press for renegotiation of the Reservation treaty.

That was a sore point, our national abscess. León had promised to cure it and took the matter up with Kennedy in the most statesmanlike manner conceivable: breakfast chat during the San José presidents' meeting.

"Did you get anything?" I asked when he and Carlitos came out. "Besides ham and eggs, I mean."

"We'll get something." He walked straight on, holding his hands in front of him like a surgeon leaving the operating theater, and those of us who'd been waiting fell in beside and behind him. Carlitos was telling someone how he had quoted Kennedy's university speech back to him. "He's a decent man," León continued; then he dropped his voice: "That's the difference between a sailor and an infantryman; he's never had to stick a bayonet into anyone."

Sure enough, that fall León got a letter from him proposing negotiation of a new treaty. That was two weeks before Kennedy's assassination and six weeks before León's.

Johnson, though a navy man himself, probably wasn't as decent as Kennedy, and Bonifacio Aguado certainly wasn't as forceful as León. Some twit in the House of Representatives accused the Democrats of wanting to "give away the Reservation," and Johnson told Aguado he couldn't think about the treaty till after November. Give away the Reservation! As though it were theirs! They bleat the same way about "losing Asia," and when did they own Asia? They rented the Reservation on a sixty-five-year-old swindle and were all constipated over renegotiating the lease, and Bonifacio Aguado, who was terrified of gringos and everyone else, said he understood, he understood. So the students demonstrated and tried to haul down the flag at the U.S. Embassy, and the Guardia beat them back, and they rioted along Bolivar Avenue.

The regular politicians nodded gravely and clucked about how the students were the conscience of the country but street violence wasn't the proper instrument for vindicating the national honor, and meanwhile they were fouling their drawers in fear of revolution and thanking God for all those gringo troops next door. But not Kiki. He resigned his embassy in protest. He came home and declared that as the Reservation was Tinieblan soil, he would carry the flag through it to Roosevelt Beach (where Palmiro Inchado's head had been washed up) on the anniversary of discovery.

Some people called me a patriot; others accused me of exploiting the nation's plight for personal power. Both were wrong, though I didn't say so. The treaty irked me, but I was no insect that would confuse my personal integrity with that of the hive. As for power, I hadn't the taste for it yet. I knew it was a great delicacy which many men craved, but it didn't make my mouth water. I wanted excitement. I hadn't had any since I'd quit the gun trade, and there were the students, raising hell and fighting the Guardia and scaring their parents and annoying the gringos. Why shouldn't I have a piece of the treaty action? Wasn't it the best action around?

The day after I made my declaration, a gringo colonel, who was public information officer for the United States Hemispheric Interdiction Team, called a press conference and said I couldn't bring a Tinieblan flag into the Reservation because the commanding general wasn't authorized to display any national emblem but the Stars and Stripes. So that afternoon I told the press that the general didn't have to worry; I, not he, would do all the displaying. More, so the general wouldn't get in trouble I would swear out an affidavit that it was entirely my idea and that I would execute it without aid or comfort from the general. Another man might have been solemn, but I thought some gringo telling me I couldn't wave my own flag in my own country was much too serious a matter to be solemn about. That called for either blood or banter. Certain prominent Tinieblans, men who sat around the Club Mercantil harrumphing at each other, said I was making a mockery of the flag, but the common folk, the students especially, liked my approach, and right away I began hearing from all sorts of individuals and groups who wanted to march with me. I was also visited by a young man named Manfredo Canino Rabioso who wanted to overthrow the government. He represented a faction of a faction of the University Students' Syndicate and claimed his group would have Bonifacio out of the palace in jig time if I would give them weapons.

Canino was a resolute fellow, the leading distributor of mayhem during the romp down Bolivar. His illustrious family had fallen on hard times; he was estranged from his father, a hack whom Aguado had named to a municipal judgeship; but he managed well enough, supporting himself on the earnings of a cantina barmaid and on small sums paid him by some shop owners in return for advance warning of student demonstrations. I didn't want to blunt his initiative, so I refused to give him guns but offered to sell him some Schmeisers at cost whenever he could show me the cash. Meanwhile the general huddled with the U.S. Ambassador to Tinieblas and made and received calls on his hot line to the Pentagon and finally instructed his information officer to tell the press that Mr. Sancudo was free to enter the Reservation (restricted areas excepted) any time he wished, but that if he wanted to bring a flag or a group with him, he would have to have a parade permit. If Mr. Sancudo applied for such a permit, his application would be given all due consideration. It wasn't long before the Associated Press called asking if I was going to apply, and I said I was sure the people in the Reservation were busy defending us all from communism and I wasn't going to bother them with idle paperwork. All I was going to do was stroll out to the beach with a flag and maybe a few friends. No one in the Reservation had to go out of his way for me. I certainly wouldn't lift a finger one way or the other if the general felt like carrying a U.S. flag from, say, Sunset Boulevard to Malibu. Then Reservation gringos began writing letters to the editors of the English-language papers, calling me a communist and saying that the Tinieblan flag had no business in the Reservation, at least not till the treaty ran out in another nine-hundred-odd years. Alfonso set aside a column in the *Morning Mail* for such letters and then expanded it to a full page, and the circulation of the paper tripled, and an enterprising Jamaican set up in the Café Bahía, translating the letters aloud to a teeth-gnashing audience and drafting irate replies in English at one centavo the word. These letters, and their replies and counterreplies, inflamed tempers on both sides of Washington Avenue and contributed to the severity of the flag plague.

Quite soon after I announced my intention to carry the

Tinieblan flag out to Roosevelt Beach, U.S. flags began appearing, on houses in the Reservation. Civilians (dock workers, maintenance men, paper pushers) began it; the military took it up. As the controversy grew—and I never contributed to it or organized anything; all I did was announce my plans and, when anyone asked if he could go with me, say, "Sure, why not? Come along"—Tinieblans began putting out flags of their own. This was not a traditional practice. Stores soon ran out of Tinieblan tricolors. But a rush order was put in to manufacturers in Osaka, and by midsummer almost every house in the capital had a flag or two draped on it. This led Marta's uncle Lazarillo to comment in *Diario de la Bahía* that "una peste de banderas," a flag plague, was epidemic in the land.

Then symbols blossomed into symptoms. The first case of flag plague was recorded in the Reservation when a journeyman plumber, who had recently had an anti-flag-march letter published, showed up at an out-patient clinic with exactly fifty tiny blue stars on the back of his writing hand. The same week a man was treated at Marine barracks sick call for red and white stripes on his forearm. Then, on July 4th, fully a hundred bathers at Roosevelt Beach were amazed to discover red-white-and-blue shields on each others' chests and bikini midriffs. Meanwhile doctors at San Bruno Hospital began noting similar irritations in Tinieblans. Habitués of the Café Bahía letter sessions went purple-green-and-yellow in the face. The national colors bloomed on the biceps of student leaders and the buttocks of journalists. These stigmata were not only indelible but had an eerie way of glowing in the dark, and they burned painfully whenever the afflicted heard his national anthem played at a sporting event or on the radio. As more and more Tinieblans became obsessed with their right to fly their flag in the Reservation and gringos with their obligation to keep it out, the plague spread and waxed virulent. The entire membership of the Tinieblan College of Attorneys (which had petitioned the World Court to adjudicate the flag dispute) developed purple-green-and-yellow spirals around their penises. Flag-conscious housewives woke from their sleep with purple-green-and-yellow portraits of General Feliciano Luna and other national heroes glowing on their thighs and abdomens. The commander of American Legion Post

One in the Reservation, who was already starred and striped from crown to toe, sprouted the hooked beak and jagged talons of the heraldic bald eagle, while a colonel on the Interdiction Team Staff (who had been doing some clandestine canvassing for Goldwater) found his forehead transformed into a miniature Allied Chemical Building across which phrases like MY COUNTRY RIGHT OR WRONG AND AMERICA: LOVE HER OR LEAVE HER ran in red-white-and-blue letters. No deaths were reported nor any cases in children under six, and sufferers usually recovered after four or five weeks of isolation. Reinfection was common, however, the second affliction being generally more severe than the first, and only a few were immune. The plague spared only those who did not get worked up over flags and anthems, those who were too busy to worry about them or who, like myself, refused to take them seriously—in short, those very few who, either by reason or intuition, could detect a difference between symbol and substance.

So it went all summer and fall. The flag plague raged; the flag march was the biggest thing in Tinieblas. The only distraction came early in November when a group of university students stole two trucks and fled to the cordillera, stopping to shoot up the town of Mercedilla with Schmeiser machine pistols and issue a manifesto calling for the overthrow of Bonifacio Aguado ("Lackey of the Wall Street Imperialists and Running Dog of the Pentagon Warmongers"), but as opponents of the flag march chose to connect me with this insurrection, it only brought me more attention, and every eye in the country was focused on me on the anniversary of discovery.

That day, which was also my thirty-fourth birthday, dawned rainy. It kept raining, and my phone kept ringing. I told reporters that, yes, I would march, rain or shine, and Alfonso that, no, the gringos wouldn't kill me except by accident, and Elena (calling from Los Angeles) that, all right, I'd wear my Olympic medal, and meanwhile, despite the rain, a small crowd was gathering outside my house and a large one on Washington Avenue. At exactly four o'clock, which was the hour I'd announced for my stroll, the rain stopped. I went downstairs. Jaime had the flag I'd bought—a small one, about the size of a bath towel—rolled up on its gold-painted stick. He took it out and put it in the back seat of the car. Then I went out after him.

There were a few shouts and a scatter of applause, nothing like what I'd heard in Helsinki, but it moved me strangely. These people—perhaps there were fifty, half of them students, for I hadn't wished anyone to come to my house and had used the phrase "See you on Washington Avenue" to anyone who asked about the march—these people wanted me to lead them. They were all plague victims, some of them very far gone, and saw me as a symbol, not a human being; yet their fealty was exhilarating. Sharp, like a whiff of ether. It made my head ring slightly and brought a glow like I'd felt when I said "Now" to Angela or when I squeezed a round through Memo's lips. I all but whinnied with excitement when a girl put her foot on the bumper of my car and drew her skirt up to show me my portrait etched on her inner thigh in purple-green-and-yellow above that of Simón Mocoso. To keep this lovely feeling I put the girl up front between Jaime and me and let other kids climb in the back and on the trunk and fenders, and off we went at ten miles an hour, men jogging alongside joking with me through the window, horn tooting, kids shouting happily at pedestrians and motorists, as to a fair or wedding. I was criticized for it later. Iron-boweled mastodons in Tinieblas as well as the States decried the "carnival atmosphere," but the only thing that redeems patriotism is gaiety. Only gaiety keeps it from congealing into a glacier of fecal filth sixty-storeys tall such as engulfed the Kennedy funerals (all that solemn patriotism, when what was called for was an Irish wake and a fine, prancing revolution).

Well, we went gaily that afternoon, piping the city into our trail. I heard later that the passengers of several busses voted democratically to follow me, and the drivers stopped to debark dissenters and then abandoned their routes and tailed me to Washington Avenue and parked their busses and got down with their passengers to join the crowd. Oh, yes, there was a crowd. Some said five thousand, some said ten thousand. I don't know, but there were people massed in the avenue for blocks on either side of Alfonso's building, plague victims all with the Tinieblan colors burning on their arms and faces, and opposite them inside the

Reservation fence a goodly crew of star-spangled gringos and, of course, the troops in combat gear, helmets, and fixed bayonets. Those troops gave me a faint scare. Not for myself—the glow took care of that—but I had a fleeting worry that something might happen to these people who were smiling at me, pushing back to make room for my car, pressing in around it, slapping the roof gaily, reaching in to squeeze my shoulder, shouting, "Here he is! Here's Kiki!" But when I got out among them I was so high and glowing (as with a woman or when winning a fight) I didn't care what happened. I might have understood then the craving some men have for power, especially men who're not adept at love or combat, or men too old to gobble such bonbons any more, but I still wasn't ready to examine life. I was much too occupied with living it.

I got down, and the crowd foamed about me to sweep me up, but I shook my head, smiling, and waved my hand, no, for I'd done nothing yet to deserve being carried on men's shoulders, and after a minute they sucked back and left a little gap around me. Then I saw it wasn't just common people and students who'd come but men of my own class: Lino was there, and Meco, and others, even Alfonso, dressed to kill and carrying a furled umbrella and with a gorgeous tricolor stain spiraling up from beneath his button-down and twining across one cheek. I was their leader too. So I took my flag from Jaime and unrolled it and raised it in the air in one hand as high as I could, and there was a great shout from all those pressed and milling people. Then I laid the flag on my shoulder as a soldier does his rifle and smiled around at my troops and waved my left hand for them to make a little way and started walking toward the Reservation.

The only spot on the Reservation border not zipped up with cyclone fence was the intersection of Washington Avenue and Roosevelt Road (a street which curved through the civilian housing area out to the beach). The north corner of this intersection was commanded, as the military historians say, by the Y.M.C.A., which faced Roosevelt but whose west windows gave excellent vantage of the Tinieblan side of Washington from the Instituto Politécnico, along the block of fancy shops to the Edificio Petrolero and past the lower and less sumptuous office buildings to Alcibiades Oruga Park and the Chamber of Deputies. Above the south corner, on a considerable hill, stood the Reservation Club, a fine example of Early Gringo Imperialist architecture, whose swaybacked roof and sagging screened veranda were said to symbolize Uncle Sam straining beneath the White Man's Burden. In defiance of all Captain Liddell Hart's strictures against relinquishing the element of surprise, Sancudo (who, like Caesar and De Gaulle, enjoys third person in his war commentaries) had announced this intersection as the point where he would penetrate the Reservation. General Spear, Commander-in-Chief of the United States Hemispheric Interdiction Team, had defended it stoutly.

The windows of the Y.M.C.A. were choked with binoculared staff officers, seersuckered embassy observers, snoops from the Army Metaphysical Police, and spooks from the CIA. Roosevelt Road was held by two platoons of infantry, supported by a tanklike armored personnel carrier (with a black sergeant and a .50 caliber machine gun mounted on its top) and a squad from the 429th Airborne Vomit-Gas Battalion. A reserve platoon was posted on the Reservation Club lawn, their morale bolstered by numerous civilian spectators, many of whom were exercising their constitutional right to bear arms. Besides regular phone lines from Y.M.C.A. and Club, communications were provided by a command car with microwave telephone and three radio-equipped Military Police sedans. (One can imagine General Spear following every move on a huge mock-up of the Reservation in his A-bomb-proof War Room eighty feet beneath Fort Shafter Headquarters: white-faced WAC's with overly calm voices take messages and relay them to a trio of lieutenants with croupier sticks; these reach gingerly to maneuver toy trucks and soldiers around on the board.) Tactical command was entrusted to a full colonel with four decks of ribbons on his blouse and REMEMBER THE ALAMO in red-white-and-blue letters on his forehead. Into these formidable defenses Sancudo now hurled himself.

As I stepped out from the crowd toward the double line of troops, a helmeted captain gave them: "Attention! Port, Arms! On Guard!" Heels clomped together; rifles swung up; bayonets dipped toward my chest. Most of the front rank had stars and stripes on their faces, but there was one young fellow almost directly ahead of me with nothing but freckles, and I thought, I'll walk for him and see if he has guts enough to stick me. Then the colonel came over at a parade-ground strut and stepped in front of me. I stopped and felt the crowd stop behind me.

"Sir," puffed the colonel. "This is a U.S. military reservation. Unauthorized personnel may not enter." He bit his lip and the letters on his forehead vanished, then blinked back DON'T TREAD ON ME.

"Colonel," I snorted. "This is part of my country. I don't need your authorization." As I spoke, according to people behind me, the hack of my neck went purple-green-and-yellow.

"My orders are to keep you out."

"My intention is to walk right in."

We stared at each other and found we could communicate tele-pathically. Our thoughts crouched behind our eyes, then sprang over at each other:

I'd like to wipe you and your commie rabble out to the last snotnose greaseball.

I don't care if you kill me and everyone else on this street, I'm not giving up this lovely glow.

Lucky for you I've been ordered to use restraint.

That's your problem. In ten seconds I'm coming through.

My troops will stop you.

The first gringo that touches me gets this flag in his ear. His buddies retaliate, I defend myself, the crowd mixes in, your men open fire. A bloodbath, in short.

You'll be responsible.

No. You. I'll be dead.

You prick! You don't care!

Me? I'm enjoying myself.

Christ! Twenty years of service for this!

Better think of something.

I'll pass the buck to the C-in-C.

Good idea.

"Wait here, sir," he said. His forehead flashed STARS AND STRIPES FOREVER. "I'll communicate your intention to my superiors."

He trotted over to his command car and reached in the window for the phone. I turned and stepped back almost to the line of bayonets and held up my left hand and yelled to the crowd (which was jeering the soldiers good-humoredly) that the gringos were a little confused, that we'd have to give them time to get organized. The colonel raised a finger to test the wind, which was blowing toward the Reservation, then bent back to the phone. I wondered briefly whether I'd mind being bayoneted to death and decided I wouldn't. It would be all over before I lost my glow. The sun was out now, and flags were waving above the crowd, and purple-green-and-yellow throats were shouting, "Give it to 'em, Kiki!" and I couldn't understand why I'd waited so long to try something like this. Then the colonel returned with a miniature Old Glory fluttering at half-mast on his forehead and said I could enter the Reservation under escort and take a delegation of twelve with me.

I was tempted to turn this down—everyone goes and no escort. But all I'd said was that I was going; I hadn't organized a march. As long as I took a flag out to the beach I was keeping my promise, and I could raise a mob for something else in a week or two. So I told the colonel all right and yelled the terms to the crowd and asked who wanted to go with me. Not everyone did, not nearly everyone, but there were many more than twelve. I hesitated, not knowing how to pick, and then decided on a group of fourteen-year-olds who had got the National Museum to loan them the first Tinieblan flag, one sewn by Simón Mocoso's sister the night before we declared independence. I was later accused of seeking to shield myself behind children, but that wasn't it. I thought that particular flag would be the best one to take, but mainly I was having so much fun I wanted the kids to share it. We filed through a gap in the gringo ranks and set off, accompanied by a lieutenant and two squads from the reserve platoon and trailed by a Military Police car.

We swung jauntily along between rows of grand-old-flag-draped houses and red-white-and-blue-glaring faces, the kids taking turns carrying the flag and I chatting with them, trying to make them stop calling me Señor Sancudo. Three months later I had to recall our picnic sense of safety when a garishly-tighted and still unplowed Marta berated me across our dinner plates for risking children's lives. I wished my own kids were there, though Mito was ten and Olguita only seven and Olga, who had custody, would never have let them go even if they'd been older. It was such a fine lark, carrying the flag with all those gringos watching, and as we weren't solemn the patriotism of it did no damage. Then, where the road dipped past a movie theater and turned left toward the beach, our way was blocked by about two hundred civilians waving flags and shouting insults. The lieutenant tried halfheartedly to negotiate a passage for us, at which they called him a traitor and started singing "The Star-Spangled Banner." My kids drew in around me and took up "Hijos de Tinieblas" in return. I realized then I'd caught the plague, for at the first strains the back of my neck began burning as though from bee stings. But one of the worst things about the plague was that one actually enjoyed that burning, and when the lieutenant came to tell me we'd have to go back to the border, I began singing too.

Well, there we stood, both sides burning with plague and blaring anthems at each other, while the soldiers shuffled about sheepishly and the lieutenant struggled between his orders and his wish to be accepted by his countrymen. When the gringo crowd realized our escort sympathized with them, they began pushing in toward us. A girl was holding our flag just then, and a matron in slacks and too much lipstick leaned over a trooper's shoulder and spat juicily on her school uniform. That amazed me. The sight of that gorgon face rammed forward spitting paralyzed me as fully as I am right now, but it seemed to hearten the gringos. They pressed in, and a beefy fellow with red-and-white stars all over his face pushed a soldier aside and slapped the little girl who'd been spat on and tore our flag off its pole.

I hit him harder than I'd ever hit anyone, harder than I'd hit anyone in the brawling days with Duncan, a lot harder than I hit sailors, the big sailor in that Piraeus bar. Nothing in all my life has pleased me as much as the way I hit that man, and if I enjoy killing Ñato half as much I'll be happy. Twenty minutes later I found a broken incisor embedded in my middle-finger knuckle, and if I'd hit him once more I'd have killed him. But I yelled for the kids to run back to the border, and when I reached down to pick him up and hit him again, a soldier clubbed me with his rifle butt and I went out.

I came to in the back of the police car. My scalp was cut and my shirt was plastered to my back with my own blood and my medal had been torn away. They took me to be bandaged at Fort Shafter Dispensary. When I was led back to the car, the driver was asking over the radio if I was to be held at the stockade. "Get him off the post!" came the reply, and I realized soon enough why they wanted to be rid of me. The kids had got back to the border more or less unhurt, and when they told how we'd been attacked, the crowd broke down the fence and tried to burn the Reservation Club. The troops pushed them out with a bayonet wedge-formation, but they broke through further down opposite the Chamber, and some-one on one side or the other opened fire. By dark we had five dead, and the frustrated mob had burned Alfonso's building. A dozen looters roasted on the top floors, but you can't blame that on me, Marta. The gringos started the riot when they spat on that little girl and slapped her and tore our flag.

37

Phil clomps by the door, calling for Marta. Godspeed. Find her, firk her, fork her, and fangle her so she'll give me some peace. My blessing, boy, and accept these thought-wave pointers from a re-tired forager:

A. When in a filthy mood, as now and all too often, she will squeak, squawk, snap, and snarl; ignore it.

B. She likes it airedalewise for the sturdy swabs and the feel of your fingers.

C. If you can stay on safety till she's come three times—I used to bite my lip and count backwards—she will stay sunny for at least three hours.

Press on, good fugleman, and while you work I'll watch some scenes from your Oscar-winning movie.

Long view of Washington Avenue from the Reservation Club: gringo riflemen prone on the sloping lawn; the flattened fence; the rock-strewn street with butchered command car; the far sidewalk, mob frozen in ballet attitudes before smashed and flame-lit store-fronts. Blare of carnival music, jerky and orgiastic. Action!

Looters samba out of a department store and down the street, women with their arms crammed with clothing, bucks with TV sets balanced safari-style on their heads, six pallbearers strutting under a hi-fi console. A line of men dances in the opposite direction, each with his left hand on the one in front's shoulder and a jerrycan of gasoline clutched in his right. Howl of hoodlums gallops past them carrying Ñato Espino, who twirls a hangman's noose like a key chain. Close-up: the sweat-gobbed, singing faces of youths who stone the Tinieblas Fire Department outside Alfonso's smoking building, the fat black woman who slashes office drapes with a carving knife, the thugs who rock a car with Reservation plates, tip it over, and drag the driver out. They pass him, hand to hand, high overhead toward Ñato, who slings his rope across the arm of a streetlamp, fits the noose, and hauls away, dancing.

Fade from the dangling gringo's Popeyed face to Kiki Sancudo, who stumbles down the avenue toward Oruga Park, his head bandannaed in white gauze, his shirt liberally smeared with drying ketchup. Park full of men and boys, some crouched behind the low wall, some milling, hunched over, near the Chamber of Deputies. Pop. Pop of light rifle fire filtered through the wild saxophones; gringos answer with machine-gun burst. Men swan for cover in choreographed swoops; others pirouette deathwards in the stitching gunfire. The survivors see Kiki, who vaults the wall and circles the park in Jerome Robbins leaps. Trumpets on the sound track. All rise joyfully and sing...

No. Phil hasn't the guts to film the riots as a musical, and the scene at the Chamber wasn't that gay. All the gaiety was up by Alfonso's building with the looters and burners. Some of the kids who'd been with me in the Reservation had reported my injury as fatal, and the men in the park were inspired enough by my resur-

rection to follow me if I led them in another charge, but there were
too many Tinieblans down already, and I was much more sober
than I'd been that afternoon. I had a fine, black anger that craved
results not gestures. Unarmed charges were futile, as were the wild
shots from the upper storeys and the bravery of kids who crept
across the avenue to toss rocks at the gringos. Colonel Tolete,
afraid of the mob and the gringos, had confined the Guardia to
barracks. No one from the government was on the avenue, and a
radio announcer was reporting all sorts of crazy lies from a cantina
six blocks away. So when I'd learned what had happened and then
seen what was happening, I moved among the people there, duck-
ing with the machine-gun bursts, and told them to stay down, that
I'd see to it our country was properly defended. Then I found a
man who had his car parked nearby and went down to the palace
to tell Bonifacio Aguado what to do.

It is traditional for responsible Tinieblans, men of the ruling
class, to go to the palace in time of crisis. You don't have to be a
member of the government; you go to give your advice and support. I didn't go to the palace that night to overthrow Bonifacio
Aguado, contrary to what everyone said later. I went to tell him
what to do, and it was all right with me if he remained President
so long as he did it. He had shilly-shallied over the negotiations, but
now men were dying and the city was being sacked. Firm action
was called for. We needed the Guardia Civil on Washington Avenue
to disperse the mobs and face the gringos. That's what I meant to
tell Aguado, and I didn't care if he took credit for it.

But President Aguado was in no condition to do anything
which might bring him credit. All day he had sheltered in his office
—the same office where Alejo had received Lieutenant Colonel
Domingo Azote—with the blinds drawn and the lights out, listening to endless repetitions of the funeral scene from *Götterdäm-
merung*. He gave orders he was not to be disturbed; he took his
private phone off the hook and unplugged his intercom. No note
of discord leaked into his office or his mind until six o'clock, when
Lino Piojo pushed his way past three secretaries and an aide-de-
camp with some of the kids who had gone into the Reservation.
Aguado listened in silence to the tale of flag-tearing and mob vio-

lence. Then he rose and switched off the phonograph and began
to curse. He cursed the day he went into politics and the night he
was nominated for vice president, the afternoon when León Fuertes
was killed and the evening when he, Bonifacio Aguado, was sworn
in as President. He cursed the two hundred thousand people who
had voted for León and the person or persons unknown who had
blown him up, the gringos in the Reservation and the Tinieblans in
the streets. He cursed the U.S. flag and the Tinieblan flag and all
other flags, flag by flag, down the roll of sovereign nations from
Afganistan to Zambia, and the companies which manufactures
flags and the stores which sold flags and the people who bought
flags and the flag plague and all those who suffered from it and
spread it. He cursed Simón Mocoso's sister for sewing the first flag
and the children for carrying it; he cursed me for thinking up the
flag march and Alfonso for publishing the flag letters and Lino for
bringing him the news that the flag had been torn. Then, after having cursed without interruption for the space of half an hour, he
switched the phonograph back on and sat down behind his desk.
He summoned a secretary and dictated an order to his Minister of
Justice. Then he summoned another secretary and dictated another
order countermanding the first. He would dispatch one man on a
vital mission, then send another man to call him back, so that the
whole government was soon gyrating futilely about the city—
Carlitos Gavilán on his way to the airport to catch a plane for
Miami and Washington, Nacho Hormiga racing after him to call
him back, and so on—while men stood about the palace discussing
the situation in excited, uninformed accents, batting rumors about
like badminton cocks from one group to the next; and, in Aguado's
office, Brunhilde mourned.

   Then—it was while I was pushing my way through the foyer
and up the stairs, getting evil blinks from old rhinos and friendly
nods from young cocks, while I was listening to Lino tell me how
Boni had gone bats, while I was trying to persuade the aide-de-
camp to let me in to see the President—Manfredo Canino, with
twelve disciples, forced his way into Radio Patria and pointed a
Schmeiser machine pistol at the announcer on duty and took possession of the microphone and the airwaves, and proclaimed a stu-

dent and workers' soviet government, accusing the gringos of invading Tinieblas, denouncing Aguado as a quisling, and calling on the people's republics of China and Albania for recognition and aid. Our radio stations were monitored in the Reservation. I imagine an officer trotting across the War Room to inform General Spear, General Spear lifting the red phone to inform the Pentagon, and someone in the Pentagon lifting a similar phone to inform the White House. Whether or not this imagining is true, at exactly eight o'clock on the evening of November 28, 1964, Bonifacio Aguado's private secretary, who liked to eavesdrop on his calls, stood up behind her desk near where I was arguing with the aide-de-camp and exclaimed to no one in particular:

"The American Ambassador says the communists are making a revolution. American troops are going to invade us. He wants President Aguado to say he asked them to!"

"What did Aguado say?" asked I.

"He said, 'All right.'"

I held my palm out to Aguado's aide-de-camp. "Give me your pistol."

He stared at me for about two seconds, then unflapped his holster and put his little Browning in my hand. I pushed him aside gently and entered Aguado's office. He was leaning back in his swivel chair, gazing at the ceiling. Only the desk lamp was lit, and with Wagner's music swelling augustly the atmosphere of the room was properly funereal.

"Go home," I said.

"What?" blinking at me.

I switched on the main lights. "Go home. I'm in charge now."

A recent reference work, *Monarchs, Potentates, and Strong Men,* fails to list me among the numerous presidents of the Republic of Tinieblas; I can scarcely blame its compilers. During my half-hour's occupation of the palace I levied no taxes, concluded no treaties, and signed no bills. I declared a war and ordered a mobilization, but Camilo Araña, Tinieblan Ambassador to the United States, declined to take my declaration to the White House and Colonel Tolete refused to send his men against the gringo tanks, though I offered to lead them personally. It was not so much that I lacked personal authority. I later learned that my call to Camilo caught him in bed with the daughter of a prominent member of the House of Representatives and that Colonel Tolete was in the process of being relieved of command by a group of his younger officers. I managed to clear the palace of such men who favored gringo intervention. I issued a statement, broadcast over Radio Tinieblas, Uncle Erasmo's station, proclaiming myself President, denouncing both Canino and the gringos, and calling on all citizens to resist internal subversion and foreign attack. But my only real achievement came near the end of my administration when my secretary (until recently Bonifacio Aguado's secretary) rushed into my office with word that the White House was on the line. I picked up the phone.

"Is this the President of Tinieblas?"

"Yes."

"Hold on please."

Then molasses began oozing through the international cable into my ear:

"Mistah Prezdent, Ah'm deeply distressed that citizens of ow two countries came to blows this afternoon, an even moe distressed at this grave threat to yo intunnel security an the freedom of ow hemisphere, an Ah wont you to know Ah'll do evathin necessary to see that democratic govment doesn't go undah down theah in yo little republic. Ah know you don't have much of an army, an I think you made a wise decision requestin my assistance."

"Mister President, we neither need nor want your assistance."

"Now wait just a minute, Mistah Prezdent! My ambassadah just called an said he'd spoken with you an that you an he had made a deal."

"Your ambassador spoke to the former President. The new President doesn't make deals with gringos."

"Down in Texas we don't like the word 'gringo.'"

I answered with my one phrase of Texan: "Fuck you, pardner." Then I hung up.

But I had no time to congratulate myself, for Dmitri Látigo came in with a squad of civil guards and my term in office was over.

* * *

One of the marvelous things about Tinieblas is that every cit-izen, no matter how ignorant or unprepared, is convinced he can run the country better than whoever is trying to at the moment and, consequently, always has at least part of his mind occupied with how he and his friends might take power. Since the junior officers of the Civil Guard have little to do and, lacking wars, small hope of quick promotion, they dream of power constantly, more or less the way adolescents dream of screwing movie stars. When the risks disappear, they pounce. So since I had already sent Bonifacio home and gringo tanks were humping into the capital, a group of young officers led by Dmitri Látigo and Narses Puñete decided to take over the state. They relieved Aiax Tolete of command, promising him a seat on their junta, sent General Spear word that they would deal firmly with all com-munists, and dispatched troops to secure the means of commu-nication, the ministries, and, of course, the palace. I think Puñete would have tried to make a deal with me, for he and Látigo lacked popularity while I had abundance. But Látigo hated me, and not only demanded I be imprisoned but came personally to drag me to La Bondadosa.

Dmitri Látigo's father was the son of an Otán landowner and the only Tinieblan I know of to devote himself exclusively to liter-ature. He wrote more than a dozen novels, none of which was ever published. At least he carried a number of fat copy books around with him wherever he went, claiming they were novels, and no one dared to doubt him publicly for fear he might begin reading aloud. His master was Dostoevski. He complained that his career had been thwarted by the lack of political persecution in Tinieblas, his inability to develop epilepsy, and his wife's iron refusal to be unfaithful to him. He managed to lose most of his inheritance gam-bling, however, and he named his three sons Ivan, Dmitri, and Alyosha, and his daughter Grushenka. Impressionable children all, Ivan became a professor of philosophy, Dmitri an officer in the Guardia Civil, Alyosha a priest, and Grushenka the most affection-ate girl in Tinieblas.

She was small, bright, pretty, good-natured, sly in a soft feline way, tender, calm, and loving, as adept at love as Angela though in no way fierce about it. She wasn't the most beautiful girl in the country, but she got the best men. The French Ambassador, one of Malraux's protégés, a war hero and a poet, was at the point of divorcing his wife over her a few years ago, and they say that León Fuertes was on his way to visit her when he got blown up. Two years before that, when she was nineteen or so, we spent some time together. That was just while I was divorcing Olga, before León took office and I went to Madrid. Perhaps she loved me or had hopes of respectability; perhaps it was all Dmitri's idea, but he came up to me one afternoon as I was having a drink at the Hotel Excelsior and, in front of other men and very seriously, declared it was about time I announced my engagement to his sister. I'd had some drinks. Marriage wasn't a very congenial topic to me at the time. It was annoying to be badgered in public. So I said that as I was in the process of divorcing one whore, it would be foolish for me to think of marrying another one. Látigo went white and reached for his pistol. I threw my drink in his eyes and broke his jaw. And for this, in his rancorous way, he hated me, and no doubt still does.

Látigo had his pistol out this time before he came through the door. "I arrest you in the name of the Provisional Military junta of the Tinieblan Civil Guard," he said. "Why don't you try to escape?"

"I'm too tired," getting up from Bonifacio Aguado's swivel chair and holding out my wrists for a sergeant's handcuffs. "It's been a fatiguing afternoon."

Two soldiers shouldered me down the stairs, with Látigo right behind me, his pistol pointed at the back of my neck. My head hurt, but I managed to hold it high. An old palace chambermaid who watched them take me out to their truck told *Time* magazine that I looked just like Alejo when the gringos deposed him in 1942; but there was at least one significant difference: the blood on my clothes was my own.

It was my last stay in La Bondadosa and my most unpleasant. Látigo, who was a modern militarist, had me interrogated daily for the first week, trying to get me to admit collusion with Canino, whom neither the Guardia nor the gringos ever captured. His questioners used automobile radiator hoses and worked in relays, and as I'd been in poor shape when I went in—the gringo rifle butt had given me a concussion—I weakened quickly. Látigo would have put me in one of the coffins, but they were all filled with communists, and Puñete insisted that they get priority lest the gringos lose confidence in the new regime. Látigo was threatening to put me on the Costaguano Lie Detector—a kind of knitting-needle gadget which they stick up your ass and stab your prostate with—when Elena made the gringos make him stop torturing me.

She declared she was going to Tinieblas, with a field hospital outfitted at her own expense, to rescue her patriot husband and tend the victims of fascist repression and U.S. intervention. When Tinieblas refused her a visa, she swooped to Miami with a considerable entourage and set up at the Fontainebleau, holding twice-daily press conferences in the grand ballroom. These were orchestrated by Schicksal (who had one Elena Delfi picture in the first-run houses and another ready for release) and made the lead stories of every paper in the States and, of course, the network news coverage. For Miami Elena created a new role, a grand pastiche of Tosca, Antigone, and Saint Joan; in it she gave some of her most stirring performances. She attended Mass in the Cuban ghetto (black veil, deep eye shadow) accompanied by the widow of a butchered civil rights leader, a famous novelist, and two former White House aides. In one conference she appeared decked in rich jewels which she offered in my ransom; in another she clasped hands at the neck of a white surplice and appealed to His Holiness. She never mentioned Puñete or Látigo but accused Lyndon Johnson of persecuting me because of the way I'd ended our phone conversation (reported by Aguado's nosy secretary to Lino, hence to Alfonso, hence to Elena). *How strange that such a beeg, fat man should have such a teeny, leetle soul* (thumb and forefinger held toward the camera two centimeters apart). She scoffed at the official declaration that U.S. troops had been ordered into Ciudad Tinieblas to protect American citizens: Mussolini had invaded Ethiopia, Hitler had invaded Poland, Stalin had invaded Hungary—no, that was Khrushchev, but it didn't matter, all despots were the same—so of course *Meester Johnson was bound to invade some leetle country, and send tanks to kill defenseless civilians, and engineer a military coup d'état, and ask the fascists to please put in jail and torture the man who had been rude to him, because you mustn't be rude to people who have tanks, even if they invade your country.* She held Johnson accountable for every hair on my head—which wasn't too illogical as there were five thousand gringo troops in Ciudad Tinieblas with more pouring in from Guantánamo and the Canal Zone and Fort Bragg—and since she was a famous actress and very popular with Italian-American bloc voters, word was passed that I oughtn't be too badly mutilated. I still had to worry about being shot while attempting to escape, however, and I was happy when they gave me a cell mate, Major Dorindo Azote, the only Guard officer who had refused to go along with the captains' coup.

Puñete and Látigo were no longer captains, of course. They promoted themselves to major the morning after they took over, became lieutenant colonels the next week, and celebrated U.S. recognition of their regime by leaping to brigadier general. Then Látigo proposed a Christmas promotion for all ranks, and Puñete, who was afraid of being outbid in popularity, recommended two grades for enlisted men and three for officers. So they became full generals, and everyone expected the New Year to see them field marshals, with batons and new uniforms, for their insignia were large seven-pointed stars (a point for each province), and a regulation officer's jacket could accommodate no more than four of these, and that not without some crowding. Puñete personally undertook to solve this problem, appointing a Council of Sartorial Advisers from the leading tailors and dressmakers of the country and working closely with them. It was, in fact, the only work he allowed himself. He would rise late, zoom to headquarters amid a cluster of motorcycles, and secrete himself in the atelier he had set up in Tolete's former office, letting one modiste convince him of the functional efficiency of the Hungarian epaulet and another one extol the swash of the Brazilian tunic. After an hour or so of this and having briskly indicated directions for new research, he would remove to the permanent bacchanal he and his cronies had installed in Club de Oficiales. He might snatch an hour or two from his pleasures to review this or that unit, but in the main he left the tedious tasks of running the Guard and the country to Dmitri Látigo, who accepted them in the most magnanimous spirit of self-sacrifice. The two never lost a chance to declare toothily that they were bound as brother officers and comrades in arms by ties which transcended any mundane ambition or jealousy, until the most ignorant peasant in the farthest bog of Selva Trópica was aware that it was only a matter of time before one betrayed the other. Most Tinieblans expected it would be Látigo who got rid of Puñete, and we prisoners knew the date and hour when the garrison at Córdoba would turn its rifles on its illustrious inspector, the guardroom where he would be confined, and the name of the man—Sergeant Puñal, Dmitri Látigo's personal bodyguard—who would string him up with his own belt to make it look like suicide. Since Puñete's reverence for gringos was the only thing that kept Dmitri Látigo from having me tortured to death, I used every argument with the guard who brought the food and slop cans to have him take a message upstairs for me. He was aware that Látigo wanted me shown no favors, however, and I would never have succeeded without Azote, who, though ill-disposed toward my family and perfectly content to let either general destroy the other, finally agreed to intercede. On the morning before the scheduled inspection, General Narses Puñete received word that Elena was a bosom friend of Yves St. Laurent and could easily secure his collaboration on the new uniform. I was sent for immediately and managed to have the office cleared long enough to persuade Puñete that his life was in danger. He was capable of action when he felt like and had the confidence of General Spear, who suspected Látigo of communism because of his Russian first name. By midnight both Látigo and I were at the airport, he manacled and gagged for the plane to Peru, I shaved and suited for the plane to Miami.

38

"I'm sorry, Kiki." Jaime mopes in the doorway. "I wasn't alert."

"My fault. Stupid to send you. You all right?"

"Yes, Kiki. I wasn't worried. I knew you'd get me out."

Nod. Make my smile. "I'm glad you're back."

"I saw him, Kiki."

Nod.

"His mother called him. He came to the screen and looked at me. He was scared, Kiki."

"Good."

"Later he came out. When they had me handcuffed, when they were putting me in their car, he came out and yelled at me. He called me dumb indian. He said you're finished, Kiki. That everyone knows it but you and me."

"What did you say?"

"I didn't say anything. If you're finished, Kiki, why is he so scared?"

Smile. "Come. Push me inside. Quick bath."

"All right, Kiki."

"How'd he look?" as Jaime rolls me out into the hall.

"He looked all right, Kiki. A little fat."

"Fat?"

"Well, you know, Kiki. As if he lives well."

Nod.

"What's the house like?" as Jaime comes out from opening the taps.

"It's a nice house, Kiki." He swings me to the bed to undress me. "They have a rosebush in front near the door."

"A rosebush?"

"Yes, Kiki." He pulls off my trousers. "All the houses are the same. Not big like this one, but all right, nice. His has a rosebush."

Jaime hoists me in his arms and sidesteps to the bathroom cranes me down into the warm water.

"He lives well, you say?"

"Yes, Kiki." He slips the washcloth glove on his right hand, holds my shoulder with his left hand. "It looks that way." He looks away from my face and swabs my pasty flesh with the soaped cloth. "We're going to kill him, aren't we, Kiki?"

"Yes, Jaime. We're going to kill him."

39

They'll bring him drugged, not to La Yegua—here. Marta will be gone, and Elena. Who'll complain? and we'll have the cellar ready for him. They'll bring him at night, wrapped up in a rug, like Cleopatra.

Jaime will undress him and lay him out. We'll have three ten-foot four-by-fours bridging two sawhorses. Jaime will drape him there and cinch him tight. Leather straps at his hips, chest, and naves; a belt for his ankles; a strand of telephone cord twining his wrists beneath the boards; another strand pulled around his head. Fit it between his lips, Jaime, and twist it tight. I don't want him pleading. Groans and choked screams will do.

Then we'll wait for him to waken. We'll want the place well-lighted, and a mirror on the ceiling so he can watch. And the sawhorses low, the level of my knees. Instruments ready on the long worktable: the charcoal oven Franca broils meat on, Otilio's machete with the blade-end plunged among the coals, a steel E-string with each end fitted to a wooden handle, the saw. Cauterization's the key. Less mess, and he won't bleed to death. We'll start as soon as he comes to, before the drugs worn off completely. Mental pain's worth more than physical, and I don't want him dying of shock. He'll open his eyes, and blink, and stare around wildly, and see himself in the mirror, and I'll tell him—I'm sure he'll understand if I speak slowly—that he's in my cellar and we won't be disturbed. Then we'll get started.

Shall we geld him first? I don't want the taste of it blurred by pain, but I think we should leave that for dessert. Right arm first and work in a circle. Jaime will take the saw—one of those electric hand numbers. Zizz! Go through a plank like butter. Jaime will take it and switch it on, nudge the blade into Ñato's armpit. Muffled squeak, blood spurts, and the arm flops, swinging by the wrist-cord. Saw switched off, dropped on the table. Quick with the machete to sizzle the wound. Old Ñato will have probably fainted, and we'll wait till he wakes up for the other arm.

We'll trim him like a weeviled oak, Jaime. We'll prune him like a poxed plum tree. Arms at the shoulder, legs at the hip, and when you've lopped his limbs and seared the sawings, you'll loop the E-string around his parts and pinch them off. Flick your fists apart and snap the steel, and they'll drop like clipped figs.

Then Jaime will pat Ñato's new twat with the white-hot machete blade and undo the straps and lift him down into Neira's zinc washtub. He'll pile the arms and legs on Ñato's stomach; he'll clasp the parts into Ñato's right hand. Then he'll take Ñato over to that nice little house and leave him on his mother's doorstep, beside the rosebush.

40

That's the way it will be, that way or the other way. Or simple pesticide without the poetry: hanging for example. Hang him and be done with him. Or drive a spike through his temples. Or bury him. Dig a hole and plant him; see if he sprouts. So many ways. Dostoevski's father had his nuts crushed by peasants. Or so they say. Died of shock. Drape Ñato's ballocks on an anvil and swat 'em with a sledge; if it doesn't kill him try something else. Burning, say; I haven't studied that. Pittsburg Phil Schwartz, a somewhat colleague of Ñato's (since they both did work for the syndicate), tied a man—and no one's found out who—to a tree and burned off his face and prints with a blowtorch. That would be scanned. Or douse him with gas and light him up, a Mississippi cook-out. Such game as Ñato may be roasted, seethed, broiled, or fried, oven-baked, or fricasseed. So many ways and only one Ñato, but I'll find the right recipe.

Something to aim my mind at while the day seeps out through my bathroom louvers, while Jaime lifts me toward the bath towel spread out on my bed, while Elena rises from her own bath in a flutter of invisible attendant cupids, while Phil and Marta tremble in the thunder clap of love.

Or I can imagine Bolívar Plaza brimming with life, tides of people foaming up from the poor quarters, rivers of people flowing down from the bus station. Along the side streets and on the plaza's rim men sway behind their braziers swabbing spice on smoke-fragrant meat chunks speared on sticks; old women crouch on produce boxes beside their trays of meat-filled yucca cakes, boys swing zinc buckets full of beaded beer and soda bottles. A band crammed on a truck back blares choruses of the old Acción Dinámica song. A bald electrician with sweat stains on his shirt tests the loudspeakers: "Dos, uno, cero, arriba Alejo!" In front of the Hotel Excelsior two guardias are frog-marching a pickpocket toward their van. The sky darkens; streetlamps go on; the square fills.

Or I can go to Nacho's mansion where the flag-decked, dust-caked cars wait at the curb; where thirsty politicians jumble the salon and terrace, drinks in hand; where Alfonso arrives, cologned and talcumed, to huddle in the vestibule, still uneasy after all these years in the ambiance of his lost love Irene; where Alejo stands, pants dropped scowling, in the guest room, waiting for Furetto to squeeze him full of youth from a syringe of hormones and vitamins.

Still itching to be president. To seize his destiny, he would say, and perhaps he's right. A drive to rule so deep only the stars could have forged it. With me the itch was chosen, not imposed; I gave it to myself. On the eighth night of my last stay in prison, when I came to lying in rat filth and my own vomit, too sick to move, unable to urinate, sure of more torment and a degrading death, I began to think about my life. I didn't stay long at it. I passed out again, and since I wasn't beaten the next day and began recovering strength and hope, I felt no further call to self-inspection. In fact I avoided the contemplative life for another year until Ñato Espino rubbed my face in it for good. But that night I considered my life and found it as unplanned and purposeless as any animal's: some rash enthusiasms, some squandered gifts, some heady pleasures over-priced in pain, an accidental progress to a dingy end. That wasn't odd, for the world was unplanned too. But I wasn't responsible for the world, I was responsible for my life, and I groaned to have lived it so clumsily. I even envied Dmitri Látigo—not because he was in power and could turn his foes to bugs, but because his hate for me had lent his life some purpose while mine had had none. I thought such thoughts; then I lost consciousness. Later on I more or less forgot the interlude, which a self-dramatizing person might have called a Dark Night of the Soul. It sowed a seed of angst which sprouted a year later when I was on campaign and led to things which have convinced me that it's riskier to hunt for meaning in your life than to run guns to Costaguana, but I wasn't aware of that then. All I could say my hour of self-examination had left me was the hunger for a long-term goal, and when I was out of prison I remembered the glow I'd felt when people followed me and the stimulation offered when you grab for something other people want, and I put it in my mind to become president. Scarcely odd for a Tinieblan. Crassly common in fact. But it was the first distant mark I'd set myself since, twenty-some years before, I'd decided to get strong.

I took my glossy new ambition off to Miami and Paris and kept it combed and curried in a back stall of my mind. At night I'd let it out to prance, and on quiet mornings in my office with the taste of Marta still fresh on me. How pleasant to watch it trot across my desk; how good to hear it whinny. It gave me more paternal joy than Mito did when he learned to pa-pa. I'd watch it go through its gaits while Elena dozed beside me and a volume full of someone else's glory drooped unread to my lap. I'd dream views of the course we'd run together, then thwack it back to stable lest it blow its wind untried. And no one knew I had it. It reared its pride in secret till I vaulted it and cantered off toward power.

Yet, though I kept it hidden, my ambition changed me. I grew more youthful in my step and smile; I felt flooded by an excess of energy, as though plugged in to some unlimited reserve. My strength returned more quickly than the doctors had thought possible, and with no special training grew beyond what it had been before I went to prison. That spring an open wrestling meet was held in Istanbul, and on a whim I went and won the free-style trophy in my weight class, pinning twelve opponents including the man who'd got the silver medal the year before at Tokyo. My early skill at handbalancing came back. One morning as I sat in my ambassadorial chair imagining campaigns and speeches, all unawares I gripped the chair arms and swung myself, legs tucked, into a handstand, and then stepped up onto my desk with my left palm and poised there, one-handed, still musing politics, until my secretary came in with the mail and squeaked me back to earth. I acquired puzzling mental gifts. Elena gave me a script to read, and I glanced through it and made a note or two and six weeks later found myself reciting it, lead parts and walk-ons, directions and suggested camera shots, to an amazed audience of Elena, Schicksal, and the author. I took up chess, a game I'd learned years before by hovering, invisible, at Uncle Erasmo's elbow while he and Felix Ardilla slammed the pieces about the board and yelped taunts at each other, and brewed up such magnetic fields of concentration that I divined opponents' strategies as though tapping their minds and watched my hand leap through successful lines of play twenty moves long without once giving it a conscious order. I recalled conversations between Alejo and my mother which I'd overheard from my cradle and quoted verbatim from books I'd read in grammar school. I received presentiments of the future. One midnight the phone rang, and, as I reached for it, I said aloud: "It's Juanchi Tábano calling from Tinieblas; his son is hurt"; and, sure enough, the operator asked me to hold for an overseas call, and, after clicks and crackles, I heard Juanchi yell that his son had broken both legs in a car crash outside Cannes, and would I see he got the best doctors. In April I went to a reception at the Dominican Embassy, and some ribboned gorilla was thumping his chest about how stable his country was now that the generals were in power, and I heard myself laugh and whisper to one of the Venezuelans, "Let them talk; they'll be up to their ass in gringos inside a month." Strangest of all was the repose I felt in the midst of vitality, the sense of being ready, the knack for savoring the interim until my name was called. Women were more drawn to me than ever, but I was spared the wasp-sting thirst to gulp them all. Men also sought me out: artists and scholars welcomed me to their society; men hardened in the fires of war and commerce confided their cares to me, asked my counsel, proffered me favor. All year long my fine, streamlined life whistled downslope with the wind behind it, sun-flecked down through its alpine morning, toward the dark wood and Ñato's bullets.

Ñato nursed his own ambition: a fief to hold for the gringo crime kings. In this dream he swiveled behind an immense desk in an office guarded by merciless gunmen. A murmur into an ivory phone, and clouds of powdered pleasure-death were wafted about the hemisphere; a nod and brothels rose; a shake and rivals perished. Below, visible through the two-way mirror at his feet, a casino bulged with gaudy bettors, and each departing plane bore a courier with a satchel of cash for his numbered account.

So clear were Ñato's visions of this paradise that he believed it attainable. After Castro de-gangstered Cuba, Ñato approached one of Meyer Lansky's exiled men-at-arms and suggested the syndicate invest Tinieblas. Some months later three Sicilians appeared with funds for a casino at El Opulento and a dope franchise for Ñato. Then León Fuertes took office and nationalized the casino and expelled the Sicilians and formed a narcotics squad. Ñato thought León had cost him a dukedom. He was convinced that, with the right government, he could realize his dream. But Lansky would never have picked you, Ñato, even if I'd lived up to your hopes. You were never more than a beast of burden, fit to lug junk and bray for leavings. You were born a companion to spiders, to scutter through a sputum-lobbied world trailing a slime of fear. Your sewer universe is narrow, low, and dark, a haven for roaches lighted only where the deepest drift of mine plummets to graze it.

Our universes touched again that fall when a cocaine famine scourged the Côte d'Azur. Ñato left Ciudad Tinieblas for Lima at one o'clock in the morning aboard Hemispheric's Flight 959, *El Imperialista,* the same flight that had carried Dmitri Látigo half a year before. He wore pointy black Mexican pumps and nylon stretch socks, beltless dark blue dacron-and-wool slacks, a marine-blue silk sport shirt buttoned at the neck, and a light blue Palm Beach jacket. His baggage contained four similar shirts in various pastel colors; his passport was visaed for Peru and France. During the flight he cheerfully but unsuccessfully propositioned all three tourist-class stewardesses. At a little before eight o'clock he debarked the aircraft, passed customs and immigration, taxied to the city, and checked in at a small hotel near the shrine of San Martín de Porres. He had coffee in the dining room, chatting with and unsuccessfully propositioning a vacationing Chilean dental assistant who was having breakfast at the next table. Then he walked to the offices of the Cagliostro Lines and booked a third-class passage to Marseilles on the *Cola di Rienzo,* arriving Callao that afternoon from Valparaíso and sailing the next evening for Guayaquil, Balboa, La Guaira, Barcelona, Marseilles, and Genoa. While ascertaining that the ship would have cargo space available for his car, he unsuccessfully propositioned a female clerk. Then he returned to his hotel, successfully propositioned an indian chamber-maid, committed an act of darkness with her, did not get up to see her out, and slept all afternoon. That evening after dinner he received a blue envelope containing a parking lot stub, a set of car keys, and the registration papers (filed in his name) to a 1964 Leviathan Regal Imperator. At seven the next morning he assumed command of this machine and piloted it to Callao, stopping at every pump along the way. The tank was partitioned to accommo-date one gallon of fuel and twenty-three of superfine Andean cocaine. Car and Ñato went aboard ship that afternoon; *Cola di Rienzo* cleared the breakwater at seven P.M.

During the first week of the voyage Ñato stained his blue silk sport shirt three times and his green silk sport shirt twice with spaghetti sauce and unsuccessfully propositioned a number of female passengers. He heard a great deal more than he cared to about pilgrimages to Rome from a Bolivian priest who shared his cabin and compensated by boring the priest with fabricated travels of his own. He played seven-card rummy with two undershirted Chilean mechanics bound for Volkswagen training in Germany, cheating steadily from Guayaquil to Balboa, getting caught halfway through the Panama Canal, whining to no avail as Pedro pinned his arms and Pablo kneed him roundly in the testicles. He hobbled moaning to his cabin and spent the next twenty-four hours in his bunk feeling sorry for himself. While the ship crossed the Caribbean he played double-deck solitaire in a dark corner of the lounge, pausing between deals to mine his nose with discreet industry and deposit his finds along the leg of his chair.

During the second week of the voyage he reached an understanding with a thirty-one-year-old Italian demi-vièrge, the secretary to a Caracas importer, who was returning to Brindisi to get married. They sambaed in the lounge and tussled on the fantail until he managed to assure her that he had no designs on her hymen. After that they spent four mornings playing with each other in his cabin while the priest said Mass for all passengers in the first-class lounge.

During the third week of the voyage French customs officials began probing Ñato's dreams for cocaine. One morning a French policeman with drooping mustache and a blue kepi peered in through the porthole while his Italian friend was wristing him, and he went noodle-ish and thrust her out the door. His waiter, a French spy, put something in his food, and he developed diarrhea and cramps. The Mediterranean sun spilled an excess of light from horizon to horizon, flooding the crannies where a fugitive might hide, and in the night narcotics agents padded the companionway beyond his door and held stethoscopes to his bulkhead. After Barcelona he huddled in his bunk while the aroma of cocaine seeped from the soldered gas tank of his car and rose three decks to choke his cabin. The ship's horn, blasting to the Marseilles pilot, so frighted him he fouled his sheets. He cuddled quaking in his mess till the priest went up on deck. He pulled the sheets off the bunk and wiped himself with them and stuffed them out the porthole. Then he did what he had promised himself and his *capo* he would not do: he pried off the heel of his Mexican shoe and took a packet from the hollowed-out leather and poured a little mound of white powder onto the back of his left hand and pressed his right nostril with the index knuckle of his right hand and held his left hand under his left nostril and sniffed himself full of courage, well-being, and good cheer.

At eight o'clock on the morning of September 5th Ñato Espino tangoed down the gangway of the *Cola di Rienzo* onto the Marseilles quay. Swinging his valise like a polo mallet, he headed for the bow of the ship, from which cars were being unloaded. In his path a stevedore bent to tie a shoelace, and Ñato leapfrogged over him, turned to flash him a grin, flipped him a Peruvian sol de oro, pirouetted five-hundred-forty degrees, tipped an invisible boater, and cakewalked toward his car, which was settling to earth ahead of him in a steel cradle.

"Belle voiture!" said a dockman, patting the Leviathan's haunch.

"Formidable!" replied Ñato, bowing from the hip.

"Papiers," said a customs man, approaching with clipboard.

"But of course," said Ñato in English with a Chevalier accent, sweeping the registration from his jacket pocket.

While the car was being inspected, a man came by with a jerrycan of gasoline to moisten the tanks which had been drained upon loading. He regretted that he could only give four liters to each driver; Ñato assured him that was quite all right. The customs man licked a sticker and slapped it on the windshield. Ñato flung his bag into the front seat and leaped in after it. He fired the Leviathan's engine, waved to the customs man, flipped the car into reverse instead of drive, stomped on the accelerator, whizzed backward, bashed thunderously into a steel hawser post, jammed the car into low, squealed forward past the chalk-faced customs man, zoomed through the gate trailing white powder, and rammed squarely into a motorcycle van full of fresh eggs.

Four hours later an inspector of the judicial police called on me at my embassy. Was I acquainted with a Tinieblan national named Jesús Maria Espino Amaro? Espino . . . Espino . . . Also known as Ñato? Ñato . . . Ñato . . . Did I know the man? It might come to me. Would the Ambassador have the kindness to notify the Quai des Orfèvres should Espino contact the embassy? Would the inspector have the kindness to reveal his interest in this citizen of my country? Very well: Espino was wanted for questioning in regard to the illicit traffic in narcotic stupeficants. He had escaped apprehension that morning in Marseilles and had been reported to have debarked an Air France flight at Orly. I noted the name carefully. I assured the inspector that the Republic of Tinieblas was eager to discourage crime on the part of its citizens and to cooperate with the authorities of all civilized nations, of which France was surely one of the most illustrious. I doubted that Monsieur Espino would show his face about the embassy but pledged to inform the Quai des Orfèvres immediately if he did. Then I showed the inspector to the door and let Ñato out of the closet.

He had crawled in a few minutes before the inspector, dripping fear across my rug, whining about his bad luck, pleading for sanctuary. It was the third time I saved him, and each time I might have looked away and saved myself. He was my other self, my mirror image, buffooned reflection of a prince. I loved the contest more than the prize; he dreamed of ease and feared the means to it. He was edgy where I was calm, grinning where I was grave, complaining where I was stoical, cowardly where I was valiant, clown where I was hero. And totally shameless. He's bragged for years about the steel-nerved acumen with which he eluded the French police. I should have let him show it. I should have flung him out and let him save himself. That would have been a kindness beside what he did to me. Instead I stooped to save him. I hid him at the embassy. I gave him the extra suit of clothes I kept there. I issued him a fresh passport. And when he blubbered that he hadn't nerve to boldface out of France, I smuggled him to Spain.

That was a fine lark, whisking Ñato 'cross the border. I grabbed a pair of ballet sprites as cover, and we left at dawn in my embassy Comanche with the diplomatic plates and the flags on the fenders. We stopped in Chartres for coffee and rolls and stayed half an hour to stroll the cathedral. Ñato whined about that: we might be seen; we ought to hurry, so I let him sniff what was left of his shoe packet, and he waxed gay and courageous. Down into the Loire country with me driving and Josette tucked alongside, Ñato in the back with his arm round Nicole. Lunch at Poitiers: fois gras, langouste, entrecôte, fromages, fruits; Chablis with the lobster, Lafitte with the beef, port with the cheese, Armagnac with our coffee. On to Bordeaux with a liter of brandy for the road; across the moorlands, flashing between the elms, with the girls and I singing "Chevaliers de la table ronde" and "Jeanneton" and "la Ballade du fier Ñato," which I composed extempore to the tune of "Malbrouche s'en va t'en guerre" and whose refrains Ñato and Nicole punctuated with kisses. I knew an excellent restaurant at Biarritz, but Ñato, growing nervous, wished to get across the border as quickly as possible, so we stopped only long enough to stow him in the trunk under a lap rug, and swept down to Hendaye and passed French customs, and crossed the bridge to Irún and passed Spanish customs, *courtesy diplomatique* and *cortesía diplomática*, scarcely slowing the car and certainly not having to give Ñato the three-knock danger signal we'd agreed on. Then the girls suggested I let Ñato out, but I felt he deserved more durance for the grave crime of trafficking in narcotic stupeficants, so we pressed on to the outskirts of San Sebastián, where I knew a very decent inn. When we got out, I rapped three times on the trunk. Then we went in and had fish soup and shrimp Basque and half a chicken each and white Riojo wine—I stepping out between each course to slam the car doors and make gruff noises—until Nicole declared that if I didn't let Ñato out at once, she would sleep with Josette, so we took our brandies and trooped out to the car, and when I opened the trunk, there lay Ñato, white with terror and marinated in piss, curled in a fetal lump with his lips drawn back and his rat-teeth gleaming.

The girls cooed about "le pauvre," but I went cold. I heard a crowd scream and saw a spurt of flame beside my shoulder. I reached to close the trunk lid; in half an hour I could have him back in France, trapped away where he couldn't kill me.

"What's wrong?" asked Josette. "You look as though you've seen a ghost."

"My own. Ce salaud me tuera un jour."

But I was making an ass of myself. Me afraid of Ñato? I forced a smile and dropped my hand to help him up.

"Some friend you are! Searing me, keeping me locked in when there wasn't need. You don't care about me, Kiki. All you want is to have fun with this pair of whores!"

"I got you out, didn't I? Shut up or I'll hand you over."

I meant it, though I couldn't understand why. Ñato snarled at me, then grinned, embraced me, called me brother, swore he'd never forget. I shook the future out of my head, and we went inside. The girls and I had another bottle while Ñato ate, squeezing for gaiety, but the day's wine was drawn. Josette said she was tired, and I didn't bother her. She fell asleep at once with her cheek on my bicep, but I lay for hours in a demoned half-sleep where phantoms lurked behind me and I couldn't turn my head. At first light I drove Ñato to the airport at San Sebastián where he could get a plane for Madrid, and from Madrid a plane home. Then I fled into Josette's body. Voices whispered of horrors, so I pulled her young warmth down over my mind. I should have listened. I should have listened.

Next month I had a premonition I didn't dismiss. Narses Puñete had promised elections, but all military dictators promise that. Tinieblans in and out of the country made plans to live with him till the end of the decade. Then one morning I read an item about a gringo mission to Central America, and though the gringos love military governments and send out missions every year when it gets chilly in Washington, I heard myself remark to Marta that Johnson was feeling righteous and we'd have elections in the spring.

I wrote to Gonzalo and suggested he begin putting the party in shape. I sent a problem to Armando Loza in Boston: Assume elections in Tinieblas in 1966; which issues were important and how should they be treated? I began liquidating some investments to build a war chest. I asked Elena not to sign any contract that would keep her busy during March and April. Finally, early in November, I went to see Alejo.

He was living in Montreux in a large house about a quarter of a mile above the Château of Chillon. He had Furetto with him, and Gunther and Egon, and an East German woman who reminded me faintly of Angela, though her teeth weren't pointed and she didn't look as if she had a tail. As far as I could learn he did nothing but read political philosophy and pay monthly visits to a Lausanne monkey-glander, but when Egon had convoyed me by the Dobermans and into his presence, he advised me to tell him what I wanted without foolishness; he could give me five minutes.

He sat in a leather chair with his book on his knee, his place kept with an index finger. He wore tweed slacks and a cardigan and a cashmere scarf. He was quite pale, and with his glowing eyes and his skin stretched paper-thin over his cheekbones he looked like what a clever director might cast if called upon to use the medieval figure of Death in a modern-dress melodrama. The German woman was curled on a leather couch with a copy of *Der*

Stern. He flicked her out of the room with his free hand and waved me into a chair.

"What do you want?"

"I want to tell you something. I think there will be elections soon at home. I think I will run for president."

"Why tell me?"

"So you don't have to hear it from someone else. Or read it in the papers."

"Have you told anyone else?"

"No."

"Good. I have given you everything I intend to give you, but since I know you will not take it, I will offer you some advice: avoid politics. No, it's not what you think. If, as you say, elections will be held soon, I have no intention of running in them. I am destined to be President of Tinieblas once more before I die, but not for some years. Not for some years. I have learned how to wait. You should learn. For you it would be a profitable study. And you should forget politics. No one can escape destiny, but perhaps one can postpone it."

"I only came to inform you. I don't know yet if there will be elections or if I'll have a chance to win. But if they're held, and if I have a chance, I'll run."

He nodded. He smiled. "I knew you would not listen. But don't you find it strange, this desire to 'inform' me? Inform your wife. She is a beautiful woman; I have seen her in magazines. Inform her. Inform your brother. Inform your friends. But why inform me?"

I didn't know why. It was strange. I didn't care how Alejo learned of my ambition, and yet I'd gone to see him. I felt a chill like I'd felt when I looked down at Ñato huddled in the trunk of my car. I heard excited voices as though above me. They faded, then grew louder, and there was fire in my neck. I raised my hand to my forehead and wiped these signs away.

"Why give me advice?"

"As I said, I know you won't listen." He flapped his book on his knee. "If you have nothing else to tell me . . ."

The next time I saw him was four years later, six weeks ago, at Alfonso's house, when I offered to campaign for him if he'd give me

Ñato. He agreed at once. Then he looked at my wasted flesh piled in a wheelchair, and said in exactly the same tone, with exactly the same half-smile: "I knew you wouldn't listen."

On November 28th, 1965, my thirty-fifth birthday and the four hundred fifty-first anniversary of the discovery of Tinieblas, General Narses Puñete announced that elections would be held the following spring. That night I woke from sleep with my nostrils full of ether and the murmured tones of doctors worrying my cars. But I paid no more heed to this sign than I had to any of the others. The next morning I took the plane for home.

41

Trails to guide my mind down while Jaime dries and dresses me. Quick gallop into next month, and a trot through five years ago. To keep the beast from turning on me. I trained my body, taught it entrancing tricks and to be my uncomplaining servant. Got much good use and pleasure from it till Ñato killed it. Now I tame my mind to keep it from trampling me, to make it lift me from this wheelchair.

Some men have taught their minds to bear them up among the galaxies or down into the atom's core, or to find countries unicorned with marvels, lands rich in order and excitement, where splintery nature's beveled down with dreams. I have Tinieblas and my storm-drenched past, the circle that's marked out for Ñato's execution, and a sharp-hoofed mind to take me if I keep it bridled, to lift and carry me as Jaime does now.

Downstairs in his brown arms, but not into the *sala*, where Carl and Sonny are checking their equipment. He sets me in my folding chair, and I grunt him to the library. Cool and quiet. Wait here for Elena and Marta, for Alejo and his motorcade, and ride my mind along another path.

42

I spoke to people. I spoke to them one by one in my air-conditioned study and beside the pool and on the porch at La Yegua and at Alfonso's house at Medusa Beach and by overseas phone to Armando in Boston. And of the men I spoke to I asked thirteen to supper.

That was two weeks after I returned "on leave," while the last rains of December torrented against the louvers of the dining room and flailed across the terrace. I can't paint that scene in Leonardo's mode—we sat around the table, not all bunched at one side—but I could film it as well as Phil. I'd sit myself just where I sat at lunch-not in this baby stroller, but in the master chair with sturdy arms and lion faces carved where I rest my hands—and hang the camera over my right shoulder. Mid-shot across the supper plates to Uncle Erasmo, who sits at the far end sipping Vichy instead of Brandy Lepanto, sucking a toothpick instead of an Uppmann cigar. Zoom into his mind, to the lavishly appointed, cypress wood coffin which lies in his study at the foot of his books, which he sleeps in each night, fully clothed, to spare Cousin Raquel the annoyance of dressing his cancered cadaver. And perhaps reach forward to the morning after I announced my candidacy when he told the maid he would not get up and died as discreetly as he had lived.

Zoom back through Uncle Erasmo's old lizard's eyes to a beardless Alfonso, on his right, who licks a bit of éclair cream from the top of his lip, harrumphs portentously, and then says nothing. Swing left again to Aquilino Piojo, silver-haired at thirty-nine, sufficiently sleek in pearl-gray sharkskin to remind all present of his membership in General Puñete's governing junta. Then on to the Verdun landscape of Gonzalo's face, where pill-box warts, bristling with black hairs, sit among the smallpox craters in a trenched wilderness of wrinkles, and over to Armando Loza, or, rather, just his hands, which have pushed back his dessert plate and dab with felt-tipped pen in a tiny notebook.

Now I slide my camera left again to a coffee saucer in which Parliament ash is being tapped by a manicured finger attached to a lotioned hand (which has never lifted anything heavier than a balance sheet) coifed by a soft linen cuff clasped by white-gold links half hidden by an Italian silk sleeve; ascend this to a narrow shoulder, a smooth cheek, puppy-brown eyes, a pallid brow—face which, like a palimpsest, imperfectly conceals the child who got so many presents he was never happy: Hunfredo Ladilla. And on to a black bear in a brown suit, the Reverend Dr. Gladstone Archer, who aims hooded eyes diagonally across at the irreverent Dr. Garibaldi Saenz (on Uncle Erasmo's left), who listens with his eyes closed and his left thumb hooked in the lip of his nostril.

And on Saenz's left Juanchi Tábano, like an albino hippo, with his chalky jowls and small pink eyes and pudgy arms clasped over a gut-swelled, sauce-specked white *guayavera*. Then Olga's brother Edgardo, who is whispering something to Pedro Oruga, who is looking at Pablo Chinche, who is directing remarks to a spot just below and to the right of the camera, an unseen me. And next to him, on my right hand, his mustache straightened by an expectant grin, Ñato Espino, faithful Ñato.

They talked and I listened. Gonzalo Garbanzo promised the nomination and the Tinieblist machine, if I could promise sufficient money. Juanchi said, "Politics is a business, you invest so much to get so much back," and promised a hundred thousand, if I would promise him Finance or Public Works. Uncle Erasmo promised the papers and the radio station, if I could promise him there'd be no flak from the gringos, and Armando Loza, whom I'd asked to stop in Washington on his way down, said he'd talked with Watson and had lunch with Mann and that the gringos promised not to bother me when Armando promised I was anticommunist. Dr. Gladstone Archer promised the loyal Tinieblans of West Indian descent, if I would promise to make their leader UN Ambassador.

"Which leader?" asked Gonzalo a bit maliciously, and Dr. Archer replied, "The leader who can deliver their vote."

Dr. Saenz promised the banana pickers of Tuquetá and the oil drillers of Salinas, whose unions he counseled at law, if I would promise to support him for deputy.

"What do you mean by support?" asked Gonzalo.

"A party nomination, of course, and money."

"How much?" pressed Gonzalo, and Uncle Erasmo wagged a finger at him and said, "That's a detail; we can work that out."

Hunfredo promised his TV station and as much cash as Juanchi, if I would keep the promise I'd made him in private, and Lino promised General Puñete would stay neutral, if I would promise to reappoint him commandant of the Guard. Edgardo Luciérnaga promised to organize professional men, and Pedro to give me the ranchers of Otán, and Pablo to help me in Selva Trópica, and Ñato, faithful Ñato, promised me the poor quarters of the capital and two hundred strong fellows to do what others might be squeamish to do. Lino asked Ñato if he could also promise to stay out of trouble, but just then Marta came in saying my call had gone through to Elena in Rome.

"Is there something wrong? It's five in the morning."

"Nothing's wrong. I've decided to run."

"Oh, caro! Securo?"

"Yes. I want to announce in two weeks, on Christmas day. Can you be here?"

"Sì, caro. Certo. Ma, tuto va bene?"

"Sure. I just wanted to tell you first."

"Grazie, caro. È maraviglioso! But now I won't be able to sleep."

"I wish I were there to help you."

"Ti voglio bene, Kiki!"

"Anche io a ti. Ciaou, Elena."

"Ciaou, caro. E buona fortuna!"

"What'd you tell her, Kiki?" Ñato jumped up as I reentered the room. "Are you going to run?"

I stood beside my chair and tried to put a worried face to the faces turned toward me. "Have I got the party, Gonzalo?"

"You've got the party if you've got the money."

"And I have the money, don't I, Juanchi?"

"You've got my share."

"And Hunfredo's. And I'll match your share and his. I have TV."

"And the papers, and the station," said Alfonso.

"And the gringos won't bother me."

"Nor will the Guardia," said Lino Piojo. "If you don't bother them."

"And I've an M.I.T. sociologist to invent me a program, right, Armando?"

"Right, Kiki. I'll even make you believe in it."

"And a ruthless brother to run my campaign. You are ruthless, aren't you, Alfonso?"

"Merciless, Kiki. Like a lion."

"And Uncle Erasmo, I've got him too, the foxiest uncle in Latin America. He was making presidents while the rest of us were sucking teat."

"Alfonso hasn't quit yet," observed Edgardo.

"Well, he's going to quit till election day. And I've got the West Indians, don't I, Doctor Archer?"

"Your father never had them, Ambassador Sancudo, but you're going to."

"Good, Doctor. I need them. And the oil workers and the banana workers, right, Doctor Saenz? And a strong running mate, an aristocrat to balance the ticket. I'm making it public, Hunfredo. Gentlemen, your next vice president, Don Hunfredo Ladilla!"

Applause from all, and I shouted over it, "So I can't lose, can I?" Cries of "No!"

"So I'm going to run! There's your answer, Ñato."

And Ñato let out a Mexican yelp and ran around to Lino and grabbed his shoulder and said, "Hear that, Mr. Member of the Junta? He's going to run, and he's going to win, and when my brother Kiki"—here Alfonso winced and looked away—"is President of the Republic, I won't be able to get into trouble!"

43

My campaign was born on the twenty-fifth of December and died on the Ides of March. It shook the country for eighty days, then dissolved like a dream in a puff of gunsmoke. I was picked to run last and was so far in front on the day Ñato shot me that I nearly won while still in coma and put three-fifths of my deputies into the Chamber. Had Ñato missed I would have been the youngest elected president in Tinieblan history with a mandate to lead a united country, but he got a round home, so instead I'm a plant. Win a few, lose a few, as the gringos say.

No star shone in the east when I announced my candidacy. I wanted a rally in Oruga Park, a sprig of violence to evoke the flag march, but my managers told me to change my image. "Running for election isn't the same as leading a mob," Gonzalo told me. "You've got to prove you're not a wild man." So I took the ballroom at El Opulento and trundled out a certifiably tame Kiki who mewed a speech by Armando Loza while reporters coughed and the cameras watched Elena. This specimen had rubber privates and a styrofoam heart. His adrenal glands had been replaced with vials of Valium. Pepe Fuertes and Felix Grillo watched his performance and slept soundly, dreaming of triumphs.

The next morning Uncle Erasmo decided not to get up from his coffin. In accord with his last wishes he did not receive the state funeral the Republic of Tinieblas grants former presidents: the archiepiscopal Mass, the florid oratory, the honor guard with unsheathed sabers, the rococo coach drawn by six black horses, the hallowed plot in the National Cemetery, the marble pillar, the memorial bust. He was buried beside his mother in the graveyard at Angostura with simple rites and a rude granite headstone:

ERASMO SANCUDO MONTES

1893-1965

"Let not thy left hand know
what thy right hand doeth."

He left the bulk of his large estate to his daughter Raquel. Alfonso got a controlling bloc of newspaper shares; I, an uncultivated tract in Otán Province. A final codicil, composed *in extremis,* left me twenty thousand inchados in cash with the provision, whispered to me by Uncle Erasmo's law partner and executor, Inocencio Ahumada, that the money be used to buy votes or bribe members of the

Electoral Jury. He had an unbroken string of victorious candidates, and it is just as well he didn't live to see the end of my campaign.

I was still pretending to be tame at the Tinieblista Party Convention four days later. Armando wrote me another speech; I was nominated on a sedate first ballot. I had the name and the cash and a good team behind me. "Give us a chance to line up the bloc votes," said Dr. Saenz. "Don't scare the gringos," said Gonzalo Garbanzo. "Let Pepe and Felix make the mistakes," said Alfonso. "Don't peak too early," said Armando Loza. "Take it easy," said Hunfredo Ladilla. But I have never enjoyed taking it easy, and acting tame was giving me blotches, so I went into the streets to stir things up.

On New Year's afternoon I was at the big open house Lino Piojo gives every year. Armando was there, and we were supposed to go over the big loose-leaf notebook he'd prepared with a section on every national problem, but I got bored with that and took my shirt off and kicked a soccer ball around the lawn with Lino's kids. Alfonso was splashing in the shallow end of the pool with a pair of stewardesses. (Years pass; Alfonso grays at the temples and sags in the gut, but the stewardesses remain gene for gene and chromosome for chromosome the same.) Well, around five o'clock I yelled for him to put his clothes on; we were going campaigning.

"You're drunk, Kiki."

"No. I'm bored."

"Stick to the schedule." We were leaving at five the next morning for a week in the interior: Córdoba, Bastidas, Angostura, Otán, Puerto Ospino, Otán, La Merced, Córdoba, then home to the capital for the first big rally.

"Put your clothes on."

He took his cloud nymphs up to dress, and twenty minutes later the four of us and Elena were in his big Grosse Pointe Conquistador convertible, with Hunfredo and Armando and Edgardo Luciérnaga and their wives following in one car and Lino and some of his more sober guests in another, riding into the old part of the city down avenues yet streamer-strewn and groggy from the night before. Just past Bolívar Plaza I had Alfonso stop the car and put the top down—though the sun was still strong enough to bubble tar in cracks along the pavement—and then turn right into the slums that fold down toward the harbor. I boosted myself up on the trunk and sat there with my arms raised, and as we wound through alleys overhung with drooping balconies, I drew the people out into our wake, pried women from their gossip and their kitchens, sucked men from shadow-cool cantinas, jerked drowsing couples from their tousled beds, and dragged them all behind me. We twisted to the docks and bent back toward the avenue, yanking knots of men from street-corner palavers, pulling a score of youths from a vacant-lot ball field, trolling at five miles an hour with the whole quarter netted in my smile, and towed it up onto Cervantes Plaza. And when I jumped down and stepped into the square, the audience in the Cine Cervantes felt my presence and forsook their movie, and sullen drinkers binged since Christmas Eve drained from a bar called Viva Mi Desgracia, and a squabble of young toughs in Kiki T-shirts (SOBERANÍA Y HONOR—KIKI on the back, me on the front with my head bandaged and a flag waved at arm's length) stomped blinking from El Palacio del Billar, and a skulk of priests flapped out of the Church of San Geronimo, and women kneeling at novena put away their beads, and old men playing checkers six blocks away in the Plaza Inchado left their boards, and shoeshine boys outside the Hotel Excelsior ten blocks the other way snatched up their boxes, and street vendors all along Bolívar Avenue picked up their trays of food or flowers, and strollers broke off their chats, and holiday drivers parked their cars, and all joined the crowd that was filling up the plaza.

I didn't go to the covered bandstand but told Edgardo to take the ladies there and walked instead to the empty pedestal where, sixty years ago, the city fathers had intended to put a statue of Don Quixote but ran out of money. I garnished the front edge with a couple of kids and sprang up and raised my arms, and yelled, "Viva Kiki!" and they all yelled with me, "Viva! Viva!" and all the church bells in the city began ringing, and foghorns boomed on vessels in the roadstead, and the big air-raid siren on Dewey Hill in the Reservation moaned and wailed and screamed. Then I spread my fingers and held out my palms, and the square and the city grew silent. I had no idea what else to say or do, but I glimpsed Armando, thick notebook clutched to thin chest, being jostled against the pedestal, and I reached down and plucked the book from him.

"Here's my program," waving the book. "Prepared by the smartest man in Tinieblas, Doctor Armando Loza Quebrada. A man so smart the gringos stole him for their best university. And I stole him back for you. A yell for Armando! Viva el doctor Loza!"

I cued them, and they howled, and their power tugged the bell ropes and threw the switches on the horns and sirens. I raised my palms, and there was stony silence. All through my speech and through my whole campaign I played the crowds that way.

"Now this book says . . ."opening the book. "But it says everything," closing the book. "It has something for everything, just like a drugstore. And when I'm President of the Republic, I'm going to read it through and do just what it says. It's the most beautiful, the most scientific program ever offered anywhere, and it goes into action the day I take office. But we don't have to worry about it now. I'm not going to bother you with it now. People of Tinieblas," holding out the book, "I dedicate this beautiful and brilliant program to you!" Then I flipped the book back over my head like a matador's hat.

Cheers from the crowd; a blanch from Armando. It occurred to me then, while they were cheering, that I could do or say whatever I liked. I drew the crowd's brute, unformed energies, refined them to a glow, then beamed it back. It didn't matter what I told them; there was no reason why it shouldn't be the truth. So I motioned them to silence and said I'd tell them why I was running for President. But first I'd tell them why some other people ran.

"Consider Señor Don Felix Grillo del Campo. He says he doesn't really want to be president. 'The presidency of the republic is a heavy burden, a grave responsibility.'" I sucked my chin in and stuck my upper lip out—Felix looks like Eleanor Roosevelt—and puffed the phrase, to the great good humor of one and all, myself included. "But he says he's got to accept this burden and this responsibility so that this country will have a decent government. It's his duty, Don Felix says, and Don Felix was brought up to be a serious man and do his duty. Now Don Felix is convinced it's his duty to run for President. I won't deny him that. But it doesn't have anything to do with what you or I would call decent government. Don Felix has a duty to himself and his family and his class to insulate Tinieblas from change. Because Don Felix and his family and his class are diarrheic with terror that this country will go communist. Because then they'd all be shot or, worse maybe, be exiled to Miami and have to live off their Swiss bank accounts. And that's why Don Felix is running.

"Now take Pepe Fuertes. Excuse me—Doctor José Fuertes. A good dentist. He made a great set of teeth for my father. But why is he running for President? He says he wants to complete his brother León's program. Now León was a good president, but I'll tell you this, there never were two brothers more different than León and Pepe Fuertes. León was generous, and Pepe wouldn't loan you a razor blade to cut your throat with. León was open, and Pepe's so tricky he doesn't dare tell himself what he's going to do. And Pepe never cared for León's program while León was alive. Every time León felt like doing something for the people, Pepe would jump up and say, 'Wait a minute, León, do something for me first.' And it's not hard to understand. León was a healthy fellow, a baseball player, a good dancer, and Pepe has a bad foot. You can't blame him. Imagine how bitter a kid could get dragging a twisted foot around. That's why he's running for President. He wants you to straighten out his foot. If enough of you vote for him, he'll be President. And if he's President, he can tell people what to do and they'll have to listen. And everyone will ask him for favors. And call him Señor Presidente. And take off their hats. And that will make up a little for all the baseball he never played and all the girls he never danced with and all the times mean people laughed at him and called him cripple. He's got a better reason for running than Felix.

"All right. What about me? Maybe you think I'm like my father, that I think the stars intend me to be President. Well, I don't think the stars care one way or another about you and me. I'm running for President because I feel like it."

I saw something move below me and looked down, and there was Alfonso shaking his head like crazy, mouthing, "No!" I had to laugh, and my speech stopped for my laughter.

"Excuse me," still laughing. "But my brother Alfonso's down here, my campaign manager, and he's having a fit. He thinks I'm going to blow the race right here by telling you the truth. But you don't care what I tell you, do you? You're going to vote for me anyway, aren't you? Whatever I say. Come on, let's have a yell to reassure Alfonso! Viva Kiki! Viva Kiki! Viva Kiki!"

Vivas, bells, and whistles.

"That's great! Thank you! Feel better, Fonso?

"Alfonso feels a little better now. Thanks. Where was I? Oh, yes, I said I'm running because I feel like it. Yes, that's it. It seems like an interesting thing to do. You go out and try to get people to vote for you. You speak to them and see if you can make them cheer. You promise people this and threaten people with that. You insult the other candidates and they insult you. If you win, you get to be President, which is what everyone in this country seems to want. If you lose, you look like a sap. That's the exciting part, the risk. I used to wrestle, but you know that. Well, a man looks so foolish when his opponent turns him over and pins his shoulders to the mat. No one ever pinned me—no gringo and no Russian. That's my foreign policy, by the way: not to get pinned down by either the gringos or the reds. But, I was saying, I never got pinned, but I was always aware it might happen, and that's what made wrestling exciting. Knowing that every time you went out on the mat, you might end up looking like a sap. And feeling like a sap and a weakling. So think how much more exciting it is to run for President. Because can you imagine how horrible it would be to get beat by Felix Grillo? Can you imagine how sick I'd feel if I couldn't get more votes than Pepe Fuertes? Kiki Sancudo, who was in Oruga Park—some of you were there that night, some of you were with me—when the gringos were shooting real bullets, while Felix Grillo and his family were on a plane for Ticamala and Pepe Fuertes was hiding under his bed. I'm risking my honor as a man, and when you risk that much, there's got to be excitement. Running for President is the most exciting thing I've ever done, and that includes winning the Olympics and marrying a movie star. That's why I'm running, for the joy of it. That's the best reason there is.

"Now, perhaps you're asking yourselves this: If he's running for the joy of it, what's he going to do when he wins." I paused, not so much to let the question sink in as to think up an answer. I looked out at those upturned brown and olive faces, those sweat-stained bodies, sun-flecked close to me, shade-spotted farther back in the creeping shadow of the church, and felt I was riding an immensely powerful and capricious beast who would snap me up like a titbit if I ever loosed control. At that moment I hadn't an idea of what I'd do when I was President, not a plan beyond the greed of my supporters and some idealistic aims of Armando's which the rest of the team considered smoke puffs to bamboozle the electorate. But it was a lovely ride so far, and the beast was snorting gaily, so I thought, I hurt Armando before, now I'll make him happy.

"Well," I said, "that's why I've got Armando and my program. You have another copy, don't you, Armando? Yes. He's got one. Good. Well, when I win this election, I'm going to do something even more exciting than running for President. I'm going to take that book of Armando's, and I'm going to use it to give you the country. Yes, I'm going to give this country to the people. And if you don't think that will be exciting, just stick around and watch. Exciting and risky, because they'll all be after us then. My own friends first, my own team and ticket. They don't think I mean it. There's Hunfredo Ladilla down there. He's running with me. Come on, a yell for Hunfredo! Viva Hunfredo!" I cued them, and they vivaed, and the bells and whistles sounded as before. "Good," holding up my palms. "There's Hunfredo—and he's going to be a great Vice President—and he loves to hear you cheer, but he doesn't believe I mean to give you the country. None of them believe it, not even my brother Alfonso. If they did they'd run like hell and find a place with Felix or with Pepe. They think I'm lying to you like any other politician. But I don't have to lie. I can tell you anything, even the truth. They can't believe I mean it because it's never been tried. Not once. Not anywhere. No one else has ever really meant it. And when they see I mean it, they'll try to stop me. I'm talking about my friends now. I don't have to tell you what my enemies will do. Or the gringos. Because to give this country to the people of Tinieblas I'll have to take a lot of it back from the gringos. And they won't like it. But we'll teach them all to enjoy a little excitement. Because that's what I'm going to do. I'm going to give this country to the people who live in it. And won't we have a grand time doing it?"

When I cued them this time, their roar broke every window in the Hotel Colón opposite the church, and the stomping of their feet shook the ground as far away as the Alameda, and of course the bells rang and the horns and sirens blew, but besides that every light in the city went on, even those in empty buildings where the current wasn't connected, and the Wurlitzer organ in the bar of El Opulento played "Hijos de Tinieblas" by itself, and appliances started up and doorbells rang, all without the slightest drop in power on the gauges of the Compañía Tinieblina de Electricidad y Gas, and the horns on all the cars and busses tooted "Viva Kiki!" in Morse code, and the doors of all the cells in La Bondadosa Prison swung open, and the guards couldn't close them, not even when they tried ten to a door, until the crowd stopped cheering. I didn't stop them. I stood there grinning for three minutes or so; then I moved to jump down from the pedestal, but hands seized me, and I was lifted onto shoulders. I had a glimpse of Elena smiling at me from the bandstand; then I was borne away on that strange camel-swaying ride I got to know well during my campaign, up Bolívar and out Bahía, all the way to my house more than a mile away, and all of them still cheering.

Later, when Alfonso brought Elena back, he pulled me into this room and shut the door and stood there by the desk and asked me if I was serious about "giving the country to the people." I smiled at him and said, "What do you think?" He laughed and clapped me on the shoulder and said, "All right, Kiki. I understand. But you sounded so convincing up there."

That's how I played it with Hunfredo and Armando and the others. Each asked a version of Alfonso's question, and I let each think what he wanted. The truth was I didn't know whether I was serious or not. I'd never been the kind to fret about the welfare of the masses or any other thing beyond my own sweet lusts, yet I wasn't a liar either. I hadn't calculated the phrase one way or another; a gap of silence opened, and the words jumped out to fill it. I had to agree when Juanchi Tábano compared idealism to the mumps: no more than a discomfort when you catch it young and get over it; dangerous, painful, and ridiculous if you pick it up in later life. Still I resented it when Marta accused me of lying to win votes. So I decided to win the election and then see what I'd meant. Meanwhile I kept promising to "give the country to the people," and every time I said it, it sounded better, and more and more I thought, Jesus! I might just do it; Christ! won't that make them jump!

I had no more trouble from my managers anyway, no warnings about "peaking" early, no pleas to take it easy. They'd seen me draw a crowd; they'd seen the way I moved it. From then on they hung on with both hands while I moved the way I pleased. They hung on over in Bastidas when I told a big crowd they were suckers. I was in a black mood for some reason—maybe because Marta had begun call ing me a demagogue—and I said they were a nation of suckers; everyone cheated them and they didn't care. The gringos cheated them on the Reservation rent—the best part of their country for less than a desert airstrip in Libya; the government cheated them on their taxes—no medicine in the hospitals, no desks in the schools; landlords cheated them on their rent—all that good money for tumbledown roach farms; politicians cheated them on their vote. "I don't want to talk to suckers," I told them. "I'm sick of talking to shit-eaters!" For a while it looked as if we'd all get lynched. Dr. Gladstone Archer turned whiter than me—he'd introduced me and they were mostly his people. But they ended up cheering. They ended up carrying me around on their shoulders. And if I'd asked them to burn down the town, they'd have done that too. When I left that town, Pepe and Felix didn't have twelve votes there between them.

I drew the crowds. I pulled the people to me like iron filings gathered by a magnet; then I moved them whichever way I pleased. No one in Tinieblas had seen anything like it since Alejo's '48 campaign, and then he polarized people, attracting some, repelling others, whereas I drew everyone. People of every class came out to cheer for me, and while some thought better of it the next day when I was in another town or another quarter of the capital, while some told themselves, I don't trust that Kiki, and wondered why they'd cheered, they came out again to cheer me when I returned. Clever men who'd seen and suffered our divisions remarked the strangeness of it and spoke or wrote about "charisma" and "irrational appeal," but the strangest thing about my campaign wasn't what it was doing to the country. The eerie thing was what it did to me.

It began in Salinas, at the end of my first swing through the interior. I'd come down through the oil fields speaking to groups of workers gathered near their rigs, joking with them, chatting about whatever came into my head, easing up after a week of crowds and car trips over broken roads, and that evening I spoke in a pasture outside Córdoba. The party's candidates for the province's five Chamber seats had made a barbecue: butchered steers, a band, plenty of rum and *aguardiente*. The whole town was there, and people from towns forty miles north and south along the highway, and peasants who'd walked down from hill villages carrying their machetes wrapped in newspaper. I meant to eat and drink with them and wire them to my "irrational appeal" and set them cheering and boost the party's candidates and then go down to the capital for a decent night of sleep.

Salinas isn't a rich province, not like Otán, where you scarcely need to plow—"just throw some seeds down," they say, "and jump back." Many rice gamblers in Salinas, and they'd had three bad years: drought through July and August; floods and downpours in December making what crops had sprouted impossible to reap. The drought had hurt the cattle people too, and in October foot-and-mouth had broken out. It's a province of small holders; many of them had gone under and the rest were mortgaged to their eyes. But the struggle for existence winnowed all the whiners from Salinas centuries ago, and the people there know how to feast an evening, bad times or no. And I had no land there. I didn't feed my family on salary from a rice mill that was folding. My rivered ranch was two hundred miles northwest, and every cow that sickened in Salinas made my fat, healthy ones worth more. I didn't have to share those people's troubles.

But while I was mixing through the crowd, being introduced by Rosendo Salmón, who's Vice President of the Chamber now, I met a wiry chap about my age, and when I shook his hand a wave of anguish swept me.

"You lost your harvest," I said softly. I didn't have to ask. I knew he'd lost his crop and his credit and his freedom, that the best he could hope for was to find a place in some more fertile province administering some luckier man's fields, that he'd never be his own man again. I knew this, though I didn't know his name, and, more, I winced his hurt and choked his helpless rage as though they were my own.

"That's right, Don Kiki. She rotted in the field."

I nodded to him—what could I say?—and shook his hand again, and it seemed to draw off some of his pain, for he smiled and wished me luck, but I stayed with his suffering. And before I could grasp what was happening to me, Rosendo led me up to a bunch of barefoot peasants, all munching avidly on stick-speared strips of beef, and I was pierced by hunger. But not food-hunger, I realized, and I said:

"Land's what you want."

They all nodded, and one man said, "That's clear, Don Kiki. Everyone wants land."

I nodded back. "I'll have to find a way to give you some then."

They liked that, but I kept their hunger.

The worst was when I met a man, a rancher of fifty-odd, who'd had land, land his great-grandfather had wrested from the Spanish Crown, and his grandfather had held, and his father had added to, and he had lost to a bank the month before. I didn't speak to him. I only shook his hand, and his shame buckled me. I had to brace to hold my shoulders straight under the frowned contempt of those disgruntled forebears.

I wanted to speak soberly that evening. By the time I got up I wanted to speak about land reform, and an agricultural development bank, and irrigation projects. I started out that way because I was in pain and that kind of talk seemed to ease it. But then I saw I was ruining the fiesta, reminding those people of their grief, piling it back on top of them. So instead I picked it up and carried it myself. I told them to enjoy their food and drink, the music and the speeches. I told them not to fret about their trouble;

it was my trouble now. The problems of Salinas were my own personal problems from now on, and I would solve them. And when I said I'd give this country to its people, I meant it, Marta. I meant it.

I reconsidered later. On our dark journey to the capital, propped beside Jaime as he hurled the car along the tunnel chiseled by our headlamps, I wondered, Do I mean it? Do I want to do such things? And many times I told myself, the phrase wins votes, that's all, and that's enough. But wherever I went I felt the people's pain and worry. The night after Salinas I faced a crowd dredged from the shack-towns which stretch like a girdle of misery around the sleek paunch of the capital, and I felt those people's frightful weakness, the helplessness we others know in dreams where monsters gnaw us while our fists flail punily. I lifted it from them, and took it on myself, and told them that I'd make them strong and free. And once the words were out, I knew I'd meant them; those people's weakness was my own. I went to the new Club Mercantil and spoke with bankers and landlords and felt their fear-guilt as my own—fear for their perfumed comforts, guilt over luxuries spilled out amid rasped want—though I'd never sought comfort, hence couldn't fear to lose it, and hadn't known guilt. I drew it from them as they accused me of being power-wild like Alejo, ready to pitch the country into chaos on a whim. I told them that we'd have to work together, all the country working together so that everyone might thrive, and they felt better once they'd passed some of their fear and guilt to me.

I didn't plan my words or actions. I was aware, quite suddenly, of people. They stumbled through their lives in pain and terror, and now I felt it with them. One afternoon, in one of the strange showers which, that year, broke the dry season, I saw a monster child, a stunted mongol with a gross, bulged head, standing beneath the drainpipe on the Ministry of Commerce, letting a flood of filthy water ram on his tilted crown, and I felt that child's bewilderment and sorrow so strongly that I nearly went to stand beside him. It was as though I went out of myself into other people's minds and bodies, or that they entered me. Yes, they passed their pain to me; I sponged their trouble from them.

It went beyond the human. As I moved round the country I felt the longing of parched fields, the twined confusion of dark jungle. I had all Tinieblas inside me, and it filled my brain to bursting.

For seven weeks I tried to seal myself against the suffering of others and the torment of the land, and each week brought me a new anguish. I had the famines, where I ate and ate, yet remained hungry, and the thirsts, and the sorrows, where every sight set my eyes burning and I wept all night tears held back through the day. I had the guilts, where I repented four hundred and fifty years of injustice as though I'd done it all myself, and the resentments, where I sulked a countryful of injuries and slights, and the terrors, where I shuddered everybody else's fears. Worst was the plague of hopes, where every night I dreamed the dreams of others: slum-dreams of lottery, peasant-dreams of land, invalid-dreams of health, whore-dreams of dignity. I carried with the rush of my campaign like a cork in a torrent, scarcely aware of where I went or what I did. I'd sit the long miles in an idiot daze. We'd reach some town, and I'd blink and go out to draw the people to me, to drain them of their pain and worry and to set them cheering. Then I'd lapse back into my trance. I would hear Gonzalo or Alfonso as from a great distance, and my answers would go back like rays from beyond the sun. Those about me wondered at my strange. placidity, but inside all was maelstrom. Only Elena understood.

"I think you're going through what I do when I work up a new role," she told me. "But I'm much more malleable than you are, Kiki. And I make the changes on purpose. I think the part through and decide what voice I'll use, what gestures I'll put on. But you're like a poor caterpillar who's got to become a butterfly and doesn't know why or how to go about it. It must be painful."

Then, at the beginning of March, I found my ease. I was speaking in Tuquetá, in a little town far up against the Ticamalan border, and when I said I was going to give the country to the people, I knew once and for all I meant it. I knew I wouldn't wonder any more. I had the whole country inside me the way an author wombs his characters and settings—things grander and more various than himself—inside his heart and mind. I was at one with the people. I shared their emotions and could order them so that the strains of class and interest might meld in harmony. The idea of the country for the people—a new idea for me—had come unthought, and I'd doubted it. The suffering of others had come unsought, and I'd struggled with it. Now I accepted the vision and the gift. I claim no credit. A man can be possessed by grace as well as by demons. And it was brief. Ñato the exorcist purged me of it soon enough.

A new country was swelling inside me; no scandal ought attend its birth. I gave Uncle Erasmo's legacy back to his executor. I told Gonzalo and the others that, whatever frauds Pepe or Felix tried, I wanted none from us. A clever candidate from La Merced had xeroxed up some thousand twenty-dollar bills—not much gringo money is seen in the interior—to pass out to voters on election day. I told him, "Burn them," and when he carped, I kicked him off the ticket. And I sent for Ñato, who'd disappeared somewhere, to tell him to disband his goon squads.

The where he'd disappeared to was Miami. He'd sneaked up with his cousin Pio's passport. Which showed a certain rodent courage, not just because the French and Interpol both wanted him, but because his Miami friends could hardly write off his cocaine bungle as a tax loss. He was alive, in fact, only because they hadn't thought him worth the price of an assassin. But now he offered them the new Havana, almost as close with jet planes flying and ten times as corrupt. Wasn't the president-to-be a former smuggler? Wasn't old Ñato his best pal? The pranks they'd played together, the capers that they'd pulled! With syndicate funds and know-how they'd turn Tinieblas into a border-to-border vice farm.

He had great plans. Casinos? Of course. Run by the mob and rigged by smart mechanics. But that was peanuts. Why not poppy plantations and a junk refinery? What about the world's first machine-rolled joint? ESPINOS: a choice blend of Panama red and Acapulco gold. A bank or two to launder grimy money. So many things were possible when you owned a country. Poor Ñato. He never dreamed I'd start believing my own speeches.

He got the news at Alfonso's house at Medusa Beach. I went with only Elena and Marta to get three days of rest before my final drive—the rally in Bolívar, the last swing round the country, the

TV speech before the vote on April first—and left word for Ñato where I'd be. Alfonso had developed both his part and the tract Alejo still retained, but it was mid-week, and the cottages were empty. We rose early, my ladies and I, and walked beside the sea and talked about the future. I remember Marta commenting that this was the last tranquility I'd have for four years.

"I'll have plenty once I'm dead," I answered. But that's not true.

I was trying to find a way to speak to Elena about her career —I didn't think the First Lady should make movies—when she declared she was canceling her contracts.

"I think it's time I had some babies," she said.

And Marta would go back to school in Paris. How neatly we had everything arranged.

The house where Angela had lived stood empty behind its high walls topped with glass shards, and the last morning I went over there and entered as I had fifteen years before, between the gate top and the wire. Wild flowers had sprung up on the spot I'd burrowed in and sunlight drenched the terrace that I'd run across. Instead of tangos, the dry slap of a loose shutter, the rapping of wan ghosts. I studied the leaves at the bottom of the empty swimming pool for some clue to the relation between the pirate who'd stealthed in to board his father's mistress and the candidate who was going to give Tinieblas to its people. We had strong urges, I decided, and made the risky play. On balance it seemed more rational to be lured by a fair-skinned whore than by one's own rhetoric. Some people's dreams grow wilder as they age. I climbed out and swam round the point back to Alfonso's, and when I got there, Ñato was waiting.

He bubbled with delight. We were going to be rich. Not Tinieblas rich, gringo rich.

I said sure. I sat down in one of the canvas deck chairs Alfonso has beside his pool and yelled for Marta to bring us some iced tea and said sure, but first I had to tell him something.

"No, hombres I have to tell you."

He sat down in the shade of a table umbrella and opened the neck of his silk sport shirt and whispered to me the oracles from Miami. When Marta came with the tea, he stopped as if unplugged, then whispered on again when she'd left. I watched his kid-with-ice-cream grin for a while, then gazed the prismed sunlight in the beads of sea-water on my chest. I waited till he'd finished, then said, "No."

"What do you mean no, Kiki?"

"I mean no."

"Sure, Kiki, but what? You don't like the junk part? I know you never liked that, but it's big money, Kiki. You see, it grows in Turkey, and they refine it in France, and the gringo government is leaning on those countries, and that makes everything difficult and puts the price up and could maybe even cut off the supply. But I told them in Miami how you don't take shit from the gringos. Ah, ho, Kiki! You should have seen their face when I told them what you said to Johnson on the phone. And if they move in here, they can control the whole thing from the poppies to the horse, and we get a big cut. And, Kiki, if they don't do it here, they'll just do it somewhere else, and someone else will get the money. All right, Kiki. You don't like it. You don't like it. I can see you don't like it. All right, I'll tell them no junk. You're the President, Kiki. I know that. I know when you don't like something. I know enough not to try to push you. All right. I'll tell them. We'll still get rich. The gambling is big money. They'll set it all up and bring down tours of rich gringos, and . . ."

"No, Ñato."

"What do you mean, Kiki?"

"I mean no. No drugs, no gambling, no weird banks, no grass, no pre-teen whorehouses, no syndicate in Tinieblas. The country's not for sale. I'm not for sale."

"They don't want to buy you, Kiki. They'll make you a partner. There's a guy coming down tomorrow to make all the deals. He's got a hundred thousand for your campaign, Kiki."

"You better call and tell him not to come, Ñato."

"But it's all set, Kiki."

I started laughing. "Did you tell them I'd sent you?"

"Well, Kiki. I know you. And it'll be good for the country, all that money coming in. And you were out on the stump. And, Kiki, I didn't know when I left here whether I'd swing the deal or end up on the bottom of Biscayne Bay, so I thought if it worked out I'd make it a surprise. And you can't say no to this, Kiki. It's too big. Do you know who's coming down?" He breathed the name of an august crime magnate. "He says he wants to meet you, Kiki. And he's a big fan of Elena's."

I laughed again. "No."

"Ah, ho, Kiki! Be serious! Let me tell you again. Let me give you the figures. It's millions and millions and millions, and we get a cut of everything. You get a cut. You get a big cut. And you don't have to do anything. All you have to do is look the other way and take the money."

"No."

"You don't understand, Kiki. It's my big chance."

"No, Ñato. You don't understand. Listen. I'm not going to sell this country to the Mafia."

"It's not the Mafia, Kiki. The Mafia's only a branch of the outfit I'm talking about. Like Buick is a branch of General Motors."

"Still no, Ñato."

"Kiki . . ."

"No!"

He pulled the front of his shirt from where it was sweat-stuck to his chest. "You're hard, Kiki. You don't care, do you? You don't care about anyone but yourself. Everything's fine for you now. You're going to be President, so you don't care what happens to me. You don't have any feeling. Everyone else, when they're President, they take care of their friends, but not you. Everything for you and nothing for anyone else. That's the way you are."

"I'll take care of you Ñato." I looked over in the direction of the house where Angela had been and remembered Lalo Marañon. "I'll make you consul in Macao. You'll have diplomatic immunity, and you can make a nice little bundle."

"Consul in Macao! That's peanuts! This is my big chance, Kiki!"

"I said no, Ñato."!

"Kiki! I can't tell"—he breathed the name—"to stay in Miami. It's all set, Kiki! You can't say no!"

"I've already said it."

"Then, Kiki, you'll be sorry!" He jumped up. "You'll be sorry for treating me like this. You think you can have everything for yourself and leave me with nothing, but you'll be sorry!" And he ran off to his car.

At lunch I told it all to Elena and Marta. I told it as a joke. Sell Tinieblas to the gringo crime conglomerate! What an ideal I might have thought of it myself some years before if it hadn't involved mere leisured riches. And it was amusing to be threatened by Ñato Espino.

But later on that day something occurred that might have shaken me had I been less certain in my coming victory and the rightness of what I meant to do. Near the end of our drive home, as we were rolled down Washington between unpainted slum buildings and the Reservation fence, I saw my mongol urchin grubbing in a waste can and stopped the car. He didn't understand me when I called him over, but when I showed him a tin of cookies, he came over to gobble avidly, heehawing about like I do now.

"What an ugly child!" whispered Elena.

The monster looked up at her, smiled and said clearly: "Not as ugly as what will happen tomorrow."

44

"Kiki?"

"Yes, Marta." She stands in the doorway, the fringes of her hair damp from her shower, her face smeared with pleasure and contrition like a child who's been at the icing bowl.

"Can I come in, Kiki?"

Nod.

Shuts the door. "I'm sorry, Kiki."

"For what?"

"For what I said before."

"Oh!"

"I didn't mean it, Kiki. I'm not glad about what happened to you. You know that. I only said it to hurt you. I'm sorry. It's that . . . lately I've been confused."

"I know. Forgiven. I thought you were apologizing for your romp with Phil."

Big blush. "Does it show that clearly?"

"I know that look. I remember it. I didn't see it this morning, so I suppose last night's round misfired. I telepathed Phil some advice this afternoon, so I'll take part credit and a kiss in thanks. On the cheek is all right. And to absolve you for using my house as a pushbutton I'll take another in penance. Good."

"You're feeling better."

"High on memories. Very strong today. I hadn't thought of it till you came in, but that creamy look of yours brings back an afternoon four years ago when you assaulted me during my siesta and gave me my very last taste of love."

"You weren't very eager."

"Elena and I had been planting sons all morning. God knows why none of them took. That memory's got me high, and I'm a little nervous about going to the plaza."

"Don't go, Kiki."

"Of course I'll go! Why shouldn't I?"

"It might bring back . . ."

"That's the best reason for going."

"Do you mind if I stay home?"

Shake my head.

"I'm still leaving tomorrow."

"All right. And I'm still staying."

"I know. You won't accept reality." Bites her lip. "Kiki, I want to say . . ."

"Don't say it."

". . . that I never . . ."

"Don't."

"What will you do, Kiki?"

"Things marvelous and bloody. Things you don't even want to think about, Martita."

"No. I mean, how will you . . ."

"Live? I'll live. And if I come to miss you," make my smile, "the city's full of girls. I'll let one seduce me and take your place. Come on! None of that. I've seen girls cry sometimes after a good orgasm, but not from sadness."

"Kiki . . ."

"Stop. Red eyes will only make Phil feel protective. He won't concentrate on his movie. Is Elena ready?"

Nods.

"Then wheel me out. Alejo will be by soon. Politics will be honking horns outside."

"Filthy politics."

"That's it. Get mad. I like you better bitchy than all soft. Come. Come on, Martita. Wheel me back to 'reality.'"

As if this maimed reality, whose edge I won't be bound by, were the only one!

She sniffs, opens the door, pushes me out. Sonny, Phil, and Carl by the bar, Elena on the left horn of the crescent couch, sipping tea, flipping, yes, *Réalités*. And Alfonso sweeping in, all agitated and important, saying we must get ready, the caravan will be here any minute.

Moviemen swing up their gear and lug it out to Alfonso's convertible. Marta goes to tell Jaime to bring my car around. Elena leaves her tea and magazine, comes to embrace Alfonso and ask me in Italian if I feel all right. And he rolls me to the door and eases me down the step.

Now over all the land the tropic dusk is falling. Shrimp boats run in from the wide gulf; peasants trudge home across sere pastures. In the deep forest monkey chatter stills; parrot wings beat against the darkling sky; the jaguar yawns and stretches. And I set off for the place my mind has circled toward all day, all day and longer, since Alejo set the rally and I said I'd go, since I left the clinic and returned here to Tinieblas. My life was arrowed all too fast for thought. Now I plod back along its flight to the place my mind shies from, to meet death-monster fear again and steal a meaning from between his paws.

45

Alfonso's car curbed on Bahía, pointed downtown. Alfonso at the wheel, Sonny behind him, Carl kneeling on the rear seat with his camera shouldered, Phil on the sidewalk, slung with light meters. My car behind Alfonso's with the motor ticking. Jaime at the wheel, Elena behind him, Kiki right-front, safety-strapped at lap and chest. Superplant mounted and ready to move out.

Ready ahead of time, or Alejo's late. Motorcade slowed by throngs, no doubt. Which gives my mind time to catch up with my body. So both can leave for the plaza together.

"Are you all right, caro?"

"Tucked in tight, Elena. And you?"

"I was happier last time."

Exactly. So was I. That day I also woke at dawn, but got out of bed all by myself. And bathed and shaved myself, imagine that! And sat down on the toilet with Charles de Gaulle and did my duty. Then I tucked the book away in my night table and put on shorts and old desert boots and a shirt with a crocodile on it, and went out on the balcony for coffee.

The pelicans were fishing that day too. I watched them while Edilma brought my tray. I spooned my sugar and poured my milk all by myself. I drained the cup, and poured a second from the thermos, and sipped it slowly. "KIKI SPEAKS!" shouted Correo *Matinal*, "PEPE TO SELVA TRÓPICA," whimpered *La Patria*.

I saw the shrimp fleet off. Beneath blue skies I smoked a blue Galoise. Warmed by the infant sun, half-swollen by a languorous fantasy, I rose and stretched and went to Elena.

She had the drapes pulled, the machine on high, the covers piled about her. I dropped my clothes and slithered in. My fingers crept under her nightgown into her dream. She half-turned toward me, making sweet moan. I rolled her back and hitched her gown up and spread her petals and climbed between them (with her already shuddering, half in sleep) and slipped into her as into a warm sea. Plunged, and caught her at the bottom—oh!

Then soaked a bit while she waked. And curled in her warm fragrance while she bathed. And imagined her soaping her breasts. And was ready again when she returned.

"Good. I want to be awake when my first child's conceived."

"Too late."

"If you're so sure, I might as well get dressed."

"No, no. Let's stay on the safe side."

Later we dozed. And later still we hedged our bets again. Then we dressed and went downstairs, she to feed the triplets an egg apiece, I to practice politics.

There should be time, before Alejo's juggernaut toots up, to daub a triptych of my morning. The central panel shows Don Kiki with his shirt peeled off, baking healthily in the poolside sun. Gonzalo and Armando hug the umbrella's shade beside him: Gonzalo, his face gold-red and pitted like a pomegranate, his lips drawn back, a fist balled on the table top, a forefinger stabbed toward Armando's face (he was saying, I believe—and the squabble churned throughout my whole campaign—that ideology is mental masturbation if you don't get the votes); Armando with his arms folded, his chin and nose and eyebrows raised (he had just finished saying that votes are worthless without a program). Both look to Kiki, who smiles like Solomon and lifts his hands in reconciliation. In the left background a round man with a shiny face (a hard-pressed candidate for deputy who craved a seat nearby me on the rally stand that night) peers through the glass door of the *sala* at Kiki and his counselors. Behind him a tall, sallow gringo with bad teeth and a wrinkled seersucker (the noted journalist Kerry Pimpton, who got an interview that morning and a box seat at a murder the same night) flirts desultorily with Marta, while a squat old man with an Alejo-style white suit and a face carved from a chunk of mahogany which had lain out on a beach till it was sun-cracked and sea-streaked (Doroteo Aranque, Felix Grillo's ward boss in San Felipe, who was prepared to deal three hundred votes, all relatives and debtors, for a niche on my bandwagon) paces nearby. The head, like an eight ball fuzzed with cotton, of the Reverend Dr.

Gladstone Archer, is visible over Pimpton's shoulder, and the top of the panel is crowded with the figures of associates, retainers, petitioners, and advisers. To the right of the Kiki-Gonzalo-Armando group the dining-room window frames a picture within the picture touched in the Vermeer mode: Donna Elena at breakfast, holding a triangle of toast halfway to her mouth as she gazes softly into a dream of heirs, and, through the doorway to the kitchen, bent-backed Edilma husking crayfish for the first course of our lunch.

The left-hand panel shows the pool at noon. Kiki stands waist-deep at the shallow end, the top of his shorts visible beneath an inch of transparent water, holding nine-year-old Olguita, her heels cupped in his upstretched palms, her eyes clamped shut, her hands bladed over her head. Water streams his sun-brassed chest and crinkles in the corners of his smile and beads the sunlight in his hair and slicks his shoulders as he lifts his daughter for her dive. At his side twelve-year-old Mito waits his turn, while in the background, Olga in a smart Miami pantsuit (she has just remarked, a trifle bitchily, that Elena and I ought to have children of our own) and Elena in a print dress (she smiles in secretive contentment) watch the performance from a pair of aluminum chairs set back in the shade of the trellis. The sunlight-shimmered sala door reflects Kiki's V-ed torso and Olguita's rump, but a careful look through it will be rewarded by a glimpse of a delicious houri in a micro-skirt (Alfonso's stewardess of stewardesses—she made *Time*'s "PEOPLE" section six months later when she married Spitzer the hedge-fund wizard), who stands in the cool of the *sala* tinkling a heraldic gin-and-tonic.

On the right we are coming out from lunch: Olguita with a dab of chocolate at the corner of her mouth, Mito preening his gold-buttoned blazer, Alfonso the Suave with Elena on one arm and Mouche (who looks over her shoulder to send me my last sweet message), Kiki and Olga (I have just complimented her on our children's table manners, and she replies, "I feel the same way about having married you as Edgardo does about having fought in Korea: I was crazy to do it, but I'm glad I did, now that I've managed to survive."), and Marta, as fetching as the sprite on Sparkling Water labels, in a light-purple shift, who raps the doorway molding with a knuckle when Armando Loza says we'll all be lunching in the palace in ten weeks.

But all this sunny, viand-rich well-being fogs me from Ñato whom, I confess, I didn't give a thought to all that morning. Hindsight reveals I'd best have spent an hour picking in Ñato's mind—roached and spidered like the top slab of a basement cell in La Bondadosa, strewn with elliptical black rat turds and staled by drying urine. I might have flushed the scorpion that stung me later on. Instead I took my joy at work and love, so now I mustn't snip him from this replay.

He drove, then, from Medusa Beach to the capital at *grand prix* speed, cursing me without interruption and escaping a spectacular death two or three times through the skill of certain anonymous motorists, whom I will not take trouble to imagine since they chose to preserve themselves rather than spare me my paralysis. Immediately on arriving at his mother's house, he went to the bathroom, lifted the top of the toilet tank, untaped a packet of cocaine, and inhaled it. Then he left for the Compañía Interplanetaria de Telecommunicaciones to place a call to Miami but arrived instead at the Alameda. A pig-tailed nine-year-old fell from her swing and scuffed her knees; Ñato soothed her with ice cream. He and the child were lifted to his car and whisked magically to an obscure dirt road beyond the airport. A blue inchado note—on which Simón Mocoso was smoking a marijuana joint stuck on a toothpick—flapped from Ñato's fingers to the girl's, but when his thing cobraed from his trousers to brush the steering wheel, she grew frightened, so he grabbed her dusty hand and made her do it, though she sniveled distractingly and squeaked when he gooed her thumb. Then he was sitting on his toilet, his pants gauded with dried starch and a hillock of cocaine trembling on the back of his hand. He sniffed it up, and Kiki Sancudo came in wearing a wet bathing suit to apologize for joking so cruelly the day before. Ñato forgave him, since they were going to be partners again and millionaires, and went to the Palmita to celebrate. While he was on his third rum, or his fourth, he got an overseas call from Miami, which he took on a pair of leather dice cups, speaking through one and listening through the other. Meyer Lansky congratulated him personally. Ñato passed the earpiece to his friend Fidel Acha, but as Acha didn't know much English, he couldn't comprehend the

importance of the call. Then they were in the men's room of the
Hueco Negro with Acha zipping beside the sink and Ñato parked
on the toilet with a young fag squatting between his knees. But
nothing happened and Acha started cackling, so Ñato pushed the
kid away and said he'd bit him, and Acha got angry and coshed the
kid with his revolver and kicked him in the face, and Ñato got up
and pissed on him a little, trying to hose the blood from his lower
lip. Then he stood outside his car, which was rammed, radiator
split and steaming, into the rear of a sedan, scuffling his feet in
shattered headlight glass, while Acha flashed his Guardia badge at
the other driver and counseled him to forget all about the minor
scratch on his bumper, the imaginary ache in his neck, and to watch
his driving, and to think who he might be talking to before he
started shooting off his mouth. And next morning, just as I was
letting Mito push me in the pool with my shorts on, Ñato woke up
with a bad headache and sat naked on a corner of his bed, gouging
pale chunklets of dead skin from between the small toes of his left
foot and carrying them to his nostrils for appreciative sniffs, trying
to recall where he'd been and what he'd done, remembering only
that Kiki had betrayed him, had denied him a fair share of the electoral booty—out of plain spite, since Kiki stood to gain as much as
he—after all he'd done for Kiki, and that the capo from Miami was
already airborne, expecting to close a deal that wasn't there.

So he inhaled a packet full of hope and set off to buy his dream
from pawn. He wandered in the driveway looking for his car; then
he recalled the crunch of twisting metal. But a neighbor had left
the keys in hers, so he took it to Tinieblista Party Headquarters.

Kiki had gone insane, he told Gonzalo. A spender from Miami
wanted to contribute a hundred thousand to the campaign, and
Kiki wouldn't take it!

Gonzalo commiserated. It was true Kiki had been acting
strangely lately. He'd ordered a clean campaign, for instance, something so foreign to Tinieblan traditions—to politics in any country,
for that matter—that it made one doubt his reason. More, there
were rumors that he meant to keep his campaign promises, which
would prove what Gonzalo had suspected all along, that Kiki was
a dilettante, an amateur, gifted to be sure, but not serious. Still, he

was winning the election, and everyone knew it, even his opponents. This wasn't the moment to cross him. Young Mani Liso from La Merced had had a marvelous idea; you know, xeroxing gringo twenties, and Kiki had given him the boot. Right off the ticket, and since there wasn't time to file another Tinieblista for the race, he'd pledged support to a Christian Democrat. He was capable of anything, even firing him, Gonzalo. It was true, nobody turned down a hundred thousand in the last two weeks of a campaign, but Gonzalo had learned not to judge Sancudos by ordinary standards. He'd seen Alejo win on astrology! No, Gonzalo wouldn't say anything to Kiki. He had enough trouble trying to rig a ward or two without Kiki's finding out. No, the most he'd do—since the wheel was flying in today—was loan Ñato a party car and a driver. Maybe if Ñato took the man to beg in person, Kiki would take his money.

While Gonzalo talked, six-inch cockroaches in Dior gowns mamboed across his desk in time to the vein beating in Ñato's forehead. Ñato howled hysterically at the final quip, snatched up the order for the car, and left. In the hall he met a Boston bull terrier who suggested that Pepe Fuertes might accept the deal Kiki had rejected; the syndicate could keep its hundred thousand and dynamite Kiki instead. He located his driver and ordered him posthaste to Pepe's house, but when he got there, he learned that Pepe was campaigning in Selva Trópica. Lansky's lieutenant would land in forty minutes. Home to change and sniff another packet, and before leaving, a desperation call to Kiki.

Ñato's first ring synched with Marta's second rap.

"I'll get it," said Alfonso, relinquishing two lovely arms and heading for the library.

"We've a layover till tomorrow night," Mouche remarked to Elena, a bit louder than necessary, "and I'm going to play the lottery. The Excelsior has put me in room 1007 for the third straight time."

"I wish you luck," said Elena, turning to smile at Kiki, on whom life continued to lavish goodies.

"It's your 'brother' Ñato," said Alfonso, who emerged from the library tapping two fingers to his nascent right horn.

"Hang it up."

"He says it's life or death."

I went in and picked up the receiver. "Have you decided to join the Consular Service?"

"Beep, beep."

"What?"

"This bus will run you over if you don't give a fair share."

"Are you on snow?"

"Varruuum!"

"Sleep it off, Ñato."

"You owe me, so don't cheat me. I know what's right. Correct in the rectum, you son of a bitch!"

I hung up and went to see my guests out. Alfonso came over to me. "What'd your 'brother' want?"

"Trouble. He'll get it."

"Ha!" Marta came over. "You'll probably put him in your cabinet."

Shook my head. "If I put him anywhere, it'll be outside the country." I smiled to Elena, who was standing near the door with Olga.

"Look, Kiki." Alfonso pursed his lips. "Lino called me this morning . . ."

"And?"

"And said some Guard officers are saying you and Ñato have a deal with some gringo gangsters. The deal León Fuertes turned down."

"They're saying that?"

He looked away.

"And it'll be all over the country by tomorrow?" I went on.

"And it'll cost me votes?"

"Votes!" from Marta.

"You'll still win, Kiki," Alfonso said softly.

I grinned and put my arm around his shoulder. "I have no deal, Fonso. And you!" I grinned at Marta. "You ought to be working for Pepe, the things you believe about me."

"Charm goes only so far, Kiki."

"I'm not running on charm, Marta. Charm's not my platform. But see, Fonso? Some people have no faith. Those need demonstrations. I wish this had come up at lunch, Marta. I'd have turned the water into wine for you." And I went to give Olguita a hoisting hug and to tousle Mito's hair and kiss Olga's check and shake Armando's hand and nod with simple (and hence slightly pregnant) courtesy at throaty, long-legged Mouche.

Marta came to me when I was about an hour into my siesta. Warmth fumbling near me. "Hold me, Kiki."

I let her snug her back against my chest.

"I'm sorry about before, Kiki. I believe you."

"S'all right."

"I was dreaming now, Kiki. I don't know what, except it was of death."

"No death here, Marta."

My hand hung loosely on her flank, and she moved it to her breast. "Touch me, Kiki."

I thought, Coño! ambushed while unarmed, but she wrinkled against me and moved my hand over her, and I knew I had strength and love to spare, for Marta, and for Mouche that night, and for any targets of opportunity that popped up in between or after, for all the sweet, lovely women life blew my way, and love to spare for Mito and Olguita, for Elena and the kids she'd give me, strength and love to pour out for all Tinieblas and bury death forever.

Ñato, for his part, had a talking crocodile who, like himself dressed nattily in a fawn sport coat and a pink silk shirt buttoned at the neck and dark glasses. They sat drinking rum and Coca-Cola in the bar of El Opulento. The man from Miami, who had just checked in, wanted to shower, rest a while; Ñato and his crocodile passed the time buying each other drinks.

The crocodile complimented Ñato on his sang-froid. "Those gringos like a take-charge guy," he said. "It wouldn't have done to let on that the deal's gone sour, much less tell him. You were smooth as silk out there, baby. You've got a real pair of balls."

"And when he finds out?" Ñato was close to tears.

"He won't find out. Kiki will come through, and the syndicate will never know there was a hitch."

"You don't know Kiki," Ñato whined. "He's a real prick. He used me for years, and now he's going to be President, and he doesn't need me any more, and he'll ruin my big chance just from spite."

Ñato told the crocodile how Kiki had abused him, how it was Kiki's fault Ñato was an orphan, how Kiki had run out on Ñato when they were doing so well in the gun business, how, because of Kiki, he'd gone into drugs and got hooked on cocaine. "He only cares about himself," said Ñato.

"Don't believe it," said the crocodile. "He likes you. He's your friend."

But Ñato shook his head and sulked.

Then Kiki Sancudo spoke to Ñato out of the Wurlitzer organ. The force of Kiki's voice trembled the surface of Ñato's drink and tinkled glasses behind the bar:

"Who saved you from a beating in Piraeus, Ñato? Who got you out of Greece when you were broke? Who gave you a piece of the Costaguana gun trade and stood up to Memo when he pulled his highjack? Who hid you from the French police? Who fixed you a clean passport and slipped you across the border? Who always took care of you when you were in jams?"

"You did," whined Ñato, "but now you're against me."

"Don't doubt me, Ñato," Kiki boomed from the Wurlitzer. "Don't doubt me, and don't try to figure me out!"

"You were testing me, weren't you, Kiki? That was it, wasn't it?"

"Don't bother yourself with why, Ñato. Just trust me."

"See?" said the crocodile. "What'd I tell you? All you've got to do is take Don Vito to him before the rally."

"Ah, ho!" said Ñato, slapping the table so that the waiter turned to stare at him. "Ah, ho!" grinning behind his shades. "I knew Kiki wouldn't let me down!"

So Ñato and his crocodile had a drink in celebration while Don Vito enjoyed his shower and Marta kissed me, smiling, and wrapped herself in her robe and went back to her room. Then, for the very last time in all my life, I got up from bed on my own power and stretched before the mirror, admiring my fine, hard body, and, having more strength than I knew what to do with, dropped naked to the floor for push-ups. Then I washed and dressed myself for the last time, thinking nothing special of it at all, and tied my own shoes and buttoned my own shirt, and went in to watch Elena dress, for there were people downstairs, and I wanted us to go down together,

"Giovanni Alfonso," I said, zipping her dress. "After your father and my brother. Giovanni Alfonso Sancudo. Born in the palace just like his old man."

"And if it's a girl?"

"Elena. Elenita."

"And if it's triplets?"

"Harpo, Chico, and Groucho. Come on. You look good enough. I'm the star today, remember?"

Now, downstairs were Juanchi Tábano and Gonzalo Garbanzo, Armando Loza and Dr. Garibaldi Saenz, and Pedro Oruga, who'd flown down from Otán in his own Cessna, and Hunfredo Ladilla with his new wife, and Aquilino Piojo with Hunfredo's old one, and Pablo Chinche, up from Selva Trópica, and Rosendo Salmón from Salinas, and Olga's brother Edgardo Luciérnaga with his wife, and the Reverend Dr. Gladstone Archer, and the candidate for deputy who'd petitioned me that morning, and Alfonso with Mouche, and Marta with the same post-orgasmic glow she showed me in the library ten minutes ago, and several others, including one Jesús Maria Espino Amaro ("They call me Ñato"), who pushed up to Elena and me as we reached the bottom step, with a man who looked more like an accountant than a gangster, a round-shouldered, bespectacled man who tried not to gawk at Elena.

"This is him, Kiki," said joyful Ñato. "This is Don Vito, just tell him 'OK.'"

There was an audible hush. All eyes were on us, Alfonso watching nervously and Marta watching apprehensively and Elena watching in regal calm.

"I don't know you," I told Ñato in English. Then I pointed to him and looked about. "I don't know this man."

Ñato and Don Vito dissolved onto the tiles like two gouts of spilled grease, and Elena and I walked past them, into a garden of smiling faces.

46

Din of horns behind us, and Nacho's Lincoln whooshes by. Glimpse of Alejo through the rear window, then another car, and another, and Alfonso swings out from the curb, wedging left hand and fender into the motorcade, and Jaime lurches after, rocking me against the door, then against the chest strap, and we are off down Bahía, gunning to keep up, with Carl swaying to his feet in the car ahead to sight his camera down the avenue, while Phil kneels backward on the front seat, clasping Carl's waist, and pedestrians jerk their heads to peer at us through the gloom and drivers stare from cars we've elbowed to the right, as the long, honking line of cars is yanked with Alejo in his spring toward a last bite of power.

That day we walked. I was too charged with energy to wait while the plaza filled, and so I called my friends and teammates out. The sea was high that day, and as we gathered on the corner —a handsome group, fit for a racing meet or garden party—the west wind rolled a great swell, building, down across the bay and flung it to the sea wall. A roiling tower rose and boomed and glittered in the sun, and then it shattered, sighing salt mist across the avenue to brush our faces.

Now we knife in darkness, but that day we strolled, and the declining sun filtered among us through the palm fronds. Arm-in-arm with Elena I led them, all the E-string tension that had held me in the weeks of my campaign softened, and my pulse beating with the rhythm of the world. Each action of my life, acts that had seemed disordered blunderings when I reviewed them that foul night in prison, were now revealed as careful moves to shape me for this moment. I'd gorged my ego on the world around me, and the world had suffered for it. A sleeping man had had his head smashed so I might stand an equal to my father. Men had died in Costaguano to prove my courage and along Washington Avenue to show me I could lead. Olga had wept to sensitize my heart to love, and more, and more, and now poor Ñato had been publicly denied so that I might deny and slough all that was mean and greedy in my spirit. And I was ready now to give back all I'd grabbed. My life, the world itself, seemed planned and ordered, and I walked smiling toward that shimmering mirage.

Up on the Avenida Simón Mocoso offices were letting out, and clerks and secretaries crowded to us, and people clambered down from busses to mingle with us, and businessmen called to me from their cars and pulled them to the curb to walk with us. Hands glanced in toward mine over other people's shoulders, and eyes groped for my eyes, and I took them, feeling at once serious and gay, and said, "Yes, come along, come on with us." I'd go five steps or ten, then stop to take somebody's hand or greeting, and the whole avenue moved with me at that pace, while to the east, bus-loads of people were rocking in along the Vía Venezuela, and to the north others were rolling down the highway from the interior, and Ñato was sniffing up his last packet of courage and fumbling under socks and handkerchiefs for a pistol.

Now Alejo's cortege slows, turning up from Bahía, and people lean from the sidewalk to squint darkly at us through the insulating sheen of uprolled windows, faces inquisitive, or frenzied, or an-gered as the guardias press them back; but that day I walked among them, they smiled. I was bringing them the fire of new life and had taken up their problems. I needed no protection.

Now I can see Alejo climbing from his car to strut along the corridor carved by policemen, looking neither left nor right as the mob howls its excitement. The streetlights gleam on sweatstreaked, shout-strained faces hot for blood and retribution like myself— *Two guardias will bring him to the ranch*—men yeasted in old hates and snarled to plunge toward violence, but that day I came in concord, stepping out into the square with the people all about me, all the people, rich and poor, light and dark, gathered for me and marching with me, opening a way for me and trooping in my wake, all bound as one, graced by my grace, while Ñato snaked his way among the crowd with death clasped in his pocket.

Now Elena unbuckles me while Jaime assembles my chair, and now he lifts me to it and settles me inside, and Elena rolls me down the corridor where Carl stands, spraying the crowd with his camera and dropping it to squeeze a burst at me, and someone to my left screams, "Venganza para Kiki!" and others take it up, "Vengeance! Vengeance!" I make my smile —*Jaime will probe with the smeared barrel*—hate-stuffed, maimed abortion trundling on rubbered wheels, but that day I strode proudly with my woman on my arm and all the country nested in my palm for me to mold it fresh.

Now they lift me, Jaime on one side, Alfonso on the other, up toward where Alejo and Nacho and the others sit, and the roars pound and eddy, and the faces leer and twitch, and the mob moans for its plunder—*there will be a dull pop, a seismic bulge in Ñato's belly, a rainbow arc from heels to shoulders and pig squeals stabbing at the ceiling.* They turn and settle me beside Nacho, and I look out at the groom that folds in about the howling pack, but that day there was still sunlight as I mounted with Elena and the others, the whole land laved in the last glow of afternoon, and the people shouting gaily.

Now Elena sits down beside me and takes my handkerchief to wipe the spittle from my chin and asks, "Va bene, caro?" and I have strength enough to nod, and to my left Alejo rises and holds up his gaunt hands and lifts his dried death's-head and rasps his ancient incantation—"I am Alejandro Sancudo. I have been your President. I will be your President again."—his voodoo prayer to darkness and decay, but that day I stood up myself and raised my hands to weigh the people's hope, and I was going to say, I was going to, I was . . .

"Are you all right, Kiki?"

But my brother Ñato, my double cleverly reversed, stood up behind me, a little to my left, and pierced my words with bullets, and skewered my life, and drained the power from my hands so that they dropped the people's hope, and smashed my body, and broke my sex, and soured my soul, and . . .

"Kiki!"

Flashbulbs bursting in my brain, head lolling wildly, long donkey bray erupting from my throat. Nacho twists to stare at me in horror as Elena grasps my checks.

"Kiki!"

Grope for control along thin, overloaded circuits. Grope for

control. Another one, another one could kill me. And then we'd
. . . And then we'd never . . . And then he'd be safe.

"Kiki! Are you all right?"

Make myself nod. "Yes. Elena." Lifting the words like weights.

"Are you sure?" Smooths my cheek. "I'll make them stop. I'll
get you home."

Shake my head. "All. Right. Now."

Alejo ranting, and the mob howling back. Touch of grace gone
from them forever. And from me. But there are other joys.

"Are you sure, Kiki?" dabbing my lips with the handkerchief.

"Yes, Elena. Fine now." Make my smile. "We're going to win."

*The gun will be blown free. Or Jaime will withdraw it. Then
he'll undo the cords and irons and put a pillow under Ñato's head
and dress him neatly. Then he'll bring a chair to wait with me for
Ñato to regain consciousness. With any luck Ñato will scream for
days.*

December, 1968–November, 1970